W9-ADH-002

HOLIDAY CITY WEST
LIBRARY

THE
14TH
COLONY

ALSO BY STEVE BERRY

COTTON MALONE NOVELS

The Patriot Threat

The Lincoln Myth

The King's Deception

The Jefferson Key

The Emperor's Tomb

The Paris Vendetta

The Charlemagne Pursuit

The Venetian Betrayal

The Alexandria Link

The Templar Legacy

STAND-ALONE NOVELS

The Columbus Affair

The Third Secret

The Romanov Prophecy

The Amber Room

THE
14TH
COLONY

STEVE
BERRY

MINOTAUR BOOKS
NEW YORK

This is a work of fiction. All of the characters, organizations, and events portrayed in this novel are either products of the author's imagination or are used fictitiously.

THE 14TH COLONY. Copyright © 2016 by Magellan Billet, Inc. All rights reserved. Printed in the United States of America. For information, address St. Martin's Press, 175 Fifth Avenue, New York, N.Y. 10010.

www.minotaurbooks.com

Designed by Steven Seighman

Library of Congress Cataloging-in-Publication Data

Names: Berry, Steve, 1955– author.
Title: The 14th colony / Steve Berry.
Other titles: Fourteenth colony
Description: First edition. | New York : Minotaur Books, 2016. | Series: Cotton Malone
Identifiers: LCCN 2015045816| ISBN 9781250056245 (hardcover) | ISBN 9781250091796 (signed edition) | ISBN 9781466862616 (e-book)
Subjects: LCSH: Malone, Cotton (Fictitious character)—Fiction. | National security—United States—Fiction. | Presidents—Succession—United States—Fiction. | Targeted killing—Fiction. | Secret societies—Fiction. | Political fiction. | BISAC: FICTION / Espionage. | GSAFD: Suspense fiction. | Spy stories.
Classification: LCC PS3602.E764 A615 2016 | DDC 813/.6—dc23
LC record available at http://lccn.loc.gov/2015045816

Our books may be purchased in bulk for promotional, educational, or business use. Please contact your local bookseller or the Macmillan Corporate and Premium Sales Department at 1-800-221-7945, extension 5442, or by e-mail at MacmillanSpecialMarkets@macmillan.com.

First Edition: April 2016

10 9 8 7 6 5 4 3 2 1

For the Ducks,
Larry and Sue Begyn, Brad and Kathleen Charon,
Glenn and Kris Cox, John and Esther Garver,
Peter Hedlund and Leah Barna, Jamie and Colleen Kelly,
Marianna McLoughlin, Terry and Lea Morse,
Joe Perko, Diane and Alex Sherwood,
Fritz and Debi Strobl, Warren and Taisley Weston.

ACKNOWLEDGMENTS

My sincere thanks to John Sargent, head of Macmillan, Sally Richardson who captains St. Martin's, and my publisher, Andrew Martin. Also, a huge debt of gratitude is offered to Hector DeJean in Publicity; Jeff Dodes and everyone in Marketing and Sales, especially Paul Hochman; Jen Enderlin, the sage of all things paperback; David Rotstein, who produced the cover; Steven Seighman for the excellent interior design work; and Mary Beth Roche and her folks in Audio.

As always, a bow to Simon Lipskar for another great job.

And to my editor, Kelley Ragland, thank you.

A few extra mentions: Meryl Moss and her extraordinary publicity team (especially Deb Zipf and JeriAnn Geller); Jessica Johns and Esther Garver who continue to keep Steve Berry Enterprises running smoothly; Colonel Barry King for his help with military hardware; Hayden Bryan at St. John's Episcopal Church for opening doors and showing me around; and Doug Scofield for introducing me to Fool's Mate.

Without fail, to my wife, Elizabeth, who's quite brilliant.

In 2013 Elizabeth and I hosted a Danube River cruise with fans. We were unsure what to expect, being confined for eight days on a small riverboat with a group of total strangers. Anyone would be a little apprehensive. But the experience was marvelous and 20 new friends emerged from that trip. During the cruise, as we toured the various stops, collectively we'd all follow Elizabeth, who carried an orange paddle. After a while we began to call her Mama Duck. Naturally, we became baby ducks. Since that time we've visited with nearly all of those 20 new friends, some more than once. A few of the characters in this story are even named for them. For those of you I missed, don't worry, your time will come.

So this one's for the Ducks.

Of which Elizabeth and I are proud members.

The terms of the President and Vice President
shall end at noon on the 20th day of January.

—U.S. CONSTITUTION
20TH AMENDMENT

PROLOGUE

VATICAN CITY
MONDAY, JUNE 7, 1982

RONALD REAGAN KNEW THAT THE HAND OF GOD HAD BROUGHT him here. How else could it be explained? Two years ago he was locked in a bitter primary fight against ten contenders, vying a third time for the Republican party's presidential nomination. He won that battle and the election, defeating the Democrat incumbent Jimmy Carter and claiming forty-four states. Then fourteen months ago an assassin tried to kill him, but he became the first American president to survive being shot. Now he was here, on the third floor of the Apostolic Palace, at the pope's private study where the leader of nearly a billion Catholics waited to speak to him.

He entered the room and marveled at its modesty. Heavy curtains blocked the summer sun. But he knew that from those windows, each Sunday, the pope prayed with thousands of visitors in St. Peter's Square. Sparse furniture, the most prominent being a plain wooden desk, more reminiscent of a table, with two high-backed, upholstered armchairs fronting each long side. Only a gold clock, a crucifix, and a leather blotter sat atop. An Oriental rug lay beneath on the marble floor.

John Paul II stood near the desk, regaled in papal white. Over the past several months they'd secretly exchanged over a dozen letters, each delivered by a special envoy, both speaking to the horror of nuclear weapons and the plight of Eastern Europe. Seven months ago the Soviets had declared martial law in Poland and clamped down on all talk of reform. In retaliation, the United States had ordered sanctions imposed on both the USSR and Poland's puppet government. Those punitive measures would stay in place until martial law ended, all political prisoners were freed, and a dialogue resumed. To further ingratiate himself with the Vatican, he'd directed his special envoy to provide a mountain of covert intelligence on Poland, keeping the pope fully informed, though he doubted he'd passed on much that had not already been known.

But he'd learned one thing.

This cagey priest, who'd risen to one of the most influential positions in the world, believed as he did that the Soviet Union was destined for collapse.

He shook hands with the pope, exchanged pleasantries, and posed for the cameras. John Paul then motioned for them to sit at the desk, facing each other, a panel depicting the Madonna keeping a mindful watch from the wall behind. The photographers withdrew, as did all of the aides. The doors were closed and, for the first time in history, a pope and a president of the United States sat alone. He'd asked for that extraordinary gesture and John Paul had not objected. No official staff had been involved with the preparations for this private discussion. Only his special envoy had quietly worked to lay its groundwork.

So both men knew why they were there.

"I'll come straight to the point, Holiness. I want to end the Yalta agreement."

John Paul nodded. "As do I. That was an illegitimate concept. A great mistake. I have always believed the Yalta lines should be dissolved."

On this first point his special envoy had read the pope correctly. Yalta happened in February 1945. Stalin, Roosevelt, and Churchill met for the last time, deciding how a postwar Europe would both look and be governed. Boundary lines were drawn, some quite arbitrary, others deliberate as appeasement to the Soviets. Part of those concessions entailed an agreement that Poland remain under the sphere of the USSR, with Stalin pledging to hold free elections. Of course, that never happened and the communists had ruled there ever since.

"Yalta created artificial divisions," John Paul said. "I, and millions of other Poles, greatly resented that our homeland was given away. We fought and died in that war, yet it mattered not to anyone. We have suffered brutality for forty years, starting with the Nazis, then the Soviets."

He agreed. "I also believe that Solidarity is the way to end Yalta."

That tear in the Iron Curtain happened two years ago at the Gdansk shipyards, the first non-communist-controlled trade union ever allowed. Now over nine million Poles were members, one-third of the entire workforce. A scrappy electrician named Lech Walesa served as its head. The movement had acquired power, force, and appeal. So much that last December the Polish government had imposed martial law to quell it.

"They made a mistake trying to quash Solidarity," he said. "You can't allow something to exist for sixteen months then, just as it catches on, reverse course and outlaw it. The government has overestimated its reach."

"I have made overtures to the Polish authorities," John Paul said. "We must open talks on the future of Solidarity and the end to martial law."

"Why fight it?"

And he watched as this novel overture registered. His special envoy had urged him to broach the subject, thinking that the Vatican would be receptive.

A grin came to the pope's lips. "I see. Let them be. All they are doing is alienating the people. So why stop it?"

He nodded. "Any rebuttal the government mounts to Solidarity is a cancer. Let it grow. Every word in opposition the government speaks just makes the movement stronger. All Solidarity needs is money to keep it alive, and the United States is prepared to supply that."

The pope nodded, seemingly considering what he was proposing. That was far more than Reagan's people had been willing to do. The State Department strongly disagreed with the tactic, saying the Polish regime was stable, solid, and popular. They provided a similar assessment for Moscow and the USSR.

But they were wrong.

He said, "Pressure is building every day from within, and the Soviets have no idea how to deal with that. Communism is not equipped to handle dissent, short of dishing out terror and violence. The only morality Moscow recognizes is what will further its own cause. Communists reserve unto themselves the right to commit any crime. To lie. To cheat. To do anything they want. No political system like that has ever survived. It's inevitable their system will collapse." He paused. "But we can hasten it."

John Paul nodded. "The tree is rotten, all it needs is a good shake and the bad apples will fall. Communism is evil. It prevents people from being free."

That was another sentiment his special envoy had reported, and what he'd been hoping to hear. Never had a pope and a president conspired in this way, and never could either of them admit it had happened. The church openly forbade itself from interfering in politics. Recently the world had seen evidence of that when John Paul scolded a priest for resisting a papal order to resign a government position. But that did not mean the church was oblivious to oppression. Especially when it hit so close. Which was more proof that God was clearly at work here. At this precise moment in human history the storm seemed centered on Poland. For the first time in 450 years a non-Italian, a Pole, occupied the chair of St. Peter. And nearly 90 percent of all Poles were Catholic.

A screenwriter could not have imagined it better.

The Soviet Union was about to be gripped by a great revolutionary crisis. He could feel it coming. That nation was not immune to revolt, and Poland was the pivot that could send everything over the edge. Cliché as hell, but right on target. As with dominoes, one country falls—they all fall. Czechoslovakia, Bulgaria, Hungary, Romania, and all of the other Soviet satellites. The entire Eastern Bloc. One by one they would drop away.

So why not provide a push?

"If I may," he said to John Paul. "I was once asked, how do you tell a communist? The answer is easy. It's someone who reads Marx and Lenin. But how do you tell an *anti*-communist?" He paused. "It's someone who understands Marx and Lenin."

The pope smiled.

But it was true.

"I agreed to this private talk," the pope said, "because I wanted us to have the opportunity to be honest with each other. I thought the time had come for that. So I must ask, what of the cruise missiles that you wish to deploy in Europe? At present, you are presiding over an unprecedented rearming of America, spending many billions of dollars. This concerns me."

His special envoy had warned him about this reservation, so he was prepared to reply. "There is no one in this world who hates war and nuclear weapons more than I do. We must rid this planet of the scourge of both. My goal is peace and disarmament. But to accomplish that I have to use what's at my immediate command. Yes, we are rearming. But I'm doing that not only to make America strong, but also to bankrupt the USSR."

He could see that John Paul was listening.

"You're correct. We are spending billions. The Soviets will have no choice but to match us, spending that much and more. The difference is we can sustain that spending and they can't. When the United States spends money on government projects, those funds make their way back into our economy through wages paid and profits made. When the Soviets spend, it's just a drain on their treasury. There's no free market. The money simply goes out and doesn't return. Wages are controlled, profits are regulated, so they have to constantly generate new money just to pay their bills. We recycle ours. They can't match us dollar for ruble, year after year. It's impossible. They'll implode."

He could see that the pope was intrigued.

"Communism has never attained the legitimacy of public support. Its rule depends solely on force, supplied by terror. Time has worked against them, as does the world, which has changed. Communism is just a modern form of serfdom, with no advantages that I can see over capitalism. Do you realize, Holiness, that less than one family in seven owns a car in the USSR? If a person wants to buy a car, there's a ten-year wait for delivery. You tell me, how can a system like that be deemed stable or solid?"

John Paul smiled. "The regime stands on a cracked foundation. It always has, from the beginning."

"I want you to know that I am not a warmonger. The American people are not bent on conquest. We want a lasting peace."

And he meant that. Inside his coat pocket he carried a plastic-coated card with codes that could be used to launch a nuclear arsenal. Just outside sat a military aide toting a black leather satchel that could make that happen. All totaled the United States owned 23,464 nuclear warheads. The Soviet Union stockpiled 32,049. He called them the tools of Armageddon. Just a handful of those could destroy all human civilization.

His goal was that they never be used.

"I believe you," the pope said. "Your envoy made a good case for you on that point. She is a bright woman. You chose her well."

He hadn't chosen her at all. Al Haig had made that selection from among his attachés at the State Department. John Paul was right, though. She was young, smart, and intuitive—and he'd come to rely on her judgment when it came to the Vatican.

"So long as we are being frank," he said, "let me say that you sell yourself short. You are also engaging in a bit of deception. That priest you scolded on the runway in Nicaragua, in such a show of anger. You told him to quit his government post, but he defied you. And he still defies you. I suspect that man is now an excellent source of Vatican information on what the Sandinistas are doing. And who would suspect him, after such a public admonition."

John Paul said nothing, but he could see that his conclusion was correct. The Sandinistas were nothing but Soviet puppets. His people were already working on ways to rid Central America of them, as apparently was John Paul.

"We must have a farsighted policy," the pope said. "One that stretches across the globe and favors justice, freedom, love, and truth. Peace must always be our goal."

"Without a doubt. I have a theory." And he now thought it would be okay to share it. "To me, the USSR is essentially a Christian nation. Russians were Christians long before they were communists. If we stay this course, I think we can tip the balance where the Soviet people will revert to Christianity, allowing those long-held ideals to eclipse communism."

He wondered if the pope thought he was pandering. Based on his special envoy's visits he'd been provided with a detailed personality assessment. John Paul valued order and security, preferring to deal in known entities. He lived by reason and thought, in clear no-nonsense terms. He was repelled by ambiguity, impulsiveness, and extremism, always thinking everything through before deciding. But he particularly despised being told what someone thought he wanted to hear.

"You believe this?" the pope said. "In your heart? Your mind? Your soul?"

"I must say, Holiness, that I am not a man who attends church regularly. I don't even consider myself overtly religious. But I am spiritual. I believe in God. And I draw strength from those deeply held beliefs."

He truly meant that.

"You and I share a common bond," he said.

John Paul clearly realized the connection. Last year, within two months, both of them had been shot. All three bullets were fired from close range, barely missing their aortas, which would have meant certain death. His lodged in a lung, while John Paul's two rounds passed right through, yet incredibly spared the vital organs.

"God saved us both," he said, "so that we can do what we are about to do. How else can it be explained?"

He'd long thought that every person possessed a divine purpose. A plan for the world outside of human control. He knew that this pope also believed in the power of symbolic acts and the role of providence.

"I agree with you, Mr. President," the pope said in a near whisper. "We must do this. Together."

"In my case, the shooter was simply insane. But in yours, I would say you owe the Soviets."

The CIA had learned of a connection between John Paul's would-be assassin and Bulgaria, one that led straight to Moscow. The White House had provided that information to the Vatican. True, conclusive proof was lacking, but the idea had been to end Solidarity by ending its spiritual and moral leader. Of course, the Soviets could never afford to be directly implicated in a plot to kill the leader of a billion Catholics.

But they were involved.

"*If possible, so far as it depends on you, be at peace with all men,*" John Paul said. "Revenge would be a bit un-Christian, would it not?"

He decided to keep to the Bible and Romans. "*Never take your own revenge, but leave room for the wrath of God.*"

"*But if your enemy is hungry, feed him, and if he is thirsty, give him a drink. For in so doing you will heap burning coals on his head.*"

That they would.

This priest had witnessed Nazi atrocities. Karol Wojtyla was there when Poland suffered that unimaginable horror, working with the resistance. After the war he'd then done what he could to thwart the Soviets as they prolonged Poland's suffering. By all accounts John Paul was a heroic figure, an extraordinary man, learned and courageous.

People drew strength from him.

And he was in the right place at the right time with the right thoughts.

"The moment I fell in St. Peter's Square," the pope said. "I had a vivid presentiment that I would be saved, and this certainty never left me. The Virgin Mary herself stepped in that day and allowed me to survive. That I believe, with all my heart. And may God forgive me, but I do owe the Soviets. Not only for what they may have done to me, but for what they have done to so many millions for so long. I forgave my would-be assassin. I went to his cell, knelt and prayed with him, and he wept for his sin. Now it is time for those who sent him to know their sin, too."

He saw resolve in John Paul's strong eyes, which seemed ready for the fight. He was, too. At seventy-one he'd never felt better. His whole countenance had revivified after the assassination attempt, as if he'd truly been born again. He'd read what the pundits were saying. Expectations for his presidency seemed low. In past decades, the sheer weight of the job had annihilated many good men. Kennedy died. Vietnam drove Johnson from office. Nixon had been forced to resign. Ford lasted only two years, and Carter was sent home after one term. Critics called Ronald Reagan a reckless cowboy, an old actor, a man who relied on others to tell him what to do.

But they were wrong.

He was a former Democrat who'd long ago switched parties, which meant he did not fit into any clear political mold. Many feared and distrusted him. Others held him in contempt. But he was the fortieth president of the United States, intent on remaining in office seven more years, and he planned to use that time for one purpose.

To end the evil empire.

That was exactly what the Union of Soviet Socialist Republics represented. But he could not do it alone. Nor would he have to. He now had an ally. One with two thousand years of experience dealing with despots.

"I'll keep the pressure on from my end," he said. "Both political and economic. And you from yours with spiritual encouragement. Another trip to Poland would be good, but not quite yet. In a year or so."

John Paul had already visited his homeland once, in 1979. Three million people came to mass in Warsaw's Victory Square. As a candidate for the White House he'd watched that spectacle on television, while the man in white descended from the papal plane and kissed the ground. He remembered vividly what the pope told his countrymen over and over.

Be not afraid.

And he realized then what the religious leader of a billion people could accomplish, particularly one who held the hearts and minds of millions of Poles. He was one of them. They would listen to what he had to say. But the pope could never be obvious. Instead, the message from Rome must always be one of truth, love, and peace. There is a God and it is everyone's inalienable right to freely worship Him. Moscow would ignore that at first, but eventually it would respond with threats and violence and the startling contrast between the two messages would speak volumes. And while that happened America would encourage reform in the Eastern Bloc, finance free-market reforms, and isolate the Soviet Union both economically and technologically, slowly but surely leading them into bankruptcy. They would play to the paranoia and fear communism loved to exploit in others, but could not handle on its own.

A perfect two-front war.

He checked the clock.

They'd been talking about fifty minutes.

Each seemed to clearly understand both the task and their individual responsibilities. Time for the final move. He stood and extended a hand across the table.

The pope likewise rose to his feet.

He said, "May we both successfully carry out our responsibilities to mankind."

The pope nodded and they again shook hands.

"Together," he said. "We will eliminate the USSR."

PRESENT DAY

CHAPTER ONE

Bitter experience had taught Cotton Malone that the middle of nowhere usually signaled trouble.

And today was no exception.

He banked the plane 180 degrees for another peek downward before he landed. The pale orb of a brassy sun hung low to the west. Lake Baikal lay sheathed in winter ice thick enough to drive across. He'd already spotted transport trucks, buses, and passenger cars speeding in all directions atop milky-white fracture lines, their wheel marks defining temporary highways. Other cars sat parked around fishing holes. He recalled from history that in the early 20th century rail lines had been laid across the ice to move supplies east during the Russo-Japanese War.

The lake's statistics seemed otherworldly. Formed from an ancient rift valley thirty million years old, it reigned as the world's oldest reservoir and contained one-fifth of the planet's freshwater. Three hundred rivers fed into it but only one drained out. Nearly four hundred miles long and up to fifty miles wide, its deepest point lay five thousand feet down. Twelve hundred miles of shoreline stretched in every direction and thirty islands dotted its crystalline surface. On maps it was a crescent-shaped arc in southern Siberia, 2,000 miles west from the Pacific and 3,200 miles east of Moscow, part of Russia's great empty quarter near the Mongolian border. A World

Heritage Site. Which likewise gave him pause, as those usually meant trouble, too.

Winter had claimed a tight hold on both water and land. The temperature hovered right at zero, snow lay everywhere, but thankfully none was currently falling. He worked the controls and leveled off at 700 feet. Warm air blasted his feet from the cabin heater. The plane had been supplied by the Russian air force from a small airport outside Irkutsk. Why there was so much Russian–American cooperation he did not know, but Stephanie Nelle had told him to take advantage of it. Usually visas were required for entry into Russia. He'd used fake ones many times in his day as a Magellan Billet agent. Customs could also be a problem. But this time there was no paperwork, nor had any officials impeded his arrival. Instead, he'd flown into the country on a Russian Sukhoi/HAL fighter, a new version with two seats, to an air base north of Irkutsk where twenty-five Tupolev Tu-22M medium-range bombers lined the tarmac. An Ilyushin Il-78 tanker had provided refueling along the way. A helicopter had been waiting at the air base, which ferried him south to where the plane waited.

The An-2 came with a single engine, two pairs of wings, an enclosed cockpit, and a rear cabin large enough to hold twelve passengers. Its thin aluminum fuselage constantly shook from a four-blade propeller that bit a choppy path through the frigid air. He knew little about this World War II Soviet workhorse, which flew slow and steady with barely any zip to its controls, this one equipped with skis that had allowed him to take off from a snowy field.

He completed the turn and readjusted his course northeast, skirting heavily timbered ground. Large boulders, like the teeth of an animal, protruded in ragged lines down ridges. Along a distant slope sunlight glinted on phalanxes of high-voltage power lines. Beyond the lakeshore, the terrain varied from flat empty earth, punctuated by small wooden houses clustered together, to forests of birch, fir, and larch, finally to snow-topped mountains. He even spotted some old artillery batteries situated along the crest of a rocky ridge. He'd come to examine a cluster of buildings that hugged close to the eastern shore, just north of where the Selenga River ended its long trek from Mongolia. The river's mouth, choked with sand, formed an impressive delta of channels, islands, and reed beds, all frozen together in an angular disorder.

"What do you see?" Stephanie Nelle asked him through his headset.

The An-2's communications system was connected through his cell phone so they could talk. His former boss was monitoring things from DC.

"A lot of ice. It's incredible that something so large can be frozen so solid."

Deep-blue vapor seemed embedded in the ice. A swirling mist of powdered snow blew across the surface, its diamondlike dust brilliant in the sun. He made another pass and studied the buildings below. He'd been briefed on the locale with satellite images.

Now he had a bird's-eye view.

"The main house is away from the village, maybe a quarter mile due north," he said.

"Any activity?"

The village with log houses seemed quiet, only fleecy clouds of smoke curling from chimneys indicating occupancy. The settlement rambled with no focal point, a single black road leading in, then out, outlined by snow. A church comprising yellow and pink plank walls and two onion domes dominated the center. It nestled close to the shore, a pebbly beach separating the houses from the lake. He'd been told that the eastern shore was less visited and less populated. Only about 80,000 people lived in fifty or so communities. The lake's southern rim had developed into a tourist attraction, popular in summer, but the rest of the shoreline, stretching for hundreds of miles, remained remote.

Which was exactly why the place below existed.

Its occupants called the town Chayaniye, which meant "hope." Their only desire was to be left alone and the Russian government, for over twenty years, had accommodated them. They were the Red Guard. The last bastion of die-hard communists remaining in the new Russia.

He'd been told that the main house was an old dacha. Every respectable Soviet leader back to Lenin had owned a country place, and those who'd administered the far eastern provinces had been no exception. The one below sat atop a whaleback of rock jutting out into the frozen lake, at the end of a twisting black road among a dense entanglement of trailing pines feathered with snow. And it was no small, wooden garden hut, either. Instead, its ocher façade had been constructed from what appeared to be brick and concrete, rising two stories and topped by a slate roof. Two four-wheeled vehicles were parked off to one side. Smoke curled thick from its chimneys and from one of several wooden outbuildings.

No one was in sight.

He completed his pass and banked west back out over the lake for another tight circle. He loved flying and had a talent for controlling machinery in motion. Shortly, he'd make use of the skis and touch down on the ice five miles south near the town of Babushkin, then taxi to its dock—which, he'd been told, handled no water traffic this time of year. Ground transportation should be waiting there so he could head north for an even closer look.

He flew over Chayaniye and the dacha one last time, dipping for a final approach toward Babushkin. He knew about the Great Siberian March during the Russian Civil War. Thirty thousand soldiers had retreated across the frozen Baikal, most dying in the process, their bodies locked in the ice until spring when they finally disappeared down into the deep water. This was a cruel and brutal place. What had one writer once said? *Insolent to strangers, vengeful to the unprepared.*

And he could believe it.

A flash caught his attention from among the tall pines and larch, whose green branches stood in stark contrast with the white ground beneath them. Something flew from the trees, hurtling toward him, trailing a plume of smoke.

A missile?

"I've got problems," he said. "Somebody is shooting at me."

An instinctive reaction from years of experience threw him into autopilot. He banked hard right and dove further, losing altitude. The An-2 handled like an eighteen-wheeler, so he banked steeper to increase the dive. The man who'd turned the plane over earlier had warned him about keeping a tight grip on the controls, and he'd been right about that. The yoke bucked like a bull. Every rivet seemed on the verge of vibrating loose. The missile roared past, clipping both left wings. The fuselage shuddered from the impact and he leveled off out of the dive and assessed the damage. Only fabric had covered the lift surfaces, and many of the struts were now exposed and damaged, ragged edges whipping in the airflow.

Stability immediately became an issue.

The plane rocked and he fought to maintain control. He was now headed straight into a stiff north wind, his airspeed less than 50 knots. The danger of stalling became real.

"What's happening?" Stephanie asked.

The yoke continued to fight to be free, but he held tight and gained altitude. The engine roared like a rumble of motorcycles, the prop digging in, fighting to keep him airborne.

He heard a sputter.

Then a backfire.

He knew what was happening. Too much stress was being applied to the prop, which the engine resisted.

Power to the controls winked in and out.

"I've been hit by a surface-to-air missile," he told Stephanie. "I'm losing control and going down."

The engine died.

All of the instruments stopped working.

Windows wrapped the cockpit, front and side, the copilot's seat empty. He searched below and saw only the blue ice of Lake Baikal. The An-2 rapidly changed from a plane to eight thousand pounds of deadweight.

Dread swept through him, along with one thought.

Was this how he would die?

CHAPTER TWO

Stephanie Nelle stared at the speaker on the desk. Her direct link to Cotton's phone had gone quiet.

"Are you there?" she asked again.

Only silence continued to answer her.

Cotton's last words rang in her ears.

I'm losing control and going down.

She stared across the desk at Bruce Litchfield, the current acting attorney general and her boss for two more days. "He's in trouble. Someone shot his plane down with a surface-to-air missile."

She was working out of an office in the Justice Department. Usually she would be ensconced inside her own secure space at Magellan Billet headquarters in Atlanta. But that was not possible anymore, and with the impending inauguration of a new president she'd been ordered north to DC.

And she knew why.

So that Litchfield could keep an eye on her.

Back in December Harriett Engle, who'd served as President Danny Daniels' third attorney general, had tendered her resignation. The Daniels administration's two terms were over and not only would there be a new president but a new party had seized control of both the White House and half the Congress. Danny had tried hard to get his man elected, but failed. It seemed the Daniels magic only

applied to the man himself. Litchfield was here at this ungodly hour since he was in temporary command of both the Justice Department and what remained of the Magellan Billet.

Two months ago, on the day after Thanksgiving, she'd been informed that not only would she be reassigned from the head of the Magellan Billet, but the entire unit would be dismantled. The new attorney general, who would be confirmed by the Senate next week, had already stated that he considered the Billet duplicative of the countless other intelligence and counterintelligence units that populated the government. The Justice Department had no further need for those services, so the Billet would be abolished and all of its agents dispersed.

"Let the Russians deal with it," Litchfield said. "They asked for our help, you gave it to them, now it's their problem."

"You can't be serious. We have a man down. We don't rely on others to take care of our own."

"We do here. And don't forget, *you* sent Malone in there without my okay."

"The president of the United States asked me to do it."

Litchfield seemed unfazed. "You and I agreed that *all* operational decisions would be run through me. But that didn't happen. And we both know why. Because I would not have authorized it."

"I didn't need your authorization."

"Actually, you did. You know there's a working agreement that the current administration will keep the new one informed and that all operational decisions, starting last week, would be joint. It's my job to keep the new administration informed. For some reason, though, this operation became unilateral across the board."

Litchfield was career Justice with a respectable eighteen years. He was a Daniels appointee, confirmed by the Senate, and had served as deputy AG for the past five years. The new attorney general had yet to decide who, at the top level, would be kept on. Stephanie knew Litchfield was jockeying for a high-level post, so when the new president's AG appointee indicated a desire to end the Magellan Billet Litchfield had seized the opportunity to show he could play with the new team. Any other time she'd never tolerate this level of bureaucratic interference, but with the inauguration so close everything had gone fluid.

Authority swirled in a state of flux. Change, not consistency, ruled the day.

"You tried to keep this close," Litchfield said. "But I found out about it anyway. Which is why I'm here, in the middle of the damn night. White House approval or not, this is over."

"You better hope Cotton doesn't make it out," she said, with equal casualness.

"What's that supposed to mean?"

"You don't want to know."

"Inform the Russians about what happened," he said. "Let them handle it. And you never really explained why the president wanted Malone there in the first place."

No, she hadn't, even though Litchfield would surely understand the value of doing someone a favor. "Coin of the realm" is what they called it in DC. A favor done is a favor returned. That was the way things worked, especially years ago when she first started the Billet. Then her twelve agents were all lawyers, each additionally trained in intelligence and espionage. Cotton had been one of her first hires, brought over from the navy and JAG with a Georgetown law degree. He worked for her a dozen years before retiring out early and moving to Copenhagen, where he now owned an old bookshop. Periodically over the past few years, because of circumstances, he'd been drawn back into her world. Of late she'd hired him as contract help. Today's assignment, a simple recon mission, was one of those hires.

But something had gone wrong.

"Make it happen," he said to her.

Like hell. "Bruce, I'm still in charge of this agency for two more days. Until that time, I'll run it as I see fit. If you don't like that, fire me. But then you are going to have to explain yourself to the White House."

She knew that threat could not be ignored. Danny Daniels was still president and the Billet had been his go-to agency for quite some time. Litchfield was a typical DC panderer. His only goal was to survive and keep his job. How he accomplished that mattered not. She'd dealt with him on only a few occasions in the past, but she'd heard the talk about being an opportunist. So the last thing he could afford was a pissing contest with the current president of the United States, not only one that he would lose but one that would draw a lot of attention, too.

If this man wanted to be a part of the new administration, he had first to survive the old one.

"Look, don't take this in a mean way, but your time is over," he said to her. "So is the president's. Can't you both just let it go? Yes, you're in charge of the Billet. But no agents work for you anymore. They're all gone. You're all that's left. There's nothing left to do except some cleanup. Go home. Retire. Enjoy yourself."

The thought had occurred to her. She'd started back in the Reagan administration at State, then moved to Justice, eventually assigned to the Magellan Billet. She'd run the agency a long time, but now all that seemed over. Her sources had reported that the $10 million it took to fund the Billet would be redirected to social outreach, public relations, and other tools to bolster the new AG's image. Apparently that was deemed more important than covert intelligence work. Justice would leave the spying to the CIA, the NSA, and all the other alphabet agencies.

"Tell me, Bruce, what's it like to be second? Never the captain. Always the lieutenant."

He shook his head. "You *are* an insolent old bitch."

She grinned. "Insolent? Sure. Bitch? Probably. But I'm not old. What I am, though, is head of the Magellan Billet, for two more days. I may be its only employee left, but I'm still in charge. So either fire me—or get the hell out of here."

And she meant every word.

Especially the *"not old"* part. To this day her personnel file contained no reference to age, only the letters N/A in the space designated for a date of birth.

Litchfield stood. "Okay, Stephanie. We'll do this your way."

He couldn't fire her and they both knew it. But he could at noon on January 20. That was why she'd authorized Cotton to immediately head for Russia without seeking approval. The new AG was wrong. The Justice Department needed the Magellan Billet. Its whole purpose had been to work outside the scope of other intelligence agencies. That was why its headquarters had sat 550 miles south in Atlanta, far away from DC politics. That one decision, made by her years ago, had bred both an independence and an efficiency, and she was proud of that legacy.

Litchfield left the room, but he was right about one thing. All of her agents were gone, the offices in Atlanta shut down.

She had no intention of taking some other post within Justice or allowing herself to be fired. Instead, she was quitting. Time to cash in her pension and find something else to occupy her time. No way she was going to sit around the house all day.

Her mind raced, thinking with a comforting familiarity. Cotton was in trouble and she wasn't banking on the Russians to help. She hadn't particularly liked trusting them in the first place but there'd been no choice. All of the risks had been explained to Cotton, who'd assured her he'd stay alert. Now there seemed only one place left for her to turn.

She reached for her smartphone.

And sent a text.

CHAPTER THREE

LUKE DANIELS LOVED A FIGHT, BUT WHAT TENNESSEE COUNTRY boy didn't. He'd enjoyed many in high school, especially ones over a girl, then relished them even more during his six years as an Army Ranger. For the past year he'd had his share as a Magellan Billet agent, but sadly those days were over. He'd already received his marching orders, reassigned to the Defense Intelligence Agency, his first day on the job coming Monday, one day after the new president assumed office.

Until then, he was officially on leave.

Yet here he was, in the wee hours of the morning, following another car.

His uncle, the current president of the United States, had personally asked for his assistance. Normally he and his uncle did not see eye-to-eye but, of late, they'd both been trying harder on that relationship. Truth be told, he was glad to help. He loved the Magellan Billet and he liked Stephanie Nelle. She was being dished a raw deal by a bunch of politicians who thought they knew better. Uncle Danny was on his way out to pasture, his political career over. Yet there seemed one more problem, one more something that had captured both the president's and Stephanie's attention.

Characteristically, not much had been explained in the way of why he was following the car. His target was a Russian national named

Anya Petrova, a curvy blonde with a fine-featured, almond-shaped face and a pair of high cheekbones. Her legs were long and muscled, like a dancer, her movements poised and calculated. Her favorite ensemble seemed to be tight Levi's tucked into knee-high boots. No makeup either, lending her a slight air of severity, which might have been intentional. She was quite impressive and he wished they'd met under different circumstances. Watching her the past two days had not been all that unpleasant.

She seemed to like Cracker Barrel, visiting twice today, once for lunch, and the other for dinner a few hours ago. After eating she'd hung out in a Virginia motel west of DC, just off Interstate 66. Uncle Danny had provided all the pertinent information. She was thirty-four, the lover of Aleksandr Zorin, an aging former KGB officer now living in southern Siberia. Apparently no one had paid Zorin much mind until a week ago. Then something spooked both the Russians and Uncle Danny, enough that Luke had been dispatched as a hound dog and Cotton Malone sent overseas as point man.

"Just don't get made," the president said to him. *"Stay with her. Wherever she goes. Can you handle that?"*

Their relationship was testy at best, but he had to admit his uncle did know how to run things. The country would miss him, as Luke would miss his former job. He wasn't looking forward to the Defense Intelligence Agency. After graduating high school, avoiding college, and enlisting in the army, he'd finally found a home at the Billet.

Unfortunately, that was now gone.

He was a mile behind his target, providing a wide berth since there were few cars on the interstate, the winter night clear and calm. Half an hour ago he'd been watching the motel when Anya, carrying an ax, suddenly emerged and left, driving west into Virginia. They were now near Manassas and she was signaling for an exit. He followed suit, coming to the ramp's end after she turned south on a two-laned, rural highway. He'd have to allow a greater gap to open between them here as there were nowhere near the distractions an interstate highway offered.

Where was she headed in the middle of the friggin' night?

With an ax?

He thought about calling Uncle Danny and waking him up. He'd

been provided with a direct phone number and ordered to report anything immediately, but all they'd done so far was take a ride out in the
country.

Anya, half a mile ahead, turned again.

No cars were coming in either direction, the landscape pitch-black
for as far as he could see, so he doused his headlights and approached
the point where the car had veered from the highway.

He was behind the wheel of his pride and joy. A 1967 silver Mustang, a gift to himself while still in the army. He kept it tucked away
inside a garage adjacent to his DC apartment, one of the few possessions he truly cherished. He liked to drive it during the downtime
Stephanie Nelle required all Magellan Billet agents to take every four
weeks. He paid nearly $25,000 for it from a guy desperate for cash, a
bargain considering what the open market charged. It had come in
mint condition with a four-speed manual transmission and a souped-
up 320hp V-8. Not the best on fuel, but this thing had been built to
enjoy when gas was twenty-five cents a gallon.

He saw a driveway, framed on either side by heavy stone pillars,
capped with a wrought-iron archway. An iron gate hung askew, the path
beyond paved and leading into dark trees. No way he could drive in,
since he had no idea how far the path extended or what awaited. The
better tack was to use his feet, so he turned onto the drive, passed
through the entrance, and parked off into the trees never switching on
his headlights. He slipped from the Mustang and quietly closed the
door. The night was cold but not bone chilling. The mid-Atlantic states
had been enjoying a uncharacteristically mild winter, the heavy
snows of recent years bypassing them so far. He wore thick cord trousers and a sweater, along with an insulated jacket and gloves, his
Magellan Billet–issued Beretta tucked into a shoulder holster. He
didn't have a flashlight, but he did carry a cell phone that could do in
a pinch. He made sure the phone, though, was on silent.

He trotted ahead.

The run was only a couple hundred yards, leading to the black hulk
of a rambling two-story house with wings, annexes, and outbuildings.
To his left stretched a grassy field stiff under a dusting of frost. Movement caught his attention and he followed the shape of an owl winging
out over the field. He remembered those all too clearly from his days

growing up in rural Tennessee. Stars sharp as needles dotted a black velvet sky, only a quarter moon animating the heavens. He spotted a car parked in front of the house, a flashlight beam near the front door. He wondered who lived here as there'd been no name, mailbox, or anything identifying the address.

He kept to the trees and snaked a path clear of the snatching brambles. Cold worked its way toward his skin, but the burst of exertion and rising levels of anticipation caused him to sweat. He counted over thirty 16-paned windows along the front façade. No lights burned anywhere. He heard a rap, like metal on metal, then a splinter of wood. He settled against a tree and peered around its trunk, seeing the flashlight beam fifty yards away disappearing into the house. He wondered about the lack of finesse on entering and, as he came closer, realized the house was derelict and abandoned. Its outside had a Victorian look, most of its clapboard still intact, the walls splotchy with mold and scoured by weather. A few of the ground-floor windows were sheathed in plywood, the ones along the upper floor all exposed. Weeds and brush littered its base, as if no one had offered the place much attention in a long time.

He'd sure love to know who owned it. And why was a Russian national paying it a visit in the middle of the night? Only one way to find out, so he stepped from the copse at the edge of the drive and approached the front doorway, where thick paneled doors had been forced open.

He found his Beretta and gripped the weapon, then entered, careful with his steps. He stood inside a spacious foyer, a rug still covering the floor. A few pieces of furniture remained. A staircase wound upward and open doorways led into adjacent rooms where window treatments hung. Paint had peeled, plaster crumbled, the wallpaper pregnant in too many spots to count, the elements slowly reclaiming what was once theirs.

A hallway stretched ahead.

He listened, feeling as though he were standing in a tomb.

Then a sound.

Banging.

From across the ground floor.

Spears of light appeared in the hallway fifty feet ahead.

He crept forward, using the commotion from the far room as cover for his steps. Anya Petrova seemed unconcerned about attracting attention. She most likely assumed that there was nobody around for miles. And normally she'd be right.

He came to the open doorway where the light leaked out into the hall. Carefully, he peered around the jamb and saw what was once a large paneled study, one wall floor-to-ceiling with bookcases, the empty shelves collapsed and lying askew. He caught a glimpse of the ceiling overhead. Coffered with plastered decorations. No furniture. Anya seemed focused on the far wall, where she was gouging a hole in the wood paneling. And not subtly, either. She clearly knew how to use the ax. Her flashlight lay on the floor, splashing enough illumination for her to judge the progress.

His assignment was to watch, not engage.

"Don't get made."

She kept pounding, hacking away chucks of wood until a hole appeared. He noticed that the wall was an interior one, the space being opened up beyond it hollow. She used her right boot to splinter more wood, completing her incision and inspecting the area past the opening with her flashlight.

She laid the ax down.

Then she disappeared through the gash.

CHAPTER FOUR

CASSIOPEIA VITT REALIZED TOO LATE THAT SOMETHING WASN'T right. Two days ago her quarrymen had bored a series of holes into the limestone, not with modern drills and concrete bits, but the way it had been done 800 years ago. A long, metal, star-shaped chisel, the bit as thick as a man's thumb, had been pounded into the rock, then turned and pounded again, the process repeated over and over until a neat tunnel penetrated several inches deep. The holes had been spaced a full hand apart, ten meters across the entire cliff face. No rulers had been used. As in olden times a long rope with knots had served that purpose. Each cavity had then been filled with water, capped, and allowed to freeze. If it had been summer they would have been packed with wet wood or split with metal wedges. Thankfully, the temperature had plummeted enough that Mother Nature could offer a helping hand.

The quarry sat three kilometers from her French estate. For nearly a decade she'd been hard at work trying to build a castle using only tools, materials, and techniques available in the 13th century. The site she'd purchased had first been occupied by the only canonized king of France, Louis IX. It contained not only the castle ruins but also a 16th-century château that she'd remodeled into her home. She'd named the property Royal Champagne, after one of Louis XV's cavalry regiments.

A mason tower was once the symbol of a nobleman's power, and the castle that stood at Givors had been designed as a military fortress with curtain walls, a moat, corner posts, and a large keep. Razed nearly three hundred years ago, its resurrection had become her life's mission. And just as in medieval times, the surrounding environs still provided an abundance of water, stone, earth, sand, and wood—everything needed for construction. Quarrymen, hewers, masons, carpenters, blacksmiths, and potters, all on her payroll, labored six days a week, living and dressing exactly as they would have eight centuries ago. The site was open to the public and admission fees helped defray costs, but most of the work had been funded from her own extensive resources, with a current estimate of another twenty years needed to complete.

The quarrymen examined the holes, the water inside frozen solid, expansion cracks radiating outward signaling all was ready. The cliff face towered many meters, the rock face bare with few cracks, crevices, or protrusions. Months ago they'd extracted all of the usable material at or near ground level, now they were twenty meters up, atop scaffolding built of wood and rope. Three men with mallets began pounding *chase masses*. The impact tools looked like hammers, but one side was forged into two sharp edges joined by a concave curve. That side was nestled to the rock, then struck with a hammer to expose a seam. By moving the *chase masse* along that seam, striking over and over, shock waves pulsated through the rock causing splits along natural fissures. A tedious process, for sure, but it worked.

She stood and watched as the men kept maneuvering the *chase masses*, metal-to-metal clashing in an almost lyrical beat. A series of long cracks indicated that enough fissures had fractured.

"It's about to break," one of the quarrymen warned.

Which was the signal for the others to stop.

They all stood silent and studied the cliff face that rose another twenty meters above them. Tests had shown that this gray-white stone came loaded with magnesium, which made it extra-hard, perfect for building. Below them a horse-drawn cart stuffed with hay waited to take the man-sized chucks—those one person could lift on his own—straight back to the construction site. The hay acted as natural padding to minimize chipping. Larger pieces would be hewn here, then transported. This was ground zero for her entire endeavor.

She watched as the cracks increased in length and frequency, gravity now their ally. Finally, a slab the size of a Mercedes broke free and dropped from the rock face, crashing to the ground below. The men seemed pleased with their effort. So was she. Many stone blocks could be extracted from that prize. A gaping indentation remained in the cliff, their first excavation at this level. They'd now move left and right and drop more of the limestone before raising the scaffolding higher. She liked to watch her people at work, all of them dressed as men would have been long ago, the only exception being that the coats and gloves were modern. As were hard hats and safety goggles, accommodations her insurer had insisted upon and that history would have to forgive.

"Good job, everyone," the foreman said.

And she nodded her agreement.

The men started shimmying down the wood supports. She lingered a moment and admired the quarry. Most of the workers had been with her for years. She paid good wages, year-round, and included room and board. French universities provided a steady supply of interns, all anxious to be part of such an innovative project. During the summer she employed seasonal help but here, in the dead of winter, only the hardcores kept at it. She'd reserved today to be at the construction site, starting with this extraction. Three of the four curtain walls were nearly complete and the stone just acquired would go a long way toward finishing the fourth.

She heard a crack.

Followed by another.

Not unusual since they'd affected the cliff's integrity.

She turned back toward the rock face. Another series of snaps and pops from above drew her attention.

"Get everybody away," she screamed to the workers below. "Now. Go."

She waved her arms signaling for them to flee the scaffolding. She wasn't sure what was happening, but caution seemed the right course. The breaks came louder and quicker, like rounds from a distant automatic weapon, a sound she knew all too well. She needed to go and turned for the far side of the platform where it was easier to climb down. But a limestone chuck split from the cliff face and crashed into the top-level planks. The wooden scaffolding pulsated beneath her feet. There was nothing for her to hold on to and balancing was tricky, so she dropped to the cold wood and clung to the edges until the rocking subsided. The tower holding her aloft seemed to have survived the assault, its rope bindings able to give and take. Voices from below asked if she was all right.

She came to her knees and glanced over the side. "I'm okay."

She stood and shook off the dirt and dust.

"We're going to need to examine the scaffolding," she yelled down. "That was a hard hit."

A new pop drew her attention.

She glanced up and knew what was happening. Rock from above where they'd just extracted was freeing itself along a sedimentary layer, gravity now becoming their enemy and exploiting every weak point. For all its seeming invincibility stone could be as finicky as wood.

Two cracking explosions shook the rock wall.

Dust and scree rained down from overhead and fouled the air. Another boulder-sized piece fell and just missed the scaffolding. She could not flee ahead, as that would lead her directly into the problem. So she turned and rushed toward the other end of the platform. Behind her, more limestone found the planks and obliterated part of the supports.

She saw that all of the workers had fled out of harm's way.

Only she remained.

Another huge piece slammed into the exposed wooden beams. In an instant she'd have nothing to stand on. She glanced down and spotted the hay cart, still in place, ten meters below. The pile looked sufficient but there was no way to know for sure.

Unfortunately, she had no choice.

She leaped out, headfirst, and flipped over midair so that her spine led the way. If she'd calculated correctly the hay should be right beneath her. She heard the wooden tower collapse from the rocky onslaught. She closed her eyes and waited. A second later she found the hay, which cushioned her impact and brought her to an abrupt stop. She opened her eyes, lying faceup, and listened to the crescendo of rock and wood finding the ground.

She stood and surveyed the destruction.

Clouds of dust rolled skyward.

Her employees rushed over and asked if she was hurt. She shook her head and made sure again that all of them were all right.

"Looks like we have a mess to clean up," she said.

She rolled out of the cart, her nerves rattled, but accidents happen, especially on a project of this magnitude. Thankfully, to date, none of the on-site injuries had been substantial.

She held a degree in medieval architecture from l'École pratique des hautes études in Paris, her master's thesis on Pierre de Montreuil, the 13th-century proponent of Gothic style. She'd taken nearly a year to design her castle and hoped to be around when it was finished. She was not yet forty, so age wasn't the problem. It was the risks she sometimes took, and not just the ones that came from falling rock. Through the years she'd been involved with some scary stuff. She'd worked with foreign governments, intelligence agencies, even presidents, never allowing the inevitability of a routine to capture her. But if you stayed around people with guns long enough, eventually something bad happened. So far, though, she'd been lucky.

Like today.

The workers headed for the rubble.

Her cell phone vibrated in her coat pocket.

Over the past couple of weeks she'd been working more closely with her family corporation, headquartered in Barcelona. Her mother and father had bequeathed the company to her as their sole heir and she was its only shareholder, its assets totaling in the billions and stretching across six continents. Usually business was one of her least favorite tasks, the day-to-day operations left to competent officers, but work of late had taken her mind off other things. She assumed this was another call from the chief executive officer. They'd already talked once today.

But the alert had been for a text.

She tapped the icon and saw the sender.

STEPHANIE NELLE.

Her spine stiffened, as this the last, or at least next-to-last person she wanted to hear from.

She read the message.

Cotton's in trouble and I wouldn't be telling you this if it wasn't bad.

CHAPTER FIVE

Lake Baikal, Russia

Malone shut his eyes in a bid to clear his mind. He had one shot to survive, so he held on to the yoke and kept the nose straight into the headwind, intentionally trying to stall. The guy who'd turned the plane over to him had bragged that the An-2 was capable of flying backward in a thirty-knot headwind. Pilots had even managed to maneuver themselves to the ground like a parachute. He'd wondered about such a boast, but was about to find out if it was true.

The plane bucked in the turbulence and he yanked the control column full aft, keeping the wings level, which wasn't easy considering that a respectable part of the two left ones was gone. The engine remained dead, instruments not working, the cockpit turning cold from the lack of a heater, his exhales evident in gray fogs. Luckily, he was dressed properly. Thermals close to the skin, windproof on the outside, insulation in between, all Russian army issue. Gloves protected his hands, boots his feet, and a fur-lined hood part of his fiber-pile coat.

He felt airspeed diminish, the plane being held aloft by the headwind. Two loud snaps drew his attention. Stress on the wings had buckled the leading edge slats. He began to lose altitude and not at a steady rate, more a steep drop. He worked the control surfaces and managed to regain some stability, the plane leveling but still falling. He stole a quick glance out the windows and saw the blue ice and sugared surface of the lake approaching. The plane rocked right, then left, but he was able to counter the motion and keep the fuselage pointing into the wind. Sunlight blared back in reflection from the windows. A buffeting blast of icy air blew straight at him, the stiff wind acting like his engine and providing lift, the plane heading down backward against the gusts. He had no idea where or what he would hit and realized the landing would be anything but smooth, so he quickly made sure his harness was tight and braced himself.

He found the ground, tail-first, the landing skis smacking, then recoiling, strong surface winds assaulting the An-2. A rasp of steel edges on the crusted ice told him he was no longer airborne. Pain from the sharp impact shot through his head, short-circuiting his brain in a starburst of sparks that exploded before his eyes. He tasted blood on his tongue. Nothing he could do but hope the slide ended soon. The plane's weight finally allowed it to settle on the surface, skidding backward then spinning like an amusement park ride. Thank goodness there was plenty of room.

He juddered to a stop.

Nothing but the pulsating blood in his ears and the puff of his exhales broke the silence.

He smiled.

That was a first.

He was once a fighter pilot, trained by the navy, and he still maintained a commercial licence. He'd flown a variety of aircraft, just about everything. But he bet few had ever stalled out then landed backward and lived to tell the tale.

He released his harness and squinted out at the shimmering blue plate. A weather-scarred truck, painted a dull red beneath a gray dribble of slush on its hood and sides, approached. From the fuselage, he noticed liquid gushing out on the ice, the stench of fuel strong in the freezing air. He'd sprung a leak, big time. The truck was speeding straight at him across the lake through a light mist that wreathed the surface. It could be someone coming to help. He could definitely use a ride to Babushkin, where his own ground transportation was waiting. He needed to not only investigate the dacha but also discover who'd tried to shoot him down.

The truck kept coming, its treaded tires spitting out snow. Wind buffeted the plane and the temperature inside the cockpit turned colder. He slipped the hood of his coat up over his freezing ears. His Magellan Billet–issued Beretta was tucked inside a shoulder harness beneath his coat. His cell phone remained connected to the An-2's communications equipment. He was about to disconnect it when the truck glided to a stop thirty yards away and two men emerged, both carrying automatic rifles, their eyes staring out from apertures in ski masks.

Not the usual Welcome Wagon fare.

They crouched and aimed.

He rolled from his seat just as gunfire erupted.

Rounds obliterated the forward windscreen. Shrouds of glass rained down. The plane's aluminum skin was no match for high-caliber bullets, which penetrated at will. He needed to leave. Now. He crawled through the doorway into the aft compartment.

So much for a simple recon mission.

He reached beneath his coat and found his gun. Then he realized that the exit door was on the side of the plane opposite from where the truck had stopped. He wrenched the latch open and launched himself out onto the blue ice. Gunfire continued to echo, the plane peppered with rounds. He hoped he'd have a few seconds of freedom before his assailants realized he was gone.

He kept the plane between him and them and ran.

Twenty yards out he stopped and turned.

The firing had stopped.

He saw one of the men near the propeller, the other rounding the tail, their attention on the plane, then on him. Fuel continued to pour from the center of the fuselage to the ice, the orangey liquid oozing out across the frozen surface. Normally a bullet would not ignite anything. That only happened on television. But he knew that rule did not apply to aviation juice. Not much was needed to set it off.

He aimed mid-center and fired two rounds.

Neither man got a chance to do a thing.

An explosion lit the sky and a maelstrom of forced air rushed his way. He was thrown down to the ice, which felt like slamming onto concrete. He rolled twice then refocused on the plane, which was gone, along with the two problems, which were now charred lumps of blackened flesh and carbonized bone.

As was his phone.

Which meant he had no way of immediately contacting anybody.

He trotted around the holocaust of flames and smoke and found the truck. Thankfully, keys remained in the ignition. A handheld radio lay on one of the seats. He climbed inside, pushed the SEND button, and said, "Who's listening?"

"I am," a male voice said in perfect English.

"And you are?"

"How about you go first?"

"I'm the guy who just took out two men with rifles."

"That would make you a problem."

"I get that a lot. Why did you shoot me down?"

"Why are *you* here?"

He could not reveal the real reason, so he decided on another tack. "How about we meet, face-to-face, and have a chat. I'm American, not Russian. If that matters to you."

"You were spying on my home."

Then he realized who was speaking.

"My name is Cotton Malone. You must be Aleksandr Zorin."

Silence signaled he was right.

"I'm assuming you now have the truck," Zorin said.

He thumbed the mike button, his own mouth dry, and let the man wait. Finally, he said, "It's all mine."

"Head due east from where you are. Come off the lake onto the main highway. There's only one road. Follow that north until you see the observatory. I'll wait for you there."

CHAPTER SIX

Aleksandr Zorin left his clothes inside the rude entryway and stooped low through a fur-clad door. The space he entered was dark and gloomy. A tallow candle burned feebly in one corner, throwing off barely enough light to define a circular room built of hewn logs. The windowless walls were midnight black from the sooty deposits of fires that had baked them for decades. A pile of stones dominated the center, a strong blaze from birch logs burning beneath. A series of pine benches descended from one side like steps. A chimney hole high above allowed smoke to vent, leaving only dry heat from the stones, which made breathing painful and perspiration a necessity.

"Do you like my black bath?" he asked the other man already inside, sitting on one of the benches.

"I have missed them."

Both men were naked, neither ashamed of his body. His own remained hard, a barrel chest and ridges of muscles still there, though he would be sixty-two later in the year. The only scar was white and puckered across the left breast, an old knife wound from his former days. He stood tall with a face that tried hard to express perpetual confidence. His hair was an unruly black mane that always looked in need of a brush and scissors. He had boyish features women had always found attractive, especially the thin nose and lips of his father. His right eye was green, the left brown or gray depending on the light, a trait that his mother bestowed. Sometimes it was as though he had two faces superimposed, and he'd many times used that anomaly to maximum advantage. He prided himself on being a man of education, both formal and self-taught. He'd suffered for decades through a life of exile but had learned to stifle his needs and habits, accepting his forced descent to a lower sphere, where he breathed noticeably differ-ent air—like a fish tossed upon the sand.

He stepped over and sat on a bench, the slats wet and warm. "I built this to replicate the black baths of the old days."

Every village had once provided a *banya* similar to this one, a place to escape Siberia's nearly year-round cold. Most of those, like his for-mer world, were now gone.

His guest was a stolid, brutal-looking Russian at least ten years older with an agreeable voice and teeth stained yellow from years of nicotine. Receding blond hair swept back from a steep forehead and did nothing to strengthen an overall weak appearance. His name was Vadim Belchenko and, unlike himself, this man had never suffered exile.

But Belchenko did know rejection.

Once, he'd been a person of great importance, the chief archivist for the First Chief Directorate, the KGB's foreign intelligence arm. When the Soviet Union fell and the Cold War ended, Belchenko's job immediately became obsolete, as those secrets mattered no longer.

"I am glad you agreed to come," he told his guest. "It has been too long, and things must be resolved."

Belchenko was nearly blind, his eyes wearing their cataracts like ac-quired wisdom. He'd had the older man brought east two days ago. A request that would have turned into an order, but that had proved un-necessary. Since arriving, his guest had stayed inside the black bath most of the time, soaking in the silence and heat.

"I heard a plane," Belchenko said.

"We had a visitor. I suspect the government is looking for you."

The older man shrugged. "They fear what I know."

"And do they have reason?"

He and Belchenko had talked many times. Nearly every person they ever knew or respected was dead, in hiding, or disgraced. Where they all once proudly called themselves Soviets, now that word bordered on obscene. In 1917 the Bolsheviks had cried with pride *All power to the Soviets*, but the phrase today would be regarded as treason. How the world had changed since 1991 when the Union of Soviet Socialist Republics dissolved. What a magnificent state it had been. The world's largest, covering a sixth of the planet. Over 10,000 kilometers from east to west across eleven time zones. Seven thousand kilometers north to south. In between lay tundra, taiga, steppes, desert, mountains, rivers, and lakes. Tartars, tsars, and communists had ruled there for 800 years. Fifteen nationalities, a hundred ethnic groups, 127 languages. All ruled by the Communist party, the army, and the KGB. Now it was the Russian Federation—which had evolved into barely a shadow of what had once existed. And instead of trying to reverse the inevitable and fight a battle that could not be won, in 1992 he and a hundred others had retreated east to Baikal, where they'd lived beside the lake ever since. An old Soviet dacha served as their headquarters and a cluster of homes and shops not far away became Chayaniye.

Hope.

Which seemed all that remained.

"What of the plane?" Belchenko asked.

"I ordered it shot down."

The old man chuckled. "With what? British Javelins? MANPADs? Or some of those ancient Redeyes?"

Impressive how the old mind remained sharp for details. "I used what's available. But you're right, what we fired was defective. It still managed to accomplish the task."

He bent down to a pail of cold water and tossed a ladleful onto the hot stones. They hissed like a locomotive, tossing off welcomed steam. The candle across the room burned bluer through a deeper halo. Temperatures rose and his muscles relaxed. Steam burned his eyes, which he closed.

"Is the pilot alive?" Belchenko asked.

"He survived the landing. An American."

"Now, that is interesting."

In decades past they would have spread their bodies out on the lowest of the pine benches while attendants doused them with hot water. Then they would have then been scrubbed, rolled, pounded, and drenched with cold water, then more hot, their muscles pelted with bundles of birch twigs and washed with wads of hemp. More long douses of cold water would have ended the experience, leaving them cleansed and feeling disembodied.

The black baths had been a wonderful thing.

"You know what I want to know," he said to Belchenko. "It's time you tell me. You can't allow that knowledge to die with you."

"Should this not be left alone?"

He'd asked himself that question many times, the answer always the same, so he voiced it. "No."

"It still matters to you?"

He nodded.

The older man sat with his arms extended outward up to the next level of bench. "My muscles feel so alive in here."

"You're dying, Vadim. We both know that."

He'd already noticed the painful breathing, deep and irregular. The emaciated frame, the rattling in the throat, and the trembling hands.

"I kept so many secrets," Belchenko said, barely in a whisper. "They trusted me with everything. Archivists were once so important. And I knew America. I studied the United States. I knew its strengths and weaknesses. History taught me a great deal." The old man's eyes stayed closed as he ranted. "History matters, Aleksandr. Never forget that."

As if he had to be told. "Which is why I cannot let this go. The time has come. The moment is right. I, too, have studied the United States. I know its *current* strengths and weakness. There is a way for us to extract a measure of satisfaction, one we both have craved for a long time. We owe that to our Soviet brothers."

And he told his old friend exactly what he had in mind.

"So you have solved Fool's Mate?" Belchenko asked when he finished.

"I'm close. The documents you provided last year were a great help. Then I found more. Anya is in Washington, DC, right now, attempting to locate a critical piece."

He could see that the ancient archivist seemed fully conscious of his remaining influence. And forty years of keeping the KGB's secrets had definitely empowered him. So much that the Russian government still kept watch. Which might explain their visitor.

But an American?

That puzzled him.

For twenty years he'd fought time and circumstances, both of which had tried hard to turn him into a corpse. Luckily, that had not happened. Instead, vengeance had kept him alive. What remained unknown was how much hate still lingered inside his guest.

"I thought Fool's Mate a dead end," Belchenko said.

He'd not been sure, either. But thankfully, his dominant characteristic had always been boundless energy and an immovable will. And if exile had taught him nothing else, it had crystallized the value of patience. Hopefully, Anya would be successful and they could move forward.

"The time to strike," he said, "is soon. There will not be another opportunity for years."

"But is it relevant anymore?"

"You hesitate?"

Belchenko frowned. "I merely asked a question."

"It matters to me."

"The zero amendment," his guest muttered.

"That's part of it. What I need is what you personally know. Tell me, Vadim. Let me be the one to use what's out there."

For so long he'd felt like a man buried alive who suddenly wakes and pushes against the lid of his coffin, all the while realizing the futility of his efforts. But not anymore. He now saw a way out of that coffin. A way to be free. And this was not about the pursuit of his own legend or politics or any specific agenda. No other purpose existed for what he was about to do save vengeance.

He owed the world.

"All right, Aleksandr, I will tell you. He lives in Canada."

"Can you direct me to him?"

Belchenko nodded.

So he listened as everything was explained. Then he stood from the bench and checked his watch. Sequins of sweat glistened across his skin.

Only 56 hours remained.

An urgency enveloped him, choking, yet electric, quick spasms to his muscles and brain urging action. The years of dull, nerve-grinding non-accomplishment might finally be over.

"I have to go."

"To find out why that American is here?" Belchenko asked.

"What makes you think I will see him?"

"Where else would you be going?"

Indeed. Where else? But an American being here at this precise moment was no coincidence.

"I might require your help with him," he said.

"An adventure?" Belchenko asked, doubt in the voice.

He smiled. "More a precaution."

CHAPTER SEVEN

FRANCE

CASSIOPEIA STARED AT THE PHONE AND SAW A SECOND TEXT APpear from Stephanie Nelle, this one with a phone number and the words CALL ME.

The past few weeks had been anything but calm. Life for her had taken a 180-degree turn. She'd made some major decisions that had deeply affected others, particularly Cotton. At first with all that happened in Utah she'd thought herself on the side of right, but hindsight had allowed her to see that she may have been wrong. And the results? A man she'd cared about in her youth was dead, and a man she loved now had been driven away.

She'd thought a lot about Cotton. His last phone call came a few weeks ago, which she'd not answered. Her reply by email—LEAVE ME ALONE—had obviously been heeded since there'd been no further contact. Cotton was a proud man, never would he grovel, nor would she expect him to. She'd made her feelings clear and he'd obviously respected them.

But she missed him.

Everything still weighed heavy. Part of her psyche screamed that Cotton and Stephanie had simply done their jobs and circumstances had left them little choice. But another part of her was tired of the lies that came with working intelligence operations. She'd been used. Even worse. She'd used herself, thinking she could keep things under control. But she'd been wrong and people had died.

She read Stephanie's first message again, hoping the words might be different. No mistake, though. Cotton was in trouble. Stephanie had been the one who'd drawn her into Utah. She blamed Stephanie more than Cotton for what ultimately happened. In response, she'd cut off all contact with Stephanie, too. If she never spoke to the woman again that was fine by her. But where was Cotton? What was he doing? And why had Stephanie felt the need to call for help? She should follow her own directive and leave it alone, but realized that was not an option.

She retreated from the commotion in the quarry, back down a tree-lined path toward her château. Bright rays of morning sun rained down from a cloudless sky through bare winter limbs. In summer the leafy oaks and elms high overhead closed into a natural cloister that cast a perpetual evening-like gloom. Purple heather, broom, and wild-flowers would carpet the dark earth on both sides. But not today. All was winter-dead, the air brisk enough to warrant a coat, which she wore, now streaked in limestone dust. She knew what had to be done and tapped the blue number in the text, allowing the smartphone to dial.

"How have you been?" Stephanie asked her.

She wasn't interested in small talk. "What's wrong?"

"Cotton is in Russia, doing something for me. He was piloting a small plane that was attacked from the ground. He went down."

She stopped walking, closed her eyes, and bit her lip.

"I've lost all contact with him."

"Is he alive?"

"I have no way of knowing."

"Send an agent."

"I don't have any more agents. The Magellan Billet is over. All my people are gone. Our new president has different priorities, which don't include me."

"Then how did Cotton get to Russia?"

"We have a developing situation here, one that warranted action. The White House okayed me hiring him to have a look. He's done a couple of jobs for me since Utah. But something went wrong."

That seemed a recurring theme in her life, particularly when fate was so consciously tempted. Luckily, she wasn't fooling herself anymore. The past few weeks of quiet reflection had brought things into sharp focus. She now knew that she bore as much responsibility for what had happened as Stephanie and Cotton. Which, more than anything else, explained why she'd called.

"The Russians asked for our help," Stephanie said.

"Help with what?"

"A look at some living, breathing relics from the past that might be a big problem."

"If you want *my* help, tell me everything."

And she hoped Stephanie understood what had not been said. *Not like last time when you held back, then lied to me.*

She listened as Stephanie told her that after the 1991 fall of the Soviet Union, most communists inside Russia assumed a low profile and kept to themselves. A small group of diehards, though, migrated east and settled on the shores of Lake Baikal. The Russian government periodically kept a watch but by and large left them alone, and the favor was returned. Then something changed.

"One of them is here, in DC," Stephanie said. "Luke Daniels is engaging her, as we speak."

She recalled the handsome, young Magellan Billet agent who'd been there in Utah with the rest of them. "I thought you didn't have any more agents?"

"The president enlisted him."

She knew the uncle–nephew connection. "Why are the Russians so cooperative?"

"I don't know the answer to that. But I'm about to find out."

"You and I have a problem," she said.

"I get that. But I did what had to be done. I'm not making any apologies for what happened in that cave."

Nor had she expected any. Stephanie Nelle was tough. She ran the Magellan Billet with dictatorial efficiency. They'd first met right here, on her estate, a few years ago. Since then she'd several times been involved with Stephanie, never regretting any of that until a month ago.

Her nerves were still rattled from the incident on the scaffolding. None of the people who worked for her knew the extent of her extracurricular activities. No one was aware how she could handle a gun and deal with trouble. She kept all of that to herself. That was another reason Cotton had been so special. They were so alike.

"Why are you telling me this?" she asked Stephanie. "I'm a long way from Russia."

She heard the far-off baritone beat of rotors pelting the air, growing louder. She squinted through the trees and saw the outline of a military helicopter sweeping in from the north across the nearby foothills.

"Did you send a chopper here?" she asked.

"There's a French military base not ten miles from you. I made a call and can have you in Russia within five hours. I need you to make a decision. Either get on that chopper or send it back."

"Why would I go?"

"I can give you the practical reasons. You're highly skilled. More than capable. Discreet. And you speak fluent Russian. But you and I know the real reason."

A moment of silence filled her ear.

"You love him, and he needs you."

CHAPTER EIGHT

LUKE MADE A DECISION. HE WOULD FOLLOW ORDERS AND JUST observe. Malone had taught him that field agents could pretty much do whatever they wanted, as long as they delivered results.

But not tonight.

This was clearly an off-the-grid, unofficial op being done at the personal request of the president of the United States. So he remained a good boy and stayed put as the light played off whatever lay beyond the gash in the wall.

He heard a series of soft thuds, like something hitting the floor.

A pause.

Then a few more.

Anya Petrova was obviously here for something specific. After all, she'd traveled thousands of miles to this exact spot. He had to admit, his curiosity was getting the best of him, but he kept telling himself he could come back later and see what was there.

The light beams re-angled toward the makeshift entrance and an instant later Anya appeared, climbing through the gash with nothing in her hand besides the flashlight. He did not linger. Instead, he retreated into a room across the hall and hoped she didn't come his way. He heard a click and the flashlight beam extinguished, plunging the interior back into darkness. He flattened himself against the wall and listened to her determined steps, one click after another, as she marched back toward the front door. He assumed she was wearing the same pair of leather boots from the past couple of days.

He hesitated an instant, then peered out to see her about to leave through the front door. He waited a few seconds more, then, making little to no sound, hustled in the same direction, coming to the outside door and expecting to see her departing.

But no one was in sight and the car was still there.

Before he could react to the obvious repercussions she pounced, leaping onto his back, wrapping a cord around his throat, forming a garrote, which she tightened, cutting off his breathing. She'd apparently twisted the rope as it had been applied, making it easier for her to choke the life out of him, and he had to admit she was doing a pretty fair job of it.

Oxygen to his brain rapidly depleted.

His head exploded in lights and black circles that whirled before him.

But he was no amateur.

So he broke with the code of a southern gentleman and rammed his right boot into her knee, moving closer to reduce her advantage, which kept the rope from accomplishing its fatal duty.

Never pull away when someone is choking you.

Self-defense 101.

She absorbed his first blow, but a second gave her pause.

He spun and jammed his elbow into her shoulder, wrenching her backward and freeing her grip on the rope. She spun on her heels, steadied herself with outstretched arms, and laughed.

"That all?" she asked.

He lunged forward swinging his right leg around for a full body blow. But she was quick as a bird and dodged his attack, landing a kick of her own to the small of his back.

Which hurt.

He was still recovering from the choking, grabbing as many breaths as possible, and she seemed to sense his quandary, vaulting into the air and planting her right boot into his chest. The blow propelled him backward and he lost all balance, dropping down where the back of his head found something hard.

Everything winked in and out.

She fled out the front door.

He climbed to his feet. That woman was strong and knew how to fight. She also seemed to have enjoyed it, and apparently her orders were not similar to his own.

"Don't get made."

She'd gone out of her way to engage him.

He staggered out and heard an engine growl to life, then watched as she made her escape. He grabbed hold of himself and rushed into the night, reaching for the Beretta and a shot at her tires or the rear window, but the receding taillights trailed away like a meteor down the lane.

He ran toward the Mustang.

Cold air seared his lungs and throat, but he kept moving, glad that he maintained a steady physical regimen that included five miles of jogging each week. His thirty-year-old body was mainly muscle and he intended on keeping it that way for as long as the good Lord allowed.

He made it to the Mustang, hopped inside, and fired up the V-8. Time to put that power to use. Tires spun on the cold ground as he backed out then sped through the wrought-iron entrance to the highway. No cars were in sight either way. He assumed she'd headed back the same way she came, so he turned left and floored the accelerator. Being in the middle of nowhere in the dead of night had advantages, so he gained speed trying to catch up. The road ahead remained devoid of taillights and nothing appeared in his rearview mirror. He recalled from earlier that the highway was fairly straight all the way from the interstate.

So where was she?

The answer came with a bang as something popped into his rear bumper. Headlights suddenly ignited in his mirror and he realized the bitch had waited for him.

No problem.

He relaxed on the accelerator and veered left into the oncoming lane. She matched his move and slammed once again into his bumper.

She was about to really piss him off.

Tires squealed and he was forced back to the right, the steering wheel nearly torn from his grip. He drifted too far and found the road edge, wobbling in the soft shoulder. At this speed that could lead to disaster. He yanked the wheel left and once again acquired hard pavement. Anya had used his moment of distraction to maneuver into the left-hand lane and come parallel. He glanced over but could see little in the pitch dark. The interior cabin light in her vehicle came on and he saw her face, staring at him through the windows.

She puckered her lips and threw him a kiss.

Then the lights extinguished.

And she veered her car into his.

Now she had pissed him off.

This was a 1967 Mustang in mint condition. But not anymore. So he jammed the accelerator to the floor and decided to see how fast she wanted to go. He alternated his attention from her on the left to the road ahead. They'd already passed beneath I-66, now heading north into rural Virginia. The road ahead vaulted up a short hill. She was still beside him in the other lane seemingly unconcerned with what might lie over that rise.

So he decided to amplify her problems.

He yanked the wheel and started to force her from the road. What did it matter? That side of the car needed a body shop now anyway.

A guardrail protected her on the left side.

He heard the grinding screech of metal hitting metal and realized she was pinned. From the corner of his eye he caught movement. A quick glance and he saw the passenger-side window in her car descend. Anya's right arm extended and he saw a gun. No time to do anything but duck, which he did, shifting right and trying to drop below the window while keeping his foot on the accelerator and hands on the steering wheel.

He heard a bang, then the driver's-side window exploded inward. He shut his eyes as glass spewed across the front seats. Fragments stung his face and hands. His foot slipped from the accelerator, which instantly slowed the car enough for her to scoot past. He settled back in his seat and was about to head her way when she veered into his lane and slowed, challenging him to hit her from the rear.

He spun the wheel left.

The Mustang hurled into the oncoming lane and he passed her. But as he did, a spray of bullets peppered the car's right side, thudding into the panels, obliterating one of the rear windows.

Two loud bangs signaled a new problem.

Tires blown.

He jerked the wheel hard right. The rear end swished side-to-side. A curve was approaching that he knew could not be negotiated on two tires. The risk of flipping loomed great, and this car came with no shoulder harnesses. Sweat stung his eyes and he eased off the gas, trying to regain equilibrium as his speed slowed. The wheels chattered. A loud clatter of metal against roadway signaled the end of the line.

Anya sped ahead, then fishtailed around a curve and disappeared into the night.

He stopped, opened the door, and stepped out to the road.

He rounded the car and saw smoke billowing from the two gone tires. Bullet holes dotted the entire side, along with massive dents, missing paint, and a shattered window.

A friggin' 1967 first-generation Mustang.

Destroyed.

He slammed the palm of his hand onto the hood and cursed. He kicked the side of the car and cursed some more. Thank goodness his mother wasn't here to hear him. She never had liked a foul mouth.

"Don't get made."

The last thing Uncle Danny told him.

That hadn't worked out.

CHAPTER NINE

STEPHANIE HEADED TOWARD THE GROUND FLOOR OF THE JUSTICE Department building. There was little she could do from here with a dead telephone line as her sole means of communication. She hoped Cotton's phone was simply broken or out of service, not destroyed in a plane crash. She'd called her Russian counterpart, the man who'd first requested American assistance, who assured her he would have the situation assessed. He also agreed, though, that Cassiopeia could come, acting as American eyes and ears. Whatever was happening seemed unusual, to say the least. But soon none of this would be her problem anymore.

She buttoned her coat and left out the front doors, past a security checkpoint. Though her watch read 3:40 A.M. she wasn't the least bit tired. She decided to head back to the Mandarin Oriental and wait for news in her hotel room. At least there she was free of Litchfield, though she doubted he'd be bothering her again until he was truly in charge.

Normally there would be a car waiting to drive her but that perk went with the end of the Magellan Billet. She was, for all intents and purposes, a private citizen, on her own, which wasn't so bad. She'd learned long ago how to take care of herself.

Up near Constitution Avenue she caught sight of three cabs parked at the curb. One of those would be her chariot. The night air was cold, but thankfully arid. She stuffed her bare hands into her coat pockets and headed for the cab line. DC lingered in an early-morning slumber with little street noise and light traffic. The government buildings all around her sat dark, their business day not beginning for a few more hours. Her job, unfortunately, had never respected the clock. Running the Magellan Billet had been a twenty-four-hour-a-day task, and she could not remember the last time she took an actual vacation.

Many times she'd wondered how it would all end. Never had she imagined that it would simply disintegrate into nothing. Not that she expected any pomp or ceremony, but a simple thank-you would have been appreciated. And not from Danny. She knew how he felt. But from the new people. Seemed like common courtesy would mandate that the AG designee tell her face-to-face. But the ignominious bastard told the press instead and sent Litchfield to do the dirty work. She should not have been surprised. Politics had no memory, and no one cared that the Magellan Billet was gone. If truth be told the other intelligence agencies would be glad to be rid of it. Her relationship with the White House had long been their envy. But she'd earned that trust with proven results, a large part of which was thanks to Cotton. That was why she would see this last operation through, right until the new president finished his oath of office and shook the chief justice's hand.

A black Cadillac sedan eased to the curb next to her and its rear window whined down. Alarm bells rang in her brain until she recognized a face.

Nikolai Osin.

Supposedly working for the Russian trade mission, Osin's primary responsibilities were with the Sluzhba Vneshney Razvedki, the SVR, the successor to the First Chief Directorate of the now debunked KGB, tasked with all Russian foreign intelligence operations. Osin headed the Washington, DC, *rezidentura*. And unlike during the Cold War days, the SVR and CIA now routinely identified their chiefs of station, the idea being so they could work faster and better together to counter global terrorism. Russia and the United States were supposedly allies, but tensions remained high, the old distrust never fading entirely. One problem came from simply defining terrorism. Caucasus separatists and Chechens were freedom fighters to the United States, as was Hamas or Hezbollah to Russia. More disagreements than cooperation seemed to exist. Which made Osin's request, the one that had led to Cotton heading for Lake Baikal, all the more unusual.

She stopped and faced him. "Are you having me watched?"

He smiled. "I drove over after our call, hoping you might be leaving. I wanted to speak with you privately."

She'd never known this man to play fast and loose. His reputation was one of skill and caution. "About what?"

"Forward Pass."

How many years had it been since she last heard those words? At least twenty-five. And not far from here. Just a mile or so west on Pennsylvania Avenue. She wondered if the intelligence operation named Forward Pass remained classified. Nearly all of the once sensitive documents from the 1980s had been released, the passage of three decades and the fall of the Soviet Union transforming them from state secrets into historical perspective. Countless books had been written about Reagan and his war on communism. She'd even read a few. Some on target, others close, most missing the mark. But never had she seen the words *Forward Pass*.

"How do you know about that?" she asked.

"Come now, Stephanie. Ronald Reagan himself gave your operation that name."

She stared at the president of the United States, having never before been this close to the most powerful man in the world.

"Al Haig tells me you're a smart lawyer," Reagan said. "He has great confidence in you."

They sat in the Oval Office, she on a small settee, Reagan in an armchair, his tall frame perched upright, head high, legs crossed, looking like the actor he'd once been. A late-night call from Secretary of State Haig had told her she was expected at the White House and should head there immediately. A bit unusual to say the least for a lower-level State Department lawyer. She'd been home, about to go to bed, but she'd dressed and caught a cab. Now she was talking alone to the commander in chief.

"I'm told," Reagan said, "that you came on board during President Carter's time."

She nodded. "In 1979. I decided that private practice was not for me. International relations have always interested me, so I applied to the State Department and was hired."

"Cyrus Vance says you're top-notch."

She smiled at the compliment. Her former boss, secretary of state during most of the Carter administration, had become a friend and mentor. Like her, Vance deemed public service a duty and an honor.

"You spoke to Secretary Vance?"

Reagan nodded. "I wanted his assessment. He says you could even be secretary of state one day yourself."

She didn't know what to say to that, so she kept silent.

"How old are you?" Reagan asked.

She normally dodged that question, but not tonight. "Twenty-seven."

"So you lived through the 1960s and 1970s. You know what the Cold War means."

That she did.

"What is your assessment of the Soviet Union?" he asked.

A fair question considering she was assigned to the Soviet division at State. "A system flawed to the core. My father used to say that if you have to build fences to keep people in, you've got a serious problem."

Reagan smiled. "Your father was right. I'm going to end the Soviet Union."

Bold words, spoken nonchalantly. But not as bragging or bravado, just a simple statement of a purpose he seemed to truly believe in.

"And you're going to help me."

Her mind snapped back to the face in the car window. She hadn't thought about that night at the White House in a long time. The seven years after that had changed her life forever.

"Stephanie," Osin said, "I have confirmed that the plane your man was flying exploded on the lake."

Her heart sank.

"But that was after it made a landing. Two bodies were found, burned to nothing. We know they are Russian."

"No sign of Malone?"

"None. But those two men were probably driving something."

She agreed, and felt better. Cotton could be on the move.

"Will my second envoy be given free rein?" she asked.

"Of course, just as I said."

All of this was beyond odd. Only a mile away workers were erecting the scaffolding and platform for the pending inauguration. Years ago that ceremony was held on the eastern side of the Capitol building, but Reagan had wanted to face west, toward California, so every president since had followed suit. Normally, this was the slow time for government, a transition from one administration to another. The old group short on power, the new learning how to acquire it. Little was ever done in this limbo. Yet Russia seemed to need American assistance.

And now a mention of Forward Pass.

"Would you take a ride with me?" he asked.

"You never told me how you learned that code name."

"It is my business to know such things. You were there, Stephanie. Reagan's eyes and ears to the Vatican. His special envoy, who helped broker a deal that ended the USSR. That matters not to me. Frankly, I'm glad the regime is gone. But it does matter to another man."

Finally, something substantive.

"Aleksandr Zorin. He wants revenge."

CHAPTER TEN

ZORIN FOLLOWED THE GRAVELED LANE ALONG THE LAKESHORE, then turned inland and drove up toward the odd-looking gray-and-white observatory. The building rose in sharp angles and planes with a long rectangular chute leaning skyward, the whole thing resembling some modern work of art. It had been built twenty years ago for solar research, since Lake Baikal received more than two hundred days of sunshine each year. An ancillary stellar observatory sat a kilometer away, on an adjacent hill, round with a dome, more reminiscent of what such a place should look like. This time of year no one occupied either facility, the sun too low in the sky, the nights too cloudy. That was why he'd chosen the locale to confront the American.

His talk with Vadim Belchenko had been exhilarating. Other than Anya, Belchenko was now the only other person who knew what he was planning. And it was interesting to learn where the man he sought now lived.

Canada.

For all its power, all its wars won and arrogance across the globe, Canada remained a U.S. failure. Twice it invaded, both times soundly defeated. A bit of inspiration, he'd always thought. It showed that the so-called mighty nation was not invincible. For him, Canada was familiar territory. He served three years there in the 1980s, commanding an expansive KGB intelligence network, milking an army of informants—government officials, journalists, police, factory workers—anyone and everyone who could provide useful intelligence. Incredibly, most of them worked unknowingly for free, their information volunteered simply in answer to a casual inquiry. Canada traditionally stayed neutral on the world stage—especially in the Cold War—which explained the ease of gathering information there. People seemed to talk more freely in a place that wasn't on either side, and much as in Switzerland and Sweden, that element of detachment had made it the perfect place for espionage.

He'd been headquartered in Ottawa, a midlevel KGB posting, nothing like London, Washington, DC, Paris, or Bonn. No major general was ever assigned, a mere colonel like himself would do, but it wasn't unimportant. Canada sat right next door to the USSR's main adversary. And that alone had made it of keen interest to both sides of the Cold War. Resources had been freely allocated to the post, his mission focused on preparations for the inevitable war with America. Like the tens of thousands of other KGB officers around the world he became one of the troops on the invisible front. His bases had been embassies, trade missions, Aeroflot offices, and an assortment of other cover companies. And unlike the military that spent its time drilling, studying, and training soldiers, a KGB operative went to war the moment he or she stepped onto foreign soil.

He stopped the car and climbed out into the frigid air. No fences protected the observatory grounds. Why would they? Nothing here but a few scientists and some unimportant equipment. The perch upon which the building sat overlooked the lake and he stared out at the frozen blue expanse. In the fading winter sunshine he caught sight of an old Lada speeding across the surface. Occasionally he heard the familiar symphony of bangs and snaps as the ice plates shifted, creating new patterns of white lines. Though locked in cold, the water remained alive, never yielding, constantly adapting.

Just like himself.

He wore an overcoat, gloves, boots, and a fur hat. A gray, heavy-knit turtleneck sweater circled under his chin, wreathed by a scarf. Winter always made him think of his childhood in central Russia. His parents were not of the elite, the apparatchiks, whose birthright automatically ensured them a lifetime of official privilege. No luxury apartments, summer dachas, or access to the best goods and services came their way. His father worked as a lumberjack, his mother on a farm. He was the youngest of three sons and his life fundamentally changed at age sixteen when a factory worker handed him some party literature. For the first time he read about Lenin, the Soviets, and a workers' utopia, beginning then and there to believe. He joined the Communist Youth, at first for the organized games—but he stayed for the politics. As his own family fractured apart, the Soviets became more and more important. His father lived in another town for most of his childhood, his visits back home every few weeks still vivid memories. He would talk about the Great War and his life as a soldier surviving Stalingrad, which not many could claim. Once he'd dreamed of going to war with his father, fighting side by side, but that never came to pass.

His parents always had the highest hopes for their youngest son. They wanted him to be schooled, unlike his two older brothers who'd been forced to go to work early. *"I will make you an educated man. What you do with that education is your choice."* And for all his personal shortcomings his father kept that promise, making sure his youngest attended preparatory school where, thanks to his perception, bearing, and organizational talents, he caught the party's eye. He became one of the *nomenklatura,* those rewarded for being in political favor with those in charge. He then spent seven years at military school, studying Marxism, Leninism, the Communist party, philosophy, and economics. He changed from a wild, impulsive, somewhat arrogant boy who never accepted a mistake into a smart, patient, and determined man. As Lenin had said, *"Give us your child for eight years and it will be a Bolshevik forever."*

During his final year at school a colonel in the GRU recommended him for the military intelligence agency. He took the entrance exams and passed, eventually gaining admittance to the KGB's Red Banner Institute in Moscow, equal parts boot camp, university, and spy school. Only three hundred candidates a year were taken. Graduating meant becoming a foreign intelligence operative with possible assignment overseas. The institute taught him about the West and how to speak perfect English. He studied banking, credit cards, mortgages, taxes, all things nonexistent in the USSR but vital to someone living on the outside. He'd also been taught first aid, reconnaissance, Morse code, survival skills, and how to navigate by the sun and stars. He'd learned nuclear, biological, and chemical defense techniques. Parachuting, scuba diving, and flight training, too. He'd first driven a car there and mastered the rules of the road, as few inside the old regime had owned vehicles.

Most students never earned a passing grade, relegated to searching for spies within the Soviet Union, the homeland becoming their safe, warm womb. He earned a passing grade, was commissioned a lieutenant, and assigned to the coveted North American desk. As a further reward he'd been given an apartment near the Kremlin with a private bath, which signified the hopes his superiors held for him. Within three years he was posted overseas. First to Western Europe, then North America. And where many of his colleagues succumbed to the lure—that startling contrast between the image of capitalism pressed back home and the reality of living in the West—he resisted and remained loyal.

The Ministry of Fear.

That was how many once referred to the KGB.

Its twenty directorates had been all-encompassing, yet none of that mattered on December 26, 1991, when Declaration 142-H acknowledged the independence of the twelve republics of the Soviet Union, creating the Commonwealth of Independent States and ending the USSR. Mikhail Gorbachev declared the office of general secretary extinct and handed over all power to the new Russian president, Boris Yeltsin.

His stomach turned simply at the thought of Yeltsin.

A drunk—incompetent and corrupt—surrounded by men who stole the country so they could become billionaires. Himself and millions of others felt betrayed by both Yeltsin and the oligarchs who emerged from the ashes, most either relatives or friends of Yeltsin who skimmed off the cream and left sour milk for the rest. At least in the Soviet system there'd been order. None existed in the Russian Federation. Contract killings became big business. The mobsters controlled everything of value, including the banks and many corporations, far more feared than the KGB had ever been. From the first socialist nation in the world emerged a criminal state. Authoritarianism, but without authority. Two failed revolts, one in 1991, the other in 1993, soured the people on communism forever.

He still recalled that December night when the Soviet flag was low-ered from the Kremlin for the last time, replaced with the Russian tricolor.

And the Cold War ended.

Then the horror started.

Inflation rose 250%. The national economy shrank 15%. Pensions went unpaid, salaries were deferred, money became nearly nonexistent. The end for him came one day when he'd ventured out to buy some bread. At the store he encountered an old man wearing his World War II medals, asking the clerk if he could buy but a quarter loaf, as that was all he could afford. The clerk refused, so he'd stepped forward and offered to buy the man a full loaf, but the veteran brushed him off, say-ing, *"I am still proud."*

As was he.

So he moved east where he no longer had to witness failure.

He rubbed his hands together for warmth and checked his watch.

The American should be here by now.

Twenty years he worked as an officer. Never were the KGB referred to as agents. Always either "officer" or "operative," which he liked. It had been an honorable job. He'd fought for the motherland without bias or prejudice, preparing for the inevitable fight with the United States. During the 20th century 75 million Soviets died from revolution, con-flict, famine, or terror. Not since the mid-19th century had war visited American soil. Russians had been continuously ravaged. He'd been taught that the only way to defeat an enemy was to bring war to its home, and that had been a big part of his mission. The new Russian Federa-tion eventually created its own foreign intelligence arm, the SVR, but it was nothing like its predecessor. Commercial and industrial espionage replaced national security as top priorities. The SVR seemed to exist only to make mobsters rich. He wanted to serve the nation, not crimi-nals, so he resigned. Many of his colleagues did, too, most going to work for the syndicates, which valued their skills. He'd been tempted, but resisted, and for the first time in his life he became unemployed.

He was thrilled when, in 1999, Yeltsin finally resigned. He'd watched on television as the drunken fool had said, *"I want to beg forgive-ness for your dreams that never came true. And also I would like to beg forgiveness not to have justified your hopes."*

A little late by then.

The damage was irreversible.

To this day he still held a Russian passport and carried his Communist party and KGB pension card, though he never saw a ruble from retirement. Only a few understood how the USSR had truly been brought to its knees. He'd made a point to become one of those, reading everything he could. And Vadim Belchenko, waiting for him back at the dacha, knew every detail, too.

He checked his watch again and wondered about Anya and her progress in Virginia. She carried a throwaway cell phone he'd purchased in Irkutsk. He carried one, too, and they'd agreed that contact would be made only when necessary. That type of portable technology did not exist in his day, but he'd stayed current, learning to use a computer and work the Internet.

Twenty-seven years separated him and Anya. His first wife died of cancer, his only son before that from a drug overdose. Both deaths hit him hard. He'd been taught all of his life to operate off known facts and assumed realities. Be careful and be prepared. Self-possessed? Absolutely. At his core, though, was integrity, which forced him to always be honest with himself.

Anya, too, was strong, full of lust and anger, two emotions that he understood with great clarity. She'd come into his life a few years ago when he desperately needed someone to share his passions. Thankfully, she was drawn to older men, especially those without pretenses. The day he finally explained his goal and desire her response had been immediate.

"We shall do it together."

Which had pleased him.

One more check of the watch.

55 hours remained.

He'd thought the American might actually show, but apparently that was not the case.

Which was okay.

Like any good officer, he'd anticipated deceit.

CHAPTER ELEVEN

STEPHANIE WANTED TO KNOW MORE ABOUT ALEKSANDR ZORIN, so she asked Nikolai Osin to explain.

"He's former KGB and GRU, and also headed a *spetsnaz* team."

Those she knew. Ruthless units of paramilitary specialists who once carried out assassinations, raids, and sabotage. They were created after World War II when the Soviet Union wanted to emulate the success of American commandos. Eventually the Red Army organized "troops of special purpose," *spetsialnoye nazranie,* or *spetsnaz* for short. To lead one of those squads meant Zorin was not a man to be taken lightly. He would be highly trained, far more accustomed to offense than defense.

"And what does Zorin want revenge for?"

"He longs for communism."

"Move to China."

"I doubt he has much love for the Chinese. He's more a Lenin-traditionalist, and a dangerous one. He was also part of the special destinations group."

Those she also knew. The Soviets trained them to penetrate an enemy either before or just after a war started. Their job would be to disrupt power stations, communications grids, dams, highways, and any other strategic target. They were experts in weapons, explosives, mines, and killing. They were also all pilots, required to be fluent in at least two other languages, English nearly always one of those.

"He served in Afghanistan during our war there," Osin said. "Quite effectively, too."

"Nikolai, please tell me what's really happening here."

She hoped her conciliatory tone would loosen this spy's tongue. All of this had started for her with a call from Osin. The initial inquiry had come days earlier from the Kremlin to the White House, the matter then referred her way by President Danny Daniels.

The facts, as originally told, were relatively simple. A former KGB archivist, an old man named Vadim Belchenko, had gone missing. Russian internal security kept tabs on Belchenko, since they'd learned long ago that archivists could be their biggest security problem. Archivists once enjoyed unfettered access to both the highest intelligence and the most sensitive policy papers. They knew everything, so to ignore them could be fatal. That lesson was taught by one named Mitrokhin, who smuggled out 25,000 pages of sensitive documents, which in 1992 made their way westward, offering the clearest picture ever of Soviet espionage and proving that the KGB had evolved into the largest foreign intelligence service in the world.

Sharp of sword, tough of shield.

That was its motto.

And the main way the West knew anything about how dangerous it became was from archivists. So she understood why Belchenko may have been on a watch list. What remained unclear was why this man was so important right now, and how Zorin fit in.

"He is a profoundly troubled man," Osin said. "He fled east after the Soviet collapse, along with a hundred or so other expatriates. They've lived by Lake Baikal without incident for a long time. Lately, though, this calm has changed. Zorin knows Belchenko. They have communicated many times through the years. But never has Belchenko himself gone east."

That had been Cotton's mission. To recon the dacha and the village and see if he could locate Belchenko.

"Why not send your own people," she said. "Why call me?"

"There are several reasons for that. But the most relevant is that this has nothing to do with Russia. It's an external problem."

"Care to explain that one?"

"If your agent finds Belchenko, I will gladly. For now, let's just say that I like to think that we are not enemies, though sometimes it's hard to know for sure. I was told to involve you as a show of our good faith."

And, she realized, to also give Moscow some deniability if things went terribly wrong. *At least we brought you in from the start* would be their line. And he was right about the enemies part. No longer were Russia and the United States open adversaries. But while the Cold War had been over a long time, a more frozen version had slowly come into existence. She sensed, though, that this mess was something more akin to the old days.

"For now," he said, "let me say that this is a fight that may involve only Zorin and the United States. Or at least that's our hope. So I thought it prudent to now make you aware of it. We don't want to see you lose."

A strange comment, which she added to the growing list of anomalies.

He stared at her through eyes that were surprisingly congenial. "Do you know of Stanislav Lunev?"

Absolutely. A former Soviet military officer and the highest-ranking intelligence operative to ever defect to the United States. He turned in 1992 and remained to this day hidden away. He did, though, write a memoir. *Through the Eyes of the Enemy*. She'd read it several times. One comment from the book always stayed with her. *The best spy will be everyone's best friend, not a shadowy figure in the corner.*

"Lunev's claims are true," Osin said.

She knew what he meant. In his memoir Lunev had revealed something shocking. He wrote about a Soviet weapon identified as RA-115. In the United States they called them suitcase nukes. Each weighed about fifty pounds and delivered six kilotons of firepower, which by Hiroshima and Nagaski standards was small. Those bombs had packed punches of sixteen and twenty kilotons. Still, at short range six kilotons could do extreme damage. Congress outlawed the weapon in 1994, but that provision was repealed in 2004. To her knowledge, though, the U.S. did not have any in its nuclear arsenal. The old Soviet Union and the new Russia were another matter. She recalled the concerns from 1997 when a Russian national security adviser claimed on *60 Minutes* that more than a hundred RA-115s remained unaccounted for. No one knew if they had been destroyed or stolen. Congress held hearings, where experts differed on whether the weapon even existed.

"Are you saying RA-115s are real?"

He nodded. "The Soviets produced 250. They are about so big." He used his hands to describe a package about twenty-four inches long, sixteen inches wide, and eight inches tall.

"They were distributed to military intelligence units of the KGB and the GRU, tagged for special operations. After the Soviet collapse, they fell under the jurisdiction of the SVR. There they have remained."

She wondered about his frankness. This was not the type of information nations shared with one another. Warnings about poor security over Russia's nuclear weapons dated back to 1990. A congressional act in 1991 provided American technical aid to help eliminate Russian warheads and account for their nuclear material. Thankfully, to date, no rogue bombs had ever surfaced. Eventually, the furor over any potential problems faded and suitcase nukes entered the realm of movies and television. None was ever seen in real life. Now she was being told that 250 of them existed.

"Our counterintelligence units worked hard to downplay any threat and discredit press attention to the potential containment problem," he said. "We diffused all of that publicity."

That they had. She remembered the shadow cast across the *60 Minutes* story when it was revealed that, at the time of the broadcast, its producer had written and was promoting a book on the dangers of nuclear terrorism. That same producer had been involved with a just-released movie called *The Peacemaker,* which involved a missing Soviet nuclear weapon used for terrorism. Talk about casting doubt on credibility.

"You people do stay busy," she said. "Always up to something."

He smiled. "I could say the same for you."

"What does this have to do with Vadim Belchenko?"

"Eighty-four of those RA-115s remain unaccounted for."

That was startling information, but she kept her cool and simply said, "And you're just now mentioning this?"

"There is good and bad to this reality. The good is that those weapons are hidden away, in places only a handful of people know. The bad is that one of the people who know is Vadim Belchenko."

Now she caught the urgency. "And you think Aleksandr Zorin is after one of those suitcase nukes?"

"It's a possibility."

They were still driving through Washington's deserted streets, cruising past closed buildings and empty sidewalks. She'd thought something was seriously wrong from the moment Osin had first called. A second call from Osin had alerted her to the fact that a woman was in the United States, someone who bore careful watching.

"Tell me more about Anya Petrova."

"As I told you before, she is Zorin's lover. About twenty-five years younger, police-trained, and seems to share Zorin's passion for revenge. He sent her here for a reason. Hopefully you'll determine what that is."

Her mind went to Luke Daniels, who'd been recruited as Petrova's shadow. He could handle things.

"An RA-115," Osin said, "is engineered to last for years, so long as it's wired to a power source. In case of a loss of power, a battery backup is provided. If the battery runs low, the weapon has a transmitter that sends a coded message by satellite to a Russian embassy or consulate."

"Has any such signal ever been received?"

He nodded. "Seventy-nine. None was ever followed up on."

"Which means they're out of juice and harmless."

He nodded. "That's right. Then there are the other five. No signal has ever been received from those weapons."

"Is it possible they still have power?" She paused. "After twenty-plus years."

"Zorin apparently thinks so."

"Go get them."

"We don't know where to look. Any records relevant to them are gone. We think Vadim Belchenko purged them."

"Insurance for a long life?"

Osin smiled. "Probably. Unfortunately, Zorin may have discovered what Belchenko knows."

Which explained the urgency in finding the old man.

Her phone vibrated.

Normally, she would ignore it, but since only the White House was still in her communications loop she decided to check the display.

LUKE DANIELS.

Which raised more alarms.

"This call could be relevant to what we're discussing."

"Please answer it."

She did, and listened as Luke explained what had happened in Virginia ending with, "I assume you know what I'm doing, so I decided to call you instead of him. I don't want to hear how I blew it. But I know I will. That woman's long gone."

"Where are you?"

"I called a tow truck and they hauled my Mustang to a lot just off I-66."

He told her where.

"That house," he said, "bears another look. I don't want it to sit there wide open for long."

Neither did she, so she said, "Hold on."

She faced Osin. He'd been straight with her, and since she was short on resources and did not want Bruce Litchfield to know her business, she had little choice. "I need your help. We have to go to Virginia. It bears on Anya Petrova."

"Tell me where and I'll have the driver take us."

CHAPTER TWELVE

MALONE NEVER HAD ANY INTENTION OF MEETING ZORIN AT some observatory. That would be the precise definition of stupidity. So he'd avoided the unusual-looking facility on a rocky hilltop and driven another fifteen miles north to the dacha. The two-laned highway framed by snow paralleled the lakeshore, and he'd passed no cars coming from the opposite direction, which made him wonder even more about Zorin. More than likely, the only thing waiting for him at that observatory was trouble. So he decided to just plunge straight into the lion's den.

His sense of direction was excellent, thanks in large part to his eidetic memory, a blessing bestowed upon him in the womb. He often wondered where the genetic trait came from and was finally told by his mother that her father had likewise been blessed. He'd actually grown accustomed to never forgetting a detail. He could remember word-for-word essays he'd written in grammar school, and exactly what happened at every Christmas. It had certainly come in handy as a lawyer, then when he worked for the Magellan Billet. Now it helped him keep inventory on the rare books at his shop in Copenhagen. But it also prevented the memories of Cassiopeia Vitt from fading. He recalled every detail of their time together, and that was not necessarily a good thing.

He found the winding lane he recalled seeing from the air that led up to the perch where the dacha waited. He eased the truck off the highway and into the trees, stopping atop a snowy patch of ground. He parked and trekked up toward the house, scrambling from one tree trunk to another through the drifts, his boots crunching atop dry snow. Evergreen boughs and the spiny tentacles of leafless trees reached for the ever-darkening sky. His eyes smarted from the wind and cold. A daily regimen of squats and sit-ups had definitely kept his muscles toned, but the frigid climb taxed him.

He found the top, glancing back and noticing how the snow betrayed his presence with a trail of footsteps. A rusted, waist-high wire fence blocked the way ahead. A draft of icy air off the nearby lake stung his throat. He settled behind a thick pine and gazed at the dacha. Smoke continued to waft skyward from three chimneys. One of the two vehicles that had been there earlier was gone. Strains of folk music floated through the frosty air. He located the source. An outbuilding, this one round, all of wood, no windows and a single door, a thin spire of vapor steadily escaping from the top of its conical roof.

His mission was to search for Vadim Belchenko. He'd been shown a picture taken a few years back. The man was some kind of former KGB archivist. If found, he was to retreat and report the location. The first part would be relatively easy, the second not so much as his cell phone had been destroyed. But he had the truck and could find a phone somewhere.

He stepped over the fence and scampered across a blacktopped area that spread out from the end of the drive to the house, the smoking round building leaking music situated to one side. He negotiated the pavement with care since he could not afford a fall on black ice. He came to the round building's doorway and quickly entered, assaulted by a welcomed wave of warm, dry air. Another doorway led farther inside, blocked by a fur blanket that hung from its jamb. He peeled back a small section of the blanket—enough for him to see that the building was some sort of sauna. A fire burned in the center beneath a bed of hot stones. An old man sat on the lower level of a series of pine benches that rose against the far wall. He was naked, laid out with his legs extended straight, gnarled hands intertwined behind his head. The features matched the picture he'd been shown.

Vadim Belchenko.

Music swelled from a small CD player that lay on the bench. He slipped inside and approached the old man. The face looked like a bland mask, broad and flat with skin the color of dirty snow. The closed eyes were set back into wrinkled cups of folded flesh. Wet, blondish hair covered the scalp, and the only indications of advanced age came from the sunken chest and cheeks. The older man calmly smoked on a potent-smelling cigar.

He reached down and shut off the music.

Belchenko opened his eyes and sat up. Both pupils were clouded with cataracts.

"My name is Cotton Malone," he said in English.

Belchenko stared at him. "And what are you doing here?"

"I've come to see if you're okay."

"Why would I not be?"

"You disappeared and people were wondering."

"You mean Russian state security was wondering. And why would they send an American to see about me?"

The voice was low and throaty, with no inflection, emotion, or concern.

"That's a question I've been wondering, too."

Belchenko exhaled a cloud of blue smoke that drifted upward. "Are you a spy?"

"Not anymore."

The hot air was drying his nostrils, so he kept his breathing shallow and through his mouth. Sweat began to trickle down his spine, leaving a chilly path.

"Let's just say I'm a part-time spy."

"We had a few of those in my day. I never cared for them."

"Where is Zorin?"

"He went to meet with you."

He hadn't come to chitchat. In fact, his mission was done. He'd found Belchenko and now he had to report in. But old habits were hard to break, so he had to ask one more question. "Why does the Russian government give a damn what you do?"

"Because I know things, Mr. Malone. And they want to know those things, too, before I die."

Now he understood. "And you promised to tell them."

"It seemed a small price to pay in order to stay alive. Once they know, I will have no value. You really do not understand what you have been thrust into, do you?"

"Not a clue. Care to tell me?"

Belchenko chuckled. "Why would I do such a thing?"

Good question, one he decided to leave for another time. "I have to go. Nice to meet you."

"Did you know that every story ever conceived by the human mind can be whittled down into three parts?"

He didn't like the sound of that odd statement.

"A beginning. Middle. Then, the end," Belchenko said. "There's a symmetry and satisfaction that occurs when those three parts ultimately join to form a complete tale. It's truly magical. We have already had the beginning, then a long middle. Now, Mr. Malone, it is time for the end of the story."

Nothing about this seemed right. He'd thought himself clever avoiding Zorin, coming straight here, but something told him that his move had been anticipated. The old man's left hand held the cigar, but the right arm reached back behind to the bench and a gun appeared.

"Don't think, Mr. Malone, that I can't see you clearly enough to shoot."

Movement caught his attention. The fur blanket across the jamb had been disturbed. He turned to see two men, dressed in winter gear, both toting automatic rifles.

"And why would you shoot me?" he asked.

Belchenko shrugged. "Because Zorin says there's no way you can leave here alive."

CHAPTER THIRTEEN

CASSIOPEIA SQUIRMED IN THE BACKSEAT OF A FRENCH FIGHTER, the pilot settled in the front. She'd flown in the helicopter from her estate to an air base, where the high-performance jet had been waiting. They were cruising at 2200 kilometers per hour nearly eight kilometers up, following the same route Cotton had taken less than twelve hours ago.

She disliked high places, avoiding them wherever possible. The scaffolding earlier had been bad enough, but flying was a necessary evil that she endured. At the moment she was stuffed into an ill-fitting flight suit and packed tight into a cockpit with little to no room to maneuver. They'd already dropped to a lower altitude and taken on fuel from an airborne tanker that had met them along the way. She'd never witnessed that operation firsthand and it had been fascinating to watch. It had also helped take her mind off the fact that she was presently a long, long way up in the air.

The entire trip from France to Siberia would take a little over four hours, which was amazing. The world had truly shrunk. Stephanie had read her perfectly, knowing that she did indeed still love Cotton. There'd been many men in her life, a few of the relationships quite serious, but none was Cotton Malone. They'd met at her château a few years ago, at the same time she'd first been introduced to Stephanie Nelle. A mutual friend, Henrik Thorvaldsen, had made all of that possible. Sadly, Henrik was gone, murdered in Paris, another of those unfortunate circumstances that seemed to follow her life.

When she'd broken off all contact with Cotton, she'd known even then that it would not be permanent. He was too much a part of her. She felt comfortable in his presence. He treated her as an equal and respected her as a person. True, he could sometimes be an ass. But she was no angel, either. That was the thing about relationships. A constant give-and-take. She'd wondered how they might reconnect. Both of them were proud, and a lot of bitterness had passed between them. It had taken many months for either of them to say the L-word. But finally, it had been spoken, then acted upon. Hopefully, the division between them had not grown past the point of no return.

Stephanie said she would advise her if anything new developed. She'd also told her about a dacha and a village named Chayaniye. Hope. An interesting designation, but fitting for the expatriates who'd created the place.

Communism was truly a dead theology. No such thing as a workers' paradise with no social classes, where everyone owned everything. What the old USSR created had all been an illusion, a place where fear and force had been the only means for it to survive. That so-called classless society evolved into haves and have-nots. The ruling privileged enjoyed the best and everyone else fought over the leftovers. Far from everyone owning everything, a select few had enjoyed it all. Only lies had kept the masses from revolting, along with daily doses of terror and violence. In the end, though, nothing could prevent the truth from causing its downfall.

And fall it had.

She'd been fifteen years old when it happened, living at her parents' estate in Spain. Her father had always remained apolitical, but she recalled his utter joy at the dissolution of the Soviet Union. And something he said. A quote from the American Thomas Jefferson. *"A government big enough to give you everything you want is strong enough to take everything you have."*

She never forgot that.

Her entire adult life had been one without the pressures of the Cold War. Instead, threats and terror today came from other places, East and West finding common ground, as those new enemies did not discriminate between Russians and Americans.

So what had Cotton been drawn into?

"I hired him to have a look. He's done a couple of jobs for me since Utah."

That's what Stephanie had said on the phone. So Cotton had become an agent-for-hire. *"Since Utah."* Maybe that was his way of trying to forget. She'd tried business and her castle, neither one of which had done much to quell her anxieties. Throughout her nearly forty years she'd thought herself in love several times. But now she knew that only one of those relationships had meant anything.

"Something went wrong here."

Her heart had sunk at Stephanie's words. Was Cotton hurt? Or dead? She hoped neither, wishing this jet could fly faster.

"How much longer?" she asked the pilot in French through her headset.

"Less than two hours. We're making good time."

Her mind drifted back to the first conversation she and Cotton ever had. At her estate, on a warm June afternoon. Prior to that their encounters had been quick and violent, each taking gunshots at the other, she looking after him, he unsure just exactly who she was. On that day she'd followed him outside into the bright sunshine, walking with him down the same tree-shaded lane from earlier toward the construction site.

"When I'm finished," she said, "a 13th-century castle will stand exactly as it did eight hundred years ago."

"Quite an endeavor."

"I thrive on grand endeavors."

They kept walking and entered the construction site through a broad wooden gate and strolled into a barn with sandstone walls that housed a visitor reception center. Beyond loomed the smell of dust, horses, and debris, where a hundred or so visitors milled about.

"The entire foundation for the perimeter has been laid and the west curtain wall is coming along," she said, pointing. "We're about to start the corner towers and central buildings."

She led him through the construction site and up the slope of a steep hill to a modest promontory, where everything could be clearly seen.

"I come up here often and watch. One hundred and twenty men and women are employed down there full-time."

"Quite a payroll."

"A small price to pay for history to be seen."

"Your nickname, Ingénieur," *he said. "Is that what they call you? Engineer?"*

She smiled. "The staff gave me that label. I've designed this entire project."

"You know, on the one hand, you're awfully arrogant. But on the other, you can be rather interesting."

She was not offended by his observation, which bore truth, and asked, "You're retired from the government?"

"You never really quit. You just stay out of the line of fire more often than not."

"So you're helping Stephanie Nelle simply as a friend?"

"Shocking, isn't it?"

"Not at all. In fact, it's entirely consistent with your personality."

"How do you know about my personality?"

"I've learned a great deal about you. I have friends in your former profession. They all spoke highly of you."

"Glad to know folks remember."

"Do you know much about me?" she asked.

"Just the thumbnail sketch."

"I have many peculiarities."

That she did, the worst of which was an inability to say what she felt. Cotton suffered from the same malady, which helped further explain why they found themselves currently estranged. They cared deeply for each other, but neither was willing to admit it. There was that one time, though, high in the mountains of China, after another ordeal, when they both gathered the courage to say how they felt.

"No more games," she said.

He nodded and cupped her hand in his.

"Cotton—"

He silenced her lips with two fingers. "Me too."

And he kissed her.

She remembered that moment, both of them knowing without either actually uttering the word *love*. But she did love Cotton. The past month had made that abundantly clear.

Was it too late?

With all her heart, she hoped not.

CHAPTER FOURTEEN

Virginia

Luke stood propped against his Mustang, watching as a black SUV eased through the open gate into the tow lot. He'd just checked his watch, which read a little after 5:00 A.M. The predawn air was freezing but he felt only anger at one, being bested by a stranger, and two, the demise of his most prized possession. The tow truck operator had just shaken his head when he arrived at the scene, loading the Mustang's hulk onto the back of his truck and ferrying it here among a litter of other cars that had definitely seen better days.

The SUV came to a stop and Stephanie emerged on one side, another man in a dark overcoat from the opposite side.

"Tough night?" she asked.

The Mustang sat with the passenger side facing out, which bore the evidence of his encounter.

"Anya Petrova," the other man said, "is quite dangerous. She was trained by the police and worked as one for several years."

Which explained some of what had happened. She definitely knew how to handle herself. "And who might you be?"

The man introduced himself as Nikolai Osin, then Stephanie added, "He's head of station for the SVR."

"Officially, I am a trade delegate and know nothing of any SVR."

"I like that," Luke said. "We'll go with it. But would you mind telling me more about Anya Petrova?"

They stood alone in the lit lot, among a deserted heap of cars.

"She is connected to a man who could cause this country many problems. He sent her here for a reason, which is why I advised Stephanie to watch her carefully. Apparently, Petrova did not appreciate that."

Luke was still trying to figure out how she'd made him. He'd been real careful, but sometimes crap happens. And though his question had not been fully answered, he decided to let it pass and said, "We need to check out that house."

They drove back south into the Virginia countryside and found the same wrought-iron-topped entrance. At any other time Magellan Billet headquarters could have traced ownership in a matter of minutes, but he knew that was now impossible. Of course, the White House could accomplish the same thing, but that required his reporting in. Stephanie had suggested they wait before making that call and he hadn't argued. Perhaps they might even learn enough to soften the sting sure to come from Uncle Danny over screwing up the one thing he'd asked him not to do.

The SUV stopped in front of the abandoned dwelling and they climbed out.

"Virginia's loaded with relics like this," Stephanie said.

"Such a large place," Nikolai said.

"And it appears," she said, "to have been abandoned for a while."

During the drive Luke learned that Malone might be in trouble and that Cassiopeia had been sent to see about him, which seemed both good and bad. He hoped everything was okay, but their SVR ally had not been able to gather much new information from folks in Siberia. Of course, the $64,000 question that nobody would answer was why someone would shoot down Malone's plane in the first place. Whoever *they* were, they possessed surface-to-air missiles, which meant far more was going on here than the Russkies wanted to admit—and far more than Uncle Danny had revealed.

Their driver produced a flashlight with a bright halogen beam. A faint hint of dawn was beginning to form to the east, but it would still be another two hours before the sun rose.

Luke grabbed the light and led the way back inside, which still cast the hollow atmosphere of a mausoleum. "She came straight here and knew exactly where she was going."

"Any idea what she was after?" Stephanie asked Osin.

"Can I reserve that answer until after we have a look? I'll try to be as direct as possible."

Luke doubted that observation. From the few times he'd encountered the SVR, *coy* would be the most generous word he'd use to describe them. Totally untrustworthy? Liars? Both fit them to a T. But he understood that this was supposed to be sort of a joint operation, one he wanted to be part of, so he kept his comments to himself.

They followed him down the hall and into the study, where the light revealed the gash in the paneled wall.

"She knew how to handle that ax," he said, pointing to it on the floor.

He was anxious to see what was beyond the opening, so he shone the beam inside. The room was small, maybe ten feet square, lined floor-to-ceiling on three sides with shelves. But unlike the ones out in the study, which sat empty and askew, these were brimming with books. A table sat in the center, on which rested a wooden easel, under glass, that displayed an open volume. A small chandelier dangled from the ceiling, sparkling in the light, its dusty bulbs useless without power.

"Some sort of concealed chamber," he muttered. "Which sweet Anya knew all about. She busted through exactly where she needed to."

He stepped inside, followed by Stephanie and Osin. With the flashlight he surveyed the shelves, studying the exposed spines. Most were books, others bound manuscripts, still more were wooden file cases holding loose sheets. He caught a few of the labels. MILITARY COMMAND CORRESPONDENCE. BATTLE OF PRINCETON. SIEGE OF BOSTON. CAPTURE OF TICONDEROGA. He scanned the entire room and read more spines.

One theme rang clear.

"It's a Revolutionary War library," he said.

"More than that," Stephanie added. "These books are late-18th- and early-19th- and 20th-century histories of that time, leading up to the War of 1812."

He estimated they were looking at several hundred volumes, everything sheathed in a thick coat of dust. Clearly, no one had been here for a long time. Here and there, sections of the shelves were empty, books that had once been there lying askew on the floor, their dust clearly disturbed.

"That's what I heard," Luke said. "Lots of thuds. She was raking those off."

"Tell us, Nikolai," Stephanie said. "What was she looking for?"

Osin did not reply. Instead, he removed the glass dome that protected the book on the easel and slowly turned the pages. He then closed the book so that its cover could be read.

Gold letters were etched into a black leather binding.

THE
ORIGINAL INSTITUTION
OF THE
GENERAL SOCIETY OF THE
CINCINNATI
AS FORMED BY THE OFFICERS OF THE ARMY OF THE UNITED STATES
AT THE CONCLUSION OF THE
REVOLUTIONARY WAR
WHICH GAVE INDEPENDENCE TO
AMERICA

Stephanie stepped closer and reopened the book, reading from a few of the pages. "It's a history of the society. Its general proceedings, minutes of meetings, and constitution. The copyright is from 1847."

"What's the Cincinnati?" Luke asked her.

She ignored him and restudied the shelves that surrounded them. "This is an archive, one I bet the Society of Cincinnati has no idea still exists." She paused. "Otherwise it would have been retrieved." Stephanie faced Osin. "Why is Anya Petrova interested in something like this?"

No reply.

"Earlier, you mentioned Forward Pass," she tried. "To my knowledge, that operation is still classified. The only way you could know anything about it is from your own records."

"We know exactly what was done," Osin said.

Which Luke immediately wanted to know, too.

"Does that mean Aleksandr Zorin knows?" she asked.

"I'm sure he does. And Belchenko knows even more."

"Including where those missing nukes are located?"

Luke stood silent and allowed the sparring to continue uninterrupted. But had he heard right? *"Missing nukes"*? He figured Stephanie would clue him in when the time was right.

She turned toward him. "Did Petrova leave here with anything?"

He shook his head. "Not that I saw."

"Then this was a dead end for her. Nikolai, you said you would be direct. Why did she come here?"

Uncharacteristically, Stephanie's voice had risen.

"I will answer that after I speak with Moscow. Some things I must discuss in private first."

"I sent my man to Siberia on your request," she said. "He went in blind, and now he's missing."

"We've allowed you to send another asset to investigate."

"Not good enough. What's going on?"

"I cannot say. At least for the moment."

Luke heard concern in the voice, which seemed genuine, and unusual for the SVR.

"I have to report all of this to the president," she said. "It'll be his call what to do next."

"I understand."

The Russian left the secret room without saying another word.

Luke stared at his former boss. "This is a deep pile of crap, isn't it?"

She carefully replaced the glass dome atop the book and the easel. Dust gently cascaded off the sides and onto the tabletop, glistening in the light.

"That'd be a good way to describe it," she whispered.

"Do you know what the Cincinnati is?" he asked again.

She slowly nodded.

"Can you tell me?"

She turned to leave.

"Not here."

CHAPTER FIFTEEN

Zorin returned to the dacha and immediately headed into the main house. He'd been told on arrival that the American, Malone, had been captured. So he took his time removing his coat and gloves. He'd be glad to leave this weather behind. Summer was so fleeting in this part of the world, and he longed for a steady warm breeze. What the next few days held for him was hard to say. All that he could hope for was that his recollections were correct, his research accurate, his planning thorough, and his resolve intact. He'd been idle far too long and he liked the feeling of being on the move again. Everything about him was primed and ready. Only this new wrinkle—the presence of an American—had proved unexpected.

Yet even that excited him.

He passed through the great room with its high ceiling and unobstructed views of the frozen lake. A welcomed fire burned in the hearth. He found the staircase to the basement and descended to where Malone stood handcuffed to a thick iron pipe. Light came from bare bulbs wrapped in iron cages that cut sharply etched shadows. The American's coat had been removed, as had apparently a weapon since a shoulder holster hung empty.

"You killed two of my men," he said.

Malone shrugged. "That's what happens when you start shooting at someone."

"Why are you here?"

"To find the old man, Belchenko, who clearly doesn't want to be found. My mistake."

"And two of my men are dead."

"Whom you sent to kill me."

"Are you a spy?"

"I'm a bookseller."

He chuckled. "You told me on the radio that you are Cotton Malone. Where did you acquire such a name? Cotton."

"It's a long story, but since we have the time I'd be glad to tell you."

"I have to leave."

"Are you one of the Red Guard?"

This man was informed. "I served my country until the day my country dissolved."

"And then you ended up here—in the middle of nowhere."

"I came on my own, with others who believed as I did. We founded this place and have lived here peacefully for a long time. We have bothered no one, yet the government feels a need to spy on us."

"I imagine millions of dead, innocent people would have said the same thing about the USSR."

"I suppose they might. We did have a tendency to overdo things."

Which seemed an understatement. Torture and death had been Soviet mainstays. He and every other KGB officer had been trained in their subtleties. Millions had indeed perished. When he first started with the KGB pain and violence had been its main tools of persuasion. He'd been trained extensively in how to twist their levels until the mind screamed. Then drugs became the more common tool to open closed mouths. After that, psychological tricks took over. Toward the end, physical stress rose in popularity. He'd read all about the CIA's "enhanced interrogation techniques." Just a fancy way to say torture. Which he, personally, didn't mind. But judging by the look of this American—who appeared strong and confident—breaking him would take effort.

And he simply didn't have the time.

"America has no idea what it meant to be Soviet," he said. "Seventy-five million of us died in the 20th century, and no one gave a damn."

"Most of whom were killed by either corrupt or stupid leaders. The

Nazis were rank amateurs when it came to slaughtering people. You communists became the real pros. What were you, KGB?"

He nodded. "I led a *spetsnaz* unit, preparing for war with the United States."

Which he liked saying.

"That's all over now," Malone said.

"Maybe not."

He clearly remembered that horrible August day in 1991, watching from KGB headquarters as a mob stormed Lubyanka Square, spray-painting HANGMAN, BUTCHER, and swastikas across the building. They'd shaken their fists and cursed, then tried to topple Dzerzhinsky's statue but could not bring the Iron Felix down. Finally a crane arrived and completed the task, leaving only a bare pedestal. Not a single person that day feared any retribution for desecrating the memory of the once feared head of the state police.

Their message came loud and clear.

Your time is over.

He recalled the paralyzing horror that had gripped him. The shouts, requests for calm, then a cacophony of sirens and chaos. For the first time in his life he had felt fear, that chilly sliver in the small of his back, something he'd made a career out of instilling in others. The incomprehensible possibilities in the future had sent a wave of doubt surging through his body that finally settled at his bladder, which voided. He'd stood at the window, watching below, feeling the shame of warm urine saturating his crouch and pant legs.

An awful moment.

Which he'd never described to anyone.

"Reagan was quite clever," he said. "Much more so than Gorbachev. He set out to destroy us, and he accomplished the task."

Thank goodness Americans believed in openness. Democracy thrived on a clash of ideas, a tolerance of viewpoints, and robust debate. Its proponents foolishly believed that truth would always prevail and the people were its best arbiter. The widest circulation of information was deemed good. Many American documents, once classified, had come to light thanks simply to the passage of time. Books had been written, which he'd read, that hinted at how the White House and the Vatican had worked together to bring Moscow to its knees. But where those books dealt only in speculation and conjecture, he knew things those authors did not. There had indeed been a plan, a conspiracy, a concerted effort to undermine the Soviet Union.

And it had worked.

He even knew its name.

Forward Pass.

"America has no idea the chaos it caused," he said. "When you destroyed the Soviet political system all order ended, which allowed the criminals to take over. Everything I, and so many others, spent a lifetime defending disappeared. And did you give a damn?" He did not wait for a reply. "No one gave a damn. We were left on our own to wallow in failure." He pointed a finger. "So we owe America. And I think it is time we repay that debt."

It felt good to say those words. They'd lingered too long in the pit of his stomach. And though he was now in his sixties, the lessons learned from his youth had never been forgotten. In fact, those memories had helped sustain him for the past twenty-plus years. From this point on his actions would come swift and natural with no hesitation. There'd be no rationalization or quarrels of conscience.

Just results.

And he'd liked the freshness of that freedom.

Lately, he'd thought more and more about his time at the infantry academy, where before he became a spy he'd learned to be a soldier. His favorite instructor, a lieutenant colonel, had hammered into all of his students that the United States was *glavny protivnik,* the main adversary.

"To forget that will mean your death."

And he hadn't forgotten.

Many times in his career he'd been called upon to kill a foreign asset and, each time, he'd accomplished the task.

"Hate your neighbors, your classmates, even your friends, but never your fellow soldier. Remember, when the war comes all of you will have a common enemy. You must know and respect that enemy. Learn how America is organized. How it works. Know its strengths and weaknesses, and America makes that easy. They air their grievances to the world. Pay attention to them."

And that war came.

But not from the main adversary he'd imagined. Instead, the battles had been fought with stealth, few even realizing they were being waged. Two generals, Reagan and the cursed Polish pope, had led the armies. Their weapons had not been bullets or bombs. Rather God, morality, and money had combined to pin the Soviet Union into a political and economic corner from which it could not emerge.

No one saw it coming—until it was far too late.

Communists must thoroughly, carefully, attentively, and skillfully exploit every fissure, however small, among their enemies.

Lenin's words from the 1920s, which the United States of America had followed with consummate skill.

Now it was his turn to follow that lead.

"You do know," Malone said, "that the world has changed? The Cold War is over."

"For you, perhaps. But not for me. I have a debt to pay, and I intend to pay it."

In exactly 52 hours, but he kept that to himself.

His life as a spy had been both challenging and exhausting. He'd traveled the world, entering countries under false identities, hiding his true self and thoughts, his every action intended to manipulate, exploit, and betray. Cut off from his culture, language, and family he'd adapted, but never succumbed to the capitalist appeal. Survival had been his main concern, and he'd lived in fear every day of exposure, which could come from places far away and unexpected. Only an invincible loyalty to the Soviet cause had overcome that daily anxiety.

Which he still possessed.

He wore the pride of his past like a mantle on his shoulders. A KGB officer must have clean hands, an ardent heart, and a clear head. He hated all those who'd stolen that pride from him, both domestic and foreign. Once he was told that the only honorable way to leave the KGB was through death, and he'd come to believe that to be true.

He headed for the stairs. "I will send down the men you met earlier in the black bath. They have some business with you, and they are particularly motivated since the two you killed were their comrades."

"Don't get too comfortable," Malone called out.

He stopped, turned, and offered a thin, self-satisfying smile.

"I never do."

CHAPTER SIXTEEN

Stephanie led Luke inside the Mandarin Oriental, the hotel she always frequented when in DC. They'd been dropped off by Nikolai Osin, who'd remained silent on the drive back from Virginia. She could tell that Luke wanted to press him for answers, but she'd telegraphed with her eyes that now was not the time. It was good to have the younger Daniels back on her team. She'd hired him originally as a favor to his uncle with the proviso that if he did not work out she was free to fire him. Danny had no problem with nepotism, but he despised incompetence no matter the source. Nobody got a free ride. Not even himself. Thankfully, Luke had proved to be an excellent agent, his Ranger training a valuable asset along with a brash personality, handsome looks, and a devil-may-care attitude. She also liked the fact that he called his mother every Sunday, regardless of where or what he was doing. Any thirty-year-old man who respected a parent that much was okay in her book.

"At some point," Luke said, "am I going to be told what's going on? I heard something back there about missing nukes. And I did just lose a car."

They fled the cold morning air and entered the elegant lobby, people in overcoats hustling back and forth, the Friday business day beginning.

"And, by the way," he said, "you let that Russkie off easy."

"It's clear he has a problem. We need to give him time to work it through."

She turned and headed for the elevators.

"Where are we going?" he asked.

"To my room."

"I'm not that kind of guy, if you know what I mean. And I don't even work for you anymore."

She smiled and kept walking.

They stepped onto the elevator and she pressed the button for the fourth floor. She could sympathize with Osin. Moscow had deliberately involved Washington in some internal affair. Surely they had a good reason, but that might have changed over the past few hours. The fact that 250 RA-115s once existed was disturbing enough, but the reality that five of those remained unaccounted for bordered on a crisis. She reminded herself that over twenty-five years had passed, and she doubted if any of those bombs would still be viable. Something that dangerous, that valuable, does not stay hidden that long. So the simple fact that none of those potential problems had ever surfaced brought her some comfort. She had to report this to the White House.

But first things first.

They left the elevator and she led the way down the quiet corridor to her suite. Inside, she sat before her laptop and sent an email that described the country and the house in Virginia, along with a grainy photo of the exterior she'd snapped with her phone.

"Is that to the White House?" Luke asked.

She nodded. "They're all we have left. Officially, through the Justice Department, I'm not even supposed to be doing what I'm doing."

"Pappy says you follow the rules about as good as he does."

She knew the nickname Luke used for Malone, done more to irritate than anything else. The favor had been returned by Cotton with the label Frat Boy, which Luke was anything but.

"You need to stay away from him," she said. "He's a bad influence."

"How bad is it for him right now?"

She'd tried not to think about it. "Enough I had to involve Cassiopeia. She didn't like it, but she also didn't refuse. She should be there shortly, if not already."

"No idea if Malone's dead or alive?"

She shook her head. "He's good, so we have to assume he's okay. You do realize, though, that by helping me out here you might kill your career."

Luke shrugged. "Could be worse."

He was just like his uncle. Both men loved swagger and bravado, and both could also back it up with action. Years ago, early in Danny Daniels' first term, she and the president had not necessarily cared for each other. But a series of crises eventually drew them together until finally they both realized that feelings existed between them. Only Cassiopeia knew the whole truth. Cotton might know some, but he'd never insinuated a thing. It was a subject neither of them would ever broach. She knew that soon Danny would become the first American president, whether current or former, to divorce, his longtime marriage over, both Danielses having already amicably agreed to go their separate ways once they left the White House. Pauline had already found love somewhere else and her husband was happy for her. *She deserves it,* he'd said many times. Danny did, too, and he might find that happiness with her.

But that remained to be seen.

"Since I'm assuming you aren't going to tell me a thing about those nukes, what is the Cincinnati?" Luke asked. "You said back at the house, not there. How about here?"

"It was America's first homegrown boys' club. It's been around a long time, not bothering a soul."

But for some reason the lover of a former communist spy had come all the way from Siberia to rifle through one of the society's forgotten archives. How had Petrova even become aware that the cache existed? Stephanie knew enough about the Society of Cincinnati to know that they kept things fairly close, so she had to wonder if the group itself knew about the archive.

The laptop indicated an incoming message.

She and Luke read the response on the screen from Edwin Davis, the White House chief of staff.

The property in Virginia belongs to Bradley Charon. He died unexpectedly in a plane crash in 2002. An Internet search shows that the children and the second wife never got along. A probate fight is ongoing, lots of trials and appeals, the estate is nearly bankrupt. A fire six years ago destroyed part of the house. Definitely arson, probably started by one of the children, but nothing could ever be proved. Which is why no insurance claim was paid and the place fell into disrepair. Back taxes total in the hundreds of thousands of dollars. The county recently moved to sell the property at public auction. Hope that helps.

It helped a great deal since it provided a much-needed starting point. So she typed BRADLEY CHARON into Google and waited.

42,800 results.

She narrowed the search by adding VIRGINIA, PROBATE FIGHT, and CINCINNATI.

The first page of results led to several newspaper accounts.

Charon had held a doctorate in political science, his family old money, he the last of a long line whose roots traced back to before the Revolution. He served as either a provost, dean, or president to three colleges and enjoyed a reputation as a learned man. He was married twice, the first for forty years, resulting in three children, the second for less than five, which seemed to have provided nothing but grief since the widow claimed she was entitled to everything.

"That's a greedy bitch," Luke said over her shoulder.

And she agreed. "Nobody wins those fights but the lawyers."

"Kind of the way of the world, isn't it?"

"It can be, when people lose sight of things."

And losing seemed to be a Charon family trait. No one had emerged from the legal war with anything, the case bouncing between the local probate court and the Virginia appellate courts. So far, there'd been four judicial opinions and no resolution.

"After the house burned," she said, "everybody apparently just abandoned it. The insurance company surely refused to pay on the claim, and none of the beneficiaries was going to sink a dime into the place. No one knew about the archive, or it would have been taken. Those books and manuscripts are worth a fortune."

"So how does our foreign visitor know?"

That was the question of the moment.

Another of the entries on the Google page caught her attention and she clicked on it.

Charon's obituary.

He'd been buried not far from the estate in a family plot near Manassas. It spoke of his family and his ties to the community, but it was the last paragraph that grabbed her attention.

> He was an honored member of the Society of Cincinnati, responsible for the expansion of the society's research library. Reminding America of the debt owed to the heroes of the Revolution was his life's work. The honorary pallbearers at his funeral will include the society's current president general.

"Seems all roads point to this Society of Cincinnati," Luke said.

She agreed.

"I'm assuming you know where we head next?"

That she did.

But more importantly she wanted to know what was happening in Siberia.

CHAPTER
SEVENTEEN

MALONE DID NOT LIKE THE SITUATION. ZORIN SEEMED QUITE confident, as evident from the calculation and contempt that filled the older man's face. He'd also noticed the firm easy strides across the basement which signaled the unmistakable air of a conquering hero. And the voice, clearly sour with bitterness, still held suggestions of energy that belied his years, reinforced by an impressive physical appearance that included bearish shoulders, a thick chest, and huge veined hands.

"I have a debt to pay and I intend to pay it."

Those words had been delivered with a hard stare and macabre grin, both of which contained only defiance. Outwardly, Zorin gave the appearance of a coarse, uneducated man. And though Malone had spent only a few moments with him there was no doubt that here was a bold and barnacled Cold War veteran. Most likely a dangerous sociopath, too. He knew the type. Highly motivated achievers, alarmingly efficient, with few to no elements of conscience, their greatest fault came from actions governed by faulty reasoning.

And here seemed the perfect example.

Zorin was still fighting the Cold War.

Which ended a long time ago.

He'd been led into the house at gunpoint, a naked Belchenko remaining in the hothouse. His two minders had forced him down to the chilly basement, a windowless space with hewn-stone walls. They'd removed his coat and weapon, cuffing both of his hands with steel manacles between an iron pipe. What they hadn't touched was the wallet in his back pocket, and that omission offered him hope.

He just needed a little privacy.

Which he now had.

Zorin was gone, back up to ground level. The sound of a door closing above signaled opportunity so he twisted his body, slid his cuffed hands down the pipe, and used the little bit of play that he had to retrieve his wallet. Inside, he quickly found the pick. The cuffs sported a simple lock that should be easy to trip.

Zorin apparently carried a hard-on for the United States. Why he longed for the old Soviet Union seemed odd. Its mortality rate had been nearly 50 percent, the life expectancy dismal. If the communist regime had not imploded it most likely would have died out through attrition. Shortages of goods and services had been epidemic. Alcoholism soared. Prices stayed in orbit, while wages had plummeted and corruption ran rampant. Lenin's pledge of equality and autonomy for all never happened. Instead, a system emerged that ordained a succession of tyrannies, each existing solely to perpetuate both itself and the privileged few who ran it.

So what was there to miss?

More of that dangerous sociopath *faulty reasoning,* he assumed.

He continued to work the lock on his right wrist, the damn thing more stubborn than he'd thought it would be. Something Oscar Wilde said came to mind. *Truth is rarely pure and never simple.* Yet it seemed so to Zorin, who apparently had taken a perverse enjoyment in his former life.

Where was he headed? What was this all about?

Stephanie needed to know everything.

He heard a door open, then a rush of footfalls down the stairs and the two men from earlier appeared. Both were burly and unshaven, with Mongoloid faces and shoulders strong as plowmen.

He slipped the pick from the lock and palmed it in his right hand.

The two wasted no time, pouncing on him, slamming their fists into his gut. Nothing cracked, which was probably intentional. As Zorin

had noted, these guys didn't want the fun to end too soon. He'd prepared himself for the blows, but they still hurt. The men shed their
coats, then yanked the sleeves to their sweaters up to the elbow, ready
to go to work. They both smiled, knowing there was nothing he could
do. He sucked a few breaths of the fetid air, which smelled of dust and
heating oil.

"You guys are pretty tough with my hands cuffed," he tried. "Cut
me loose and let's do this like men."

Red Sweater drove a fist the size of a small ham into his stomach.

He decided, what the hell, and pivoted with his spine off the iron
pipe, driving his right leg into Red's knee, buckling the joint and sending the Russian screaming to the floor. Black Sweater lunged and
tried to plant another fist. But Malone repeated the move, this time
using the iron pipe for maximum leverage to drive both feet into his
attacker's chest, sending Black reeling backward.

Red stood and rubbed his knee. Anger filled his eyes.

He doubted he could buy himself enough time to get the cuffs off.
Both men readied themselves to attack at the same time. So they
weren't near as stupid as they looked. He figured after a few blows to
the head he'd see nothing but stars, which should daze him enough so
they could smash at will. And these guys appeared no longer interested
in subtlety.

They wanted him dead.

Two loud bangs pierced the cellar.

Both men gasped, their eyes wide open. Blood oozed from Red's
mouth. Then all muscular control ceased and they dropped to the
ground, like marionettes off their strings. Behind them, at the foot of
the stairs, stood Vadim Belchenko. The older man was dressed in a
long-sleeved shirt and jeans that would have sagged off save for a belt
tightly wrapped at the waist. The right hand held Malone's Beretta.

Belchenko stepped over the two bodies. The face was even more
pale and splotchy than in the bath, the colorless eyes devoid of expression. "I told you I could still shoot."

"And the reason you killed them?" he asked.

Belchenko produced a key from his pocket and tossed it over. "To
help you. Why else?"

He caught the key and freed his wrists from the cuffs.

"I heard what Zorin told you," Belchenko said. "You realize that he is insane."

He felt like a shuttlecock in a game of badminton. Confusion swamped him. He wasn't sure what he realized. "I thought you two were on the same side?" The gun was still pointed his way, so he motioned toward it and said, "You going to shoot me, too?"

Belchenko handed over the Beretta. "I found it upstairs. I hope you don't mind my borrowing it."

"Not at all. In fact, you're welcome to it anytime. I wasn't quite sure how I was going to get clear of those two."

"These men are all fanatics. They live down in the village and worship Zorin. He's the senior man here. Together, they cling to an ideal that really never existed."

"And you?"

"How could anyone believe that a political system could provide all of the goods and services a people needed without cost? A daily gratification that would eliminate greed, selfishness, miserliness, and infidelity. A place where man could become noble, strong, and courageous. Crime, violence, and social ills would vanish. It's absurd. The experiment called the Soviet Union only proved that none of that is possible."

He should be leaving. His mission was done. But a new one was forming, one that involved an obsessed communist. "What is it Zorin's after? He said he had a debt to pay."

Belchenko's wizened head nodded. "That he does. In his mind he feels he owes the United States."

Stephanie had passed on that Belchenko was a former KGB archivist. So he asked, "What did you tell him?"

"If I hadn't told Zorin what he wanted to know, he would have killed me. If I lied, he would have gone, discovered the truth, then returned and killed me. So I opted to tell him the truth. But I doubt it matters any longer. So much time has passed. There is nothing left to find."

He had a barrage of questions, but one seemed the most important. "So why are you talking to me?"

"Because I have never been an idealist. Instead, I was simply born into an evil and corrupt system and learned to survive. Eventually, I became the guardian of communist secrets, important to the privileged. They trusted me, and I kept their trust. But they're all gone now. Like you said to Zorin. The Cold War is over and the world is different. Only a few like these two here, dead on the floor, and Zorin think otherwise. What he wants to do is foolishness. It will accomplish nothing. So on the off chance that danger still exists, I decided to save your life and tell you the truth, too." Belchenko paused. "You asked what Zorin is after."

He waited.

"Nuclear weapons—that no one knows exist."

CHAPTER EIGHTEEN

STEPHANIE AND LUKE STEPPED FROM THE CAB IN FRONT OF Anderson House. The limestone Beaux-Arts mansion sat on Massachusetts Avenue, a few blocks away from Dupont Circle, in the heart of Embassy Row. She knew all about the palatial building. It'd been built during the Gilded Age by an American diplomat named Anderson as one of the largest and most expensive residences in DC. It served as his family home during the winter social season, designed to both entertain and showcase a collection of fine art and furniture. When Anderson died in 1937, his wife gave the house to a group near and dear to his heart.

The Society of Cincinnati.

America's mistreatment of war veterans seemed to stay in the news. But that shame was nothing new. It actually started in 1783 when the Revolutionary War ended. At the time most Continental officers had not been paid in four years. Needless to say discontent was widespread. Rumors abounded that the army would soon be disbanded with those debts remaining unsettled. Serious talk of a military coup began to circulate, which could have succeeded since the fledging nation had no way to defend itself. George Washington had to personally intervene and quell any new revolutionary fever. Then General Henry Knox seized on an idea to form a fraternal society that would look after the officers' collective interests, even after the army dissolved. He envisioned the group as a way to channel anger into constructive talk, and the idea drew approval.

Its name came naturally.

Latin classics were a mainstay of study for any 18th-century learned man. Lucius Quinctius Cincinnatus lived as a 5th-century Roman aristocrat, banished to poverty on his farm. When war threatened, the Roman Senate voted him absolute authority for a period of six months to deal with the crisis. Victory came within two weeks and Cincinnatus, citing the greater good, civic virtue, and personal modesty, resigned his dictatorial post and returned to his farm. That example fit those Continental officers perfectly, since they, too, were headed back to their own plows. And, like Cincinnatus, the prospect of poverty loomed great. The society's long-standing motto reflected a sense of selfless service.

Omnia reliquit servare rempublicam.

He relinquished everything to save the republic.

Nearly half of the 5,500 eligible officers initially joined the society. Washington was elected its first president general, a position he held until his death in 1799. He was succeeded by Alexander Hamilton. Twenty-three signers of the Constitution became members. The town of Cincinnati, Ohio, was named to honor the society, as the first governor of that territory had been a member and hoped others would come west and settle there. Membership had always depended on sex and heredity. Originally, any male officer of the Continental army could join. Once that officer died, he could be represented in the society by only one male descendant at a time. A collateral heir could assume the role if the direct male line died out.

And that tradition remained today.

She knew all of this because her late husband had been a member of the Maryland branch. Originally, each of the thirteen colonies organized a local group. Lars Nelle's paternal ancestors had fought in the Revolutionary War from Maryland, and one of them had been a society founding member. Earlier, when she saw the book under the glass cover, memories had come flooding back. Her husband had been a man not prone to much excitement. His moroseness was something she came to accept, then regret after he took his own life. Lars had not been enthusiastic about most things, but one that always brought him joy had been the Society of Cincinnati.

She checked her watch.

9:05 A.M.

Before leaving the hotel she'd scoured the society's website and learned that the house and library opened at nine, but tours of the house did not begin until after lunch. The mansion had served as a museum for decades, doubling as the group's national headquarters. Its ballroom was also available for rent to outside functions, and over the years she'd attended several.

One from long ago in particular.

August 1982.

She was impressed with the ballroom's two-story white walls lined with murals, warmly lit by a pair of magnificent crystal chandeliers. A dozen white-clothed oval tables stood ready across an inlaid oak floor. Particularly noteworthy was the flying staircase with an iron balustrade that led up to an open balcony. Twisted Baroque columns supported the perch, creating an overhead musicians' gallery that tonight accommodated a classical trio.

Six months had passed since her talk with President Reagan. Already she'd visited Rome four times, meeting the pope, establishing a rapport, building a relationship. She and John Paul II had found common ground, discussing opera and classical music, which they both enjoyed. Reagan seemed to also be a constant subject for them. The pope was curious about the American president, asking many questions and demonstrating a knowledge that surprised her. She had reported all of this to the president, as he, too, was fascinated to know more about the Roman pontiff.

Two months ago the president and the pope met privately in the Vatican. She'd laid the groundwork for those talks, pleased that a deal had been struck. She hadn't been present in June. Instead, she'd waited at a nearby hotel until the president and his entourage were gone. Then she'd worked quietly with her Rome counterparts to finalize the details of what both sides would be doing in the coming months. A lot was happening in Eastern Europe, the world changing by the day, and she was thrilled to be a part of that.

Tonight she'd been invited to a State Department reception. The invitation had come as a surprise. An envelope on her desk when she returned from lunch had requested her presence at Anderson House, near Dupont Circle, at 6:00 P.M. The summons had presented an immediate wardrobe problem, solved by a quick stop at a local boutique. She wondered about the invite, as few of the faces present were familiar. One, though, she knew. George Shultz. The secretary of state himself.

He'd assumed the post only a month ago, after Al Haig had been quietly forced out. There'd been differences of opinion as to how the administration's foreign policy should proceed. Secretary Haig liked one path, but the White House wanted another.

"I see you received my invitation," Shultz said to her as he approached.

Her boss was an economist and academician who'd made a name for himself in the private sector. He'd also managed to serve in three cabinet-level posts for Nixon, now in his fourth with Reagan as secretary of state. He was dressed in a dapper black tuxedo that snugly fit his stout frame.

"I wasn't aware that the invitation came from you," she said.

Six months ago everything about this scenario would have been intimidating. But her presidential recruitment and covert missions to Italy had fortified her confidence. She was now a player in a major game. Unfortunately, only Alexander Haig and the president knew that.

"Let's walk out to the winter garden," he said, gesturing for her to lead the way.

French doors lined one wall of the long ballroom and allowed people to flow naturally out into what was once an orangery that overlooked a terraced backyard adorned with statuary and a reflecting pond. The narrow rectangular gallery was lined with garden murals, gilded trellis work, and marble columns. The floor was polished marble, slick as glass, the ceiling faux-painted like the sky. He motioned and they entered a small room at one end that held a dining table and chairs.

"I want you to know that Forward Pass will continue," he said, his voice low. "In fact, things will now escalate."

Apparently her new boss had been briefed.

Just a few days ago Shultz had proclaimed publicly that the State Department's most important task would be Soviet and European diplomacy. Before leaving, Haig had caused some alarm by openly suggesting that a nuclear warning shot in Europe might be a good way to deter the Soviet Union. Such overtness ran contrary to everything the president wanted to achieve. Ronald Reagan hated nuclear weapons. Though the public may not have realized that fact, those close to him definitely did. Over the past few months relations had grown strained not only between Washington and Moscow but also between Washington and key foreign capitals. In response to martial law in Poland the United States had prohibited American companies, and their European subsidiaries, from involvement in the construction of a natural gas pipeline from Siberia to West Germany. European leaders had vigorously protested those sanctions since they affected their own financial interests. Haig had done little to ease that tension. So she assumed that it would now fall to the man standing beside her to deal with the problem.

"The president himself told me of your special assignment," Shultz said. "He has a grand plan, does he not?"

Haig had spoken to her only once about Forward Pass, fishing for information. She'd politely dodged his inquiries, which had created a level of tension between them.

"The president's looking for help," Shultz said. "He wants partners. He's not asking for debate on how to proceed, only that we follow his lead. I intend to do that. I want you to know that I expect you to do the same."

"You know the goal?"

He nodded. "And I think we can get there. I have to say, prior to being selected for this job I wasn't necessarily a fan of Ronald Reagan. I thought him, as many others do, unqualified for the job. He was an actor, for God's sake. But I was wrong. This man is insightful and smart. He knows what he wants and intends to get it. I like that. It's refreshing. He told me that he will make all major foreign policy decisions himself, but the details of those decisions, the actual diplomacy, will be up to me." Shultz paused. "Especially regarding Forward Pass. You and I have a tough job ahead of us."

"And do I report to you?"

She did not want to start off badly with this man. From everything she'd read and heard he knew how to play the political game. How else could he have served in four cabinet positions?

He shook his head. "Why would I squeeze you into that vise? Do your job and include me when appropriate or required. We both work for the president of the United States. He's the boss. That's why I asked you here tonight. I wanted you to hear this from me, personally." He leaned in close and whispered, "And I thought it best that we not be seen at the State Department talking together."

She grinned at both his smile and conspiratorial tone.

"I daresay," he noted, "the next few years certainly should be interesting."

And they were.

The pope and the president didn't meet face-to-face again until 1984. During that time she became the primary conduit of information between Washington and Rome. She traveled the world, logging tens of thousands of miles. She came and went from the Vatican and the White House with ease, all the while helping to coordinate the destruction of the Soviet Union.

Now here she was back at Anderson House for the first time since that summer evening in 1982.

After she talked with Shultz he'd led her back inside where the tables, heavy with flowers, awaited diners. They'd all enjoyed a lovely dinner, the ballroom noisy with music, chatter, and the clink of fine china. Amusing anecdotes had fluttered back and forth. Everything about that night had seemed reassuring—its harmonic sounds tucked safely away in her memory. Somewhere she still had the gold-edged menu card signed by Shultz, a keepsake from a time when she'd been personally recruited by the president of the United States, and the secretary of state had been her confidential ally.

So unlike now—where she'd been deemed no longer necessary.

She led Luke toward the house through an arched portal, its open iron gate providing access to a recessed carriage court, shaded from the morning sun by a columned portico. A pair of two-bay multistory wings flanked on either side. Nearly thirty-five years had passed since that evening here. George Shultz was gone. Reagan and John Paul both dead. She alone remained, matured into a world-class intelligence officer, regarded by some as one of the best in the business. Unfortunately, none of that mattered to the new president or the next attorney general. Shortly, she'd be unemployed. But something had been nagging at her ever since the car ride into Virginia, while she listened to Nikolai Osin tell her about missing nukes and more on a communist fanatic named Zorin.

He wants revenge.

She could feel it.

A certainty.

Born from experience.

Then and now were connected.

CHAPTER
NINETEEN

Lake Baikal

Malone heard what Belchenko had said and realized that the old man was deadly serious. He hadn't been prepared for such a revelation, so he stared in astonishment. "What nuclear weapons nobody knows exist?"

"We were taught from birth that America was our enemy. That everything about America ran contrary to our way of life. Our duty was to be prepared to battle that main adversary. It was our whole life."

"We were taught the same about you."

"And we wonder why we distrusted each other? Why we couldn't live together as friends? There was no chance of that happening. In the bath I told you that all stories have a beginning, a middle, and an end. The communist story started in 1918 with the Bolshevik Revolution. The middle lasted from then until now. Along the way, we've seen Stalin, Khrushchev, Brezhnev, Gorbachev, Yeltsin, and Putin. The current government is no better. One disaster after another. Men like Zorin have not forgotten what they were taught. To him America remains the main adversary. Only now, the motivations are more personal. For him, the end of the story was not then. It is now."

"He told me he headed a *spetsnaz* unit."

Belchenko nodded. "He has skills, ones that are twenty-plus years in hibernation, but ones that are never forgotten. He will be a tough opponent."

He knew that Soviet special forces were once some of the best in the world. They'd fought hard in the Afghan war back in the 1980s. So he asked, "Was he in Afghanistan?"

"Nearly five years. He thought our withdrawal a betrayal of all who died. On that I disagree. That war had to end. But when the Soviet Union fell, we both saw what betrayal truly meant. The *spetsnaz* suffered from the same corruption, low morale, and lack of money that everyone else experienced. Many of those operatives went to work for the mobsters, who paid high for their services."

"But not Zorin."

"Not back then, but he did eventually work for them some. Everyone had to at some point. They had all the money. But generally, Zorin served his country, not the ruble. When there was no more country, he simply disappeared."

And avoided, Malone realized, the disasters that came after 1991. During the Chechen War the *spetsnaz* finally lost its fierce reputation, with major defeats happening to guerrilla fighters. He recalled reading about an entire unit being massacred. Then came the 2002 Moscow theater and 2004 Beslan school siege. In one *spetsnaz* troops bungled the rescue, costing hundreds their lives, and in the other they used rockets and tanks to blast their way in causing more casualties. No finesse. No skill. Only a callous disregard for life, particularly that of their fellow citizens.

"Aleksandr is a man driven by purpose," Belchenko said. "He's lived here, in this house, a long time. His bitterness has aged and matured. And like the commandos of his time, he still possesses great initiative and an ability to think for himself."

He had to know more about those nuclear weapons, so he forced his thinking process back to their basics. "You have to tell me what's happening here?"

Belchenko leaned himself against one of the iron pillars supporting the house above. "I do not know all of the details. I know you might find that odd, considering my former career. But the *spetsnaz* had access to small, portable nuclear devices. We called them RA-115s. They were hidden inside remote arms caches."

The caches he knew about, scattered across Western and Central

Europe, Israel, Turkey, Japan, and even North America. Stores of arms and radio equipment, intended for use by forward-deployed units.

"I remember one in Switzerland," he said. "When it was found, they fired a water cannon and it exploded. Booby-trapped."

"Mitrokhin's revelations led them to that depository and others. You do know that I consider that man a traitor. He had no right to reveal all that he did. Our job was to keep those secrets."

"What did it matter?"

"It mattered a great deal. To me. To men like Zorin. We believed in what we were doing. And even when our country ended, our task did not. It was our duty to keep those secrets."

"Then why are you talking to me? Why'd you just kill two men? What's changed?"

"Zorin has lost sight of what we stood for. He has lowered himself to the level of those who ultimately caused our downfall. Men like Stalin, Beria, Brezhnev, Andropov, and all of the other so-called party leaders. They were opportunists who believed only in themselves. Zorin has become like them, though I doubt he even realizes."

"And you're telling me that one of those hidden weapons caches contains nuclear weapons?"

"I'm telling you that many contained nuclear weapons. But you only have to concern yourself with one of those caches. The rest are harmless."

"Tell me what I need to know."

"Zorin is headed for Canada."

New information. Finally.

"He's after a man named Jamie Kelly. An American, who once worked for the KGB. When the end came in 1991 Kelly faded away, like so many other officers around the globe. But he knows the location of one cache that may hold five RA-115s, which could still be operational."

How was that possible? "Don't those things need constant power to stay alive?"

"They do. But if that power has been constant, nothing can prevent the weapon from working. Our engineers designed them to last a long time—hidden away."

Malone was instantly suspicious, and rightly so. This man had spent a lifetime deceiving, so why would now be any different? "What is Zorin going to do with this weapon?"

"Unfortunately, he did not share that with me, which is understandable. He just assured me that the debt owed to America would be paid."

"So what did he want with you?"

"He needed Kelly's name and location. You see, after the Soviet Union ended the decision was made not to reveal anything about those weapons caches. We decided to allow them to remain hidden. If one was found, the booby traps would protect its secrets. Traitors like Mitrokhin ruined that strategy. What only a few knew, though—and this did not include Mitrokhin—was that some of those caches harbored a nuclear capability."

"And you don't know where this one cache is located?"

"I never learned that information. But Jamie Kelly knows. I'm told that he is still alive."

A noise from above disturbed the silence.

"Sounds like a vehicle," Malone said, heading for the stairs, gun in hand.

Belchenko followed, but not before retrieving one of the dead men's rifles.

"You going to need that?" Malone asked.

"It's entirely possible."

He grabbed his coat, donning it as they climbed the risers, which led to a kitchen equipped with an iron stove and fireplace. A cupboard filled one wall, china cups hanging from hooks. The air hung fetid with the smell of unclean floors and sour dishwater. Lights illuminated the outside. Past one of the outer windows he saw three men wearing woolen balaclavas emerge from an off-road vehicle, similar to a Jeep Wrangler.

They advanced through the glow of the lights.

He heard the familiar, hurried clicks of assault weapons.

CHAPTER TWENTY

STEPHANIE LED LUKE INTO ANDERSON HOUSE. THE SOCIETY OF Cincinnati had been headquartered here since the 1930s, though its physical presence was anything but clear. The house itself served as a period museum for the Anderson family's private collection of art and statuary—a remnant of the Gilded Age that could be enjoyed free of charge—and the society's offices were confined to the basement, all of which she knew from long ago and the time of her husband. As she'd told Luke, this was the oldest private patriotic group in the country, the nation's first hereditary organization, assuming the task of preserving the memory of the War of Independence.

And she knew its members took that task seriously.

Downstairs held one of the finest assortment of books and manuscripts from that era. Both the Revolutionary War and the War of 1812 had always fascinated her, and she'd learned years ago about the society's extensive collection of primary and secondary sources. The cache in Virginia seemed particularly precious and she still wondered if anyone here was aware of its existence. There seemed only one way to find out, so she flashed her Magellan Billet badge to an attendant inside and was directed to the basement offices.

On the walk to the stairs leading down she noticed that not much had changed. The entrance hall flowed into a long anteroom and an elegant stairway up, the ballroom and library just ahead. The same dazzling array of art, furnishings, marble, and murals dominated. Even the same waft of a musty smell from a time long past remained.

Though the society today was simply another nonprofit entity, its beginnings were anything but benign. In the 1780s many regarded a fraternal military order as a threat. No good could come from men of war banding together. An understandable fear given the brash arrogance of the British military, which till then was all the colonists knew. Then there was the hereditary aspect of membership, which smacked of nobility. Peerage was a concept the new nation considered grossly obscene. The Constitution itself forbade the granting of nobility. Several states, and even Congress, thought of banning the society. Only the presence of George Washington himself calmed fears.

She recalled how her late husband had loved attending the annual gatherings held in the ballroom. He'd been a student of history, his own colonial library impressive. She still owned the books, displayed on shelves in her house back in Georgia. She should be there now deciding on what to do with the rest of her life. Instead, she was here, violating a direct order from her immediate superior, plunging deeper by the minute into an ever-widening hole.

"This place is friggin' amazing," Luke muttered. "You seem to know your way around."

She smiled at his attempt to pry information. "Comes from being around a long time."

"Okay, I get the message. You'll talk when you're ready."

Downstairs they found the library, a more utilitarian space constructed for practicality with padded carpet, acoustical ceiling, and sturdy metal shelving that supported hundreds of books and manuscripts. Three thick wooden tables stood in its center, the air full of the sweet smell of old paper and book bindings. Shadowless fluorescent lighting emitted a faintly bluish glow. Waiting for them was a short, thin man in his late forties, the face creased with lines of good humor, who introduced himself as Fritz Strobl, the society's curator. A set of eyeglasses hung from his neck by a chain. She explained what they'd stumbled onto in Virginia.

"The owner of that house, Brad Charon," Strobl said, "was a member of the society all his adult life. It doesn't surprise me that he amassed such a collection."

"And hid it away," Luke noted.

Strobl smiled. "Mr. Charon was a tad eccentric. But he loved America and this society."

"He died suddenly?" she asked, already knowing the answer, but probing a bit.

"A plane crash. I attended his funeral. It was such a sad time. I read afterward about a probate fight between his heirs, but that was quite some time ago."

Twenty-plus years in the intelligence business had taught her many things. Among them were hardball politics, covert diplomacy, complicity, and, when necessary, duplicity. She'd dealt with an endless variety of people across the globe, good and bad, and had made too many life-and-death decisions to count. Along the way she'd developed skills, one of which was to pay attention. It amazed her how little people noticed other people. Generally, it wasn't ego or narcissism that explained the inability. Indifference seemed the most common explanation, but she'd trained herself to notice everything.

Like the slight tremble in Strobl's hands. Not just the left or the right, which might signal a physical problem. Both of his shook. And there was the tiny line of sweat at the top of his brow that gleamed in the overhead lights. The room temperature was quite comfortable, cool enough in fact that neither she nor Luke had shed their coats. The kicker, though, was the bite of the lip—which, by her count, Strobl had done four times, perhaps to quell their noticeable quiver.

"What agency did you say you were with?" Strobl asked her.

"The Justice Department."

"And why exactly are you here?"

She decided to dodge that one. "To report the archive we found. There's a rare book there, displayed under glass, that details the society's founding. It's what led us here."

She showed him a photo taken with her phone just before they left Virginia.

"That's an original edition of our founding journal," Strobl said. "Only a few members own one. I didn't know Mr. Charon possessed this one."

"It can be yours now," Luke asked.

Strobl threw them both an odd look, one that said he did not agree.

"I appreciate the information you've provided. Now, if you'll excuse me, I have work that requires my attention. We're hosting an inaugural reception Monday evening and our ballroom is being prepared."

"Big affair?" she asked.

"It won't include the president, but we're told the vice president and several of the new cabinet will be attending."

She concealed her disgust and decided not to let this man off that easy. Luke had retreated to the far side of the room, behind Strobl, ostensibly examining the books. But he tossed her a knowing glance that confirmed her own suspicions.

Strobl was lying.

She scanned the room and noticed a small dark globe attached to the ceiling tiles in one corner. A security camera. No surprise. She assumed the entire villa was wired for pictures considering the value of the art and antiques scattered across the upper floors.

"My late husband, Lars Nelle, was a society member."

She was hoping that tidbit might loosen Strobl some, but it seemed to have no effect.

"He was active in the Maryland branch," she said. "He and I visited here, Anderson House, several times."

Still, nothing.

But Luke caught the information.

"You may want to go and retrieve those books at Charon's house," she said to Strobl.

"How is that possible? As you say, it's located inside the estate. That would be stealing."

"Only if you get caught," Luke said. "But I don't think anyone is going to mind. It's been sitting there a long time. It can be our little secret."

"I'm afraid that's not how we operate here. Not at all."

The obvious strain in Strobl's voice might be explained by the fact that someone from the Justice Department had appeared on a Friday morning unannounced, flashing a badge and asking questions.

Then again, maybe not.

"On second thought," Strobl suddenly said. "Perhaps you have a point. That library could be important. Mr. Charon financed the acquisition of many of the books and papers you see here around you.

He was himself an avid collector. He *would* want us to have whatever he may have amassed."

Interesting, the change in tone.

More confident. Less anxious. Even suggestive.

Strobl reached for a pad and pen lying atop one of the tables. "Tell me the location again."

She did and he wrote as she spoke.

"Is this correct?" he asked, handing her the pad.

She read.

Russian woman in second-floor security office, just past the serving pantry, with a gun. She saw you coming. Told me to be rid of you or she would kill the man who works up there.

She nodded and handed the pad back. "That's right. It's an old house out in the woods. I'd head out there right away. The winter weather will not be kind to those old books."

"We'll do just that."

She thanked him for his time and she and Luke left the library, exiting into a windowless camera-free corridor that led to the stairs.

"Anya Petrova is here," she said. "On the second floor, in the security office just past the serving pantry. When we get to ground level we'll split up. She's going to know you're coming. Cameras are everywhere."

"Not a problem. I owe her one."

She got the message. He'd make no mistakes this time.

They climbed back up and reentered the stylish gallery. The same attendant who earlier had been stationed behind a desk in the entrance foyer was still there. Stephanie turned right and headed straight for her. Luke hustled for the stairway at the other end of the gallery.

The attendant stood and called out, "I'm sorry, you can't go—"

Stephanie calmly peeled back her coat for the woman to see her holstered Beretta.

Shock swept across her face.

Stephanie kept walking and brought her right index finger up to her lips.

Signaling quiet.

CHAPTER
TWENTY-ONE

MALONE NEEDED TO REPORT BACK TO STEPHANIE NELLE. THIS
was much bigger than he'd been led to believe, much bigger than perhaps even Stephanie realized, since when she'd called to hire him she'd
openly admitted that she knew only that the Russians had asked
for American help in finding Belchenko, and that he might run into
Zorin. Unfortunately, he had no cell phone, and three men with automatic rifles now blocked any exit from the dacha.

Belchenko appeared unfazed by what was happening outside.
"That's a *Kozlík*. Means 'Goat.' A nickname for the vehicle. It's military
only. These men have surely come on orders from the Kremlin. They
are after me."

"Any idea why?"

"I assume the government decided my usefulness has waned. You
need to leave. This does not concern you. I'll deal with it. There's a
rear door down that hall. Go find Jamie Kelly in Canada."

"You never mentioned exactly where."

"Charlottetown. Prince Edward Island. He's still employed part-
time at the local college."

"Let's both of us go find him," he said.

But Belchenko ignored the offer, yanking open the exterior door
and opening fire with the assault rifle.

Retorts banged through the house.

He doubted the old man's vision was near as good as he wanted people to think, and with forty or so rounds a minute spitting out the barrel it would not be long before the clip emptied.

And it did.

Malone lunged, wrapping his arms around the man, propelling them both away from the doorway just as incoming fire arrived. They slammed into the wood floor and he took the brunt of it.

"Are you friggin' nuts?" he yelled.

A hail of slugs thudded into the walls. The exterior stone façade provided some protection, but not the windows, which began to explode as they were pummeled by shots from the outside. Wooden splinters and flying glass crashed through the room. He stayed down and waited for an opportunity.

"I took one of them out," Belchenko said.

Darkness had enveloped outside, nightfall coming early in the Siberian winter. Which should help with their escape. The problem was getting out of the dacha without being shot.

The firing outside stopped.

He knew what was happening.

Reload time.

Which would not take long, so he used the moment to bring Belchenko to his feet and they rushed toward a corridor leading deeper into the house, crouching down but moving fast.

One of the men burst in through the kitchen doorway.

Malone whirled and fired.

A hole formed on the man's face as the bullet pierced the brain. He'd learned long ago to shoot, if possible, for the head or the legs. Too much body armor around these days. And though he'd retired from active service and was no longer required to stay proficient, he remained an excellent shot. The man dropped to the floor, the body wrenching in convulsions. He decided the rifle that clattered away could be useful so he quickly retrieved the AK-47 and noted it held a fresh clip.

Oh, yes. This would definitely come in handy.

He stepped back to the hall expecting to find Belchenko waiting for him, but the wiry old man was nowhere in sight. Only a few lights burned across the dacha's ground floor, the exterior windows all dark mattes from the night. He slid the Beretta inside its holster beneath his coat and aimed the rifle straight ahead, nestling the weapon snug to his right shoulder. The corridor stretched twenty feet, ending at another room at the far end.

The house echoed with emptiness.

He concentrated on his heartbeat and willed it to slow. How many times had he faced situations just like this?

Too many to count.

Frigid air invaded from the open exterior door and blown-out windows, his exhales now forming puffy clouds. He'd retired from the Magellan Billet to avoid these exact risks, resigning his commission as a naval commander, quitting the Justice Department, selling his house, and moving to Copenhagen, opening an old bookshop. Twenty years in the navy and ten years as a Billet agent over. The idea had been a total change in lifestyle. Unfortunately, his former world found him and he'd been embroiled in enough controversies since retirement that he finally decided that he ought to at least get paid for his trouble. The task here had been a simple meet and greet, then leave. Instead, he'd stumbled into an international hornet's nest, and now angry bees were swarming in every direction.

He kept moving down the hall, floorboards creaking under his weight, a badly worn carpet runner doing a poor job of muffling his steps. Thoughts of Gary swirled through his mind. His son was growing up fast, nearly out of high school, beginning to decide what he wanted to do with the rest of his life. There'd been talk of the navy, following in his father's and grandfather's footsteps. His ex-wife wasn't exactly keen on the idea, but they'd privately agreed to allow the boy to make up his own mind. Life was hard enough without parents forcing choices.

Then there was Cassiopeia.

He wondered where she was, what she was doing. He'd found himself thinking of her more and more of late. Their romance seemed over, his last attempt at contact drawing a curt reply.

LEAVE ME ALONE.

So he had.

But he missed her.

Hard not to—considering that he loved her.

The corridor ended.

He pressed his back to the wall and balanced on the balls of his feet. He steadied his breathing, keeping the lungs' rhythm separate from his legs. That trick had saved his hide more than once. Then he tucked his elbows and cocked his forearms, applying light tension to the wrist, fingers closed around the rifle and trigger, but nothing clenched.

He carefully peered around the jamb.

The space beyond was some sort of great room with a high vaulted ceiling and another fireplace where black, smoky logs had died to smoldering embers. A wall of dark windows faced the lake. One light burned on a far table casting a jaundiced glow. Long fingers of deep shadows clutched at every corner. The pine furnishings were austere and included a sofa and chairs facing the windows. Normally, this would be a cocoon of comfort from the cold. Tonight it seemed a trap. A closed door stood on the farthest side, Belchenko standing beside it.

"Is that the way out?" he asked.

Belchenko nodded. "I was waiting for you."

The old Russian stood partially in shadow, the rest of the room nearly dark. A tense glare signaled trouble. Something wasn't right.

Then it clicked.

Belchenko no longer held the rifle.

"Where's your weapon?" he asked, remaining behind the doorway.

"No need for it anymore."

The words came low and slow. The cat had gotten Chatty Cathy's tongue. Or maybe—

"Let's go out the other way," he said to Belchenko.

"That's not possible—"

Gunfire erupted from inside the great room, the noise bellowing in the high ceiling. Malone shifted his weight forward and dove, his body stretched outward, and landed on the wood floor, momentum gliding him across in front of the sofa, near the exterior windows. He kept the rifle steady and caught a blur of movement in the half darkness as a form emerged from the shadows. He pulled the trigger and sent a volley of rounds that way. The form recoiled and bucked against the wall, then shuddered and twitched before sliding down into a patch of shadow, losing all shape and identity. He scrambled for a heavy wooden table, uprighting it before him as cover.

He listened.

No sounds, other than a low howl from the wind outside. Three men had been on the truck. Three were now down. He slowly came to his feet, keeping the rifle aimed, finger heavy on the trigger.

He heard a grunt and cry of pain from the far side and rushed over.

Belchenko lay on the floor.

He spotted a black mass of multiple bullet wounds. Blood poured out each one in ever-widening circles. Apparently, the first shots had been aimed the old man's way.

He bent down. "Was he waiting for you?"

"Sadly," Belchenko managed. "And I so . . . wanted to get out of here."

But he wondered about that observation, considering the shooting with the rifle and the risk taken with the warning. *That's not possible.*

The alarm from Belchenko's face must have mirrored his own. Pain took hold and the older man winced, screwing up his eyes in agony.

"It appears I'm no longer . . . useful to them," the older man said. "They seem to have figured things out . . . without my help."

The wounds were bad.

"There's nothing I can do," he said.

"I know. Go. Let me die in peace."

Belchenko gazed at him dully, lips parted, breaths coming in short, uneven gasps, coughing and grunting like a wounded animal. Flaccid eruptions of blood spewed from his mouth. Not good. The lungs had been pierced.

"I lied . . . earlier. I know Zorin's plan."

Pink froth bubbled at the corner of the mouth, the body trembling in pain.

"We spent decades . . . looking for weaknesses. America . . . did the same to us. We found one. Fool's . . . Mate. But never had the chance . . . to use it. The . . . zero amendment. It's your . . . weakness."

Belchenko tried to speak again, a croaking, gargling sound, like speech, but inarticulate. A flock of spittle appeared on his lips, his eyes bulging. What he had to say seemed important. But the words didn't come. They remained trapped forever between the tongue and teeth as the eyes dilated with death and every muscle went limp.

He checked for a pulse. None.

In repose, the face looked surprisingly old.

"*Fool's Mate*"? "*Zero amendment*"?

"*Your weakness*"?

What did it mean?

No time to consider any of that at the moment. His mind shifted into survival mode. He stepped to the door, eased it open, and saw that it led out to the paved area that spanned in front of the dacha, the same space he'd negotiated earlier before entering the hot bath. Before leaving he took a moment and examined the man he'd shot. Middle-aged. Green fatigues. Black sweater. Boots. No Kevlar. Perhaps they thought this an easy kill. He searched the corpse but found nothing that identified either the man or his employer.

Were these guys military, as Belchenko had declared?

He fled the house, alert for movement. Bitter cold stung his face and a breeze from the lake dissolved his white, vaporous exhales. In the wash from the floodlights he saw the Goat from earlier parked fifty feet away. He grabbed his bearings and debated searching for a cell phone among the dead but decided that wouldn't be smart. He saw the fence, the dark skeletons of the trees, and the knoll that led down to where the truck he'd commandeered earlier waited, then decided, *Why go there and freeze along the way?*

There's a vehicle right here.

He trotted over and saw keys in the ignition, so he climbed inside beneath a canvas roof and coaxed the engine to life. Dropping the gearshift into low he swung the front end around and accelerated. The tires spat snow and the truck leaped forward, headlights searching the darkness as he left the dacha behind.

He followed the twisting black road down toward the main highway, trailing a billow of exhaust. Halfway, another set of headlights appeared coming his way, which momentarily blinded him. He swerved right and avoided the vehicle, which he saw was similar to his own, two dark shapes visible through the foggy windshield. He found the highway and turned south, the cab swaying with speed, the engine straining. In the rearview mirror another set of headlights amid a plume of snow appeared from the drive and fishtailed in a controlled arc.

The other Goat.

Headed toward him.

He saw a figure emerge from the passenger-side window.

Then the stutter of automatic weapons fire began.

CHAPTER
TWENTY-TWO

ZORIN DROVE EAST ON THE DARKENED HIGHWAY, LEAVING LAKE Baikal behind and heading toward Ulan-Ude. The town had sat beside the Uda River since the 18th century, first inhabited by Cossacks, then Mongols. He liked the name, which meant "red Uda," intentionally reflective of a Soviet ideology. The Trans-Siberian Railway brought the place prosperity, as did the major highways, which all converged there. Until 1991 its 400,000 inhabitants had been off-limits to foreigners, which explained why so many of the old ways still flourished.

When the Soviet Union fell there'd been a national rush to eradicate the past. Every statue or bust of any communist leader had been either destroyed or desecrated. There'd even been talk of closing Lenin's tomb and finally burying the corpse, but thankfully that movement never gained strength. Unlike the rest of Russia, which seemed eager to forget, the people of Ulan-Ude remembered. In its central square remained the largest bust of Lenin in the world. Nearly eight meters tall, over forty tons of bronze, the image itself striking. Thanks to some special coating its dark patina had survived the elements, the area around its base a favorite gathering spot. He'd many times driven the one hundred kilometers to simply have a black coffee nearby and remember.

Ulan-Ude also accommodated the nearest international airport, which would be his way to Canada. He wasn't wealthy. His time with the KGB had paid him minimally. When the job ended there'd been no severance, pension, or benefits. Which explained why most operatives chose to go to work for the crime syndicates. They'd offered lots of money, and for men who'd risked their lives for little to nothing the lure had been too tempting to resist. Even he finally succumbed, hiring himself out locally, mainly in and around Irkutsk, being careful never to sell his soul. He had to admit, they'd treated him fair and paid well, enough that he'd amassed twelve million rubles, about $330,000 American, which he'd kept hidden at the dacha, in cash. Some of those funds had gone to pay for Anya's journey, and the rest he would use now.

He glanced at his watch.

The American should be dead by now.

He'd left instructions for the body not to be found. Whoever sent Malone would come looking.

Three days ago he'd made arrangements for a charter jet, all pending his conversation with Belchenko. That aircraft was now waiting at Ulan-Ude. He finally knew the destination, except that a visa would be needed for him to enter Canada. Of course, he could not legally obtain one, nor was there time. Instead, he'd developed an alternative, and a promise of more cash to the charter company had secured its much-needed cooperation. He could only hope that Belchenko had told him the truth.

But why wouldn't he?

He kept driving, the frozen blacktop rumbling beneath the headlights. Weather here loomed as alien as outer space. For him winter seemed merely a prison of crystalline cold. This year's version, though, had been bearable. Perhaps an omen? A harbinger of good tidings that this mission might be successful? He'd been living on frayed nerves far too long. He'd often wondered if he was the last true communist left in the world. The ideology in its purest form seemed long gone— or perhaps it never existed, or at least not as Karl Marx had intended. The Chinese version was unrecognizable, and the various smaller regimes scattered around the globe were communist in name only. For all intents and purposes the philosophy he'd been taught had become extinct.

He inhaled the roasted air blasting from the car's heater.

The pale scimitar of a moon peeked through the clouds. His mouth was dry with tension, old instincts pricking at him in a familiar way. For him there would be no more squandered chances. And though he might be only a shadow of his former self, he no longer felt the fear he had that day in 1991 when the mob stormed Lubyanka. Instead, he was fortified with conviction, and that realization brought him calm.

Anxiety had dogged him for too long. Nothing provided much in the way of peace. His anger could not be bridled, but it could be temporarily sedated with sex and alcohol. Luckily, he'd never become addicted to either. Those were weaknesses he would never allow. He considered himself a man of heart and conscience. He stayed quiet, rarely quarreled, and avoided disputes. Life had tried to turn him into a zombie, stifling all feeling, but in the end it had only fed his vengeance. The fact that he recognized that reality seemed proof he remained in command of himself. He was not merely a piece of flesh with teeth and a stomach. He was not a relic, either. Nor was he insignificant.

Instead, he was a man.

A whiff of memory flew through his mind.

The day when he first spoke to Anya.

He'd traveled down this same highway to Ulan-Ude to savor the sounds of the city—engines, horns, sirens—to watch the hunched babushkas in head scarves and shapeless dresses, and to sit with the men in topcoats of rough bleached cloth, sprawled out on benches, most tired, pasty, and strained. He loved the bazaar, a broad paved street shaded by trees and heaved with people. Open booths of wood, turned brownish black by age, lined either side. Most displayed grain, rock salt, spices, or local produce. Some offered clothes and merchandise, others sold canned goods and candles. He'd drawn comfort from the thick smell of the crowd, an odd mix of perspiration, damp wool, garlic, cabbage, and leather.

His favorite café was a whitewashed building with a peaked roof and wide wooden veranda that sat not far from Lenin's bust. A low wall of mortared boulders separated it from the bazaar. Sturdy wooden tables sat atop an earthen floor below dark wooden beams. Framed calligraphy dotted the inside. Dim lighting and discreet corners offered privacy. In spring and summer flowers topped the outer wall. Occasionally, you'd even hear the clatter of horse hooves on pavement.

Anya had come in for some cold water, dressed in the uniform of the local police. She had a clean, natural face unspoiled by makeup and a delicious laugh that burst deep from the back of her throat. Freckles dusted her pale skin. Her teeth slightly protruded from thin lips with a tiny gap in the middle. Nothing about her signaled dumb or distant, nor had she seemed preoccupied with dreaming of her youth. Quite the contrary. Her eyes stayed filled with mystery and excitement. He'd introduced himself and she spoke to him with a candor and sincerity he never doubted.

Everything about her signaled strength.

Several times he'd seen her around town, and inquiries had informed him that she was a respected member of the police. People told the story of how a gang had burst into a local club, driving right through the doors and windows, then beating everyone up. Anya had been one of the first on the scene and took four of the men down, nearly killing two of them. People spoke her name with respect.

As they had his once, too.

He recalled the pungent aroma of barbecued beef wafting from skewers on a metal grill. The flesh had been tender and succulent with a delicious smoky flavor.

Together, they'd enjoyed a meal.

"My father was a party leader," she said to him. "He was an important man in this city."

"Is he still?"

She shook her head. "He drank himself to death."

"And your mother?"

"She is still alive and wishes her daughter would marry and have babies."

He smiled. "And why doesn't her daughter do that?"

"Because I want more than that from life."

That he could understand.

"When I was little," she told him, "in our house was a poster, from the Great Patriotic War. Mother and child clutching each other before a bloodied Nazi bayonet. And the slogan below.

WARRIORS OF THE RED ARMY, SAVE US. *I remember every detail of that poster and I wanted to be one of those warriors."*

He, too, recalled a poster from where he was raised. The image of a tall, powerful woman, her head wrapped in a kerchief, her mouth open in a shout of alarm with a timeless plea. THE MOTHERLAND CALLS YOU.

"I was but a teenager when the fall came," she said. "But I remember the days before Yeltsin. Most people in this town still remember those, too. It's why I live here. We have not forgotten."

He was intrigued. She seemed to be in extraordinary physical shape and conversed in a calm, calculated way that drew his attention. She knew nothing of him. They were strangers, yet he felt a connection. So he asked, "Do you know of Chayaniye, by the lake?"

"I've heard of it. Is that where you live?"

He nodded. "Perhaps you'd like to come for a visit."

Which happened, and led to more visits until eventually Anya quit her job and came to live with him. On those occasions when he'd taken work for the syndicates in Irkutsk, she'd gone with him. Together they'd earned the money. His fight became her fight. With him she'd found that *"more from life"* she'd been seeking. And he'd found a partner.

He forced himself free of his thoughts and slowed at an intersection to turn. The airport lay only a few kilometers ahead.

He checked his watch one last time.

10:25 P.M.

50 hours left.

CHAPTER
TWENTY-THREE

Luke rushed left toward a long staircase that hugged an interior wall, its wide risers lined with red carpet. He leaped up two steps at a time, one hand gliding along a polished wood railing, the other reaching for his Beretta. He'd meant what he said. He owed Anya Petrova and he planned to pay his debt.

He came to a landing that right-angled to another shorter set of red-carpeted risers. At the top stretched a second-floor gallery that matched the one directly beneath, this one also leading to the far side of the H-shaped villa. The dark-paneled walls were trimmed with molding, the ornate cream-colored ceiling a startling contrast. Large canvases dotted one side, tapestries the other. Three crystal chandeliers hung unlit. He noted more sculptures, flags, and swords, and a clear Asian influence. He knew only what Stephanie had said, that the security office sat adjacent to the serving pantry, which had to be close to the dining room—which he now spotted to his left through an open doorway.

He readied his weapon and entered the dining room, its walls also dark paneling, the floor an intricate inlay of stone. More tapestries were displayed, and a fireplace dominated the exterior wall. A shiny mahogany table lined with elegant chairs occupied the center, above which hung another crystal chandelier.

An open door to his left led out into a room outfitted with simple white cabinets, dark counters, and lots of drawers. A placard just inside identified it as the serving pantry. He entered and spotted another door at the opposite end, ajar. He rushed over and found a short hall that led to a small, windowless space stuffed with video monitors. A man lay sprawled on the floor. He bent down, saw no obvious wounds, and tried to rouse him.

"You okay?"

The guy came around, blinking his eyes, orienting himself. "Yeah. The bitch coldcocked me."

"She's gone?"

The eyes seemed to regain focus. "Yeah. She saw you on the screen, then smacked me."

No one was outside, and no one had been near the staircase he'd used. But in a house this big there had to be many ways up and down. He could only hope that Petrova knew as little about this place as he did.

"Stay here," he said.

He left the security room and stepped back to the serving pantry, halting his advance at the doorway to the dining room. He could feel it. She was here. Waiting for him. Like last time, thinking herself one step ahead.

He crept to the exit to the second-floor gallery.

All quiet.

Another impressive inlaid stone floor stretched from one end of the gallery to another. Maybe fifty feet. Suddenly. Anya appeared in a doorway at the far end. She aimed a gun and fired. He retreated into the dining room. A bullet tore into the wood only a few inches from where his face had been. Another round came and did more damage.

Then another.

He was waiting for a chance and decided that the other side of the room with the dining table between them would be better. This woman was bold. She liked offense. She'd purposefully waited to joust with him. So if she was coming for him at least he could be ready. He rounded the table and assumed a firing position, his gun trained on the doorway.

"What is it you say?" Anya called out. "Come. Get me."

He shook his head.

Did she think him that little of a threat?

He told himself that may be the whole idea, to taunt him into making a mistake. What would Malone say? *Walk, don't run, into trouble.* Damn right. He fled his position and approached the doorway to the gallery.

No sight of dear sweet Anya.

He eased out, gun leading the way.

Quickly, he determined that there were four ways in and out of the gallery. The stairway he'd first negotiated, the dining room where he'd been, the doorway at the far end where Anya had appeared, and a final portal ten feet away.

He approached and saw that it opened to a narrow gallery that overlooked a ballroom below. Another long staircase hugged an interior wall and led down to a polished wood floor dotted with tables devoid of linen or ornaments. What had Strobl said? They were preparing for an inaugural event. Glass doors below and windows high above allowed the sun to flood the cavernous space, made even brighter by glossy white walls. A decorative iron railing protected the outer edge of the semicircular balcony that stretched before him.

She was here.

No question.

So come and get it.

Anya appeared.

To his left, from behind a glass-paneled door.

The sole of her boot slammed into his right hand, jarring the Beretta from his grasp. He reacted by spinning just as she leaped out and faced him. She held no weapon. Apparently, she wanted to settle this hand-to-hand. Fine by him. He recalled what the SVR man had said earlier, how she'd been formally trained.

Again, fine by him. So had he.

She lunged and pivoted off one leg while driving the other his way. The balcony was narrow, maybe four to five feet wide. Not much room to maneuver. But enough. He dodged the blow and readied one of his own, planting a solid kick into the pit of her stomach, reeling her backward where she fell across a row of wooden chairs along the wall. She quickly rolled and recovered, but he could see she was a little shocked at her clumsiness.

"What's the matter?" he said. "Can't take it?"

A defiant smirk came to her lips.

Large, liquid brown eyes showed anger and rage.

She pounced like a cat, grabbing him by the neck, her fingers burrowing into his flesh. She clamped her arm around his neck and, using her other hand, formed a vise that held him in an iron grip and began to restrict his breathing. He swung around so her spine faced the solid interior wall and drove her body into it. Once. Twice. On the third time her breath exhaled in a swish and she released her grip. He swung around, giving her arm a violent twist, then slammed his right fist into her jaw.

But she had staying power.

An elbow caught the back of his head, driving his face into the wall. His arms were yanked back and up in a painful double hammerlock. She forced him to his toes, his face and chest now jammed to the wall. In movies and on television it was normal to see the tough aggressive woman taking down some larger man with a few well-placed kicks and punches. In reality, size mattered, and he had the advantage of both weight and reach.

He dropped, legs limp, allowing him to wrench free, then he whirled and threw a forearm into her knee, kicking her legs out from under her. She'd tried to avoid the move, but she was an instant too late.

Down she went.

She rebounded with the agility of a tumbler, but he thrust a straight arm into her face, the heel of his palm pounding the tip of her nose.

She staggered, weaving from disorientation.

Fool me once, shame on you. Fool me twice, shame on—

He punched her again and she collapsed across the row of wooden chairs, which clattered about, one of the legs breaking from the impact. A thin trickle of blood crawled down the corner of her mouth.

"You want some more?" he asked her, his breathing coming hard and fast. "Come on, and I'll give it to you."

His face surely had the look of coal, not candy. Or at least that's how his mother used to describe it. He'd been taught since childhood that hitting a woman was bad. But his parents had never met predators like Anya Petrova. Enough extra doses of testosterone flowed through her to disqualify the "Don't hit a woman ever" rule.

And there was still the matter of his beloved car.

Which this nutcase had shot to hell and back.

She stayed down. All her energy seemed spent.

He found his gun, then pressed his knee into her spine, pinning her to the floor.

"You're under arrest."

CHAPTER
TWENTY-FOUR

CASSIOPEIA HATED HELICOPTERS WORSE THAN AIRPLANES. THE ones she'd been always compelled to ride inside seemed to bump and grind their way through the air, like a car on a pitted highway, and all to the deafening beat of powerful rotors. Compounding the experience here was the pitch dark, the cold, and her anxiety over what may have happened to Cotton. She'd been sent no new information from Stephanie and the briefing she'd received on landing at the air base did nothing to alleviate her fears. No word had been heard or seen of Cotton since his plane went down. Or at least no word the authorities were willing to pass on.

She decided the crash site would be her starting point, so a military chopper was ferrying her east toward Lake Baikal. She'd appreciated, though, the cold-weather gear, which definitely helped, and the officer in charge seemed quite accommodating. If she weren't mistaken he may actually have been flirting with her, which was the last thing she needed to deal with at the moment.

Clouds hung low in a freezing shroud and they skirted the air just beneath the ceiling. A rim of lights blurred by distance framed a halo around Irkutsk to the south. Over the years she'd learned to sleep in snatches, and she'd caught some rest on the jet flight east. She tried again now, hoping to take her mind off the fact that she was hundreds of meters off the ground in a machine that, technically, should not even be able to stay aloft. Like the bumblebee, she'd read once. Neither should be able to fly, but somehow both managed. The local time was approaching 11:00 P.M., but her body was still seven hours behind in France.

"The wreck site is twenty kilometers ahead," the voice said through her headset.

"How far is the dacha from that location?"

"Ten kilometers north."

She nodded at the officer sitting across from her. Two pilots manned the controls. Everything had been spoken in English, Stephanie suggesting that her linguistic skills be kept to herself. She'd learned Russian in college, along with a few other languages, thinking that one day they'd all come in handy. At the time she'd had no idea how handy. Though she might try to deny it, she liked the action, and enjoyed a good fight. Most of the intrigue she'd participated in had started from some personal motivation, mainly thanks to her old friend Henrik Thorvaldsen. God rest his soul. After Henrik died, she'd occasionally outright worked for Stephanie Nelle. Never for money, more as a favor, friend-to-friend.

But Utah changed all that.

Yet here she was, flying through Russia, headed to who-knew-what.

This time for love.

MALONE ENGAGED THE CLUTCH, THEN GROUND THE SHIFT INTO second and spun the wheel. The rear end swung wide, the low gear gripping the cold road. He floored the accelerator and turned up the high revs in a straightaway before working his way through the gears on a curve.

Bullets whizzed by.

The road clung to the side of a hill, a cathedral column of trees tightly packed along sharp embankments. The chassis slewed side-to-side on the occasional ice and crusted snow. He rode the clutch. Wind buffeted the cab, rocking the vehicle. Everything in the Goat rattled.

A side window shattered from a round.

Fragments of glass stung the back of his head and neck.

He was trying to be a difficult target but was not having much luck. The road found ground level and he moved out of the trees. To his right stretched the wide-open expanse of the lake, its frozen surface offering little cover. Yet there was something to be said for room to maneuver where he would not have to worry about slamming into a tree. So he angled the front end to the right, leaped the road, and tunneled through underbrush, leaving a rugged swath before emerging onto the ice.

The chattering of the weapon continued and a bullet sang off the Goat's interior. He decided to change things around, downshifting and swinging the vehicle hard left. With a foot on the clutch, the tires glided easily across the ice and he executed a smooth 180-degree spin. He then jammed the gearshift into second and accelerated straight toward his pursuer.

The action had clearly caught the two men behind him off guard and he swerved left and right to thwart any clear shot at his windshield. The other vehicle veered hard left to avoid a collision, which showed him that his pursuers may not have the stomach for this fight. He swung around in a wide arc and set his sights on the windshield on the other vehicle.

Headlights filled his rearview mirror.

A new player.

More gunfire came his way.

CASSIOPEIA STARED DOWN AT THE WRECKAGE. A PAIR OF NIGHT-vision goggles offered her a view of the burned-out hulk of a plane and the two bodies at either end. The Russians had already reported to Stephanie that there was no third corpse. She should take a look inside the cockpit. Stephanie was interested to see if Cotton's cell phone was there, as there'd been no signal from it for several hours. The Magellan Billet tracked its phones with sophisticated software and Stephanie had suggested a retrieval, if possible.

"We have a report of gunshots on the lake," she heard in Russian through her headphones.

"Where?" the officer-in-charge asked.

"Six kilometers north."

They hovered thirty meters over the ice.

She kept up the ruse of not understanding and asked in English, "What's going on?"

The officer explained.

"It could be him," she said.

The officer motioned for the pilots to fly that way.

MALONE COUNTED THREE MORE GOATS, THE VEHICLES FANNED out in an attack pattern like fighter jets.

All that room on the lake worked both ways.

He definitely had a problem similar to the one back at the dacha with the cuffs and the iron pipe. He could keep going until he found the west shore, but that could be many miles. At least this time he was armed, as he'd brought along the assault rifle.

One of the Goats swung out, trying to flank him on the left, attempting to pass. He decided a little offense would be good, so he swerved its way, cutting in front and causing the other driver to make a fast decision.

Malone stamped on the brakes, gripped the wheel, and began skidding across the ice.

The other jeep veered left too fast, tires spinning upward, the vehicle twisting in the air then smashing back down on its side, sliding off with the grinding screech of metal on ice.

One down.

He straightened out the wheel and kept moving.

CASSIOPEIA SAW A MÉLANGE OF HEADLIGHTS LANCING THE NIGHT. Four pairs were pursuing one pair, all of them moving fast. In the night-vision goggles she saw they were off-road vehicles, like jeeps. One tried to cut off the lead one, ending up on its side skidding across the lake. Relief, disbelief, anticipation, and exhilaration tumbled through her mind.

She knew who was driving the lead vehicle.

The chopper roared north, skimming low over the lake. She watched the officer across from her as he studied the scenario. She knew the icy surface below stretched many kilometers, and if she'd not come along Cotton might have had some trouble getting out of this predicament.

The least she owed him was to save his ass.

"Let's be sure it's him," she said in English.

The chopper swung around parallel to the chase. Through her night-vision goggles, in a faint reflection of dash lights, she saw a familiar face.

One it was good to see.

"It is," she said.

Through the goggles she also saw two figures emerge from the passenger side of following jeeps.

Both aimed rifles.

"Those are *Kozliks*. Military," she heard the pilot say to the officer in Russian.

"I know," he replied. "Which is a problem. Are we to fire on our own people?"

She noted their confusion, but could not reveal she understood the concern, so she simply said in English, "We need to do something."

MALONE HAD NO CHOICE BUT TO KEEP GOING. HE WAS COLD from the lack of a window, the Goat's heater doing little to abate the frigid night. He heard pops and realized the shooting had started again, single rounds becoming repeated bursts, the lake's smooth surface allowing for a better aim.

A few deep gulps of the cold air freed his brain.

Lights appeared in the sky before him, swooping down to a hundred or so feet off the ground. In the blackness, with nearly no illumination, it was hard to know exactly what had arrived. But the powerful heartbeat-like throb echoing around him signaled a helicopter.

He hoped Zorin did not have access to one.

The lights approached fast and he heard the distinctive sound of cannon fire. Since none of the rounds came his way, he assumed they were for his pursuers. In the rearview mirror he saw headlights scatter as the Goats broke formation. He whipped his head around and stared out the open rear window. The chopper was swinging for another pass, the Goats making a beeline away.

More cannon fire kept the taillights receding.

He slewed the front wheels into a sideways skid and stopped, but left the engine running. The chopper completed its assault and, seemingly satisfied that the problems were gone, swung back around and headed his way. He assumed it was the military to the rescue, which puzzled him, considering that the military may have been the ones after him.

The dark hulk of a gunship filled the sky. A light appeared in the rear cabin and framed a helmeted man crouched in an open hatch. Malone squinted against the blinding aurora. The rotors' throbbing clatter seemed earsplitting as the chopper made a final descent, the blades' downblast churning up a cauldron of snow.

Skids touched ice.

A figure hopped out and trotted his way.

In the penumbra of his headlights he began to see that the person was slim and small, clothed in a thick coat with a hood. Ten feet from the jeep he caught the dark hair and delicate features that showed a Spanish ancestry.

Then the face.

Cassiopeia.

She stopped at the Goat's front end and stared at him through the windshield. Her dark eyes projected love and concern. The sheer joy of seeing her lifted his heart. She stepped around to the driver's-side door, which he opened. There were so many things to be said, but the first word that came to mind seemed the most obvious.

Thanks.

He stepped from the truck, and before a sound could escape his mouth she brushed his lips with her gloved fingertips and said in a soft voice, "Don't speak."

Then she kissed him.

CHAPTER TWENTY-FIVE

LUKE SHOVED ANYA PETROVA DOWN INTO ONE OF THE DINING table chairs and secured her to it with more duct tape. Back at Anderson House he'd used a roll to bind her hands behind her back, then led her from the building, making their escape just before the DC police arrived. Stephanie had stayed to deal with the authorities, made necessary by someone placing an emergency call. Not particularly what they'd wanted to happen, but understandable given the gunfire. He and Petrova had left the ballroom through a rear courtyard that opened to another street. From there, he'd found a cab that had taken them across town to his apartment, his Defense Intelligence Agency badge and a $20 tip calming the driver's anxieties.

He lived near Georgetown in an ivy-veined brick building brimming with tenants in their seventies. He liked the quiet and appreciated the fact that everyone seemed to mind their own business. He spent only a few days here each month, between assignments, enjoying the place.

"Is that your family?" Anya asked him, motioning with her head to a framed photograph.

He'd been born and raised in Blount County, Tennessee, where his father and uncle were both known, particularly his uncle, who served in local political office, then as governor and a U.S. senator before becoming president. His father died from cancer when he was seventeen. He and his three brothers had been there for every moment of those final days. His mother took the loss hard. They'd been married a long time. Her husband was everything to her, and then, suddenly, he was gone. That's why Luke called her every Sunday. Never missed. Even when on assignment. It might be late at night her time when he had the chance, but he called. His father always said that the smartest thing he ever did was marry her. Both his parents were devoutly religious—Southern Baptists—so they'd named their sons to correspond with the books of the New Testament. His two older brothers were Mathew and Mark. His younger, John. He was the third in line and acquired the name Luke.

The photo was of the family just a few weeks before his father died.

"That's them," he said.

He wondered about her interest. Most likely she was playing him, trying to relax things enough so she might be able to make a move. He should bind those legs, but that could prove dangerous as they definitely packed a punch. But she now realized he packed a punch, too, the bruise on her face evidence that he was not to be taken lightly.

"I like this place. Your home," she said. "Mine is quite different."

He hadn't had many one-on-one conversations with Russian nationals, especially one up to no good like Anya Petrova.

He slid out another of the chairs, flipped it around and positioned it behind her. He sat with the high back nestled to her neck. "What were you after in that house in Virginia?"

She chuckled. "You expect me to answer?"

"I expect you to help yourself. You're not going back home. You're going to one of our prisons, where I'm sure you'll be real popular."

Her blond hair hung to just above her shoulders in a layered bob. She wasn't overtly attractive, only alluring in a puzzling sort of way. Maybe it was her confidence—never any sign of misgiving or nerves or worry. Or the blend of femininity and athleticism. He definitely liked that.

"You and Zorin married?"

"Who is Zorin?"

He chuckled. "Don't insult me."

She kept her head facing away, toward the family photo across the room, making no effort to turn back toward him. "Are you close with your brothers?"

"As close as brothers can get."

"I have no brothers or sisters. Just me."

"Might explain why you don't play so good with others."

"Have you been to Siberia?"

"Nope."

"Then you have no idea what difficult can be."

He could not care less. "What were you after in that house?"

Another deep throaty laugh.

"Things you might wish I never find."

STEPHANIE WAS READY TO LEAVE BUT THE DC POLICE WERE NOT done with her. She'd answered their questions as vaguely as possible, but with an inaugural event scheduled for the Anderson House in three days, there were lots of inquiries. The last thing the Cincinnati people wanted was to be declared off-limits and their security clearance pulled. That would mean the end of the event, and everyone wanted the bragging rights of hosting something for the new administration. Finally, she made a call to Edwin Davis and the intervention of the White House chief of staff had sent the police packing. Edwin, of course, had wanted more details, as did the president, but she'd begged off.

At least for now.

All would have been fine except for the appearance of Bruce Litchfield, who arrived in a Justice Department car.

"You want to tell me what you've been doing," he said, not even trying to keep his voice low.

They stood outside, beyond the main portico, just past one of the iron gates that led out to the street. The Anderson House staff had retreated inside.

"When you flashed your badge," he said, "the locals called Justice to see what we were doing. Since it involved the Magellan Billet, the call came to me. I'm told there was shooting in there, and a fight, and you brandished a gun. Then you took control of some woman who'd threatened everyone in the house. Do you have her?"

She nodded.

Disgust filled his face. "I told you to leave this alone. What are you doing?"

She'd worked for a succession of AGs, some good, some bad, but all of them had shown her a measure of respect.

"My job," she said to him.

"Not anymore."

She caught the cold, satisfied look in his eyes.

"This is done. You're fired. As of right now."

She brushed past, intent on ignoring him.

He grabbed her arm. "I said, you're fired. Give me your badge and your gun."

"You know what you can do with your firing. And let go of me."

He did and smiled. "I was hoping you'd go that route."

He gestured with his free hand and three men emerged from the vehicle parked at the street, all middle-aged, short-haired, and dressed in dark suits.

Justice Department agents.

"I brought them along," he said, "since I knew you were going to be difficult. Now you can either give me your badge and gun, or go with these men and be under arrest. I assure you, the White House won't be able to help."

Which meant this fool had been given the green light from the incoming administration to drop the hammer. Amazing his lack of loyalty to the president who'd given him his job. The talk seemed right. He was nothing but an opportunist. He was also not as unsure of himself as earlier. Instead, he brimmed with confidence, knowing that no harm would come to him from anything he was about to do, regardless of what the current White House might think.

He had her.

Game over.

She'd been given a temporary license to poke around, encouraged by the White House, and she'd raked up enough to make it all real, but that license had now been revoked.

She found her gun and badge and handed both to him.

"Go home to Atlanta, Stephanie. Your career is done. And do whatever you want with that woman. No one here cares."

He started to walk away.

"Bruce."

He turned back.

Her upturned middle finger told him exactly what she thought.

He shook his head. "The great thing is, your opinion doesn't matter anymore."

And he headed for the car and climbed back inside.

She watched as it drove away.

Thirty-seven years with the government. All that she'd seen, done, and been involved with. And this was how it ended? She heard the front door to Anderson House open and turned to see Fritz Strobl walk out into the cold late-morning air.

He walked over and said, "That didn't seem good."

"You were spying?"

"I apologize. But I was waiting for everyone to leave before speaking with you. So, yes, I was watching."

She wasn't in the mood. "What is it, Mr. Strobl?"

"What you did in there with that woman. We appreciate it. We don't have incidents like that here. It was a first, actually. It was most upsetting. You seem like an honest person." He paused. "I'm afraid I lied to you."

Now he had her attention.

"When you mentioned the archive found at the Charon estate. I *was* aware of it, and we've wanted to reclaim it for some time."

She understood. "But you did not want to get in the middle of a family fight."

He nodded. "Precisely. We've kept its existence to ourselves. God knows we could not approach the Charon family. Several of our members knew of Brad's secret room, including our current historian. We even contemplated what you suggested—appropriating it."

She liked how carefully he referred to theft.

"That woman you carted off. She asked specifically about that archive. She was looking for something particular within it."

She recalled the books strewn across the floor, stripped from their shelves.

"What was she after?"

"That she did not mention to me, but she wanted to speak with our historian." Strobl hesitated. "This is a bit embarrassing. You see, an organization as old as ours certainly has . . . secrets. Most are harmless. Nearly all of them are meaningless in the overall scope of things. We have our share of those, too."

"Did you tell the police this?"

He shook his head. "No one asked. I was wondering, if I direct you to our historian, could you have that archive retrieved?"

A deal? She smiled. "I do believe, Mr. Strobl, I smell a bit of larceny in your blood."

"Heavens no. It's just that, those books and records are important. They belong to us. Can you procure them?"

"Absolutely."

She listened as he told her a name and address, the same one Petrova had been given. As he spoke, a plan formed in her mind so, when he finished, she asked, "Do you have a car?"

Strobl nodded.

"I need to borrow it."

CHAPTER TWENTY-SIX

RUSSIA

ZORIN WAITED ABOARD THE JET, HIS DEPARTURE FROM ULAN-Ude delayed now going on half an hour. He'd chartered the flight over the Internet, concluding the deal with a phone call made earlier after his talk with Belchenko in the black bath. He had to fly nonstop from Ulan-Ude to Prince Edward Island, Canada, where Jamie Kelly supposedly lived. He'd calculated the distance at just under forty-nine hundred nautical miles. The charter company understood his needs and recommended a Gulfstream G550, which they could have in Ulan-Ude by nightfall, ready to go.

He was back on duty—detached and alert—his training taking over. On arrival he'd thoroughly checked out the aircraft. About thirty meters long, it flew at a top speed of nearly Mach 1 with a range of 6,800 nautical miles. Its pressurized cabin allowed for an altitude of 51,000 feet, high above commercial traffic and any adverse weather or winds. He should be able to make a straight shot in about ten and a half hours. That would put him in Canada, compensating for the twelve-hour time difference, a little before 11:00 P.M. local time, still Friday night.

He'd been told that a representative of the company would meet him at the Ulan-Ude airport, which he assumed explained the delay, as no one had been waiting for him save the two pilots. One would fly while the other rested. The company had recommended four, but he'd nixed that idea.

Far too many witnesses.

The jet's interior was luxurious and spacious, adorned with crystal wine goblets and walnut paneling. Eight oval windows opened on each side as black spots upon pale beige walls. Nine cushy leather seats faced front and back and two long sofas stretched down one side. Galleys were forward and aft, and he'd requested meals. He'd not eaten all day and would require something in his stomach. There was a wireless network and satellite communication, both of which he might require to recon his destination and communicate with Anya.

Heaters inside kept winter at bay, the lighting low and soothing. Through the forward door a man entered bundled in a thick wool coat. He was stout with a mat of wiry black hair clinging to a squat turret of a head. High Slavic cheekbones flushed red from the cold. He wore a suit of little to no distinction and introduced himself as the company rep, here to conclude their business before takeoff. One wrist showed off a jeweled Rolex, the other sported a diamond ring on the little finger.

Neither impressed him.

"You're late," he said in Russian.

"I went for my dinner."

"And kept me sitting here?"

The man's dark eyes communicated a look of begrudging respect. "I realize you are in a hurry. But you must realize that I do business with men like you every day."

"You know what I want?" he asked as the man sat in one of the leather seats facing him.

"I was told you need to go from point A to B, without anyone knowing a thing."

The man added an irritating smile, which definitely rubbed him the wrong way. That was the thing about the new Russia. Everyone thought everyone else corrupt. No one ever considered the possibility that duty and honor might be motivators, too. But he decided to keep his irritation in check and projected a calm show of casualness. Which was unusual, since he was never casual.

"I was also told by my company to conclude our business *before* you left."

He heard the unspoken words.

Because we don't know you.

He reached down and grabbed the knapsack he'd brought from the dacha. Inside were three bundles of 5,000 ruble notes, bound with rubber bands. He tossed them on the walnut-topped table that sat between them. "Ten million rubles."

The rep hadn't flinched. "You are indeed a confident man to walk around with that much money."

He decided to make things clear. "I am a man you do not want to cross."

The rep reclined in the seat and threw back a confident stare, adding a humorless smile. "We deal with dangerous men all the time. This jet cost three hundred billion rubles. It can go anywhere on the globe. Dangerous men, like yourself, appreciate tools such as this."

"And I've shown my appreciation by paying you more than the trip is worth."

"That you have. So, to those *special* services you require. We will file a flight plan for New York City. That route will take us directly over Prince Edward Island. How do you plan to get to the ground?"

He'd considered several possibilities. No visa or forged documents meant no simple debarkation. A fake emergency could allow the jet to make an unscheduled landing, from which he could slip away. But that came with a multitude of risks. Currently, no one knew he was heading west and he wanted to keep it that way, so he'd decided on the one way that would work.

"I plan to jump."

A low laugh seeped from the rep's mouth. "I gathered as much. You are indeed a dangerous man. Jumping from a jet, at high altitude, at night?"

But he'd done it before, several times. His *spetsnaz* training had included high-risk parachuting. In Afghanistan he'd twice jumped at night into territory far more dangerous than Canada.

"We'll need to drop altitude, once there," he said. "I'm assuming that an appropriate reason can be manufactured."

The rep canted forward in the chair and swept his hands above the money. "For all this generosity, I believe we can do that. You will inform the pilots as to when you want to jump?"

He pointed to the computer terminal at another of the tables, a desk area designed as an in-flight office. "I'll find a location on there. I'll also need charts. Does your company have them for the location?"

"We have them for every spot on the globe."

The rep raked the rubles from the table and stuffed the bundles into his coat pockets.

He could not resist. "I'd be careful carrying so much money around."

"I assure you, I have men just as dangerous as you waiting for me outside." The rep stood. "It was a pleasure doing business with you. Enjoy your flight."

No names had ever passed between them. Unnecessary. The flight plan would reveal only the presence of the two pilots, the plane headed to New York to pick up a client. No one else would be noted as on board. That had been another condition of his charter.

"The parachute you specified is aft," the rep said. "In a marked compartment, along with night-vision goggles."

He'd requested both, pleased these people knew how to satisfy their customers. Unlike the old days, today nearly anything and everything could be procured by anyone.

"The pilots will not disturb you. They have their own forward compartment for rest. They have been told to ask no questions, just follow your instructions. I'm sure you know how to give them."

The rep left.

Though clearly more self-indulgent than Zorin liked, the man seemed good at what he did.

Which he appreciated.

This trip had drained nearly all his cash. He had only a few thousand rubles and some American dollars left in the knapsack. But that was okay. He could acquire anything else he might need along the way. His *spetsnaz* training had also taught him about survival. He could only hope that a remnant of the old days had likewise survived, waiting for him somewhere in North America.

But all that depended on finding Jamie Kelly.

The pilots climbed aboard.

One informed him that they would be airborne in less than fifteen minutes.

He checked his watch.

49 hours remained.

CHAPTER
TWENTY-SEVEN

MALONE HAD LISTENED ON THE RIDE BACK IN THE CHOPPER AS Cassiopeia explained about Stephanie Nelle's call and her trip east from France. She seemed like her old self, no longer lost, the sharp tongue gone, her eyes brimming with a familiar glint of mischief. Everyone had assumed the worst once contact with him had been lost. Moscow had specifically allowed her to come and investigate, and he was as perplexed by that as he was by his own presence. But he kept his misgivings to himself, realizing they were communicating across an open comm line.

Gloves had been provided to him on the chopper, which he'd quickly accepted. Cassiopeia watched him carefully. Obviously, time had added a different perspective on things, enough that she'd come to his rescue. She was a dynamic woman, of that he was sure, but she was not invincible, as Utah had proved. Over the past two years they'd each seen the other at their most vulnerable, neither judging, both only helping. He felt comfortable with her, or as comfortable as a man who had trouble expressing emotion could be with another person. He certainly never felt that way toward his ex-wife. Pam had been tough, too, only in different ways. The major difference between the two women was the amount of slack Cassiopeia cut him. Far more than Pam ever allowed. Perhaps because he and Cassiopeia were so much alike, and the fact that he always returned the favor.

The chopper touched down back at the base and they rushed into a gray, granite building surrounded by a high fence. Waiting for them was a uniformed officer who identified himself as the base commander.

"I am to inform you that we are glad you survived the ordeal," he said to them both. "We appreciate the assistance you have offered, but we no longer require your involvement. This matter will be handled internally from here on."

"Has my boss been told this?" Malone asked.

"That I do not know. I was instructed by my superiors to have you flown immediately west to wherever you instruct."

"And what if we don't want to go?" he asked.

"There is no choice. I have two fighters fueled and ready. Flight suits are waiting in the next room."

He motioned toward a doorway.

Things certainly had changed.

He debated telling this man what he knew about missing Russian nukes and a former Soviet spy now living in Canada, and the fact that Aleksandr Zorin may be headed that way. Then there were those supposed military men at the dacha who'd killed Vadim Belchenko.

Something told him these people knew all about that.

So he stayed quiet.

Malone felt the g-forces as the Sukhoi/HAL fighter shot into the night sky. He missed that feeling and wished he still could fly one of these things on a regular basis. Being a fighter pilot was supposed to have been his career, but naval friends of his late father had other ideas and he ended up in law school, then the Judge Advocate General's Corps. He'd worked hard and made a name for himself, then moved to Justice and the Magellan Billet. Now he was a bookseller, or a freelancer, or something else, he really wasn't sure what.

He realized Cassiopeia would not be happy in the rear seat of the second fighter that took off right behind him. She hated high places, especially ones capable of flying at over Mach 2. The Russians had certainly been in a hurry to see them gone, and gone they were, headed toward Europe.

"Can you hear me over there?" he asked into his mike.

"I hear you," Cassiopeia said.

"Everything good?"

"What do you think?"

"Take a nap. I'll wake you when we get close."

They'd decided to be flown to the French air base near Cassiopeia's estate. From there he would contact Stephanie. He'd wanted to do that before leaving Siberia but no one would allow him to make a call, and they sure as hell weren't going to allow him to use their communications line from the air. So any debriefing would have to wait a few hours.

Chatter between the pilots and the ground filled his ears. Of course, he could not understand a word. But Cassiopeia could.

"They found your friend," she said.

In Danish. Smart girl. She was intuitive enough to keep their conversation between them. Hopefully, there was no one on the line fluent. And he knew who she meant. Zorin.

"He's on a private charter jet nearby, headed west. The pilots have been told to intercept."

The fighter veered south.

The avionic controls before him flickered with activity. Everything was labeled in Cyrillic, and though he could pretty much tell what most of the instruments were, many of the switches remained a mystery. The aircraft was a two-seater with a duplicate set of controls forward and aft, each occupant ensconced within his own cocoon. They were still headed up, into that high space between earth and orbit. Familiar territory. Above him, slews of stars slid across the Plexiglas canopy.

The jet lurched forward and started to roll.

The other fighter joined up in formation at just under twenty thousand feet. Small traceries of ice glazed the edges of his canopy. He checked the oxygen flow, watching the pressure, the breathable air outside now just scattered molecules. Neither of the two pilots liked to talk much between themselves. He'd flown with sphinxes and motormouths, not sure which he preferred. Little to nothing had been said between these two for the past few minutes, only static crashes and the hiss of an empty channel filling his ears.

He tried to organize his thoughts.

Were there portable nuclear devices still hidden out there after twenty-plus years? Any that Zorin might possibly find? Belchenko definitely thought so. And why had those military men come to the dacha? To kill Belchenko? And possibly even Zorin? Unfortunately, the old archivist had not lived long enough to tell him much about Zorin's plan.

Just *"fool's mate"* and *"zero amendment."*

Whatever they meant.

Condensation inside the face mask wet his cheeks. A taste of metal lingered in his mouth, as did the hot plastic waft of electronics in his nose. Apparently, the onboard airflow wasn't the cleanest.

With Belchenko dead, now only Zorin could lead him. The former KGB officer seemed bitter and cynical. But was he bitter enough to do something on a grand scale with a nuclear device? True, there might be a man in Canada, Jamie Kelly, who could offer answers. But that could have been more lies. He was unsure just how much truth he'd seen over the past few hours. So the smart play was to stick with Zorin.

Conversation came through his headphones.

"The target is Zorin's ahead," Cassiopeia reported, staying with Danish. "But he's close to the Mongolian border. They want the plane taken down before he crosses."

The other fighter slid beneath them and dropped off a mile or so to port. He scanned the instrument panel, looking for a way to shift flight control to the rear cockpit. But he could not decide on the right switch. The jet shuddered as the nose dumped downward. He knew what was happening. The pilot was preparing to attack.

He watched the LCD display as the onboard systems searched. They were flying nearly due south and losing altitude, finally leveling off around ten thousand feet. He searched the sky, hard with stars, and saw the other fighter with Cassiopeia now about two miles off the port wing. He scanned south, his pupils dilated to their fullest, and caught twin pinpricks of light winking on and off, marking the outer edges of another aircraft. The specks grew larger as they drew closer.

Zorin's plane.

More talk filled his ears.

Numbers flashed on the LCD, then locked on the panel. He didn't need to read Cyrillic to know that the onboard radar had acquired a target. Before they'd left the ground he'd counted six hard points on the underbelly, none of which held air-to-air missiles. But the jet did carry two 30mm cannons.

"They're waiting on orders from the ground," Cassiopeia said in his ear.

He could just let this happen and be done with it. That would certainly end things. But something Zorin said back in the basement kept rattling through his mind. About when the USSR fell. *"No one gave a damn. We were left on our own, to wallow in failure. So we owe America. And I think it is time we repay that debt."*

We?

Was Zorin the only threat?

Or would killing him just empower the next guy?

Both jets flattened their approach and eased closer, centering the target for a quick kill with the cannons, which should draw little attention from snoopy radars. The outline of the aircraft ahead signaled Learjet or Gulfstream. Enough well-placed thirty-millimeter rounds would easily take it down. He decided to do something. But there was one problem. He had to disrupt both fighters simultaneously.

"Scan the instruments in front of you," he said into his mike, keeping to Danish. "Is there one marked override? Control override. Something like that."

"At the top right. It says REAR CONTROL."

He spotted the switch, protected by a red guard. Doubtful that anyone here knew he could fly a high-performance jet, so he flicked open the plastic shield and decided, *What the hell, go for it.*

The instant the switch engaged the stick in front of him bucked alive. The pilot immediately realized the problem, but he gave the man no time to react. He rammed the stick forward, then banked hard for the other fighter. They plunged across the sky and dropped altitude, his body thrust against the seat straps. Vibrations and a jarring series of snaps accompanied the sharp roll. The other fighter thundered past them, just below, the wake from the afterburners causing enough turbulence that the other pilot had no choice but to veer away.

Both planes were now in a retreating fall.

Neither one of them could take a shot.

He assumed Cassiopeia was not happy, since she was now hurtling through the sky in a series of steep twists and turns while her pilot regained control. Malone pulled his jet up in a steep climb, the engine sucking turbocharged air, climbing like an elevator, clawing for altitude. It would be only another moment or so before his host retook the controls. He arced over the top in perfect loop and started back down toward the other jet. He scanned the instruments and saw that the radar lock was gone. Lots of angry talk between the pilots filled his ears, and no knowledge of a foreign language was required to understand its gist.

These men were pissed.

He relaxed on the stick and allowed his body to resettle into the seat. Off the starboard side the other jet eased up, wingtip-to-wingtip. The tautness in his body relaxed. The flight controls were stripped back to the forward pilot.

Zorin's plane was gone.

"I assume that was necessary," Cassiopeia asked. "I came close to dumping my guts."

"I enjoyed it," he told her.

"You would."

"I couldn't allow them to shoot."

"And I suppose you'll explain all of that later?"

"Every detail."

He heard more chatter between the pilots and the ground. He imagined there might be an even more physical discussion on the matter once they landed, which was fine.

"They're not happy," she said.

"Where's my friend?"

"Across the border. They've been ordered not to pursue."

Which made him wonder.

How much did the Russians know?

Only one way to find out.

CHAPTER
TWENTY-EIGHT

Washington, DC

Luke had tried to coax Anya Petrova to talk more, but her silence remained unbroken. She sat calmly, her hands bound behind her back, duct tape binding her midsection to the chair. The blue-black bruise on her face had to hurt. But her eyes stayed devoid of expression, pressed into a steady, impersonal gaze, nothing about them giving off the look of someone trapped.

He stayed across the room, out of range, sunk back in one of the club chairs that faced the windows. He liked this spot, perhaps his favorite in the world, the place where he always unwound. The whole apartment was like a sanctuary to him. Petrova being here actually violated his "no women" rule. Sure, he dated and had his share of overnight visits, but never here, always at their place, a hotel, or out of town. He wasn't sure why or how the rule had developed, only that it had, and he went out of his way to respect it. Not even his mother had visited, only Stephanie that one time just before Utah.

Normally he enjoyed the silence, but today the lack of noise seemed unnerving. He wasn't sure what they planned to do with Petrova beyond squeezing her for information. She was a foreign national and their operation was off the grid, so their legal options were limited. His threat to her about prison was no more than that. Even worse, she could turn out to be one tough nut to crack. Luckily, all of those decisions rested with the White House, but time was running out on Uncle Danny.

A knock broke the quiet.

He stood and answered the door, expecting to see Stephanie. Instead, the SVR spy from the car, Nikolai Osin, stood outside, along with two other men. None of them appeared happy.

"I am here for Anya Petrova," Osin said.

"And how did you know she was here?"

"Your boss told me. I told her that we would handle Ms. Petrova ourselves. Since no one wants an international incident from this, she agreed."

Osin glanced past him, toward Petrova. "What did you do, beat her?"

"I assure you, she gives as much as she gets. You don't mind if I check out your story for myself, do you?"

He'd deliberately not invited any of them inside.

"Do what you like, but we are taking Ms. Petrova with us."

He glanced over and noticed that Anya was not all that thrilled. Still, why look a gift horse in the mouth? She was leaving, which was a good thing by any definition. Clearly, though, she had no love for her savior.

He found his phone and dialed Stephanie's number. She answered immediately, he listened for a few moments, ended the call, then gestured for them to come inside.

"She's all yours."

STEPHANIE HAD NEVER BEEN FIRED BEFORE. THERE'D BEEN MANY threats throughout her government career from both attorneys general and presidents, but none had ever manifested itself into an actual dismissal.

Until today.

Bruce Litchfield had obviously received the blessing of the incoming administration to do as he pleased. No way he would have been so bold without that okay. She could hear the new AG designate as he dismissed Danny Daniels as a man who, in only a matter of hours, would no longer matter. That was a big mistake. She'd learned that Danny would always matter, regardless of his political status. He believed in what he did and stood behind those beliefs—and politics be damned. He was a man she respected and admired and the new administration could take lessons from him.

She filled a doorway about a hundred feet from Luke Daniels' apartment building, the wind whooshing by in chilly gusts. The four-story, redbrick building stood surrounded by a brown landscaped lawn and tall trees bare to winter. It sat off a busy boulevard in northwest DC, and no one had paid a visit during the past fifteen minutes. Except one car. A black Cadillac sedan. From which Nikolai Osin and two other men had emerged.

Luke had just called and she'd told him that he was to cut Anya Petrova loose and let Osin take her. She knew that Osin would play his part to perfection, which was why she'd made a call to him just after leaving Anderson House, explaining exactly what she had in mind. Her cagey colleague had complimented her on the plan and said he would head directly for the apartment and lay claim to their problem.

Anya appeared in the front door of the building, flanked on either side by two men in dark overcoats. Osin followed them into the early-afternoon sun. She watched as the entourage headed for the Cadillac, then drove away, disappearing down the short drive, past a tall hedge. She imagined Anya Petrova to be, at best, confused.

Luke stepped from the building.

She fled her shady hiding place and found the sun.

Luke walked across the front parking lot with the bouncy gait of an athlete and said to her, "You just let that happen?"

"I made it happen."

"Care to explain? 'Cause it took a lot to corral that woman."

"Fritz Strobl told me something interesting. Brad Charon was once the society's Keeper of Secrets."

She recounted what she'd learned.

"We created the post long ago," Strobl said. "It was formally abolished in the mid-20th century, or at least that's what I thought.

*About ten years ago I discovered the position still existed as part
of the historian's duties."*

"What does this have to do with the woman we have?"

*"She knew Mr. Charon had held the Keeper position. Only a
handful of individuals, high in the society's leadership, would know
that. Even I didn't. Yet she did."*

*Which raised a whole new set of questions, the most critical of
which was, "Why is any of this important?"*

*"She wanted to know the current historian, and threatened to
kill me if I did not tell her."*

"Strobl told her the man's name and where to find him," she told
Luke. "He lives in Maryland, outside Annapolis."

"And did dear ol' Fritz mention why Petrova was so damn interested in the society's long-lost secrets?"

"He told me he honestly doesn't know. And I believe him."

He pointed a finger at her. "I smell it. You have a plan, don't you?"

"I do, but I have to warn you first. An hour ago, the acting AG fired
me. I no longer have a job, so whatever we do from this point on is
without sanction."

Luke smiled. "Just the way I like it."

CHAPTER TWENTY-NINE

ZORIN DECIDED ON SOME REST BEFORE HE BEGAN THE SERIOUS task of planning what would happen once he made it to Canada. Fatigue melted through his bones, seeping into muscles. He wasn't a young man anymore. Luckily, he had several hours of quiet time to rejuvenate.

Strangely, he'd been thinking of his mother. Odd considering she'd been dead such a long time. She'd worked her whole life as a farmer, and he could still see her kneeling in the rich black soil, the sun hot on her back, working the rows of cucumbers, tomatoes, and potatoes that sometimes swayed and rippled in the wind like waves of water. *Models of tidiness and efficiency,* was how Moscow described them. His mother simply called them her own. He'd loved the fields, the air there never thick with soot, coal, chemicals, or exhaust. Perhaps that was another reason he'd fled east to Siberia, where the same smell of cleanliness could still be found.

His mother had been a kind, gentle, naïve woman who never considered herself a Soviet. She was Russian. But she was smart enough never to be a troublemaker or instigator, keeping opinions to herself and living a long life, dying simply of old age. As a boy he'd gone with her to church because he'd liked the singing. He'd realized then that he was an atheist, a fact his mother never knew. Which was good, since

God had occupied a large part of her life. Persistent, careful, hardwork-
ing, and loyal, that had been his mother.

And her humming.

That he'd enjoyed.

One of her tunes had stayed in his mind. A song from her childhood, the words of which she'd taught her sons.

> *A hare went out for a walk.*
> *Suddenly a hunter appeared*
> *And shot the hare.*
> *Bang, bang, oh, oh, oh,*
> *My hare is going to die.*
> *He was brought home*
> *And he turned out to be alive.*

He'd loved that rhyme, and like the hare he, too, had gone out for
a walk, one that had lasted for more than twenty-five years. He'd been
figuratively shot and left for dead. But like the hare, he, too, was coming back alive.

He'd often wondered how he ended up such a violent man. Certainly not because of his mother. And his father, though once a soldier, ultimately proved weak and dependent, lacking in courage.

Yet violence was no stranger.

He'd killed and harbored no remorse. He'd ordered the death of
the American back at the dacha without a moment's hesitation. If he
ever possessed a conscience, all semblances of it were gone.

Like his brothers.

Who married, had children, and died young.

And his own wife and son.

Dead, too.

Nothing remained for him save for Anya. But there was no love
between them. More companionship that they both seemed to need.
How was she doing in America? Perhaps he would find out soon.

He'd eaten one of the meals the charter company provided, pleased
the food had been filling. The jet was surely now way beyond Russian
airspace, headed on a westerly route over the Central Asian Federation,

then on toward Europe and the open Atlantic. He was pleased to be at work again, his mind focused on the invisible front and the main adversary. He'd been a good warrior, fighting for the motherland, protecting the Soviet Union. Never had he breached his oath. Never had he placed himself before his country. Never had he made stupid mistakes.

Unlike his superiors.

Who refused to see what lay clearly before them.

He recalled his first encounter with the truth.

A winter's day in January 1989.

"Comrade Zorin, this is the man I told you about."

He studied the stranger, who oddly tried to disguise his height with a slight stoop. The thick line of a black mustache colored the space beneath a bulbous fiery-hued nose. Usually he didn't meet face-to-face with recruited sources. That was his subordinates' job. His was to evaluate and report what they gathered to Moscow. But what this source had said intrigued him to the point that he had to judge the credibility of the information for himself.

"My name is—"

He raised a hand to halt the introduction and caught a slight tightening of worry around the other man's lips. "Names are not important. Only what you are about to say matters."

His operative had tagged the man "Aladdin," a nondescript way to distinguish him from the countless other sources they'd cultivated across Canada and the United States. Aladdin worked for a defense subcontractor headquartered in California. He'd traveled north to Quebec City, supposedly on holiday to enjoy the winter carnival, but the real purpose had been this meeting.

They sat within a suite inside the Frontenac hotel, high above an ice-clogged St. Lawrence River. Aladdin had booked and paid for the room himself. Zorin's people had spent two days assuring themselves that the man had come alone, and the room had just been electronically swept for any listening devices. Zorin was taking a chance on this gathering, but he'd decided the risk was worth it.

"I am told," he said, "that you have information regarding the Strategic Defense Initiative."

"Which I've passed on, and you've paid me."

"I want to hear the information, again, myself."

"You don't believe me?"

"It doesn't matter whether I believe you. I simply want to hear it again."

Aladdin seemed perturbed, as he'd not been told why it had been necessary for him to come to Quebec. He'd first been cultivated at a Canadian university, a physicist who specialized in advanced laser research. His work had caught the eye of the Americans, who recruited him. But Zorin had kept the lines of communication open, harvesting more intelligence, paying Aladdin several thousand dollars for his continued efforts. Two weeks ago Aladdin had passed on something extraordinary.

"As I told your man here, SDI is an illusion."

The Strategic Defense Initiative had been announced by Reagan six years ago. The American president had told the world that he intended to build a shield that could repel nuclear missiles, destroying them in flight, thereby rendering their effectiveness to nothing. "The solution is well within our grasp," he'd declared. Ever since, billions had been spent on research and development, part of which involved Aladdin. Zorin's and every other KGB officer's primary objective was to secure as much intelligence on SDI as could be gathered. No issue was more important to Moscow.

"And why do you believe such a thing?" he asked.

"I've been in meetings. I've heard discussions. The technology simply does not exist to make it happen. We're decades away from being able even to try shooting a missile down. It's been studied to death. It can't be done. The American taxpayer has no idea how much money is being wasted."

Moscow feared SDI so much that its abolition had formed the cornerstone of all recent nuclear weapons talks with the United States. Any reduction in offensive weapons must include the end of strategic defensive weapons, too. Of course, America had balked at such a condition, which explained why armament talks had been stalled for the past several years. Now to hear that the whole thing was a fraud?

But he wondered. Was that truly the case or was this source the fraud?

"We're developing," Aladdin said, "missile interceptors, X-ray lasers, particle beams, chemical lasers, high-velocity cannons, improved tracking and surveillance systems. Ever heard of brilliant pebbles?"

He listened as Aladdin told him about a satellite interceptor that consisted of high-velocity, watermelon-sized tungsten projectiles that acted as kinetic warheads, capable of destroying a satellite or missile.

"It all sounds amazing," Aladdin said. "And it would be if it worked. But it's just hype. These systems exist only on paper. There's no solid, workable technology that could make them practical in the real world."

"Tell me about the Defense Department," he said.

This was the most shocking revelation his officer had reported, the main thing he'd come to hear.

"They know it's all a ruse, but they want us to keep going, and they keep pouring billions of dollars into it. Don't you see? Our job is only to convince the public that it's real."

"Reagan himself said that the task would be formidable, that it may not be achieved until the end of the century."

"There's a big difference between saying something is tough and will take time, and something that's completely non-achievable. SDI is just that. It can't be done, or more correctly it can't be done anytime in the foreseeable future. And Washington knows that. The whole program will never amount to anything, except fattening the pockets of the defense contractors who are getting paid to develop what's not possible."

Sources were ranked by reliability.

"Extremely well placed" meant access to exactly what he or she was talking about. "Unproven" denoted either a rookie or information that had yet to be verified. "Unconfirmed" was always suspect, but once a source established a track record, confirmed or not, they became "reliable."

Turning targets had been his specialty, the rules of the game common sense. He or she had to first be worth the effort and have access to desirable information. If so, contact was made—usually informal and coincidental—then a friendship cultivated. The danger of a dangle, though, loomed great. Another operative merely pretending to be receptive to spying. Which was exactly what he'd first thought Aladdin to be. That happened a lot, and it was suicide for any KGB career. Ultimately, if targets passed an extensive background check and at least seven personal encounters seemed genuine, then they were assigned a code name and brought operational.

Aladdin had passed each test, becoming "highly reliable."

Everyday field officers had to contend with their natural suspicions and the consequences that might come from believing what they were being told. He had been fed something that, at best, could be fantastical and at worst a lie.

But he'd reported the information.

Only to be chastised by his superiors.

Moscow viewed the SDI program as a move by the United States to neutralize the Soviet military and seize the initiative in arms controls. To the Kremlin, space-based missile defenses made offensive nuclear war inevitable. So their response was never in doubt. A similar Soviet initiative had to be undertaken and it was the KGB's job to shorten that development process through espionage. Yet instead of providing any useful information, Zorin had reported that the whole thing may be a fraud. Most times information from even "highly reliable" sources was trivial. Seldom did anything compromise a nation. But every once in a while luck would fall their way.

He stirred in the jet's leather seat and recalled the official response to his report on Aladdin.

Forget such nonsense and get back to work.

Yet history had proved him right.

No missile defense system has ever existed anywhere in the world.

The USSR eventually spent billions of rubles trying to create one, thinking all the while that America was actively doing the same. True, billions of U.S. dollars were also spent, just as Aladdin had said, but it had all been a ruse that Ronald Reagan himself masterminded. A way for his enemies to do themselves in. Which worked. The Soviet economy imploded from hyperinflation, fueling a total communist collapse.

His gut churned every time he thought of how it all could have been avoided. If only Moscow had listened when he, and other KGB officers, reported what they were each learning, independent of the others. Yet ignorance seemed the greatness weakness of conformity. A select few made all the decisions, and everyone else followed, regardless that those decisions could be wrong.

He closed his eyes and allowed sleep to take hold.

No longer did the Red Army march in a gorgeous phalanx, stepping high, gleaming boots springing from the cobbles of Red Square, arms slapped flat across their chests as heads angled to the top of Lenin's mausoleum.

Where fools had stood.

Those days were gone, too.

Now here he was, decades later. Alone. But not impotent. He had the blood and strength of a peasant with the resolve of a communist, and, thankfully, his body had not been fatally damaged by alcohol, cigarettes, or reckless living.

Another childhood rhyme came to him.

> *Hush you mice, a cat is near us.*
> *He can see us, he can hear us.*
> *What if he is on a diet?*
> *Even then you should be quiet.*

Excellent advice.

Decades of reflection had taught him that the entire Soviet system had run on institutionalized mistrust, the military and civilian intelligence services never close. The idea had been to keep both from becoming either complacent or too powerful, but the real effect had been to render them ineffectual. Neither listened to or cared what the other thought. Both had been masters at gathering information, neither one of them good at analyzing it. So when the obvious was placed before them—that they were engaged in a bitter and desperate race that America had manufactured—both had rejected the conclusion and stayed the course to their collective end.

He would not be that stupid.

This was *his* war.

To be fought on *his* terms.

A quick shock of nervousness coursed through him. Not unusual. Every field officer knew fear. The good ones learned how to tame it.

The main adversary, the United States of America, had taken his past, his reputation, credibility, achievements, even his probity, rank, and honor.

But not his life.

And though his brain stayed racked with alternating bouts of optimism and doubt, eased occasionally by conviction but nearly always flagged with guilt, this time—

There would be no mistakes.

CHAPTER THIRTY

LUKE DROVE THE FORD ESCAPE THAT, AS STEPHANIE TOLD HIM, belonged to Fritz Strobl. How she managed to acquire a loaner from a total stranger he could only imagine. They were headed east, out of DC, on U.S. 301 toward Annapolis.

"You heard earlier about missing nukes," she said to him from the passenger seat. "The Russians think five are still out there. Suitcase size."

"Like on 24?"

"I know. It sounds fantastic. But I think Osin is being straight with us. We've always thought the Soviets developed compact nuclear weapons. Each bomb was, maybe, six kilotons. But nothing could ever be verified. Of course, we developed the same."

"And we still have these?"

"I don't think so. They were outlawed in the 1990s. That decision was reversed after 9/11, but I haven't heard of our having anything like them in our current arsenal."

He then listened as she told him more about Aleksandr Zorin, who supposedly held a grudge against the United States, and a KGB archivist named Vadim Belchenko.

"Cotton was looking into the Belchenko angle."

The Escape's little engine packed a surprising punch, and they were making good time down the highway, the Friday-afternoon traffic light.

"Have you heard anything from Cassiopeia?" he asked.

She shook her head. "Not a word."

Which was not good. "You think Cotton's okay?"

"I'm hoping so."

He heard the concern, which he echoed.

Her cell phone dinged and they looked at each other. She studied the display and shook her head again. "It's Osin."

She took the call, which lasted only a few moments. When it ended she said to him, "Petrova's on the move."

She'd already explained that Osin had driven Petrova to Dulles International, handing her a ticket for a KLM flight straight to Moscow. Osin's men escorted her into the terminal, leaving her as she made her way through the security checks. Of course, there was no doubt that she'd promptly double back and flee, finding a cab, which should take her to a street two blocks away from Anderson House, where her dented rental car remained parked.

"She headed straight for the car," Stephanie said. "That puts her not far behind us. She'll come to Annapolis."

"You always right about people?"

"More so than not."

"What about those missing nukes?"

"It's unlikely they still exist and, even if they did, even more unlikely they're operational. Yet Zorin is definitely focused on them."

"You okay?"

He knew her well enough to know that she was bothered by what had happened with Bruce Litchfield.

"I never thought my career would end like this," she said, her voice trailing off. "Thirty-seven years."

"I was but a twinkle in my daddy's eye thirty-seven years ago."

She smiled, and he left her to her thoughts as they rode for a few minutes in silence.

"It was an exciting time back then," she said, more to herself than him. "Reagan planned to change the world. At first, we all thought he was nuts. But that's exactly what he did."

Luke knew little about the 1980s, his life focused more on the here and now. He considered himself dependable, tough, and pragmatic. He took life as it came—daydreams, nostalgia, and the charms of the world held little appeal. History was just that to him—the past—not exactly ignored, but not to be obsessed about, either.

"I was part of that great change," she said.

He could tell she wanted to talk, which was unusual. But everything about this day fit into that category.

So he kept his mouth shut and listened.

Stephanie followed the pope into a courtyard on this, her twenty-ninth visit to Rome. John Paul had specifically requested the meeting. Much was happening in the United States. Reagan's two terms as president were drawing to a close. Vice President Bush and Massachusetts governor Michael Dukakis were engaged in a bitter battle for the White House, the outcome of which remained uncertain. The pope was concerned about the future, so she'd come to alleviate his fears. A marble villa and a two-story loggia surrounded them, the courtyard dotted with statues, empty benches, and a fountain. They were deep inside the Vatican, in a space reserved for residents, of which there were but a precious few.

"President Reagan will soon be out of office," he said to her. "Will that end your service, too?"

She decided to be straight. "Most likely. Either side will select its own people to carry on."

To her knowledge Vice President Bush had never been part of Forward Pass, and an open bitterness was festering between the Bush and Reagan camps. At the Republican National Convention, when accepting the party's nomination, Bush had told the delegates that he wanted a kinder, gentler nation. Which had brought a swift rebuke from the Reagan people of, What the hell are we?

"The new wash away the old," the pope said. "It is the same here. The same all over the world. And if you are no longer here, what happens to what we've done these past six years? Does that end, too?"

A fair question.

"I don't think what has been started can be stopped," she said. "It's too far along. Too many moving parts are in motion. Our people think it will be but two or three years, at the most, until the USSR ends."

"That was October 1988, the last time John Paul and I spoke," she said. "But I was right. Bush won and a new team took over at State, one that did not include me, and other people finished what I started. That's when I moved to Justice. A few years later I was given the Magellan Billet."

"How friggin' amazing," he said. "You were there? Right in the middle of what happened when the Berlin Wall came down?"

"Which Bush got credit for," she said. "But by the time he was inaugurated, the Soviet end was a foregone conclusion."

"Didn't help him get reelected," he offered, hoping to make her feel better. He wasn't entirely oblivious to history.

She grinned. "No. It didn't."

"How did you do it?" he asked.

"That's a complicated question. But by the late 1980s pressure was coming on Moscow from nearly every angle, both internally and externally. That pressure had been building for a long time. Reagan, to his credit, developed a way to exploit it. He told me once that all we needed to create was the straw that would break the communist back. And that's what we did. The operation was called Forward Pass."

Which started with Admiral John Poindexter, a key member of the Reagan National Security Council. Others had postulated the concept before, but Poindexter hammered the idea of a strategic defense initiative into a workable concept. Why match the Soviets bomb for bomb, as had been American policy for decades? That accomplished little to nothing, except mutual assured destruction.

MAD.

An appropriate label.

Instead, America's advantage was its strong economy and innovative technology. So why not a resource shift—a change from offense to defense. The United States possessed tens of thousands of nuclear warheads to launch east. Why not develop a way to stop Russian warheads from coming west? Poindexter's idea was presented to the White House in late 1982 and the president immediately embraced it. Reagan had many times said that he considered MAD immoral, and he liked the idea of shifting to a strategic

*defense. The whole thing was kept quiet until March 1983 when
the president announced the change, on television, to the world.*

*Initially, the idea had been to actually develop SDI. But tech-
nological challenges began to overwhelm the effort. Simultaneous
with SDI came a massive defense buildup of conventional weapons and equipment. New aircraft, ships, and submarines. Billions
upon billions of new money flooded into the Defense Department
in what became the largest peacetime escalation in American military preparedness ever.*

Which the Soviets had no choice but to match.

And they did.

*The Soviets were genuinely shocked by the concept of strate-
gic defense initiative. Moscow called the plan a bid to disarm the
USSR, claiming the United States sought world supremacy. But for
the Soviets the true danger of SDI came more from the technological effort itself, one that might lead to new offensive weapons—
innovations that they may not be able to counter without a strategic
defense initiative of their own.*

So they poured billions into development.

Which they could not afford.

Creating the straw that broke the communist back.

"You're tellin' me that the U.S. worked a con on the communists?"

"Not so much a con. More we exploited the other side's clear weakness, using our strengths to maximum advantage."

He chuckled. "Like I said, a con."

"It was more complicated than that. The Vatican soothed the hearts
and minds of the Eastern Bloc, keeping the people motivated, while
we applied economic and political pressure. That wreaked havoc on
Moscow. Then SDI comes along and throws them a real curve. But
once the Soviets believed strategic defense to be a real threat, they had
only two choices. Match our effort or circumvent it. They attempted
both. The KGB was all over SDI, trying to learn every detail. The CIA
stayed a step ahead, feeding them false information, exploiting their
overeagerness. Reagan played the hand perfectly. No way Moscow
could win."

He kept an even speed down the highway toward Annapolis while maintaining a watch in the rearview mirror.

"You have to be proud of yourself," he said. "To have been a big part of that."

"The history books know little of what really happened. When I first met Reagan in 1982, he told me of his idea to use money and morality as weapons—to engage the Vatican as an active ally. He was obsessed by the fact that both he and John Paul survived assassination attempts. He thought that some sort of divine message. At first, I thought the whole plan far-fetched. But he was determined. I was there when he traveled to Rome, in June 1982, and made the pitch, face-to-face, to John Paul. That took balls."

That it did.

"Then the pope did what popes do best. He appealed to faith and God and called on the Polish people to *not be afraid*. And they weren't. So Solidarity survived. Moscow wrongly thought martial law would quell the Poles, but they were wrong there, too. Instead, a call for freedom spread throughout the Eastern Bloc and slowly weakened every one of those puppet governments. When the collapse finally came, everything fell hard. Together, Reagan and the pope were unbeatable. But it was Reagan who was smart enough to put the deal together."

"Like I said, a helluva con."

"Call it what you want. All I know is it worked. The Soviet Union and the Cold War both ended. Thanks to an actor whom many shrugged off as incompetent and ineffectual. But that actor knew the value of a good show. Communism is no longer important. Instead, militant radicals and religious fanatics have taken center stage."

"None of whom possesses a country or any allegiance to anything beyond their own insanity. Not a Cold War anymore. More a Crazy War."

"Today," she said, "one error, one small omission, a single piece of bad luck, and the next step is desperate measures. The bad guys actually act today. Back then it was all posturing."

He recalled those nukes. "But a remnant from the old days might still be around." He saw that she agreed. "One last parting shot."

She nodded. "For us to handle."

CHAPTER
THIRTY-ONE

CASSIOPEIA CLIMBED DOWN FROM THE RUSSIAN FIGHTER. SHE and Cotton had just landed at the air base not far from her château, the long flight from Siberia over. The pilots had said virtually nothing on the trip, most likely told not to engage their passengers. Cotton's stunt in thwarting their attack on Zorin apparently had not been anticipated. She'd half expected that the planes be ordered to return to Irkutsk immediately, but that had not happened. She was glad to be back on French soil.

Cotton descended from his high-speed taxi and walked over to her. "I need to call Stephanie."

"I'm assuming there's a lot more to this story than I know."

"You could say that."

They entered one of the buildings and asked for a private office. Base personnel seemed to have been expecting them, as it wasn't every day that two Russian fighters touched down at a NATO air base. The officer-in-charge directed them to a small conference room. Inside, Cassiopeia found her cell phone, the same one they'd not been allowed to use back in Siberia, and redialed Stephanie's number.

Then she hit SPEAKER.

"It's midafternoon in DC," Cotton said.

The line on the other end rang.

"Where's Zorin headed?" Cassiopeia asked him.

"Prince Edward Island, Canada. I've already done the math. He'll be on the ground around 11:00 P.M. local time."

Another two rings.

"Do we need to go there?"

Before Cotton could reply, a voice answered the phone. Not Stephanie's. Male. One she immediately recognized. Danny Daniels.

"We were worried," the president said.

"I was, too," Cotton said. "It's been an interesting few hours. And how did I get you? Is Stephanie there?"

"She's indisposed at the moment, handling Zorin's lover, who's proved to be quite a pain in the ass. You might like to know that my nephew got his butt kicked."

Cotton smiled. "I'm sure it's not as bad as you say."

"You know, I got, what, less than a day and a half left on the job. Let me tell you, there's not a whole lot for a president to do in his last two days, except pack up things. I feel as useless as tits on a boar hog. So tell me something that will cheer me up."

"Zorin's headed for Canada. He's looking for hidden nuclear weapons."

"Stephanie has reported in the same thing from this end."

Daniels told them all that he knew. She then listened as Cotton recounted what had happened over Lake Baikal, then at the dacha, culminating in Vadim Belchenko's death. "That archivist believed those men were military, sent to kill him. Any idea what he meant by 'Fool's Mate' or 'zero amendment'?"

"Not in the least, but you've given me something to do, which I greatly appreciate. Stephanie is running a little operation of her own and had all calls to her phone forwarded here to the White House. I'm waiting to hear from her. In the meantime, what do you need from us?"

"A fast ride to Canada."

Cotton told the president where they were.

"It's being arranged right now. Just stay put."

"Tracking Zorin's plane would also be a good idea."

"Already thought of that one. We'll keep you posted on its route."

"We have to know if this is real, or just wishful thinking on Zorin's part," Cotton said. "We don't know if he's working alone or what.

He certainly had help at the dacha. Then there's the Russians. They definitely wanted that old archivist dead."

"Back on the lake, in the helicopter," she said, "the men recognized the vehicles chasing Cotton as military. That fact seemed to be an issue for them."

"Hello, is that Ms. Vitt?" Daniels asked. "Long time, no see."

"It has been a while, Mr. President."

The last time they were together had been on the second floor of the White House, after another ordeal in which both she and the president discovered some surprising things about themselves.

"This whole thing stinks," the president said. "Moscow specifically asked for our help. I obliged them and sent you in, Cotton. They then alerted us to Anya Petrova, who's here for Zorin, so I sent Luke to bird-dog her. They also allowed Cassiopeia to enter the country to see about you."

"Then something changed," Cotton said. "They told us to not let the door hit us in the ass on the way out of the country."

Daniels chuckled. "Haven't heard that one in a while. But I agree. Things did change fast. Let me make some inquiries. I may be headed out to pasture, but this bull can still buck."

That she did not doubt.

"We also need any information the CIA has on a man named Jamie Kelley," Cotton said. "Supposedly an American, now living on Prince Edward Island. He works at a college there. Belchenko told me this guy was once a Soviet asset. That's who Zorin is after."

He'd done the math on the ride over. No private jet could match the speed of a military fighter. So they should be able to beat Zorin across the Atlantic by at least an hour.

"I'm told your rides are being arranged," Daniels said. "Keep us posted."

The call ended.

She stared at Cotton. This was the first time they'd been alone to actually speak to each other.

"I was wrong," she said. "I handled things horribly in Utah."

"It was tough on all of us. I'm sorry it turned out the way it did."

She genuinely believed he meant that. This man was no hardened killer. For him to pull the trigger meant that there'd been no choice, and there had not been.

"I've decided that I don't want to live my life without you." She'd told herself to be honest with him and, for once, not mince words. She was hoping he would return the favor.

"That makes two of us," he said. "I need you."

She realized what it took for him to make that admission. Neither one of them was a clingy personality.

"Can we forget about what happened," she said, "and pick up where we left off?"

"I can do that."

She smiled. So could she.

They both still wore Russian flight suits. She unzipped hers, wanting to be rid of it. "I'm assuming we have to be stuffed into another fighter and flown across the Atlantic?"

"That would be the fastest way."

"And what do we do once we get there?"

"Find a man named Jamie Kelly, before Zorin does the same."

CHAPTER
THIRTY-TWO

STEPHANIE ADMIRED THE HOUSE THAT BELONGED TO PETER Hedlund, the current historian for the Society of Cincinnatus. As explained, the colonial brick mansion had been built in the mid-1700s, and a succession of owners had kept it standing. Most of what was now visible came from a mid-20th-century remodel. She loved the artful mix of marble, walnut, and plaster, along with the careful blend of bold colors, all of which reminded her of the house she and her husband once owned, which had sat not all that far away.

Annapolis was familiar territory. Though currently only the capital of Maryland, for a short time after the Revolutionary War it served as the national capital. Always compact, less than 40,000 people living there, and it had not grown much since her time here back in the late 1980s. Fritz Strobl had called ahead and alerted Hedlund to their visit. She and Luke now sat in a lovely study with a brick hearth, in which burned a crackling fire. Hedlund had already listened to their purpose for being there, and had agreed to everything she'd asked.

"My wife is out for a few hours," he told them.

"Which will make this easier," she said. "The fewer people here the better."

"Is this woman dangerous?"

"Definitely," she said. "But I don't think she's coming here to harm you. She's after something specific and we need to find out what that is. You don't happen to know, do you?"

She watched carefully, gauging the man's consideration of her question. Strobl had offered little to nothing about Hedlund, which could have been evasive or simply meant that he did not know. She was opting for the latter, hoping the answers she sought rested with this man.

"I realize that I also have the ceremonial title Keeper of Secrets," he said with a smile. "But I assure you, that's a holdover from a long time ago when there really may have been secrets. Today our society is a philanthropic, social organization that, to my knowledge, is totally transparent."

Hedlund had already showed them his private library, a separate room devoted to early American history, especially the first fifty years of the republic. He told them that he'd been collecting colonial history books all of his adult life, delighted when he became the society's historian.

"Did you know Bradley Charon?" she asked.

Hedlund nodded. "Brad and I were close friends. When he died, which was so sudden and unexpected, I was heartbroken. The plane crash came out of nowhere."

"Did you know he kept a secret library?" Luke asked.

The younger Daniels had stayed uncharacteristically quiet for the past hour or so.

"I only knew of his collection that he kept at the estate, in his study, similar to mine. But all of those books came over to the society at his death. Thankfully, he had the foresight to gift them to us in writing. What with all the probate fighting, we would've never seen those volumes again. They're now all safe, at Anderson House."

She told him what they'd found at the Virginia estate.

"I would like to see that hidden room," Hedlund said.

That would have to wait. She checked her watch, wondering what was happening in Russia. She desperately wanted to know. She'd forwarded all calls to the White House so Edwin Davis could handle them while she dealt with matters here. She'd briefly told Edwin about being fired and he sympathized, but she knew there was nothing he could do. She and Edwin decided the best course was simply to plow ahead with what was happening both here and overseas. Something big was up, something the Russians themselves were not sure about, since Osin's aloofness at the Charon estate had quickly been replaced by active cooperation when it came to Anya Petrova.

The doorbell rang.

She signaled for Luke and Hedlund to flee upstairs. Both men retreated from the study. She stood and smoothed out her blouse and pants, catching her breath, regaining control.

The bell rang again.

She stepped from the study into a marble-floored entrance hall. Two oil paintings of Annapolis dominated the dark-blue walls. At the front door she opened the latch and smiled at the woman who stood out in the cold on the front stoop.

"Are you Mrs. Hedlund?" Anya Petrova asked.

"I am," Stephanie replied.

LUKE LISTENED TO WHAT WAS HAPPENING BELOW, SAFE INSIDE one of the upstairs bedrooms, whose door opened to a second-floor balcony that overlooked the entrance hall.

At no time had Anya Petrova ever seen Stephanie, or even known that she existed, which was why the ruse would work. It seemed the fastest way to find out what this was all about. True, there was danger, as there was no telling what Petrova might do, but that was why he was here.

To keep an eye on things or, more accurately, an ear.

STEPHANIE INVITED PETROVA INSIDE AND CLOSED THE DOOR TO the afternoon chill.

"What happened to you?" she asked her guest, pointing at the bruise on the woman's face.

"I'm clumsy and fell. It looks worse than feels."

"Are you Russian? I hear the accent."

Petrova nodded. "I was born there, but I live here now. Is your husband home?"

She shook her head. "I'm afraid not."

"When does he return?"

"I have no idea."

That lie was designed to force Petrova's hand and not unnecessarily place Peter Hedlund in any jeopardy, though it would have been preferable for him to have handled this conversation.

"I come long way to speak to him. I must ask questions. About Society of Cincinnatis. He is society historian, is he not?"

Stephanie nodded. "For some time now."

"Does he have library here, in house?"

She pointed down the short hall that led off the entranceway. "A lovely one, with many books."

"May I see it?"

She hesitated, just enough for Petrova to not get suspicious. "Why do you want to?"

A look of irritation flooded the younger woman's face. She'd wondered how much patience Petrova planned to show. They'd disarmed her at Anderson House, but there'd been the matter of her car and the fact that she may have also carried a backup weapon.

Petrova reached beneath her jacket and removed a small-caliber revolver. "I want to see books. Now."

If Luke had not been upstairs, ready to act, she might be concerned. Anya Petrova cast the wary look of someone to be feared. Which made sense, as she was a product of a place where fear had evolved into a marketable commodity. Her words came simple and direct, with not the slightest hint of false bravado. Just matter-of-fact. Their meaning clear.

I. Will. Hurt. You.

"I," Stephanie started, feigning concern, "have never had a . . . gun pointed at me before."

Petrova said nothing.

Which spoke volumes.

Time to concede.

"All right," Stephanie said. "Follow me . . . to the library."

LUKE WATCHED THROUGH A CRACKED-OPEN DOOR AS STEPHANIE and Petrova left the entrance hall. He should head down and find a closer vantage point from which to listen but, before he did, he ought to make a quick check on Hedlund. Their host had fled into another bedroom at the end of the second-floor hall. He crept down a carpet runner toward the half-open door, careful that nothing betrayed his presence.

At the door he stopped.

He heard a voice from the other side.

Low and throaty.

He carefully peered into the bedroom and saw Hedlund sitting in a chair, staring out the window, talking on his mobile phone. Odd, considering what was happening below. Earlier, Hedlund had appeared straight up, genuinely surprised, willing to help.

"It has to be that," Hedlund said. "We thought all of this was long forgotten, but apparently we were wrong. It's starting again."

A few seconds of silence passed as Hedlund listened to what was being said in his ear.

"Nothing here to find. I made sure of that years ago," Hedlund said.

More silence.

"I'll keep you posted."

He heard a beep as the call ended.

"Nothing here to find"?

This just kept getting better and better.

Which meant Stephanie could have a real problem on her hands.

CHAPTER THIRTY-THREE

ZORIN DOZED IN AND OUT, RESTLESS THOUGH THE FLIGHT ACROSS the Atlantic had been smooth. He'd managed a couple of hours of fitful sleep, grateful that the two pilots stayed forward and to themselves. He'd utilized the desktop computer and found an appropriate landing spot, a national park on the north shore that should offer plenty of privacy. Weather would not be a problem. Northern Canada was having a mild winter, little snow had fallen, the skies tonight were moisture-free. The jump would still be tricky, but he could handle it. If all went as planned, he'd be about forty kilometers northwest of Charlottetown, the island's capital, where the university was located. He'd found the college's website and learned that Jamie Kelly still worked there part-time. More checking on the Internet had also yielded a home address.

Fool's Mate.

He'd been piecing it all together for over ten years, extracting bits and pieces from old records. But his talks with Belchenko had been most productive, even though the archivist had always thought the whole thing nothing more than wishful thinking.

He knew that was not the case.

The tall man who entered the apartment was in his sixties, with thick gray hair brushed straight back from a noticeably ashen face.

He wore rimless glasses, the dark eyes intense but also full of weariness. Four aides accompanied him. They quickly searched the other rooms, then retreated outside, the door closing behind them. The apartment was a KGB safe house, kept under constant surveillance. Tonight it played host to Yuri Vladimirovich Andropov.

No introductions occurred. Instead Andropov sat at the head of a wooden table where a cold supper had been laid out, along with glasses filled with vodka. Zorin sat at the table, too, as did three other KGB officers. Two he knew. One was a stranger. He'd never before been this close to Andropov. Like himself, this man came from humble beginnings, the son of a railroad official who worked as a loader, telegraph clerk, and sailor fighting in Finland during the Great Patriotic War. Afterward, he'd begun a steady climb up the party hierarchy, eventually becoming chief of the KGB. Last November, two days after Brezhnev died, Andropov had been chosen the nation's fourth general secretary since Stalin.

"I plan to do something extraordinary," Andropov said to them in barely a whisper. "I will say tomorrow that we are stopping all work on space-based missile defense systems."

Zorin was shocked. Ever since March, when Reagan announced America would develop a strategic defense system, all Soviet research efforts had been redirected. To aid that effort all intelligence operations had likewise been refocused, the idea being to learn everything possible about SDI.

"Mr. Reagan thinks us an evil empire," Andropov said. "I will show him that is not the case. We will tell the world we are stopping."

No one said a word.

"I received a letter from a ten-year-old American child," Andropov said. "She asked me why we want to conquer the world. Why do we want a war? I told her we want neither. I plan to tell that to the world tomorrow. After that is done, I will be entering the hospital."

Zorin had heard the talk. The general secretary had supposedly suffered total kidney failure, his life now sustained only by dialysis. Characteristically, nothing had been said publicly. For Andropov to mention it himself seemed extraordinary.

"I tell you this for a reason," Andropov said. "You four have been personally selected by me to carry out a special assignment. I have come here, tonight, to instruct you myself. This is a mission that I personally conceived. Each operation will carry a name. I chose those, too. From chess, a game I love. Do any of you play?"

All of them shook their heads.

Andropov pointed around the table and said to them each, individually, "Absolute Pin. Backward Pawn. Quiet Move. Fool's Mate."

That had been August 1983, the first time Zorin had ever heard those words. He'd not known their meaning, but quickly learned.

Absolute Pin. A king cornered so tightly that it cannot legally move, except to be exposed to check.

Backward Pawn. One pawn behind another of the same color that cannot advance without the support of another pawn.

Quiet Move. Something that does not attack or capture an enemy piece.

Fool's Mate. The shortest possible game. Two moves and over.

"Each of these assignments is vital to the others," Andropov said. "Once brought together, they will change the world."

"These are totally independent operations?" one of the other assets asked.

"Precisely. Four separate and distinct efforts, the results of which only I will know. None of you will communicate with the others, unless specifically ordered to do so. Is that clear?"

They all nodded, knowing that Andropov was not to be challenged. Here was the man who convinced Khrushchev to crush the Hungarian rebels. As head of the KGB he'd spread fear and terror, trying hard to restore the party's lost legitimacy. He was more reminiscent of Stalin than any of the latest so-called reformers. His order of no contact among them was nothing unusual. Zorin knew how weaklings curried favor with their superiors by informing on others. Wives spied on husbands, children on their parents, neighbors on neighbors. Far better to never ask questions and have a poor memory. Every word, every act should be chosen with care.

Better yet, as Andropov had just ordered, was to say and do nothing at all.

"Beneath your plate is an envelope," Andropov said. "The orders inside detail your specific operational mission. The method of reporting your success is also detailed. Do not vary from those orders."

He'd noticed that there had been no mention of failure. That was not an option.

One of the officers reached for his plate.

Andropov stopped him. "Not yet. Break the seal only after you leave here. That way you have no temptation to discuss this among yourselves."

Everyone sat still.

Zorin understood a need to establish an aura of self-confidence and did not resent the clear subordination being forced upon him by Andropov. He, too, had a gift for intimidating and had played the same game with those under him many times.

"I want you to know, comrades, that what we are about to accomplish will strike America at its core. They think themselves so right, so perfect. But they have flaws. I've discovered two of those, and together, at the right time, we will teach America a lesson."

He liked the sound of that.

And he liked being a part of it.

"Minimum effort, maximum effect. That's what we want, and that is precisely what you will deliver. This will be the most important operation we have ever undertaken. So, comrades, we must be ready when the moment comes."

Andropov motioned to the food.

"Now eat. Enjoy yourselves. Then we will begin our work."

Slowly, over the past two decades, he'd pieced together each of the other three operations. Record declassification and the simple fact that the Soviet Union was no more had made his task easier. But there'd been precious little to find. His own part, Quiet Move, had involved six years of devotion, starting in 1983 with Andropov's charge and functionally ending in 1989.

Just after the meeting, Andropov had in fact entered the hospital.

The ten-year-old American girl he'd mentioned actually visited the Soviet Union, on Andropov's personal invitation, providing a perfect propaganda opportunity which the Western media had devoured. Andropov himself had been too ill to greet her. Sadly, a few years later, she died in a plane crash, which had allowed for even more pandering. Andropov himself died six months after the gathering at the safe house, serving only fifteen months as general secretary. He was succeeded by Chernenko, a frail, weak man who lasted only thirteen months. Then Gromyko acted as caretaker until Gorbachev finally rose to power in 1985.

All in all, a turbulent few years by Soviet standards. So much confusion with little direction. Yet the four missions had continued. Never was any order issued stopping them. Riding in the plane, listening to the monotonous drone of the jet engines, absorbed in the eerie stillness and quiet, he now knew what all three of the other men had accomplished.

Andropov had done exactly as he'd said, telling the world that the Soviet Union would cease development of a space-based missile defense system. Which, of course, never happened. Secretly, the research continued with rubles spent by the billions. Zorin, and all other KGB assets, continued to work their sources for every scrap of information they could discover on SDI.

Absolute Pin.

Backward Pawn.

Both operatives completed their assigned tasks.

That he knew for certain.

He prided himself on not having much of a conscience. No good officer could afford such a liability. But the past twenty-five years had caused him to reassess things.

Was that guilt?

Hard to say.

He thought back to that night in Maryland.

And the last time he'd killed a man.

CHAPTER THIRTY-FOUR

Maryland

Stephanie maintained the illusion of being Mrs. Peter Hedlund, leading Anya Petrova back to the library.

"What is it you're looking for?" she asked Petrova, concern in her voice.

"Just do as I ask, then I will be gone."

They entered the library, afternoon sun pouring past open wooden shutters and through sheers that covered a set of French doors. Books filled walnut shelves that consumed two walls.

Petrova motioned, "Sit over there, where I see you."

Stephanie retreated to a settee and watched as the shelves were carefully examined, Petrova definitely searching for something in particular.

The perusal did not take long.

"It is not here. I must find book your husband knows of. Old book, from the Cincinnati. He is Keeper of Secrets and I must know one of those."

Her hope had been that Hedlund himself would not have to be involved. Now that seemed impossible.

Petrova pointed the gun her way. "Where is your husband?"

"He should be home soon."

LUKE HAD HUSTLED AWAY FROM HEDLUND'S BEDROOM DOOR, back to the other room where he'd first been hiding. He waited a few seconds, then crept back down the hall to the master suite, where he edged the door open and motioned for Hedlund. The older man still sat in the chair on the far side by the window, his phone call over.

Hedlund rose and stepped lightly toward him.

"We need to head downstairs," Luke whispered.

They made their way through the second-floor landing to the top of the stairs. He needed to know who'd been on that call earlier without Hedlund becoming suspicious, so he mouthed, *Do you have a cell phone?*

A nod.

Give it to me.

Hedlund quickly handed it over.

He found the switch on the side and activated the silent mode. They made their way to the ground floor and he could hear Petrova and Stephanie talking in the study, noting that Petrova had not found what she came for. When Stephanie mentioned that her husband would be back home shortly, that was the code they'd arranged for the next step, if necessary.

Hedlund had to go in.

He grabbed the older man by the arm and led him to the front door, where he breathed, "You have to find out what this woman wants. I'll have your back from here. Okay? Stephanie will be with you. Like we talked about earlier, just find out what you can without provoking her." He motioned with the phone he held. "I'll keep this so there'll be no interruptions."

Hedlund nodded. "Should we not call the police?"

"We are the police."

He grabbed the doorknob and whispered, "You're home."

He opened, then slammed shut the front door, immediately seeking refuge inside a nearby closet, where he settled among heavy coats.

"It's me," he heard Hedlund say in a loud voice.

STEPHANIE REALIZED WHAT WAS HAPPENING. LUKE HAD DETER-
mined that she wanted Hedlund involved, so he'd made that happen
in an inconspicuous way. Good work. But she would have expected no
less. She glanced at Petrova, who motioned for her to alert her husband where she was waiting.

"I'm in the library."

Hedlund appeared in the doorway.

"We have a guest," she said to him. "This woman is after something
from the society. Some book. She won't say what it might be. She
threatened to hurt me if I didn't cooperate."

Petrova had the gun concealed behind her thigh, which she now revealed. Shock came to Hedlund's face.

"Are you all right?" he asked Stephanie, playing along.

"I'm fine. Really. Fine."

"Enough," Petrova said, her voice rising. "I need the Tallmadge
journal."

"How do you know of that?" Hedlund asked.

A bold inquiry.

And not part of the plan.

"Not your concern. I need the journal. Where is it?"

"It doesn't exist. It's a myth. I've certainly heard of it, but I've never
seen it. And I wonder again how you would know of it. That is something only a few within the society knew about."

"A long time ago people talked," Petrova said. "We listened. We
know."

"Russians?" he asked.

"Soviets. Tell me what you know of journal?"

Stephanie wanted to hear that answer, too.

"It was written by one of our founding members, Benjamin Tallmadge of New York. He was a spymaster from the Revolutionary War,
one of the first in this country. Colonel Tallmadge was instrumental in
our victory over the British. Afterward, he served in the society until he
died in 1835, I believe. He kept the journal, which supposedly was part
of the society's early records. But it disappeared over a century ago."

"You lie," Petrova yelled. "Do not lie to me. I know truth. It was
there thirty years ago. Soviets saw it. You know truth. Charon knew
truth. Where is that journal?"

"I told you—"

Petrova darted across the room and nestled her weapon tight to Stephanie's temple. "I will shoot your wife dead, if you do not tell truth."

The gun's hammer snapped into place.

Signaling more trouble.

LUKE HEARD WHAT ANYA HAD SAID ALONG WITH THE DISTINC-tive click of a gun being readied to fire. Bad enough that they had Hedlund in play. Now there was no telling what Petrova would do. She was definitely agitated and impatient. Stephanie had told him to use his best judgment as to when to stop the charade, but urged him to give as wide a leash as possible. This seemed their best shot at finding out what was happening, and it had to have a chance to succeed.

But they now knew what Petrova was after.

The Tallmadge journal.

He gripped his weapon.

And heard again Stephanie's last order from earlier.

"For God's sake, don't kill her."

That might be easier said than done.

STEPHANIE KEPT HER COMPOSURE BUT REALIZED THAT MRS. PE-ter Hedlund would not be so calm.

"Please," she said. "Please take that gun away from me."

But the barrel stayed pressed to her scalp.

"Where is the Tallmadge journal," Petrova asked again. "It was with Charon years ago. That I know. You are now Keeper of Secrets. Tell me, or I shoot her."

Stephanie stared straight at Hedlund, who displayed a remarkable calm.

"Do you know what I did before I retired?" he asked Petrova, who said nothing. "Thirty-two years with the FBI."

Which was news to Stephanie, but it explained the calculating eyes glaring back at her. Petrova seemed to understand what that meant, too, removing the gun from Stephanie's head and pointing it at Hedlund.

"I resent that you have come into my home and threatened us," he said. "I told you, the journal does not exist."

"You lie."

"And how do you know that?"

Challenging this woman was not necessarily a good idea.

This needed to end.

Then she heard knocks coming from the front door.

LUKE RAPPED HIS KNUCKLES ON THE PANELED WOOD.

Bursting into the confined library with a gun had not seemed like a smart idea. Somebody was likely to get shot. So he'd decided to see if he could draw Petrova his way and give himself room to maneuver. He'd listened to what Hedlund had said and realized that this man was definitely keeping things close.

So he had to do something.

STEPHANIE SAW PETROVA REACT TO THE POSSIBILITY OF A VISITOR.

"Who is that?" the Russian asked.

Hedlund shrugged. "How would I know? Do you want me to answer it?"

She caught the condescending tone, which came across as more of a challenge. Petrova clearly did not appreciate it.

The gun stayed aimed at Hedlund.

"Go see," came the order. "You, too."

And Petrova motioned with the gun for Stephanie to follow.

Hedlund disappeared out the library door.

She noticed that Petrova hesitated in the hall, just past the doorway, and suddenly realized what the woman planned to do. The French doors. In the library. They offered a quick way out and this front-door visitor could provide just enough distraction for her to make a hasty escape. Unfortunately, Stephanie was unarmed, her Beretta still inside her coat in the study where they'd first met Hedlund.

"Keep moving," Petrova ordered.

Hedlund made his way into the entrance hall.

She needed to alert Luke but, before she could, Hedlund stopped and spun around—

With a gun in his hand.

LUKE HAD ASSUMED THE HIGH GROUND, RETREATING TO THE second-floor landing, which offered a clear view of the floor below. His hope was that the prospect of being interrupted would be enough to force Petrova's hand. Since he knew that there was nothing here to find, he had to end this encounter without gunfire and with Petrova in custody.

But that now seemed like a problem.

Hedlund had armed himself, the weapon surely hidden somewhere in the master bedroom. He'd heard what the man said about being former FBI, but that wasn't going to do him much good against a pro like Petrova.

Cockiness can get you killed.

He ought to know. His own arrogance had come close to getting him whacked several times. But hell, he was thirty years old and had an excuse. Hedlund was collecting a pension and Social Security, yet acting as he were still in the game.

Options here were limited.

In fact, he had only one play.

STEPHANIE DOVE TO THE CARPET RUNNER, FLATTENING HER BODY and wondering who was going to shoot first. The answer came from

Hedlund, who fired right past her. She rolled onto her spine and saw that Petrova was gone.

"Stay down," Hedlund yelled.

She glanced back and saw Hedlund gripping the weapon with both hands, steadying his aim, his attention full ahead.

"Get back, you idiot," she said to him. "Now."

Petrova reappeared and fired twice, both bullets thudding into Hedlund, the man crying out in pain, then collapsing to the floor.

LUKE HEARD THE SHOTS AND MOVED, SLIDING DOWN THE SLICK curved railing that protected the stairway's outer edge, slipping off as he approached the bottom.

He saw Hedlund drop to the floor.

He swung left, leveled his gun, and sent two rounds in Petrova's direction, but the wiry woman had already retreated into the library. He kept his gun aimed and sought cover where the hall spilled into the foyer. Hedlund groaned on the floor. He needed to see about him, but his attention was drawn to Stephanie, who lay on her back across the hall.

Was she hit, too?

He heard doors open and felt a rush of cold air.

Stephanie came to her feet. "She's gone outside through the library. Go get her."

He looked again at Hedlund.

"I'll deal with him," she said, "Stop that bitch."

He didn't need to be told twice.

CHAPTER THIRTY-FIVE

ZORIN HUNCHED DOWN AGAINST THE MID-ATLANTIC COLD. THOUGH *he'd lived and worked in freezing temperatures all his life, he still hated it. Westerners thought that some sort of immunity against the cold developed over time, but that was the farthest thing from the truth. He'd been waiting nearly half an hour in the dark, and his patience was finally rewarded as a vehicle appeared down the street. The Ford eased to the curb and he climbed into the warm cabin. The driver was, like Zorin, in his mid-thirties, a three-day growth of beard dusting a fleshy neck and chin, a Chicago Bears cap on his head. The car sped away in a shower of snow and ice from its spinning tires.*

Fifteen minutes later they arrived at a nondescript bar on Baltimore's north side, a neon sign showing a naked dancer, beneath which read NO COVER. *He'd lived in the West long enough to know that a decadent fleshpot awaited inside. The driver had chosen the spot, which was understandable given this was the other man's turf.*

So he'd not objected.

The man now lived and worked here in Baltimore and went by the moniker Joe Perko. Zorin also had assumed an alias, one of several he possessed, using the false identity to easily gain entrance into the United States. For all its talk about a Cold War, America's borders stood more like porous screens than solid walls. Both men spoke perfect English, all courtesy of a KGB training school that they attended.

They hustled inside.

Everything was shrouded in shadows except the lit bar and il-luminated stage, where a ridiculously thin blonde with large breasts danced and stripped. He'd never cared for skinny women or lean steaks, preferring in both much more fat on the bone. He also liked women born with blond hair, as opposed to those who created an illusion from a bottle. Music played, but the woman's actions were not in tune with the melody. In fact, she appeared agitated and bored.

Topless waitresses served the tables that ringed the stage.

"I like it here," Perko said. "They all watch the women and no one pays you any attention."

He saw the wisdom in that observation.

They grabbed a table near the stage and ordered a drink from one of the servers.

"I'm done," Perko quietly said. "My part is finished."

He knew what that meant. Another portion of Andropov's plan, Backward Pawn, Perko's responsibility, had been completed.

"It took five years, but I did it," Perko said. "Hard to believe it's been that long since we sat around that table with Andropov. So much has changed."

How true. It was 1988. Andropov had died years ago and Gor-bachev now ruled the USSR. Perestroika and glasnost dominated. Restructuring and openness had become national goals. The old ways were fading by the day.

"My orders, from inside the envelope I was given, were to re-port to you," Perko said. "Once the mission was done. So that's what I'm doing."

He'd already heard from the man who'd completed another quarter of the mission, Absolute Pin, nearly two years ago. Like tonight, he'd met that officer, only in New York City, learning for the first time more than he was supposed to know.

The waitress brought their orders and he downed a long swal-low of vodka. He was not much of a drinker, good at feigning oth-erwise. Perko seemed to enjoy his, tossing it back in one gulp.

"Żubrówka. Not anything like home," Perko whispered as he tabled the glass.

He agreed. Polish vodka seemed a poor substitute.

"Have you completed your portion?" Perko asked.

He shook his head. "Not yet."

Which was true.

After Andropov had left the safe house that night, they'd eaten their dinner, the envelopes with their respective orders remaining beneath their plates. The meal consumed, all four had left, each surely waiting until he was safely away before reading the contents. For the general secretary himself to have personally chosen them carried enormous weight, and by and large they all had adhered to secrecy. None, to his knowledge, communicating with the others. Only to him, once they were through. Per the orders in their envelopes.

"I finally got them in," Perko said. "They're all here."

The blond twig on the stage had finished undressing, now offering the customers some naked bumps and grinds. A few of the patrons seemed to appreciate her newfound enthusiasm and rewarded her with money tossed to the stage.

He sipped more vodka.

"They came through Mexico, by way of Cuba," Perko said. "I had to be sure there'd be no detection. We had a man drive them across the border. I took possession in Texas and brought them north myself."

He was learning far more than he should, but he'd grown ever more curious about the whole operation, so he asked, "Everything in one piece?"

Perko nodded. "They're all in their cases, powered up. Each running exactly to specs."

"No problems?"

"Nothing. But they're scary things," Perko's voice was barely a whisper over the music. "Amazing that something so small packs a nuclear punch."

That it was.

His spetsnaz unit had been trained on the field deployment of RA-115s. He was aware of weapons caches in Europe and the Far

East that included them, but this was the first time he'd learned
specifically of one in the United States. Apparently, Andropov had
indeed envisioned a grand scheme.

"I turned them over to Fool's Mate, as my orders required,"
Perko said. *"Do you have any idea what he's to do with them?"*

He shook his head. "That is beyond both you and me."

Perko finished his drink and motioned to one of the servers for
another. "I've been recalled. I leave in two days."

Which he already knew.

But he still said, "Then let us celebrate your return home."

And they had.

For several hours, while the music played and more dancers slinked on the stage. One of those women he remembered. Tiny and dark, with Asian eyes, a broad nose, and raven-black hair. Perko had liked her, too, and had wanted to get to know her better, but he'd discouraged that and eventually led the drunk officer from the bar back to the car. He'd drunk little and still possessed all his senses. Once at the car, determining that no one was around, he'd clamped his left hand over Perko's mouth, then bent his head to one side, then the other, wrenching the neck. Flesh gave way. Bone clicked. Death came instantaneously. Another talent taught him by the KGB.

Two-thirds of his mission had been accomplished.

His orders were simple. At completion and reporting in, eliminate the other three officers.

Quiet Move.

Two were now dead.

And since neither man would be around to get him into trouble, he'd not discouraged them from talking. From Absolute Pin he'd learned of the creation of five RA-115s, specially crafted for long life and maximum output. From Perko and Backward Pawn he now knew that those RA-115s had been smuggled into America. Only Fool's Mate remained a mystery. But he could guess its portion. Preservation and concealment.

And the officer assigned that part?

That name he learned from Vadim Belchenko.

A man trained, like himself, in the ways of the West, embedded in the United States, who ultimately assumed the name Jamie Kelly, now living in Canada.

Sitting in the quiet of the Gulfstream's dimly lit interior, he thought again of the two men he'd killed, both of whom had done nothing less than their jobs, faithfully serving the motherland. It was human nature to want to talk about what they'd done, especially with someone they believed to be part of their mission. But Andropov had anticipated loose lips, which was why Quiet Move had been a part of the plan.

So he'd done his job, too.

But the two murders had always weighed on him.

The least he owed them?

That their deaths would mean something.

CHAPTER THIRTY-SIX

LUKE BOLTED OUT OF THE FRENCH DOORS AND SPOTTED ANYA Petrova as she disappeared over a chest-high hedge. He ran after her, leaping the bushes like a hurdler in an Olympic heat. He rounded the side of Hedlund's house and, once into the front yard, saw Petrova racing toward the same car that still bore the scars from their encounter in Virginia.

"You're not going to get away," he called out to her.

Her head turned and their eyes met. He thought about taking a shot, but she was a hundred yards away, now leaping into the driver's seat, revving the engine.

And he heard Stephanie's final command.

"Bring her back alive."

So he opted to veer toward the Escape that had brought him and Stephanie east from DC. He leaped inside and fired up the engine, backing from the drive and speeding in the direction Petrova had gone. The residential neighborhood came with wide streets, the kind built long ago when curbside parking was still allowed. A few cars had taken advantage of the opportunity and he wove his way around them while adding speed. Ahead, he spotted Petrova ignoring a stop sign and hanging a sharp right. He followed her, the Escape's tires sliding across the cold pavement. He told himself to be careful. It would not be hard to flip over.

He'd tossed his gun on the passenger seat within easy reach.

If he could catch her, he'd stop her.

She barreled her way through another interchange that, luckily, had attracted few cars. He saw a busy boulevard. She slowed an instant at her approach then roared into the traffic, shooting out of her lane and crossing the double line into opposing traffic. Horns blared and he heard the screech of rubber on asphalt as cars veered out of her way. She wove in and out in neatly executed maneuvers that kept her moving forward. He'd have to maintain pace or lose her, but he didn't want to place anyone at unnecessary risk. So he approached the intersection with caution, assessed the situation, then sped past the congealed traffic, using the far-left shoulder to maximum advantage.

Petrova drove hard, but didn't seem accustomed to speed in such tight confines, making small mistakes, using more brake than accelerator, misjudging corners, overcorrecting the rear-end drift. His Escape shuddered as if riding on cobblestones, not built for this kind of intense driving.

But he was.

At a patch of open road he floored the accelerator. The route here was now four-laned and medianed from oncoming traffic. He caught a glimpse as she broke out of the stream half a mile ahead.

Then trouble appeared.

Flashing blue lights, moving into position behind Petrova.

A Maryland state trooper had found her.

In his rearview mirror he saw that he had an escort of his own, tight on his rear bumper, lights flashing, siren blaring.

He retrieved his Defense Intelligence Agency badge from a pocket. With one hand tight on the wheel he punched the button for the driver's-side window to descend and stuck the badge out so the idiot behind him could see. The trooper veered into the left lane and sped up parallel, the passenger window down in the patrol car.

Luke pointed ahead and yelled, "Stop her."

The trooper nodded and gained more speed, closing on his colleague following Petrova. They, of course, had the advantage of a radio, so he was hoping some local help might, for once, prove productive.

Both hands returned to the wheel and he kept pace with the troopers. Cars obliged them by moving left and right onto the shoulders, creating a wide path. They were headed east, out of town. A bevy of buildings surrounding him on both sides of the road looked governmental. He knew that the Naval Academy was somewhere ahead, adjacent to the Chesapeake Bay.

They continued on for a good two miles, then the troopers ahead came parallel to each other, a car in each lane, and slowed. That gave Petrova room as she raced onward. He knew what they were doing. Like beaters driving an animal toward guns. A rolling roadblock, a way to contain the traffic behind them.

He realized what that meant.

He whipped the steering wheel to the right, surging the Escape onto the narrow paved shoulder, where he had enough room to scoot past the troopers. He yanked the wheel hard left and ducked back onto the roadway. Nothing now stood between him and Petrova, the troopers slowing their speed and blocking anything approaching from the rear. Traffic was still four-laned and split by a concrete median. The buildings had ended, the road a straightaway, slightly downhill, leading to a long uphill expanse and a massive bridge.

Then he saw them.

Four more trooper cars on the bridge incline, about halfway up, blocking the way forward on both sides.

Damn. These guys move fast.

No traffic was coming in the opposite lane and the officers were allowing cars ahead in this lane to pass by, ready to pinch things off once only Petrova remained.

Which happened.

Nowhere now for her to go except straight through the blockade, or a 180 that cut across the median, back in the opposite direction, where the two troopers behind him would surely cut her off.

He saw guns leveled.

This was not what he wanted. He needed her alive, but he couldn't stop what was about to happen. Everything seemed like a movie. There, but far off, not real. Yet it was. He realized that the locals only practiced scenarios like this. Here, finally, was the real thing. No way they would allow this opportunity to pass. He heard shooting. Apparently for the tires, as Petrova's vehicle suddenly swerved left, right, then slammed the bridge railing.

Sparks flew.

Forward momentum was enough to free the weight off the back axle, which launched the car upward, turning it into a projectile, responsive now only to the laws of motion and gravity.

Over the side it went.

He wheeled up, slid to a stop, and burst out, finding the smashed railing just as the car below met the first line of trees leading down to the water. Nothing could stop the assault. The mass plowed through like a cannon firing, jackknifing upward and spinning full circle, Petrova ejected outward. He heard tatters of a scream, then a thud. The car, too heavy to stop, folded onto itself like a telescope, its front end gone, finally settling on its roof, wheels spinning, engine wailing then coughing a final spasm. Petrova was thrown all the way to the water a few feet from shore.

He leaped the railing and thrashed through the tangled underbrush, slithering down the steep embankment, almost losing his footing, using exposed roots to stop his boots and keep his balance until he was within a few feet of where she lay. The sun moved in and out of the clouds, casting sharp, moving shadows. She floated half submerged in a slurry of mud, water, and ice, the torso twisted to one side.

Two of the troopers followed him down.

"Stay back from there," one of them yelled.

He was in no mood and found his badge, "You stupid assholes. Who told you to do that?"

The troopers stopped a few feet away.

He glanced down at Petrova. The sharp angles of her neck and legs signaled she was dead.

"Who the crap are you?" one of the troopers asked.

He turned back toward them and shook his head in disgust. "I'm the federal agent who's going to kick your sorry ass for killing the only lead I had."

CHAPTER THIRTY-SEVEN

PRINCE EDWARD ISLAND, CANADA
10:49 P.M.

ZORIN TIGHTENED THE STRAPS FOR HIS PARACHUTE. WHEN HE
was first trained back in the 1970s the equipment had been rudimen-
tary, unreliable, and often dangerous. More than one of his fellow students had been injured or killed. Parachuting was not popular among
KGB trainees, but he'd loved it, recording nearly a hundred jumps.
He'd specifically requested a chute designed for higher altitudes and
better maneuverability. Not quite military quality, but close enough.
Jumping at night was problematic from the start, but once the chute
opened it was like any other fall, especially with the advent of night-
vision goggles, a luxury that he'd not had the chance to experience
much in the past.

The Gulfstream had made it across the Atlantic in good time.
They'd found North America at Newfoundland, their course adjusted
from west to south, straight for New York. Over the Gulf of St. Lawrence the pilots had radioed to Canadian air traffic control that they
were having trouble with pressurization and requested permission to
drop under three thousand meters for a few minutes so they could deal
with the problem. The ground had balked at first, then consented, most
likely concerned that to refuse could court disaster.

He snugged the helmet on his head.

His gun was safely tucked inside a knapsack beneath the black
jumpsuit that had been waiting with the chute, as were his last bits of

money. Not much. Maybe $5,000 U.S., which should be plenty. The Russian rubles he'd left aboard, useless to him from this point on. Google Maps had provided a location for the jump along the north shore. Prince Edward Island was huge, stretching 220 kilometers east to west, 64 kilometers at its widest north to south. He knew the place. A low-lying hump of red sandstone and fertile soil, it was home to about 140,000 people, many descendants of the original 18th-century French and British colonists. He'd visited its capital, Charlottetown, back in his KGB days.

"We're approaching the shore," the pilot told him over the intercom.

Only a quarter moon shone tonight. The cabin had already been depressurized, the lights extinguished. The idea was to stray slightly off course, which normally would be directly over Nova Scotia, veering fifty kilometers west directly over Prince Edward. Once he was gone, the pilots would correct the deviation, blaming it on their pressurization problem, and hope no one questioned them.

"Less than a minute," the pilot said.

He grabbed the door's latch and wrenched it open. The heavy panel dropped inward on its brackets, angled to a full ninety degrees. Frigid air rushed inside, but he was wearing three layers, which included a coat beneath the jumpsuit, gloves, a full balaclava, and a helmet with goggles. One of the pilots appeared in the flight cabin doorway and raised two hands, displaying ten fingers. Force of habit caused him to check the buckles of the chute at all the control points one more time.

Everything seemed fine.

Only five fingers were now displayed.

Three.

Two.

One.

He slapped his arms across his chest.

And jumped.

Bitter cold air assaulted him, but the layering was doing its job. He knew the math. At three seconds out he was moving eighty kilometers per hour. Six seconds later his speed would increase to two hundred kilometers per hour. The whole jump should take no more than three minutes, tops. Everything in the air happened fast, the experience akin to falling nose-first into a wind tunnel. His forehead tightened. His cheeks beneath the balaclava's wool seemed as if they were running off his face.

He'd not felt those sensations in a long while.

But he liked them.

Through the night-vision goggles he saw that he was still out over the Gulf of St. Lawrence, but forward velocity was quickly driving him toward shore. He carried no altimeter, but he'd been trained the old way. Know your starting point, then count down, the idea being to pull the chute at 1,500 meters, then settle into a soft glide and work your way to a reasonably safe landing.

He threw his arms and legs out, stopping his body from spinning, leading with his belly. So much could go wrong. Tangled lines. High winds. Canopy tears. Most were fixable, provided they could be solved before 500 meters. After that, nothing really mattered since there wasn't enough time to do much of anything except die.

The jump was going great.

Ahead, past a narrow beach, he saw the blurs of cliffs, rock faces, then the jagged outlines of treetops that blanketed the shore. Large boulders, like the teeth of an animal, protruded in a ragged line down the ridges. He had to avoid those. The clearing he sought, a meadow, opened just to the right, an area that the satellite map he'd accessed online noted as being about a hectare, more than enough of a target.

The alarm in his brain sounded.

1,500 meters.

He pulled the cord and the chute exploded upward.

A violent jerk and loud pop immediately signaled trouble.

The idea was to have a square, stable, steerable canopy. Instead, his had folded onto itself like a popped balloon, the cords shooting upward twisted and tangled among themselves. His body spun like a puppet on its strings. A blooming canopy meant a slower, manageable descent, but he was falling faster, twirling along the way, blood rushing toward his feet thanks to the centrifuge effect. If he didn't stop spinning he'd black out. He carried a reserve chute, but it could prove useless since its lines might also become entangled with the disabled main chute.

He had to drop the main away.

He reached for the cutaway handle, but the force of the malfunction had yanked it upward, out of reach.

His internal clock told him that five hundred meters was coming fast.

Just a few more seconds until the ground found him.

Luckily, he'd been taught how to fight panic and think clearly. He decided there was only one option.

No matter the risk.

He released the reserve chute.

The packet shot upward, opening fully, only minimally affected by the tangled main lines. His drop slowed, as did the spinning, enough that he could grab his bearings and play with the lines. Two canopies, only one hungry for air, swung above him on opposite sides, flying him in a steep downplane to the ground.

Way too fast.

He twisted the reserve lines and began to steer his fall, angling toward the meadow. Google Maps had revealed that the national park stretched forty kilometers along the north shore. Not a light burned in sight, nothing but forested wilderness all around, which had seemed like a good thing. Now, if he was hurt, it could be days or weeks before he was found.

Three hundred meters to go.

He crossed the beach, now fully over dry land, zeroing in on the meadow.

Two hundred meters.

He fought ground rush, that alarming feeling of the earth coming toward you uncontrollably.

Fifty meters.

The trees were just below. This was a place of old growth, the stands thick and tall. He quickly decided that he should land using his whole body, as opposed to only feet, since he was moving fast enough to snap a knee. He yanked on the canopy lines and tried to create more drag.

The meadow appeared ahead.

Flat, open, inviting.

But also trouble since it was cold, hard earth.

He decided to make use of the trees, tugging on the canopy lines and adjusting his fall so that he brushed the tops of the ones near the meadow's edge. His feet caught on the limbs and the drag had the desired effect as he slowed. He angled the chute farther down and dropped more so his boots kept brushing limb after limb, which hampered his ability to keep control. But once he passed the last few trees and found the meadow he was definitely moving slowly enough that he was able to fall the remaining few meters and use his legs to absorb the impact.

His body collapsed to the ground, the chutes fluttering to rest behind him.

He stared back up into the sky.

The Gulfstream was long gone.

Surely, the bastard from the charter company had sabotaged the main chute. Jump accidents were rare. The charter company most likely had feared what he might have in mind once on the ground and wanted nothing traced back to them. So they took his money, flew him halfway across the globe, then made sure he would not survive. Not a soul would have ever known the difference. Just a corpse on the ground or, even better, in the water. How it got there would never be explained. At least they'd allowed him to jump to the right spot. Most likely assuming it didn't matter. He'd be dead regardless. Any other time he would go back and kill them all, but that was no longer possible.

He had a mission.

CHAPTER THIRTY-EIGHT

STEPHANIE SAT IN THE WAITING ROOM, WHERE SHE'D BEEN FOR the past few hours. An ambulance had rushed Peter Hedlund from his house to the nearest hospital. A lie, that she was with the Justice Department, had gained her a ride along with Hedlund. The local police had arrived just as they were leaving and followed them to the emergency room. She'd explained about Anya Petrova and Luke Daniels and the officers had reported about a hot pursuit on a local highway. Two hours ago she'd been told that Petrova was dead. When the locals started asking more and more questions, she'd referred them to the White House and the Office of the Chief of Staff. The people there, she'd said, would be more than happy to provide answers.

The day's events weighed on her.

Cotton in trouble. Speaking to Cassiopeia again. Russians. Soviets. Litchfield. Being fired. Hedlund shot. Now Petrova dead.

The bright spot had come when she'd checked in with the White House and Edwin had told her that Cotton was on the move with Cassiopeia, headed for Canada on Aleksandr Zorin's trail. Thank goodness he was okay. She could always count on Cotton to be right there when she needed him. And Cassiopeia, too, who now seemed to be fully back in the saddle. Edwin had also explained all that Cotton had reported, which filled in the gaps in what she already knew. A picture was emerging—an incomplete one, but an image nonetheless.

She heard a familiar stamp of boots to tiles and looked up to see Luke approaching down the hall. He also looked beat.

"Sorry about that," he said to her.

They were alone in the waiting room.

"The locals got overenthusiastic," he said. "But I got this."

He displayed a cell phone.

"Looks like a prepaid unit bought on the fly," he said. "It was switched off."

She told him what she knew about Cotton and Zorin and nukes.

"Looks like the players are all making their way toward us," he said.

That it did.

"How's Hedlund?" he asked.

She explained that one bullet tore into his rib cage, the other grazing across his right shoulder. He'd been lucky, as the chest round could have proved fatal. He'd been taken straight into surgery, his wife appearing a couple of hours ago. She was now with her husband in his recovery room.

"Quite a surprise that Hedlund was ex-FBI," Luke said. "He got that gun when he was upstairs in his bedroom." He shook his head. "Friggin' Lone Ranger tryin' to save the day."

"It's a miracle he's not dead."

"He's also a liar."

That caught her attention.

Luke fished another cell phone from his pocket. "It's Hedlund's. I took it from him before he headed into the library. He made a call with it while upstairs."

She listened as he told her what happened—*"Nothing here to find"*—then asked the obvious, "Who did he call?"

"I got the number from the phone's memory. It's a 703 area code."

Virginia. Near DC.

"His contacts list it for a Larry Begyn."

"I'm assuming you've checked on who that is?" she asked.

"Lawrence Paul Begyn is the current president general of the Society of the Cincinnati."

"I wonder what they're hiding," she muttered out loud.

"Enough that ex-G-man Hedlund got his gun for a fight."

She stared at Luke and nodded.

"We now know there's nothing at Hedlund's house," he said. "But there's obviously *something* to find. That Tallmadge journal. Petrova knew exactly what to ask for."

"It's time we bring in the big guns."

She saw Luke understood what that meant.

"I assume Uncle Danny already knows the details up to now."

She nodded. "We'll head back to DC, right after we do one more thing."

He clearly knew what that meant, too.

"Lead the way. I can't wait to hear what he has to say."

They found Peter Hedlund awake, sitting up in his bed, his wife, introduced as Leah, at his side.

"You do realize," Stephanie said to him, "that what you did was foolishness."

"I've been in worse situations."

"With me in the middle?"

"You know how to handle yourself."

She handed his cell phone back. "Tell me what it is Larry Begyn knows. And I don't have the time for any more lies."

Comprehension registered in Hedlund's eyes, a look that seemed to signal cooperation.

"Can this wait?" his wife asked. "He's been shot."

"I wish it could, but it can't. And if your husband had been honest with me to start with, we wouldn't be here. But, after all, he is the Keeper of Secrets." She was in no mood for more nonsense. "The woman who shot you is dead. But she knew about that Tallmadge journal. I need you to tell me what it is."

"How did she die?"

"Acting like an idiot," Luke said.

Hedlund got the message and held up a conciliatory hand. "All right. You made your point. I'll tell you."

ZORIN GATHERED UP THE PARACHUTES, THEN STEPPED OUT OF his jumpsuit. Beneath he wore a coat, black trousers, and a black turtleneck shirt. He needed to hide the bundle so it would not be found anytime soon and decided somewhere in the woods would be best. So he plunged into the trees and found a spot beneath a fallen trunk. He also left the helmet and night-vision goggles, as neither would be necessary any longer. Everything he needed he carried in his pockets or in the knapsack. If something else was required, he'd find it along the way. At the moment transportation was tops on his list. On the drop in he'd spotted a series of cabins not far away, all dark to the night, which could mean they were empty. But he decided to check them out anyway and headed off in their direction.

Night movement came with an assortment of challenges. He'd been taught to feel the ground with his toes before planting his heel, not disturbing anything along the way. Steps should be short, the feet tilted slightly, one hand out ahead. He'd not gripped his gun but, if necessary, he'd keep the weapon tight to his chest, finger on the trigger. The idea was to be aware and stay alert, head turning like a machine—oiled, regular, and thorough—ready for anything.

He found the road that ran adjacent to the shore and followed it east for a couple of kilometers until he came to the cluster of cabins in a clearing among the trees. A sharp tang of salt air filled his nostrils. His greatest fear was that a dog or two might alert anybody nearby to his presence, but the cold air remained silent, disturbed only by the muffled booms of waves that crashed in the distance against an unseen beach. By Siberian standards the cold here was more springlike.

He counted eight cabins, each rectangular, wood-sided with a gabled roof. All were dark. Three had vehicles parked to the side, one in particular drawing his attention. An older pickup truck. He'd been largely out of touch for twenty-five years. A lot had changed with cars since the day when he could hot-wire one in less than a minute. Electronic ignitions, computers, security chips—none of those existed in his day. But that old pickup might be just what he was looking for.

He hustled over and saw that the driver's door was unlocked. He carefully opened it and reached beneath the steering column, exposing the key cylinder. In the darkness he could see little, but he did not need to. Touch worked just fine and he found the customary three sets

of wires. He yanked the pairs free, keeping them apart. Each represented a different position for the key. One for lights only, another for
radio, the final pair triggering ignition. Which was which? That was
trial and error. He found the utility knife he'd brought and stripped
the ends of all six wires.

The first pair he matched together momentarily lit the headlights,
which he quickly extinguished by breaking the connection. The next
pair sparked when touched, then fired the starter, which coughed the
engine to life. He knew that holding the exposed wires together risked
a shock, one that could be nasty, so he carefully separated the wires
and stretched them as far apart as possible. No time to shield them.
He'd just have to be careful.

So far so good.

He leaped inside the truck and sped away.

A quick glance at his watch narrowed the countdown.

38 hours left.

CHAPTER THIRTY-NINE

THE AMERICAN REVOLUTION OFFICIALLY ENDED IN 1783, BUT HOSTILITIES with England continued for many more decades. The British covertly supported Indian aggression along America's borders, trying to prevent any further western expansion. They forbade some exports to their West Indies colonies. When England and France went to war, the United States proclaimed its neutrality, even though France continued to hold a special place in American hearts thanks to its support during the Revolution. But when Britain ultimately blockaded French ports, the Embargo Act of 1807 halted trade with England. In response, the Royal Navy started boarding American ships and impressing sailors into its service.

That's when Canada again became important.

During the Revolution the Continental army had invaded, the idea being to convince the French-speaking Canadians to join in the fight against the British. But the Americans were soundly defeated in 1775 during the Battle of Quebec. At the 1783 Paris peace talks negotiators tried in vain to have all of Quebec province ceded over as war spoils, but that effort failed. America's desire for Canada was so strong that in the Articles of Confederation, adopted in 1781, one provision provided that British-held Canada, if it so desired, could join the new Union automatically, without a vote from the other states.

Tensions finally reached a boiling point in 1812 when the United States declared war on England. President James Madison and his war hawks in Congress urged that the time had come to defend the country's recently won independence. But the vote to go to war only narrowly passed. Critics condemned "Mr. Madison's War" as a foolhardy adventure, motivated less by patriotism and more by expansionism.

And the offensive began with an invasion of Canada.

Madison's Democratic-Republican party drew much of its support from the rural South, along with the territories stretching up the Mississippi basin to the Great Lakes. Frontier inhabitants were eager to claim Canada because they suspected the British there of arming Indian tribes. People at the time thought the invasion would be easy, that ordinary Canadians would welcome them as liberators. Thomas Jefferson predicted that the entire campaign "will be a mere matter of marching."

But that proved not to be the case.

The American forces were poorly equipped and poorly numbered with fewer than 7,000 men, most of them untrained and lacking in discipline. They were led by an aging general named William Hull, whose own subordinates damned him as an imbecile. After an abortive foray across the Detroit River into Canada, Hull was duped into thinking that a vast Indian war party was heading his way. So he surrendered his 2,500 troops to a much smaller British force. With the war only a few months old, the entire Michigan territory fell into enemy hands.

And for the second time, an invasion to the north failed.

After 1815, America abandoned its hope that Canada would become a part of the United States. Peace reigned between the two neighbors. By the 20th century, at a length of 5,522 miles, Canada and the United States shared the longest nonmilitarized border in the world. Neither one gave the other a bad thought.

Except during World War II.

With the Battle of Britain raging in late 1940, the prospect of Hitler taking England loomed large. The United States had proclaimed its neutrality, as both the American people and Congress wanted to stay out of the war. But Roosevelt saw it another way.

He deemed it inevitable that America would enter the fight. Intelligence reports at the time indicated that one plan Hitler imagined was to place the abdicated Edward VIII back on the British throne to rule as a Nazi puppet. Edward's sympathies toward Germany were no secret. Hitler also wanted control of Britain's Commonwealth of Nations—Australia, New Zealand, South Africa, India, Canada, and an assortment of other colonies across the globe. Though by a 1931 act of Parliament, Canada, Australia, New Zealand, South Africa, and Ireland were independent of British control, many entanglements with London remained.

For the United States, securing Canada became a priority to prevent it from becoming a staging area for a German attack. Beaches were identified that could be used for amphibious landings. A strategy of a preemptive takeover was devised. A 94-page document outlined plans for stopping overseas reinforcements by taking the port of Halifax, then seizing the hydroelectric power plants at Niagara Falls while the navy blockaded all of Canada's Atlantic and Pacific ports. The navy would also take control of the Great Lakes. The army was to invade on three fronts–advancing from North Dakota toward Winnipeg, moving from Vermont to capture Montreal and Quebec, then advancing from the upper Midwest to take over the rich mines of Ontario. A military convoy was to travel to Vancouver, and simultaneously all British colonies in the Caribbean were to be seized. The goal was to claim Canada, preparing its provinces to become territories and states upon a declaration of peace.

Stephanie listened in amazement to Peter Hedlund.

"The society developed the invasion plans in 1812," Hedlund said. "We were charged with the task by James Madison. He wanted it done in secret. At that time most of our members were Revolutionary War veterans. Some even fought in the 1775 Canadian campaign. Our plan was viable, but the army and navy were simply incapable of executing it. We just weren't the military power we thought ourselves to be."

"That's ancient history," Luke said. "What about invading Canada in the 1940s?"

"We prepared that plan, too, for the War Department, in secret.

Roosevelt was familiar with the society. Some of his closest aides were members. He liked the fact that we kept the Revolutionary War alive through descendants. He was told of our work during the War of 1812. Like Madison, Roosevelt wanted to be ready, and he did not want the War Department involved with drawing up the plans to invade an ally. So he came to us and we worked up a workable strategy out of the limelight."

She was becoming impatient. "What is the Tallmadge journal?"

Hedlund shifted slightly in his bed. His wife stood on the opposite side from Stephanie and Luke, her look of concern undaunted. Stephanie wondered how much of this she already knew, as Hedlund had not asked her to leave the room.

Earlier, when Hedlund had explained about Benjamin Tallmadge to Petrova she'd recognized the name immediately. He'd served in the Continental army and led what came to be known as the Culper Ring, a network of spies that successfully operated inside British-occupied New York. He ultimately became George Washington's chief of intelligence, in essence the first American spymaster. After the war he served in Congress, and now Stephanie knew he'd also been a founding member of the Society of Cincinnati.

"Tallmadge headed our efforts in 1812 on drawing those Canadian invasion plans for Madison," Hedlund said. "He recorded his work in a journal. It's one of only a handful of sensitive documents the society ever possessed, passed down through the Keeper of Secrets. It's nothing sinister, really. We just thought it best that it never be available for public inspection."

And she could understand why. "That image of a benign social society of military officers would be shattered if the public had known you were making war plans."

Hedlund nodded. "Exactly. Everyone at the time thought it best to keep that to ourselves."

"That'll make for a great History Channel show one day," Luke said. "But on the phone, in your bedroom, before you went Batman on us, you told a guy named Begyn that it was *starting again.*' What did you mean?"

Hedlund smiled. "You're a good agent. On top of things. Observant."

"I'm shooting to be an Eagle Scout by summer. Just a few more merit badges to go."

Normally she wouldn't tolerate that Tennessee sarcasm but she could understand how he felt. Petrova was dead and this evasive man was now their only lead forward.

"We had a problem with Brad Charon," Hedlund said. "Brad was a great guy. I liked him, but he had a tendency to talk too much."

"Which is not a good thing for a Keeper of Secrets," she said.

"Hardly. About thirty years ago there was an incident. We learned that Brad had opened up our secret archives to a nonmember. Believe me when I say this, I don't know the details. I know only that it happened and Brad was removed from his post. And if that were the end of the story, then all would be fine. Instead, we had another breach. One we hoped was forgotten. But apparently, it's not."

"And Begyn?" Luke asked Hedlund again.

"He knows it all."

Not good enough. "What specifically do we ask him?"

"It's quite simple. Ask him about what the Founding Fathers wanted Canada to become after the Revolution. What we code-named the War of 1812 Canadian invasion plan. And what Roosevelt called his plan to invade during World War II. All three carried the same label."

She waited.

"The 14th Colony."

CHAPTER
FORTY

Zorin was making excellent time.

He was familiar with smartphones and GPS mapping, even the apps that came on the phones that provided precise directions, but he still preferred the old-fashioned ways. He'd stopped at a seaside motel and retrieved a map of the island, which provided directions to Charlottetown. The roads were pitch dark and lightly traveled, the trip southeast taking less than an hour. He was careful with his driving, keeping to the speed limit and obeying all signs. The last thing he needed was a nosy policeman to interfere.

He had an address for Jamie Kelly and located the street on the map. Thankfully, he was no stranger to the island. Its eastern half was heavily farmed and the most populated, the coasts dotted with countless fishing ports. The western half loomed a bit wilder, more forested, less settled. The narrow, central strip, where Charlottetown sat, stayed the most developed. The union of Canada had been born here, the confederacy arising from a famous 1864 conference. He'd visited Province House, in central Charlottetown, where that occurred.

He'd spent three years working out of Ottawa, then Quebec City, one of thirteen officers assigned to the Soviet-Canadian Friendship Society, ostensibly created to promote goodwill and cultural exchanges, but actually a KGB front. Stealing Canada's national secrets had never been a Soviet priority. If it had, the task would have been relatively simple given the ineptitude of the Canadian Security Intelligence Service. In his day that agency was less than a decade old, a baby in the spy business, no match for the much more mature KGB. Besides, it had been easy to exploit the countless pro-Canadians who despised the United States. He'd scored several coups, learning about American Arctic activities, means the United States and Canada used to track Soviet *Typhoon*-class submarines, and obtaining underwater maps of the northern seafloor, invaluable to Soviet submariners. He'd worked his job with diligence, living there alone, his wife and son staying behind in the Soviet Union. Unlike others who accompanied their spouses overseas, his wife had harbored no desire to live in the West.

He slowed the truck as he entered the Charlottetown historic district. Trees bare to winter lined wide streets. Striking churches, Victorian architecture, and clapboard houses reflected its British heritage, but he noticed how trendy cafés and modern shops now dominated. Different from his last visit so long ago. Reflective, he thought, of changing times, which suddenly made him feel old.

Many of the eateries remained open, enjoying a brisk Friday-evening business. He turned off the main boulevard and passed the Great George, the hotel where he'd stayed back in the 1980s. He noticed that another boulevard was named University, which had to be significant, but he wasn't interested in the college. Only in one of its part-time employees, and Jamie Kelly lived in Stratford, an adjacent town just past the Hillsborough River.

He followed the map across a long bridge, past a dark ribbon of wide water that stretched straight as a highway. Then he veered south on a two-laned road and headed for the address. He drove like a robot, his mind numb, body automatically reacting to the conditions. The pastoral neighborhood he found contained more stylish Victorian homes on spacious wooded lots. Lights burned in only a few windows. The address he sought sat at the end of the lane, a two-story, brick-fronted square with bowed bay windows top and bottom. He grabbed his bearings and determined that the house faced east, the river maybe a few hundred meters behind to the west through the trees.

He parked the truck on the street and noticed that lights burned

inside Kelly's house on both floors. No mailbox or anything else identified the occupant. Only a house number. He stepped from the truck
and grabbed his knapsack, deciding not to leave it outside unattended.

Whether trouble awaited him he did not know.

But he was ready.

MALONE ABSORBED EVERY DETAIL OF THE PICKUP TRUCK STOP-
ping in front of Jamie Kelly's residence. Cassiopeia sat beside him in
the car that had been waiting for them at the local airport when their
two French fighter jets landed. Edwin Davis, true to his word, had
taken care of all ground preparations. They'd been delayed a little in
flight by some weather over Greenland, but had still arrived a solid half
hour before Zorin's plane passed over the island.

Canadian air traffic controllers, working with the Royal Mounted
Police, had watched the jet carefully, noting a deviation in its flight path
that avoided Nova Scotia and found Prince Edward Island's north
coast. Whether Zorin jumped was impossible to say, but Malone had
assumed all along that would be his path. Less chance of discovery that
way, even though a night leap from a fast-moving aircraft would take
every skill of a *spetsnaz*-trained warrior, plus a little luck. If the jump
somehow killed Zorin, then this was all over. If not, the ex-KGB operative would come straight here.

And that's exactly what had happened.

"It's him," he said to Cassiopeia, studying Zorin through night-
vision binoculars that had been waiting in the car, along with two
Berettas and spare magazines.

They'd parked in one of the driveways lining the long street, hoping the occupants of the dark house were not home. That way they were
just another unnoticed car, one of several in other driveways, nothing
to arouse Zorin's suspicions. A small slit from an open window leaked
in cold air and kept the windows from fogging.

"What now?" she asked.

He slid down in the seat, leaning his head against the door frame.

"We wait."

ZORIN APPROACHED THE FRONT DOOR, BRIGHT ON BOTH SIDES from curtained sidelights. The porch was columned and covered by an extension that jutted from the second story, the eight windows on three sides above glowing a burnt amber from inside lights. What sounded like opera played beyond the door.

He knocked loud enough to be heard.

The music dimmed.

He heard the scrape of soles on a hard floor and the sound of a bolt being withdrawn. The man who peered out through the rectangular strip of light between the door and the jamb was mid-sixties, a short gray beard adorning his chin. The last time he'd seen the face, in the safe house with Andropov, the hair had been black. Now it was thin, gray, and receding. The jowls bore a solid two-day stubble, the teeth still showing a tiny gap between the front two, just as he remembered.

"Hello, comrade," he said.

The Russian who'd assumed the Western alias of Jamie Kelly appraised him with a studied glare.

Then a chilling smile came to Kelly's thin lips.

One that signaled recognition.

"Aleksandr Zorin. I've been waiting a long time for you to come."

CASSIOPEIA WATCHED AS ZORIN ENTERED THE HOUSE AND THE door closed to the night. She was glad to be back with Cotton. This was where she belonged. They'd yet to have an opportunity to fully talk, only the short exchange back in France. Everything was happening so fast, and they'd not been alone, except for the past half hour here in the car. So she'd offered him no excuses, made no appeals for sympathy or forbearance, just acknowledged again that she'd been wrong, opening herself to a rebuff that he could have easily delivered.

But he hadn't.

Instead, he'd accepted her admissions with grace and acknowledged mistakes of his own.

"Looks like the gang's all here," Cotton said.

She knew exactly what they were facing, thanks to Cotton's call to the White House. Like a hunt, she'd thought. The kind her father once enjoyed. Several times he'd taken her with him to watch as he gave the deer a wide berth, following, but not too close, just enough to know exactly what the animal might do, waiting for the right moment to take a shot. And though hunting game was not her thing, she'd loved the time with her father. She and Cotton had followed this deer all the way from Siberia, even stopping another hunter from killing him.

"I'm assuming," she said, "that we're not just going to sit here."

He smiled at her. "As impatient as ever."

"We could make out?"

"Now, that's a thought. And as tempting as the prospect is, we have a job to do." He reached to the backseat and grabbed a duffel bag that had been there when they first climbed into the car.

"I wasn't sure what would happen, but I decided to be prepared."

He unzipped the top and rummaged through, removing a small electronic unit along with a cord. "We'll need to attach this microphone to one of the windows. Then we can listen in. Not exactly state-of-the-art, but it should get the job done."

"I assume one of us will be doing the attaching?"

"Seems like the perfect job for you."

"And you?"

"I'll be watching your backside."

She tossed him a mischievous smile of her own.

"I bet you will."

CHAPTER
FORTY-ONE

Luke drove the Escape as he and Stephanie left Annapolis. Peter Hedlund would remain in the hospital for a couple more days.

"I made sure that Petrova's death would remain a secret," he told her. "The Maryland State Police agreed to cooperate, *after* the Secret Service intervened and slapped national security all over it."

He liked having the White House as an ally.

"They'll be saying publicly only that the victim is unidentified."

He could see that his former boss was tired, and could sympathize. It was approaching midnight and they'd had a long day.

"I promised Fritz Strobl I'd return his car in one piece," she said. "I appreciate your not wrecking it."

"I assume we're going to see Larry Begyn?" he asked.

"First thing tomorrow. I think we both need some sleep. Cotton has Zorin under control, and things here are at an impasse. I called Edwin and told him that some rest seems in order."

On that he could not argue.

Her cell phone vibrated.

She checked the display and he heard her say, "This is not going to be good."

She answered the call.

"You're ignoring me," Danny Daniels said through the speaker.

"Your chief of staff knows it all."

"I want to hear it from you. Directly."

"You're not going to like it."

"You have no idea how much I do not like at the moment."

Luke listened as she recounted the events of the past few hours, ending with Petrova's death and Hedlund's revelations. His uncle then told them the details about Cotton being in Canada with Zorin. For Luke, any man who could make a night jump into unknown territory from a high-speed jet commanded a high measure of respect. He'd done it twice while a Ranger, both harrowing experiences.

"But we've got a new problem," the president said.

He didn't like the solemn tone.

"Moscow has gone nuts."

MALONE LED THE WAY AS HE AND CASSIOPEIA CROSSED THE DARK street toward Jamie Kelly's house. Edwin Davis had located the address and provided some sketchy background info.

Kelly was sixty-four years old and once worked at Georgetown University as an assistant dean of students, serving the university with distinction from 1993 to 2005. He then moved to Canada, settling on Prince Edward Island, finding part-time work at the local university. No criminal record. His credit history was exemplary, and he'd never appeared on any watch list or radar screen. If Kelly had indeed been a Soviet mole, he'd apparently been damn good at what he did since not even a hint of suspicion had ever been directed his way. Once the Cold War was long gone, historians had learned that the KGB infiltrated nearly every society around the world. The United States ranked as their top priority, so there was little doubt officers were there. Occasionally, a name would pop up, an identity revealed, but by and large those assets had come and gone undetected. Little of that mattered anymore since, in theory, Russia and the United States were no longer enemies. Sometimes, though, that amicability could be difficult to see since old habits tended to die hard.

The crisp night air chilled his nostrils and parched his throat. Both he and Cassiopeia wore clothing loaded with Gore-Tex the French had provided. Darkness offered excellent cover, the quiet rural neighbor-hood bedded down for the night.

They found the end of a thick hedge that bordered the house and carefully made their way down a narrow alley between bushes and wall to the light from a ground-floor window. A murmur of voices could be heard inside. He risked a quick peek and saw Zorin and another man, with a goatee, sitting in a parlor. He nodded and watched as Cassiopeia found the listening device and carefully pressed its suction cup to the window's lower-left corner. Its cord was already plugged into the receiver.

She inserted an earpiece and signaled that all was good.

He retreated.

But kept alert for any trouble.

ZORIN ADMIRED KELLY'S HOME, WHICH WAS LIKE A DOUBLE house with rooms laid out symmetrically on either side of a central hall. Wooden details such as ceiling rosettes, cornices, fluted molding, and arches all seemed crafted with skill and precision. The décor was like-wise impressive, with lots of art on the walls and sculptures on the tables. The room where they sat in overstuffed chairs had a bay window that faced the front of the house and one on the side. His knap-sack rested on the floor near his feet. Radiators and a raging fire inside a period hearth provided welcomed heat, and he caught a faint scent of eucalyptus in the warm air.

"It's been a long time," Kelly said in perfect English.

Small talk did not interest him. "Why have you been waiting for me?"

"I miss the old days. Do you miss them?"

He told himself that this man was no amateur. Instead, he'd been successfully embedded deep within Western society, which required a measure of patience and skill. Of the three, he'd always known this one would be the greatest challenge. "The old days are why I am here."

"I thought you were dead," Kelly said. "Nearly everyone else is gone.

It saddens me to think about them. We did some great things, Aleksandr."

"Do you live here alone?"

Kelly nodded. "It is my one regret. I never married. Too risky. There were lots of girls, most not smart or pretty, but willing. Momentary diversions. But I'm a bit old for that now. How about you? Did you find someone?"

"My wife died," he said, keeping Anya to himself.

"It's not good, for either of us, to have no one. I spend most of my time reading."

"Why do you live in Canada?"

"I visited here once many years ago and decided that if I survived and wasn't shot or jailed, that this would be where I would retire. You understand what I'm saying, don't you? No way to know when or if they'll come for you. No way to know who compromised or gave you up. They just appear, with guns and badges, and then you disappear. Amazingly, that hasn't happened to me. But I have to say, to hear your knock a few minutes ago sent a chill through me. It's a bit late for visitors."

"You live well," he said, motioning to the air of affluence the room projected.

And what he'd not said hung in the air.

Like a capitalist.

"When the Soviet Union disappeared, I thought it time for me to blend totally into the West."

"You could have come back home."

"To what? Nothing I knew existed anymore."

On that they agreed. "So you became the enemy?"

Kelly smiled. "I wish it were that simple, Aleksandr. To everyone around me I was an American, so I simply kept playing the part."

"You were sent to spy."

Kelly shrugged. "That was my original mission, and the position at the university in DC gave me access to a lot of people. I knew an assistant to the chairman of the Senate Select Committee on Intelligence, another at the Rand Corporation, a friend worked at the Brookings Institute, and I had many colleagues in the State Department. I was the perfect mole, the last person you'd ever suspect as a spy. I did my job, until my job mattered no longer."

Time to get to the point. "Fool's Mate. Did you complete it?"

"And if I did, are you here to kill me, too?" Kelly's right hand slipped behind his back, beneath an untucked shirt, then reappeared holding a revolver. "You don't think I would answer the door this late at night and not be armed. I assure you, comrade, I will not be as easy as the other two."

Zorin sat still and tried to arrange his impressions into some sort of judgment. This had to go right. "How did you know?"

"Because I'm a trained officer of the KGB, just like you," Kelly said in Russian. "I pay attention."

Only here, within the confines of this home, shrouded in the lateness of the hour and a cold darkness outside, would either of them speak in their native tongue. But it seemed fitting, so he kept to it and declared, "I'm not here to kill you."

"Then what?"

"I want to complete what Andropov intended. That plan has remained dormant far too long."

"My orders were explicit. I was not to report anything, except to Andropov himself."

"My orders indicated that you were to report to me."

Kelly chuckled. "I would assume that was for your detriment."

Then he realized. Once he'd reported the success of Absolute Pin and Backward Pawn, he would have been eliminated.

Leaving only Kelly and Andropov.

With the bombs.

"I reported the second kill," he said. "But no one by then knew what I was talking about."

"Because Andropov was gone, and it didn't matter to anyone else. Surely, comrade, you can see that all of that is long past." Kelly's voice drifted off, as though weary of jousting at lost theories and forgotten ideals. "Nothing you and I ever knew still exists. In fact, all that may be left is you and I. We are probably the only people left on this planet who even know what Fool's Mate entails."

"I've waited a long time to pay the West back," he said. "They destroyed us, and I've searched hard for a way to extract some measure of retribution. Until yesterday, I did not know if you were still alive. So I have come a long way to enlist your help. You have the method and I can provide the means. Together, we can implement Fool's Mate."

Kelly was listening, that much was clear.

So he asked, "Do you remember what Andropov said that night, at the end, in the safe house?"

Kelly nodded. "Every word."

So did he.

"I want you to know, comrades, that what we are about to accomplish will strike America at its core. They think themselves so right, so perfect. But they have flaws. I've discovered two of those, and together, at the right time, we will teach America a lesson. Minimum effort, maximum effect. That's what we want, and that is precisely what you will deliver. This will be the most important operation we have ever undertaken. So, comrades, we must be ready when the moment comes."

"That moment has come," he said. "I don't know it all, but I know enough."

Kelly stayed silent, but lowered the gun.

A gesture of trust?

"You realize that it may no longer be possible," Kelly said.

He kept his optimism in check, but made clear, "It's a chance I'm willing to take. Are you?"

Cassiopeia had listened carefully, noticing the shift from English to Russian. The tone of the two men changed also, from cautious to conspiratorial. She'd also risked a look and saw as Kelly lowered a gun he'd been aiming at Zorin. She now realized that Cotton had assigned her the listening duties on the off chance that these two would revert to Russian.

Always thinking.

That was another thing she loved about him.

"I've been ready for more than twenty years," Kelly said. "I've done my duty."

"Then, comrade, tell me what I need to know."

MALONE KEPT ONE EYE ON CASSIOPEIA IN THE BUSHES NEAR THE house and the other on the street. He stood in the front lawn. His exhales hung before him in the cold air. Zorin certainly would not expect that he was being watched, and definitely not by the same American agent he'd last seen cuffed to an iron pipe in his basement. Their paths to this Canadian house had taken two totally different courses. Five suitcase-sized nuclear devices secreted away somewhere on American soil? He couldn't imagine how such a thing could have escaped detection but, unfortunately, border security in the 1980s and 1990s was nothing like today. Governments were not watching with the same intensity that the war of terrorism had taught was necessary. He'd reported all that he knew to the White House, so he assumed things were happening on Stephanie's end. But the quickest route to those hidden nukes seemed to be inside Jamie Kelly's house.

He checked his watch.

Friday had come and gone.

It was now early Saturday morning, Canadian time.

He heard a noise and turned to see a car creeping down the dark street. No headlights cut a swath of light. That was never a good thing. He was hidden behind the trunk of a sturdy oak, its width and girth signaling age. The ground just behind him sloped gently away from the house, toward the river, with more trees between here and there.

The car eased to a stop just short of Kelly's driveway, right behind Zorin's truck.

Four dark silhouettes emerged.

Each carried a short-barreled, automatic rifle.

CHAPTER
FORTY-TWO

STEPHANIE LED THE WAY INTO THE OVAL OFFICE, LUKE CLOSE ON her heels. Danny had told them to come straight here from Annapolis, sleep would have to wait. Inside she spotted the president and his chief of staff, along with one other visitor.

Nikolai Osin.

"Close the door," Danny said to Luke.

She noticed how the office had changed, the walls bare in places, the array of photographs and memorabilia that Danny liked to scatter everywhere all gone. Thirty-seven hours from now his time behind the Resolute desk would end and a new president would assume power, a man who would decorate the Oval Office to suit his own taste.

"Kind of depressing, isn't it?" Danny said, noticing her scan of the room.

"It's what makes this country great," she said.

Where other nations struggled with transitions of power, here it happened seamlessly. The Constitution originally provided that a president would be elected in November and assume office the following March 4. Eventually, those ensuing four months proved a problem. Seven states seceded during the time between Buchanan's exit and Lincoln's arrival. The Great Depression deepened waiting for Roosevelt to take control from Hoover. A lame-duck president, right or wrong, came to be perceived as no more than a default leader, his opinion irrelevant—while the incoming president suffered from not yet being legally empowered to do anything.

The 20th Amendment changed all that, ending a president's term precisely at noon on January 20. Acts of Congress followed that required the incoming president be provided a full transition team, access to all government services, training for new personnel, and funding to handle any and all costs. She knew what would happen at 12:01 P.M. Sunday, just after President Warner Scott Fox took the oath. Files and records that had not already been removed would immediately be purged. Access codes and passwords would change. New faces would flood into the White House and immediately assume their duties. Even the archives of speeches, press briefings, announcements, and videos concerning the past eight years of the Daniels administration would vanish from the White House's official website. By 12:05 the transition would be complete, without government ever losing a beat.

"That's the thing about us," Danny said. "So civilized. But it's still damn depressing. And I told my people, no pranks."

It had become commonplace for the old to leave a few surprises for the new. The most famous was when the Clinton people removed W's from keyboards before the younger George Bush took the oath.

She sat on a settee with Luke, facing Osin and Edwin Davis. Danny filled a high-backed Tennessee rocker. How many times had she been here? Too many to count. How many crises? More than her share.

And this could be her last.

"You do realize that I no longer carry a security clearance," she said. "I'm officially a civilian."

"And Edwin's looking for a job, Osin may get killed, Luke there, on Monday, has to go to work for somebody else, and I'm a lame duck. We all got our problems."

She caught his meaning and said, "What's going on, Nikolai?"

"There's a division within my government. It's been there for some time, but what's happening at the moment seems to have provided some acceleration."

She listened as he told her how he'd been initially instructed to involve the United States in looking for the archivist Vadim Belchenko. The order had come straight from the Kremlin.

"It was thought that, by involving you, it would be clear that we have no part in what Zorin might be doing. The people who issued that order wanted America to know this had nothing to do with Russia. Most likely, whatever Zorin is after doesn't even exist any longer, so there was deemed no harm in bringing you into the process. You would find Belchenko, stop Zorin, and all at our request."

"A way to show us you're to be trusted?" Luke asked.

Osin nodded. "Precisely. But there is another faction inside the Kremlin who did not agree with this course."

"The problem is," Danny said, "that what Zorin is after could damn well still be out there."

"And that other faction," Osin said, "wants what may be out there for themselves."

Earlier in the day, in the car, Osin had told her some of this. And Edwin had been coy the two times they'd talked on the phone since. That she could understand, not wanting to broadcast anything over an open cell line. But here, in one of the safest places on earth, she had to know. So she looked Osin's way and asked, "Tell me *exactly* what it is that's still out there."

"Five portable nuclear devices, planted by the KGB in the 1980s. The final part of an operation called Fool's Mate. These could still be operational."

Nothing about that sounded good.

"That division within my government," Osin said. "The main faction controls much of the SVR and the high military command. They are not progressives, or communists, but something worse. They have little allegiance to anything except what furthers their own personal goals. They live well within the new Russia. Once they learned of Fool's Mate and that it may still be active, they ordered your two agents gone. Then they ordered Zorin's plane be shot down. But your Mr. Malone interfered with that when he allowed Zorin to escape."

"Cotton and Cassiopeia are now on Prince Edward Island," Danny said. "Dealing with Zorin. I told them to bird-dog him. Give him space, but see where he's headed. We checked, the old KGB contact Zorin is looking for lives there. A damn sleeper spy who worked right here in this town for years, undetected."

"The problem now," Osin said, "is that my side of this internal struggle no longer controls things. The others have it, and there is no predicting what they might do. They see what Zorin is doing as advantageous to them, in some perverse way."

"What exactly is Fool's Mate?" she asked.

"I truly don't know. But whatever it entails, it's enough to attract an immense amount of attention."

"The bad thing," Danny said, "is they don't seem to need Zorin anymore, as evidenced by the kill order. That means they think they know enough. But we need him."

"It could be," Osin said, "that this man Kelly is the key. He alone might know the bombs' location. So far, I have no indication that anyone in Moscow has that information."

"How bad is this government division?" she asked.

"Significant enough that I am disobeying a direct order and telling you everything. This is compete and total madness. What they think can be accomplished by keeping all of this secret, I have no idea."

"Zorin apparently does," Luke said. "He's zeroed in on this for a reason. That man has a plan. He sent Petrova here for a specific purpose. Zorin knows far more than they think he does."

Osin seemed to agree. "It was unfortunate Petrova was killed. Do you have an alternative plan to discover what it is she was after?"

Though this man seemed forthcoming and truthful, thirty years in the intelligence business had taught her to keep things close. *Trust, but verify.* That was Reagan's motto and she did not disagree. And she'd noticed that no one else had mentioned the Tallmadge journal.

"Before you arrived," Edwin said, "Mr. Osin informed us that SVR assets here and in Canada have been placed on full alert."

"They intend to stop Zorin," Osin said. "Then, my guess is they will secure Kelly and whatever there is to find to themselves. That means everyone is at risk."

Her mind snapped to Canada. "Has Cotton been told?"

"I tried," Edwin said. "But I got only voice mail on his phone."

One thought shot through her brain.

Was that good or bad?

CHAPTER
FORTY-THREE

MALONE ASSESSED THE SITUATION AND DETERMINED THAT IMME-diate action was necessary. No delay. No caution. Just do something.
Now.

He found his gun, aimed at the window that Cassiopeia was standing below in the bushes, and fired one shot, making sure his bullet had an upward trajectory so that, once inside the house, it would find the ceiling.

ZORIN REACTED TO THE CRACKLE OF GLASS SHATTERING, DROP-ping from his chair and instinctively covering his head. He saw that Kelly had done the same, both men clearly surprised. He'd been lured to sleep by the calm and quiet. After all, on his approach to the house he'd seen or sensed nothing out of the ordinary.

Yet they were under attack.

CASSIOPEIA POCKETED THE MICROPHONE AND RECEIVER AND found her gun. The shot, then the window breaking had caught her off guard. She flattened onto the ground and stared out through the bushes, seeing Cotton pressed against a thick oak tree and four shadows approaching the house, then scattering in several directions, each carrying a weapon. She surmised that the first shot had to have been Cotton's way of alerting both her and Zorin.

But who were the new players?

No time at the moment to find out.

Cotton not calling out to her meant that he wanted her presence a secret, since his shot had definitely alerted the attackers that something was in their way.

Automatic weapons fire ripped through the night.

Rounds thudded into the tree where Cotton stood. Thankfully the thick trunk seemed as tough as Kevlar. But she wasn't going to lie around and let him take all the fire. Her keen eyes studied the four shadows, shifting thirty meters away.

Bare branches overhead stirred in the wind.

Two shadows moved into the open, making for other trees to use as cover.

Time to enter this fight.

MALONE HOPED HIS BULLET INTO THE HOUSE HAD WORKED. AT least Zorin and Kelly were now aware that something was happening outside, something that definitely involved them. The enemy of his enemy was a friend. Or at least he hoped that was the case. Regardless, they weren't sitting ducks any longer. He was taking fire from a shooter to his left, surely designed to keep him pinned while one or more of the others worked around behind him. Unfortunately, he had no way to sneak a look and see what was happening.

But his destruction of the window had also alerted Cassiopeia.

Who now started shooting from the bushes.

ZORIN MOTIONED THAT HE AND KELLY SHOULD FLEE THE PARLOR across the floor.

Stay low, he mouthed.

They belly-crawled toward an open archway that led back to the entrance foyer. More shots rang out from outside, but none of the rounds had found its way inside. He heard both automatic fire and single rounds.

Two different shooters?

Going at each other?

MALONE SAW ONE OF THE SHADOWS LURCH BACKWARD, THEN drop to the ground as if his joints had dissolved.

Score one for Cassiopeia.

She always could see great in the dark. The opportunity she'd provided allowed him to determine that two of the gunmen had flanked right, while the remaining one trotted left, toward Kelly's front door.

He opted for the two on his right.

Then the shadow to his left sprayed a scythe of rounds into the bushes where Cassiopeia lay hidden.

ZORIN ROLLED INTO THE ENTRANCE FOYER JUST AS BULLETS smacked into the exterior wall. The clapboard offered little resistance to the high-powered rounds and many whined their way inside, breaking more glass, ripping fabric, thudding into Sheetrock.

One of the lamps exploded in a shower of sparks.

He covered his head again.

Kelly lay to his left, behind a wall that supported a rounded arch overhead. Though the situation was dangerous, Zorin was back in his element, acutely aware of every sound and movement. His mind clicked off options as his hand crept into the knapsack and withdrew his weapon.

"I still have mine," Kelly said to him.

Someone kicked at the front door.

He looked up in alarm, then sprang to his feet and assumed a posi-tion adjacent to the jamb. The door burst open with a crash of splinter-ing wood, its lock wrenched from the casing. A man, dressed in a black jumpsuit, rushed inside the partially lit entrance, both hands tight on the grip of an automatic rifle. Zorin flexed his shoulders and twisted at the waist, ramming his palm forward with a straight arm, catching the man square in the face. Breath exploded outward and the intruder slumped forward, the hands clinging to the gun but the arms clawing for balance. A knee to the jaw sent the man into a wall, where the body slid along in a marionette's dance before collapsing to the hardwood floor. Adrenaline flooded through Zorin and knotted his stomach. He'd not done that in a long time. The intruder's head hung immobile, mouth agape, air being drawn in with short, rapid gasps. He had to know who these men were. He crouched low and dragged his prey away from the open front door, his gun jammed into the man's neck.

"Who sent you?" he asked.

No fear filled the man's eyes, but the face contorted in a helpless rage.

Kelly had assumed a position at the door, gun ready, as their train-ing had taught. Good to see that time had not dulled any instincts.

"Who?" he demanded again, yanking the man upright.

"Screw yourself, traitor."

Anger rushed through him.

Traitor?

Him?

Never.

He pulled the trigger and blew a bullet up through the man's jaw, the top of the skull exploding out in a vermillion spray.

He'd received his answer.

These men were official.

Probably SVR.

But who was shooting back at them?

CASSIOPEIA HAD ANTICIPATED WHAT MIGHT HAPPEN ONCE HER presence became known and had fled her position in the bushes, just after taking down one of the shooters. Good thing. A barrage erupted from another of the shadows, all the rounds directed at her former location. She was now at the rear of the house, crouched, waiting for an opportunity to help Cotton, who remained open and vulnerable. The shooting in her direction had stopped and she caught a glimpse of a shadow disappearing toward the front door.

That would be Zorin's problem.

Hers was to deal with the two who had turned their attention to Cotton.

MALONE DARTED LEFT AND DECIDED TO DO SOME FLANKING OF his own. Darkness was both an enemy and an ally, but his opponents carried weapons that spit out rounds by the hundreds. He had a Beretta with a full magazine, but unless he used his head it was no match for their firepower.

He hid behind a spindly fir, ears straining to catch sound, eyes searching for movement, anything that might betray their position. He kept his sights on the men and his ears on the bushes from which Cassiopeia should emerge. He hoped she'd had the foresight to get the hell out of there. She was smart and capable and never would she make that kind of rookie mistake. So he had to assume she was somewhere at the rear of the house. One of the shadows had hustled toward the front door and he'd heard wood being forced open, then a single round from inside, which might mean that Zorin or Kelly had scored a kill.

He rounded the tree, keeping the trunk between himself and where he thought danger may lurk. Everything had gone dead-quiet, which was not necessarily a good thing. A few lights had appeared in windows of the other houses on the street and he wondered if the police had been called.

One of the shadows revealed himself.

Thirty feet away.

Behind another tree.

A bright spittle of flame emitted as rounds zipped his way.

He pressed his body close to the thick trunk, counted to three, then swung around and fired twice, taking the shooter down.

"Drop the gun," a male voice said from behind.

He stood still.

"I will not say again. Drop the gun."

He had no choice, so he released his grip and allowed the weapon to fall into the grass. He turned around to see the fourth shooter, his rifle leveled and aimed.

ZORIN HEARD MORE SHOTS FROM OUTSIDE, THE SAME SEQUENCE of rapid fire, then single rounds.

"We must leave," he said to Kelly.

"I need to go upstairs for a moment. There are things we'll need."

He nodded and Kelly rushed off.

For the first time in a long while he was confused. No one should know that he was here. Only Belchenko could have betrayed him, and he doubted that was the case. And to whom? Belchenko hated the new Russia as much as he did, and there'd been no indication that Moscow was even aware of what he was doing. Only the American Malone had been a problem—which had raised red flags—but he was certainly long dead.

So who was outside?

He kept a close watch on the open front door, ready to shoot anything that moved. Kelly reappeared on the stairs and hustled down, holding a small travel bag. Like any good asset, he'd prepared for an emergency. Just like himself with his own knapsack.

"Money, passport, spare magazines," Kelly whispered. "Some other things we're going to need, too."

"Where are we going?"

"To finish Fool's Mate."

CASSIOPEIA REALIZED THAT COTTON REMAINED VULNERABLE.
She'd heard more shooting, especially the two single rounds. Then
she heard a voice that was not Cotton's ordering for a gun to drop. She
used that moment to swing back around the house and follow the
hedge line toward where two shadows stood, one facing her way,
the other with his back in her direction. She stayed low and led with
her weapon, keeping her steps light. A freshened breeze, which helped
mask her approach, caused limbs overhead to shake in protest.

"Who do you work for?" the voice said.

"I could ask you the same thing."

Cotton answering.

The tone louder, meaning he was the one facing her.

"You do realize," Cotton said, "that you're probably all alone here."

"As are you."

"Then let's figure out why we're both here. We might each learn
something."

Cotton could surely see her, so he was stalling. Good. Keep it up.
Just a few more meters.

"Zorin is in that house," Cotton said.

"He will not go far."

MALONE COULD SEE CASSIOPEIA AS SHE INCHED CLOSER TO THE
man who stood ten feet away. He was trying hard to buy her time.

"I know why you folks are after Zorin," he said. "And if I know,
guess who else knows? The people in Washington are all over this."

"Once Zorin is dead, it will not matter what you know."

A car engine suddenly roared to life.

The sound originated on the far side of Kelly's house.

Then a pair of headlights found the street and raced away at a high rate of speed. The shadow with the rifle whirled left and sent a loose spray of bullets in the car's direction, scattering the fire, hoping surely for some kind of hit.

CASSIOPEIA LEVELED THE GUN AND SHOT THE MAN SHOOTING AT the fleeing car, dropping him to the ground.

The gunfire stopped.

Silence returned.

"I was hoping you were still breathing," Cotton said.

She lowered her gun. "I thought you were supposed to be watching *my* backside."

He started running toward their parked vehicle. "As pleasant a prospect as that may be, we need to go after that car. I assume Zorin and Kelly are inside it."

And she agreed.

CHAPTER
FORTY-FOUR

STEPHANIE SAT WITH DANNY DANIELS, ALONE, IN THE OVAL OF-fice. Osin was gone with a pledge that their talk never happened. Ed-win Davis had retreated to his office, and Luke had headed to his apartment for some sleep. Midnight had passed, which meant Danny was now in his last full day as president of the United States.

"It's almost done," she said to him.

He rocked in his chair, quiet, and uncharacteristically sullen. "I don't want to go."

She smiled. "Who does?"

"Lots of folks made it this far and didn't know what the hell they were doing. So they were eager for it to end. I enjoyed the job."

"You were a good president. History will be kind."

And she meant that.

"How does it feel to be unemployed?" he said. "I'll be joining you real soon."

"Not the way I envisioned going out."

"Me either, but you know I couldn't interfere. Besides, what good would it have done? The Billet is gone. Those fools think they know more than you and me and everyone else. Remember, Fox *was* a gov-ernor."

She caught the sarcasm. The new president came straight from a governor's mansion with some administrative experience, but little to no international exposure. He'd campaigned on a platform of semi-isolationism, sensing that the country was tired of policing the world. He'd won by a solid majority in the popular vote and an even wider margin in the electoral college, which had made her wonder if public sentiment was indeed shifting. To think that America could exist independent of what was happening around the globe, no matter how far away or how remote things might appear, bordered on idiocy.

Those days were over.

"You take your eye off anybody for more than a minute," Danny said to her, "and they'll stab you in the back. The Middle East, Asia, China, now Russia. They're all rearin' up their ugly heads. And our allies? Hell, most times they're worse than enemies. Give me, take me, buy me, bring me. That's all they ever want."

She smiled, recalling the first time she heard him utter that phrase. Years ago, during another battle, one of their first, before they both realized how they felt about each other.

"Where's Pauline?" she asked.

"Gone. But she'll be back Monday for the swearing-in on Capitol Hill. Our final public appearance together as man and wife."

She heard the failure in his voice.

"Everything upstairs has been packed and shipped to Tennessee. Pauline went on a few days ago, supposedly to handle the relocation. She's anxious to start her new life and, I have to say, I was eager to see her go. It's time to move on."

"When will you divorce?"

"In a few months. Once no one gives a rat's ass about me or her. Nice and quiet. Like how Al Gore did it. Crap happens, and people understand. No one cares about some ex-vice-president or president."

She understood his remorse. Decades ago her own marriage unraveled to the point that she and Lars lived apart for years. That would have probably still been the case if he hadn't hanged himself from that bridge in France. Eventually, with Cotton and Cassiopeia's help, she came to understand why that happened, but its finality still brought a great sadness to her heart.

"Shouldn't you be asleep?" she said to him.

"I'm a night person. You know that. And I haven't slept for crap the past month or so. I don't like where this country is headed. It's scary. And I wonder if that's my fault."

"Because you did a good job protecting everyone?"

"We made it look too easy."

Which she knew it wasn't. The new president seemed 180 degrees away from Danny. But that was the thing about American politics. Its pendulum swung with predictable regularity, nothing ever lasting long, as if the country liked to continually try new things, yet complained constantly that everything seemed to stay the same. No way to please the masses and she wondered why anyone would even try. But Danny had not only tried, he'd succeeded.

"You did your job," she said. "And kept this country safe, without breaching civil rights."

"We had some challenges, didn't we?"

She smiled at him. "You do know that you can still be useful. Your life isn't over."

He shook his head. "My successor is a rookie."

"In thirty-six hours he'll be president of the United States."

"He's never dealt with anything like this. And the people he's hiring are not the sharpest tacks in the box. That scares me, too."

"It's not our problem," she said.

"I hate that this happened to you," he said. "I never would have involved you if I thought they'd fire you."

He sounded as though he really meant it.

"You've been nothing but straight with me since the first day we met," she said. "And let's get one thing clear. I do only what I want to do, and you know that. I chose to make the moves I did, so I pay the price."

He smiled at her as he kept rocking.

"Is Luke's Mustang totaled?" he asked.

"Just spare parts now."

"He loved that car."

She wondered who he was talking to. He seemed a million miles away. "You're tired."

"No, I'm worried. Something's happenin' here. I can feel it. And it's not good. You don't get an SVR station chief waltzing into the White

House and divulging state secrets every day. Five nuclear weapons are hidden around here somewhere."

"It's not like in the movies. Those things need care, and it's been a long time."

"Yet this Zorin keeps plowin' ahead. That worries me."

"The Russians were never known for smarts."

"But they are one tough competitor."

She allowed a moment of silence to pass before breaching protocol and asking, "What about us?"

His gaze focused on her. "Is there an us?"

"If you want there to be."

"I want."

A few nerves jerked along her forearms. Unusual, to say the least. She was glad to hear the admission, and she hoped the possibilities perked his spirits some over the next day and a half.

"After the swearing-in, I'm headed back to Tennessee," he said. "My little house in the woods. You're welcome to join me."

"How about you get divorced first."

He chuckled. "I thought you might say that. But you can come for a visit, right?"

"And end up on the front page of some tabloid? No thanks. I'll wait until you're a free man."

"What are you going to do now?"

She hadn't given it much thought. "I have a pension coming to me, so I think I'll collect. Then I'll see who might need the services of an ex-intelligence-officer with experience."

"I imagine there'll be many takers on that offer. How about this? Don't make a decision on what to do until you run it by me first."

She could see that he was up to something. But she would have expected no less. This man was a player. Always had been, always will be.

"I dare not ask, right?"

He grinned like a Cheshire Cat and said, "Dare not. At least for now."

Then she saw something else in his eyes.

He knew something she didn't.

Something important.

"What is it?" she asked.

CHAPTER FORTY-FIVE

ZORIN RODE IN THE PASSENGER SEAT, KELLY DRIVING A SMALL hatchback coupe. They'd fled the house out a kitchen door and found the car in the garage, managing to speed away without incident. He still was puzzled by the cacophony of gunfire at the house. They'd passed two police cars on the bridge across the river, both heading east as they drove west. But none had come their way as they passed through Charlottetown, then found a main highway.

"Where are we going?" he asked.

"Back to the *glavny protivnik.*"

The main adversary. America.

"You hid the RA-115s in a safe place?"

"My orders were clear. Find a location where they would be undetected, but remain viable. That was not easy to accomplish. But I did it."

"What happened to you?" he asked. "After we left Andropov that night?"

"I returned to my life. Unlike you, Aleksandr, I was not born in the motherland. My parents were embedded operatives in the United States. I'm a passport-carrying U.S. citizen. I came to Moscow that night on a tour group. Back in the 1980s, I daresay Russia was not a popular tourist destination, but Americans still went. I was ordered back for a face-to-face, so I booked the tour. That night, I slipped out of the hotel and came to the safe house."

He knew all about Intourist, owned by the government and once the only travel agency allowed in the Soviet Union. Stalin himself founded it. Staffed always by KGB employees, it once managed all foreign access to the Soviet Union. Officially, he'd worked out of more than one Intourist office. So he could understand how Kelly could have made it to both Moscow and the meeting.

"After that night with Andropov, I rejoined the tour group and came back to Washington. I worked at my job, followed my orders for Fool's Mate, and did a lot of listening."

Which had always proved to be the most effective means of gathering intelligence. He'd done his share during several foreign postings, but his specialty was not socializing. He was more an implementer.

"After December 1991 none of it mattered much anymore," Kelly said. "Everything just ended. I was never contacted again by the KGB or SVR. How about you, Aleksandr, what happened?"

"I tired quickly of the new Russia. Too many mobsters for me. So I moved east to Siberia. My wife and son died, so I lived alone, waiting for the right opportunity."

They were approaching the Confederation Bridge, stretching thirteen kilometers across the Northumberland Strait that separated Prince Edward Island from mainland Canada. Thirty years ago, for him, the only way across had been by ferry.

Kelly stopped and paid the toll, then sped onto the lit span.

"I, too, wondered if an opportunity would ever come," Kelly said. "For a long time I thought this all was over. Andropov died in '84. My orders had to come straight from him. But I was never told to stand down, so I kept doing my job."

"I did the same." He stared across the dark at his driver. "We owe it to all of them to finish. We never had a chance to fight the great battle against the main adversary. Instead, that adversary destroyed us."

"That it did. But we did a lot of damage to ourselves. I've spent decades reading about all that happened. So many mistakes. History has taught me many lessons."

As it had with himself. Most important, there would be no hesitation, no reservations, no mercy. Politics mattered not. Compassion and morality factored in here nowhere. Those concepts had stopped no one from destroying the Soviet Union. So he had to know, "Fool's Mate involves two moves to checkmate. Andropov himself named your mission. Is that symbolism relevant?"

"Oh, yes. And the success of any Fool's Mate in chess depends on your opponent playing extraordinarily foolishly. In this case, America has accommodated us."

"I was Quiet Move," he said.

Kelly chuckled. "How appropriate. An act that threatens nothing else on the board. Andropov was ironic, if nothing else."

"You knew about the other two dying?"

They kept cruising across the two-laned bridge, traffic nearly nonexistent in either direction. Nothing strange, considering it was the middle of the night.

"I did learn about their untimely deaths. It wasn't hard to determine why they occurred. The fewer who knew the better. I assumed the idea was for me to be the last man standing, ready to implement Fool's Mate on orders. How *did* you find me?"

"Your name exists in old records. Your location came from someone with access to secret information."

"You had an archivist's help?"

He nodded.

"They're probably the only ones who know where to look," Kelly said. "Records of my posting had to exist. Archivists have done a lot of damage. I read the Mitrokhin book when it was published back in the 1990s. It was a matter of survival, since I was terrified the traitorous fool had named me in there."

"Moscow must now be reading the same records my archivist did."

"I agree. That man in the house had to be SVR."

He thought the time right to ask, "The first move you made was hiding the weapons. What was the second move to Fool's Mate? The one that wins."

"The point of convergence."

This was what Belchenko had not been able to ascertain, or had been unwilling to share. Andropov had said that night that they would *"strike America at its core."* Two flaws had been discovered, and *"at the right time, we will teach America a lesson. Minimum effort, maximum effect."*

"I found out about the zero amendment," Zorin said. "More from those old records and that archivist. So I know the time is now." He concealed his enthusiasm and summoned a long-taught patience to keep his emotions in check. "But do you know the point of convergence?"

"My mission was to determine it. Do you remember what Andropov said to us." Kelly held up two fingers. "Two flaws. The envelope under my plate that night described both. The zero amendment is one."

Which Belchenko had explained to him.

"The second is the actual detonation spot."

They came to the end of the bridge and drove onto the Canadian mainland.

Kelly said, "I'm the only one who knows that location."

MALONE DROVE AND CASSIOPEIA KEPT WATCH AHEAD, HER TASK aided by the night-vision binoculars. They were over a mile behind Zorin, trying to blend in with the few cars out on the highway. So far he did not think they'd been made. How could they have been? They'd fled Kelly's neighborhood about two minutes behind Zorin, able to catch up when police vehicles sped across the Hillsborough River bridge and Zorin slowed, clearly trying not to draw any attention. They'd kept pace, driving west, then south, crossing what was labeled the Confederation Bridge. Along the way Cassiopeia had told him all that she'd heard at Kelly's house.

"We're in New Brunswick," she said to him.

"Have you been here before?"

She lowered the binoculars. "A few times. Pretty place."

"Any idea where they're headed?"

She found her cell phone and worked the screen. "There are airports ahead in Moncton and St. John. Could be there. And there's a choice in highways coming up. West into New Brunswick or east to Nova Scotia."

"I guess we'll just have to wait and see."

"Who do you think those guys were back there at Kelly's house?" she asked.

"Had to be Russian. Who else?"

"I agree." She returned the binoculars to her eyes. "They're turn-ing west, toward Moncton. My phone says it's about fifty kilometers."

He sped ahead, ready to make his own turn.

Two things had to be avoided.

They could not be discovered, and they could not lose that car.

CHAPTER FORTY-SIX

STEPHANIE STOOD BEHIND THE RESOLUTE DESK IN THE OVAL OF-
fice, staring down at two folders. One was thick and prominently
marked TOP SECRET—FORWARD PASS in red letters. Its edges were
worn, the classified stamp dated 1989 and authorized by the White
House. Its seal had been broken away, the inside pages disturbed, but
she recognized all of the letters, memos, notes, legal opinions, and international communiqués. Many of which she'd written.

"What was Reagan like?" Danny asked.

"Smart, clever, intuitive. He relished how others underestimated
him. But he could read people, especially the Soviets. He spent a lot of
time thinking about their demise."

She turned the pages, exposing a digest, the earliest date from
February 1982 and her first meeting with Reagan. The last was from
November 1989, when she was told that her services were no longer
required. Nothing seemed to have happened after her departure. But
what would have? The die had been cast long before the first Bush took
office. She thought back to the many meetings that had happened here,
most late in the night when few were around. She'd even gotten to
know Nancy Reagan, whom she found most gracious, sharing totally
in her husband's aspirations. They were indeed a team. She'd envied
that relationship, as her own marriage was then disintegrating.

"Reagan had an intuition about the Soviet Union, and was patient," she said. "He waited for someone like Gorbachev and, when he came along, took full advantage. It might have been the actor in him, judging the right moment to toss out the right line for maximum effect. He never rushed anything. He always told me to get it right, not fast."

"We've always been fortunate to have the right man at the right time. Washington was there in the beginning. Lincoln when the country fell apart. Wilson and Roosevelt as Depression and world wars threatened everything. Then Reagan, with the Cold War. Did it bother him that it all actually ended after his watch, when Bush took over?"

"Not in the least. He was not a man who cared about credit, only results. He wanted to leave the world a safer place than he found it, and that's exactly what he did. I saw him for the last time in 1992, at his presidential library. We met alone, and he thanked me again for all that I did. He was an extraordinary man, and history will record that Ronald Reagan won the Cold War."

"You did good," Danny said to her. "Real good. You have to be proud as hell at what you accomplished."

It meant a lot to hear his praise. He was not a man who doled out compliments lightly. The essence of the intelligence business dictated that recognition almost never came. Getting the job done had to suffice, though sometimes it could be a poor substitute. She *was* proud. More than she could ever say. She'd been there when Eastern Europe barred the one-party system, tossed aside a planned economy, and chose freedom and the rule of law. She'd helped the two most powerful men in the world bring about the total destruction of an evil empire.

Much had happened since, but nothing like that.

"It was a remarkable time," she said. "But like now, the incoming Bush administration decided they had no further need for me. That's when I moved to Justice."

"From Stettin in the Baltic to Trieste in the Adriatic, an Iron Curtain has descended across the continent. Behind that line lie all the capitals of the ancient states of Central and Eastern Europe. Warsaw, Berlin, Prague, Vienna, Budapest, Belgrade, Bucharest, and Sofia, all these famous cities and the populations around them lie in what I must call the Soviet sphere."

She was impressed. "Churchill's speech. Delivered in Fulton, Missouri, in 1946, after he lost his own reelection bid for prime minister. I never realized you were a Cold War student."

He pointed a finger at her. "What you meant was you never realized I could remember things. You're going to discover a lot about me you didn't know."

Of that she was sure.

"Truman was there in the audience when Churchill spoke," he said. "He said afterward that he agreed with every word, especially the phrase coined that day. *Iron Curtain.* Churchill was right about Stalin and the Russians."

"And it took us another forty-five years to win that Cold War."

"But win it we did. Total and complete victory."

"How'd you find out?" she asked. "Only a handful of people knew about Forward Pass."

"Osin told me yesterday."

"And you never said a word?"

"I can keep a secret."

She smiled. He could be quite adorable, when he wanted to be.

"Zorin, like you, is a Cold Warrior," he said. "But unlike you, he hasn't moved on. He's one of our problems, but the split inside the Kremlin is a whole different matter. Osin, to his credit, is trying to do the right thing. But there are more nuts inside the Russian government than Osins. Not the zealot, Lenin, Karl Marx kind. No, these are pure criminals, out for nothing more than themselves. The good thing is that they're not the world-dominating type. But five nuclear weapons hidden here? That's something that might come in handy to them. A good hammer to keep us under control."

He pointed to the other folder on the nearly empty desk. "That one I had Edwin assimilate."

She started to reach for it, but he gently clasped her hand, stopping her. An unfamiliar chill swept through her.

The phone on the desk buzzed, breaking the moment.

He pushed the lit button and activated the speaker.

"There's been a problem in Canada," Edwin said.

They both listened to what the police on Prince Edward Island had found. Four bodies at a man named Jamie Kelly's residence, just outside Charlottetown. No identification on any of them.

"Any word from Cotton?" she asked.

"Nothing. But at least we know he's been busy."

That they did.

"He'll call when he needs to," she said to Edwin. "Can you tell the Canadians to stay out of the way?"

"Already done."

"Keep me posted," Danny said, ending the call.

She saw the concern in his eyes.

"What were you going to show me?" she asked.

"Cotton reported that the archivist, Belchenko, mentioned two things before he died. Fool's Mate and zero amendment. The first term Osin has promised to work on. The second, though, we can handle." He pointed at the other folder. "It's all in there."

She stared down at the folder.

"In there are copies of documents Edwin found in an old classified CIA file. The words *zero amendment* led us straight there. Seems we have things digitally indexed at Langley now, which is a good thing. People over there tell me they haven't heard those two words associated with the Soviet Union since the 1980s. Take the folder upstairs and read. Then get some sleep. Pick any bedroom you want."

"Including yours?"

He grinned. "Like you say, not until I'm a free man."

She reached for the file. Some sleep would be great. But she was damn curious as to what was going on.

"Let's talk about this more at breakfast," he said.

She headed for the door.

"The Soviets called it the zero amendment," he said to her. "We call it the 20th Amendment to the Constitution."

CASSIOPEIA KEPT THE BINOCULARS TO HER EYES, THE GRAYISH images of the road ahead easy to see. Night-vision technology had come a long way from the everything-is-green scenario. In fact, the view through the eyepieces was clear as dusk on a summer's day. She'd been tracking their route on her smartphone, noting that they were running out of Canadian real estate, the border with Maine less than eighty kilometers away.

"Is he going to cross over into the United States?" she asked.

"Kelly could easily. Edwin told me that he's a U.S. citizen with a passport. But Zorin? No way. He dropped in on a parachute. Unless he brought some fake ID, he'd need a visa to come in legally on a Russian passport. I doubt he even has a passport. But that's not going to stop him."

They'd stayed way back, sometimes too far, but luckily the car ahead had not made any turns.

"There's a town, Digdeguash, coming up," she said, checking the map on her phone.

Cotton had done a solid job of using the few cars they'd encountered as cover. She checked her watch. Nearly 3:00 A.M.

"He's not going to drive across the border," Cotton said.

She agreed, so she used her finger to shift the map on her phone, moving the image north and south, then east and west. "We're due north of Maine, just across the Passamaquoddy Bay, maybe thirty kilometers between us."

"That's how he's going to do it," Cotton said. "On the water."

CHAPTER
FORTY-SEVEN

ZORIN HAD NOT PRESSED KELLY ON WHAT THE MAN HAD DISCOV-
ered. Any detonation spot was meaningless unless the weapons themselves had survived.

So first things first.

They'd ridden in silence for a while, passing the city of St. John and
keeping south on the four-laned highway until it shrank to two lanes,
paralleling the coastline. His driver seemed to know exactly where he
was headed.

They entered a quiet community down for the night. Kelly stopped
at an intersection, then turned south on another black highway.

"There's a lovely little village just ahead called St. Andrews by the
Sea," Kelly said. "I've visited many times. Only a couple thousand people live there, and Maine is just across the St. Croix River. I like sail-
ing and they have boats for rent. We can steal one at this hour and be
long gone before anyone realizes. We'll avoid the river and head across
the bay to Eastport, in Maine. It's not far, fifty kilometers or so. There
we can easily slip into the United States."

Zorin had to trust that this man knew what he was doing.

"I was here back in the summer. Whale-watching is big business
in St. Andrews. I like the town. It was founded by British loyalists who
fled the colonies after the Revolutionary War with no love for the new

America. It'll be a cold sail in this brisk air, but it's the smart way to go."

"Why go out onto the bay and not just cross the river? You said the border was less than three kilometers that way."

"It's patrolled, night and day. The easiest way to get into America is across the bay, through the front door. I planned this contingency long ago, though I never believed I'd use it."

A sign announced that they were entering St. Andrews. More signs directed people to an aquarium and a nature center.

"The Algonquin Hotel is lovely," Kelly said. "Old World style. It sits off in that direction, up on a hill, but the marinas are this way."

They cruised through a tiny downtown populated with colorful clapboard buildings. Mainly shops, cafés, and art galleries. A lit Canadian flag flew high above one of them. Kelly parked at the waterfront and they quickly fled the car, each carrying his bag. The night air held a bite, the freezing moisture face tightening like back in Siberia. No one was around, all quiet, except for the gentle slap of water onto the nearby shore.

They walked along a pier that extended out into the bay, boats tied to either side. Kelly seemed to be deciding, finally settling on a single-mast about six meters long and hopping down to the boat's deck.

"Untie it from the mooring cleats. We'll float out past the dock, then raise the sail. Are you much of a sailor?"

"Not in the least," he said.

"Then lucky for you that I am."

He freed the lines, then jumped into the boat. If the truth be told he was not a fan of water at all, but he recognized the wisdom in what Kelly had proposed. The boat immediately began to drift away from the dock, the tide slipping them out toward the bay. Kelly was busy releasing the main sail from the boom and preparing to catch a steady north breeze. The narrow inlet ahead seemed a couple of kilometers long, wooded on both sides to the water's edge.

What had Kelly said? Fifty kilometers across?

He could handle that.

He checked his watch.

Nearly 4:00 A.M.

36 hours left.

MALONE WITNESSED THE THEFT OF A SINGLE-MAST SAILBOAT, ZO-
rin and Kelly now floating away from shore. They'd cruised into town
a few minutes behind the Russians and stopped short of the waterfront, using darkness as cover. He lowered the night-vision binoculars
and handed them to Cassiopeia. They were a quarter mile from the
waterfront amid the few buildings that formed the main street.

"We can't follow," she said, studying what was happening out on
the black water through the lens. "There're no other boats out there
anywhere in this cold."

"Can I borrow your phone?"

She handed over the unit and he redialed the White House, the
same number used earlier to make a partial report, and Edwin Davis
answered. He told the chief of staff what was happening then said, "I'm
assuming we have drone capability up here?"

"Hold on and I'll find out."

Two minutes later the line went alive again and Edwin said, "Absolutely. The Canadians don't necessarily like it, but we have it. I've
ordered one in the air. It should be over your location in less than thirty
minutes."

He glanced at Cassiopeia, who could hear the other side of the conversation even though it was not on speaker.

She nodded and said, "We can keep a visual that long, but not much
longer. He's headed southeast, toward Maine."

"You get that?" he asked Edwin.

"We'll watch them all the way. What are you going to do?"

"Wait for your call telling me you've got 'em. Then we'll swing
around by car and come down southward on the Maine side of the border. That way we can be close to wherever they come ashore. Let's
make sure nobody bothers them. No border officers."

"I'm told things are loose there. It's the honor system coming into
the country," Davis said.

"So much for secure borders."

"If the public only knew. At least we do patrol with the drones."

"Just don't lose him. We've come this far."

"We won't."

He ended the call.

Cassiopeia kept studying the far-off bay.

He stood beside her in the cold. "Lucky for us those two have been out of touch awhile. No drones with high-res cameras in their day."

She lowered the glasses. "What do you think the endgame is here?"

He truly did not know.

"Let's just hope Stephanie is figuring that out for us."

CHAPTER FORTY-EIGHT

The issue of succession for the United States presidency has been a thorny subject since the drafting of the Constitution in 1787. Article II, Section 1, Clause 5 provides that to be eligible to serve as president, a person must be a natural-born citizen, at least thirty-five years old, and a resident within the United States for at least 14 years. In cases of removal, death, resignation, or inability to discharge the duties of president, Article II, Section 1, Clause 6 names the vice president first in the line of succession.

Seven American presidents have died in office and, each time, the vice president took the oath and served out that president's unexpired term. Whether that vice president actually became president, or merely acting president, has long been a matter of constitutional debate. No one knows for sure. The issue was finally resolved with the 1967 ratification of the 25th Amendment, which clarified Article II, Section 1, Clause 6, designating the vice president the actual president if the president dies, resigns, or is removed from office. That amendment also required any vice-presidential vacancies to be filled by the president and confirmed by Congress. Previously, when a vice president had succeeded to the presidency (or otherwise left the office empty) the vice presidency remained vacant until the next presidential election. In 1974, Gerald Ford was the first to become vice president and ultimately president through the 25th Amendment. This is all well-settled American law, and most of the confusion that once existed around a vice president's ascension to the presidency is gone.

But what about others succeeding to the presidency when there is no vice president available?

It is the 20th Amendment that deals with this contingency. That amendment also addresses issues of succession that occur *before* a president and vice president are sworn into office.

Here is the relevant language:

The terms of the President and Vice President shall end at noon on the 20th day of January. If, at the time fixed for the beginning of the term of the President, the President-elect shall have died, the Vice-President-elect shall become President. If a President shall not have been chosen before the time fixed for the beginning of his term, or if the President-elect shall have failed to qualify, then the Vice-President-elect shall act as President until a President shall have qualified; and the Congress may by law provide for the case wherein neither a President-elect nor a Vice-President-elect shall have qualified, declaring who shall then act as President, or the manner in which one who is to act shall be selected, and such person shall act accordingly until a President or Vice President shall have qualified.

First, it is clear from this constitutional amendment that the term of a president ends precisely at noon on January 20 so, by implication, the term of the next president would begin simultaneously. Second, if the president-elect dies before the term begins, the vice-president-elect becomes president on January 20 and serves the full term to which the president-elect had been elected. Third, if on January 20 a president has not been chosen, or the president-elect does not qualify for the office, the vice-president-elect acts as president until a president is chosen or the president-elect qualifies. Finally, Congress can provide by law for cases in which neither a president-elect nor a vice-president-elect is eligible or available to serve.

This last contingency was expounded on by Congress in the 1947 Presidential Succession Act, which lays out the line of succession in cases where there is no president or vice president, either before or after being sworn in. First in line comes the Speaker of the House of Representatives, then the president pro tempore of the Senate. After are various cabinet officers in a set order beginning with the secretary of state, then treasury, defense, the attorney general, and on down ending with the secretary of veterans affairs being the 16th in the line of succession.

To be eligible to succeed the cabinet officer must meet the constitutional requirements of being president and must have been appointed by and with the advice and consent of the Senate. Having taken the oath, the statute provides that the officer is automatically removed from his or her cabinet post, becoming president for the remaining term or until a person higher in the line of succession is available to serve. This law has never been called into action, but unanswered legal questions exist as to its constitutionality.

First, consider the exact language of the statute itself. Section (a)(1) provides:

> If by reason of death, resignation, removal from office, inability, or failure to qualify, there is neither a President nor Vice President to discharge the powers and duties of the office of President, then the Speaker of the House of Representatives shall, upon his resignation as Speaker and as Representative in Congress, act as President.

Initially it has to be asked, can a member of Congress even be placed in the line of succession? Article II, Section 1, Clause 6 of the Constitution specifies that only an "officer" of the United States can be designated as a presidential successor. Nearly every legal scholar who has considered this issue, including one of the American founders, James Madison, has concluded that such a term excludes members of Congress. This is buttressed by Article I, Section 6, Clause 2 (the Incompatibility Clause), which states:

> No Senator or Representative shall, during the Time for which he was elected, be appointed to any civil Office under the Authority of the United States, which shall have been created, or the Emoluments whereof shall have been increased during such time; and no Person holding any Office under the United States, shall be a Member of either House during his Continuance in Office.

Under the American constitutional system, the two branches of government, legislative and executive, must remain separate. The 1947 Succession Act deals with this prohibition by requiring that the Speaker of the House and/or the president pro tempore of the Senate first resign their congressional post prior to being sworn in as president. But how could either then be eligible to be president since, once resigned, they would no longer be Speaker or president pro tempore, hence ineligible to succeed under the statute.

When a cabinet officer succeeds under the statute there is language in subsection (d)(3) of the act that specifically provides:

> The taking of the oath of office by a [cabinet officer] shall be held to constitute his resignation from the office by virtue of the holding of which he qualifies to act as President.

No such proviso appears in the subsection of the law that provides for succession by the Speaker of the House or the president pro tempore of the Senate.

More legal questions also exist with a member of the cabinet being placed in the line of succession. The 1947 Act expressly states that any cabinet officer who succeeds serves as "Acting-President" until a new Speaker of the House or new president pro tempore of the Senate is chosen, who would then replace that cabinet officer as acting president. Scholars call this "bumping," but this statutory language conflicts with Article II, Section 1, Clause 6 of the Constitution, which says that when an officer of the United States succeeds to the presidency "such Officer shall act accordingly until the disability [of the president] be removed or a President shall be elected."

Experts agree that there is no constitutional sanction for the bumping of one officer for another, which makes sense, as the prohibition prevents the confusion that would surely arise if the American presidency were transferred to several different people in such a short period of time. It would also prevent Congress from exercising influence over the executive branch (violating the separation of powers) by threatening to replace a cabinet member acting as president with a newly elected Speaker of the House.

In short, the Presidential Succession Act of 1947 is a flawed statute. One observer calls it "an accident waiting to happen." If its statutory provisions were ever applied it would generate nothing but litigation. In the appendix attached hereto is a long list of law review and other scholarly articles (from 1947 to the present) that have come to the same conclusion. Yet the United States Congress has made no attempt to repair its deficiencies.

So consider this: If a president dies in office, clearly, under the 25th Amendment, the vice president becomes president and serves out the remaining term. If a vice president dies in office, under the same amendment the president and the Congress choose a replacement, who serves out the remaining term. If the president-elect dies before taking the oath, the 20th Amendment provides that the vice-president-elect becomes president.

But what happens when both the president-elect and the vice-president-elect die before noon on January 20?

The 20th Amendment fails to address this possibility. Instead, the amendment empowered Congress to provide an answer, which became the Presidential Succession Act of 1947. But that act would not solve anything relative to this catastrophic scenario. Instead, under the statute as it is presently drafted, the United States would be plunged into political and legal chaos.

Stephanie finished her second reading of the memorandum.

Another sheet in the file noted that the document had been intercepted on April 9, 1982, part of a cache seized from a Soviet spy captured in West Germany. Its author was unknown. But the KGB had certainly gone to a lot of trouble to learn about the Presidential Succession Act of 1947, a relatively obscure aspect of American law.

She was ensconced on the White House's third floor, inside a modest bedroom with two queen-sized beds, a lamp burning on a mahogany table between them. Danny was one floor below in the master suite. She'd tried to sleep but had been unable, deciding to read the memo once more. She considered herself well versed in the Constitution, and was aware of some of the 20th Amendment's shortcomings. But the flaws in the 1947 Succession Act surprised her, as did Congress's seeming indifference at changing them.

Although she could understand that hesitation.

What were the odds of the act ever coming into play?

Only in two instances was the American government ever congregated in a single location. One was the yearly State of the Union address, which happened each January in the House of Representatives chamber on Capitol Hill. The other was a presidential inauguration. Every major player was present for both events.

Except one.

The designated survivor.

Usually a member of the cabinet, chosen in secret by the White

House chief of staff before the event and hidden away in a remote and undisclosed location with both presidential-level security and transport. An aide even carried a nuclear "football" that could be used by the survivor to authorize any counterattack. In the event of a total catastrophe that person, in direct line to succeed thanks to the 1947 Succession Act, would become acting president. All of these plans assumed, though, no political or constitutional problems associated with such an ascension.

Yet that might not be the case.

In fact, the whole idea of the 1947 Succession Act now seemed suspect.

But what did this have to do with Aleksandr Zorin and missing Russian nukes? Was Zorin aware of this information and now planning an attack on the inauguration? That seemed the logical conclusion, given what Cotton had reported about Zorin and the zero amendment. Certainly on Monday the entire government, save for the designated survivor, would be present on the west side of the Capitol, there to watch the beginning of the Warner Fox administration.

But what would be gained by such a reckless act? *"His name is Aleksandr Zorin and he wants revenge."* That's what Osin had told her.

Then there was what else Cotton had been told.

Fool's Mate.

Danny had said he was waiting on Osin to provide more on that, too.

But she knew a quicker way that information might be found.

CHAPTER
FORTY-NINE

ZORIN STARED ACROSS THE WATER AT EASTPORT, MAINE. HE AND
Kelly had sailed from the Canadian side of the bay in just under two
hours. Finally, they'd lowered the sail and dropped anchor about half
a kilometer offshore. The cabin belowdecks came with two bunks,
some spare equipment, and life jackets. They huddled inside, with the
curtains drawn on the portholes. Peering past them he saw a dock and
marina that accommodated a variety of boats. Eastport seemed like a
quaint little town, its claim to fame being its status as the easternmost
city in the United States, as Kelly had explained.

"This is a formal port of entry," Kelly said. "A ferry sails from here
to Deer Island in New Brunswick, but only in the summer. This time
of year entry in and out is informal."

"We cannot be detained."

"We won't. I've tested this path before. What were we taught, Aleksandr? Be ready or die."

He climbed topside to the small aft deck and listened to the distant hiss of small breakers as they splashed against a rocky shore. Out
here on the water, with nothing to block the wind, the north air knifed
through him. Like another cold day, long ago on the Kamchatka Pen-
insula, when six opium-addicted soldiers seized a Tu-134 destined for
the Siberian oil fields. Two of the 74 passengers were killed and the
airplane damaged, which temporarily prevented it from being flown

to the West, which was where the soldiers wanted to go. He'd sat off-shore that day, about half a kilometer, waiting for an opportunity, another stiff Arctic wind chilling his bones. Eventually, he and three others from his *spetsnaz* unit slipped ashore and stormed the plane, killing all six of the hijackers.

He'd been good at his job.

Respected.

Feared.

And rewarded.

Unmarked buses had crisscrossed Moscow every day providing free rides for KGB employees. No shortages ever affected him or any other intelligence officer. KGB grocery stores stayed stocked with salmon, sausage, cheese, bread, even caviar. Western clothing was readily available. There were gyms, saunas, pools, and tennis courts. A private medical staff worked around the clock. A modern clinic employed dentists. Even masseuses could be hired. The headquarters of the First Directorate, just outside Moscow, came with better security than the Kremlin. And what a place. Its construction materials had been imported from Japan and Europe. The Finnish supplied all the interior furnishings. A sense of awe was evoked at every corner. Its marble façade sparkled in the sun, the wooden floors buffed to a mirror finish. No costs were spared, the whole site designed to remind everyone who worked there that they were special.

Only the best for the best.

And officers, like him, who worked the North American Department had ranked as the most important.

Then it all vanished.

"Did you ever see what happened to the Woods?" he asked. That was how they'd referred to the First Directorate headquarters.

Kelly shook his head. "I never went back after that night with Andropov. Never had an opportunity."

"You were lucky. It would have shamed you. I went in '94. The building was crumbling, paint scabbed and peeling, the inside filthy, most of the people drunk by midday. That Finnish furniture, which we so admired, was either gone or destroyed. In the bathrooms were dozens of liquor bottles. Everything reeked of alcohol and tobacco. No toilet paper or paper towels anywhere. People stole those as fast as they were laid out. You used old newspapers to wipe your ass. The place, like us, had been allowed to rot."

It sickened him to think about it. Bright, loyal, confident men broken in half. But he needed to never forget. Hate provided a powerful fuel for his aging emotions. As a foreign officer living overseas he'd learned that everything was temporary. Training taught him to suspend the mind in the surrealness around him. Home was always Moscow, familiar and comfortable, but when that world ceased to exist all logic and reason had fled him.

He'd truly felt abandoned and alone.

"I almost wish that I'd been like you," he said. "Living here you were able to avoid the failure."

"But I never forgot that I was an officer of the KGB. Not once. And I was given a mission by Andropov himself. That meant something to me, Aleksandr."

As it had to him.

He listened to the patter of water against the hull. Salmon-colored sky off to the east signaled dawn. The wind had not weakened, the water shifting like a sheet of wrinkled foil. Kelly reached into his bag, found a map and flashlight, opening the folds and spreading the paper out on the deck. Zorin saw that it showed the eastern United States, stretching from Maine to Florida.

"We're here," Kelly said, pointing the beam at the northeastern tip of Maine. "We're going to drive west to Bangor, then take Interstate 95 south. Once we get on that superhighway we can make good time. We should be where we need to be by tonight."

"I assume you don't plan to tell me any details."

"How about we discover things together, one step at a time."

He was in no position to argue, so he stayed silent. Kelly was doing what he wanted so little reason existed to complain. He stared past the deck at the town on shore. A few people moved across the dock near the marina. Headlights passed back and forth on a street that paralleled shore, then turned inland illuminating buildings on either side.

The United States of America.

It had been a long time since he last visited.

"How do we get onto those highways and head south?" he asked. "Stealing a car could be a problem."

"That's why we're going to do this the easy way and rent one. I'm a U.S. citizen with a Canadian driver's license. It shouldn't be a problem. Is anyone in America aware of you?"

He shook his head. "Not that I know of. Apparently, Moscow is watching, but they have no idea where we are now."

He wondered about Anya and how she was doing. He still carried the mobile phone that matched hers and would try and make contact tonight.

"What about the SVR?" Kelly asked. "They obviously knew you were coming to me."

Which made him wonder again about Belchenko. Had what the archivist said in the black bath been repeated to Moscow? "You're right. They knew."

"Then why haven't they made contact until now?" Kelly asked.

"Because there was no reason, or maybe they simply did not know everything until now."

"Do they know of Fool's Mate?"

"It's possible. Those old records I found, they could find, too. Other archivists could know what I was told. But you said you told no one of your success. No report was ever made. Was that true?"

Kelly nodded.

He still could not believe Belchenko had talked. "They have to be grasping in the dark, hoping you and I will lead them to the cache."

Another look across the water. Eastport had a somber, eerie quality—inviting, tranquil, yet ominous.

And he wondered.

Was the SVR here?

Waiting?

MALONE SLOWED THE CAR AS HE AND CASSIOPEIA ENTERED EAST-port, Maine. The town sat on Moose Island, connected to the mainland by a causeway. They'd kept watch from St. Andrews on the sloop as it dipped and rose across the swells, wind nudging it forward, the water giving way as it heeled over slightly to the pressure of its sail.

Once it was no longer in sight they'd fled the Canadian side of the bay and driven south, entering the United States on U.S. 1, passing through a border station, then paralleling the St. Croix River even farther south. Cassiopeia had determined from her smartphone that Eastport would give them the farthest point east.

Then they'd caught a break.

The drone, which had kept the sailboat under surveillance, revealed that it was now anchored in the lower reaches of the bay just off Eastport.

All in all they'd made good time and kept up.

Eastport's central downtown was small and eclectic, its main street lined with squatty wood buildings, some with black ironwork railings and decorative grilles. A Stars and Stripes on an eagle-topped pole blew stiff in the cold wind. The place seemed like one of those perfect weekend escapes, with Portland less than 250 miles south. Edwin Davis had just reported that all was quiet on the boat, its two occupants still aboard.

"How do they get into the country?" Cassiopeia asked.

"Believe it or not, up here this time of year it's the honor system. Somewhere down near the docks will be a video telephone booth. You're supposed to stand there so your image can be sent back to inspectors. Then you dial the phone inside and they ask you some questions. If it looks good you're given permission to enter, if not you're supposed to go back where you came from. The inspectors rely on the locals to police things for them and report problems."

"You're kidding, right?"

"I've made that call myself a couple of times in other places. Guarding a 5,500 mile border is tough and expensive. I imagine Kelly knows how loose things are with Canada. After all, he came straight here."

He eased the car to a stop in front of a bed-and-breakfast. "Zorin knows me, so I have to be scarce. But you're a different story. We'll let the drone do the seeing, until we need the personal touch. That'll be you."

She gave him a mock salute. "Yes, Captain. I'm ready to serve."

He smiled. "I've missed that attitude."

"Good thing."

Her cell phone buzzed.

She answered on speaker.

"They're leaving the boat in a dinghy," Edwin Davis said.

"Is everything clear here? If anyone calls anything in, Border Patrol will squelch it."

"All done. They should have an open-field run. I'm told we do have hidden cameras all over that dock. It's a busy place in the summer."

"Have you found out anything about Fool's Mate or zero amendment?"

"Oh, yes, and you're not going to like either one."

CHAPTER FIFTY

Stephanie left the White House and rode in a cab back to the Mandarin Oriental where she showered, changed clothes, and grabbed something to eat. She'd managed just a few hours of sleep, her mind reeling from what she'd read in the file Danny had provided.

The Soviet Union had been intently interested in the 20th Amendment to the Constitution. So intent that they'd even provided it with a nickname.

The zero amendment.

What that meant the old memo had not explained, but other memos in the file noted that references to the term appeared repeatedly in Soviet communiqués back in the late 1970s and into the 1980s, all linked directly to Yuri Andropov himself.

Then in 1984 references to the term vanished.

American intelligence paid close attention to when subject matters blossomed and wilted, as both events were significant. Analysts spent whole careers pondering why something started, then equally as much time on why it may have stopped. Linking subject matters was the Holy Grail of intelligence work and here the connection had been provided to Cotton when Vadim Belchenko, in his dying breaths, said *"Fool's Mate"* and *"zero amendment."* Stephanie needed to know more about the term *Fool's Mate,* and knew exactly where to go.

Kristina Cox lived within sight of the Cathedral Church of St. Pe-

ter and St. Paul in the city and diocese of Washington, DC. Most people simply called it the National Cathedral, as most called Kristina, Kris. Her husband, Glenn, had been an Episcopal canon, a towering man with a booming voice. For thirty-one years he'd served the church, eventually rising to bishop of the DC diocese, working from the cathedral. But one sad Sunday he'd dropped dead at the pulpit from a heart attack.

In gratitude for his long service, a small house had been provided to Kris for life, a two-story cottage that sat back from the street, its cream-colored façade dominated by tall windows whose symmetry was marred only by an air-conditioning unit set into the bottom left one. No one had thought it strange that the wife of the Episcopal bishop of DC had also been a spy. In fact, no one had ever even questioned it, her professional and personal lives never mingling. That separation was one of the first things she'd learned from Kris Cox, and only once had Stephanie ever violated that rule.

She retrieved the Saturday-morning paper at the end of a short walk leading to the front door. A shoulder-high boxwood fence protected a small garden from the street. She'd called from the hotel and knew that Kris was waiting. Her knocks were answered almost immediately, Kris greeting her with a hug in a terry-cloth robe. She hadn't visited her old friend in many months, though they occasionally talked on the phone. Kris had always been thin and trim and matronly, with short silver hair and bright blue eyes. She was approaching eighty, and for nearly fifty years worked for the CIA, first as an analyst but retiring as a deputy director. When the Magellan Billet was created it had been Kris who helped formulate its guidelines, and it had been Kris who'd encouraged that the unit be independent of DC influences. Stephanie had worked her whole career to maintain that mantra but, in the end, it had been those DC influences that had led to its destruction.

"Tell me what's wrong," Kris said. "I'd offer you coffee, but I know you hate it, and you didn't come to drink."

"No, I didn't."

They sat in the kitchen and she reported everything that had happened over the past few days ending with, "I need to know about the words *Fool's Mate*."

Neither of them dwelled on the fact that she'd been fired. It was

274 | STEVE BERRY

the way of the political world they both knew, and nobody understood those ways better than Kris. No nonsense. To the point. Get the job done. Three things she respected about this woman immensely, and three things she'd practiced every day as head of the Magellan Billet. Unfortunately, combined with those pesky DC influences, those three things had also gotten her fired.

"I remember Fool's Mate. It was a code name that we thought was associated with a rogue Soviet intelligence operation, one Andropov may have been personally involved with."

Perhaps the last of the old communists, Yuri Andropov may have been the most dangerous of all Soviets. Smart, cagey, he rarely made a false move. Definitely a throwback to the time of Lenin, Andropov had been appalled by the corruption during Brezhnev's regime. Stephanie recalled the investigations and arrests that happened after Andropov became general secretary. Many of Brezhnev's former inner circle had faced execution.

"Andropov was no friend of ours," Kris said. "He always tried to couch himself as a reformer, but he was a hard-liner. Luckily, he served as general secretary for only a short time and was really sick for most of that."

She'd thought this would be the right place to come, more so than waiting for Osin or Danny or Edwin to brief her further. That was why she'd left the White House early, deciding that knowing the answers to the questions before she asked them might prove beneficial.

"It's 1983," Kris said. "As you know, Reagan's popularity was sky-rocketing. He'd dodged an assassin's bullet and was challenging the Soviet Union on every front. Eastern Europe was imploding, Poland exploding. The Iron Curtain had begun to fall. Brezhnev dies in November 1982 and Andropov takes over. Nobody thought that would be good. He'd crushed the Hungarian Revolt in '56 and the Prague Spring in '68. As KGB head he suppressed dissidents, then advocated invading Afghanistan. He was a real badass. The Soviet Union was not going to change under him, and the Cold War definitely heated up when he became general secretary. So we redoubled our efforts and heightened intelligence operations. I spent a lot of time on Capitol Hill lobbying Congress for more money. Then, one day, Fool's Mate came across my desk."

"Is what Osin told me true? Were there Soviet weapons reposito-
ries in this country?"

"Nothing we could ever verify. But those *spetsnaz* units were good.
The KGB was good. And homeland security back then was nothing
like today. You could get things in."

She listened as Kris explained more about Andropov. "He hated
Reagan, and Reagan had a hard time dealing with Andropov. We
had an asset back then inside the Kremlin. A good one. Stuff you could
take to the bank. He told us that Andropov was readying something.
If Eastern Europe did not settle down, especially Poland, Andropov
planned to make sure there would not be a second Reagan term. If the
truth be known, the old communist was afraid of that actor."

She recalled the tension within the State Department when it was
announced Andropov had become general secretary. George Shultz
had not liked the prospect, but had dealt with the situation. Nothing
changed with Forward Pass. Everything kept moving ahead. John Paul
revisited Poland in June 1983 in a triumphant seven-day extravaganza
that reenergized every dissident. She'd helped coordinate the timing
of that visit as a way to openly challenge Andropov's reach.

"The threat of Reagan not serving a second term didn't raise alarm
bells?" she asked.

"The Soviets back then threatened stuff like that all the time. Nobody thought the USSR wanted a war with us. And that's what it would
have been, if they'd done anything. No way they could win that fight."

Maybe so, but today a threat like that would be taken much more
seriously.

And with good reason.

"When you called earlier and told me about Fool's Mate, I had to
think back long and hard. We heard that four agents were sent on a
special mission. I remember it because each was code-named with a
chess move. The last part of that mission was called Fool's Mate. But
we never learned much about any of it. Just snippets here and there,
with no substance. Andropov died in February 1984 and nothing ever
came up about it again. We figured if there was anything to worry
about, it died with him."

"It may not have," she said.

Kris had carried the highest security clearance that anyone within the government could hold, so Stephanie felt safe discussing this with her. But what did it matter? Her own security clearance had ended hours ago.

"We all thought," Kris said, "that Andropov, if he'd lived, planned on stopping reforms. He would also have cracked down on Eastern Europe. Everything would have played out differently. But then he gets sick and dies. Problem solved. A year later we had Gorbachev, who was a pussycat, and the rest is history."

"Reagan knew exactly how to handle him."

"That he did. But I'm real concerned about this current split within the Russian government you told me about. The Daniels people knew how to deal with things like that. We have no idea how the new guys will do. Transition time is always tricky. I know you realize, but I hope the Fox people realize, too, that the new Russians play for keeps."

"What's your best guess here?"

Kris seemed to consider that question carefully, especially with what she'd told her about the 20th Amendment.

"Inauguration time is only a matter of hours away," Kris said. "I do recall the Soviet fascination with presidential succession. It is a mess, no question. You would think after 9/11 Congress would be more vigilant, but nothing has changed. Of course, logic here says that Zorin wants to attack the inauguration. It certainly looks that way. But first he has to find an over-twenty-five-year-old suitcase nuke and hope it still works. Then, if it does, those things have to be positioned really close to the target. It's a nuke, but a small one. Dogs, radiation detectors, EM monitors, you name it, they've got it in DC right now, watching everything. The odds of his getting close enough to take everyone out is virtually impossible."

"Yet Zorin isn't stopping."

Kris sat back in her chair. "I know. That bothers me, also."

"So what is it he knows that we don't?"

Kris shrugged. "Impossible to say, but it must be good."

Bell chimes disturbed their solitude. Kris's cell phone. She reached for the unit lying on the table. "I've been expecting this call."

"You want me to wait in another room?"

"Not at all. It concerns you."

CHAPTER
FIFTY-ONE

LUKE DROVE NORTHWEST OUT OF DC INTO MARYLAND. FRITZ Strobl's car had been returned by the Secret Service and he'd been provided with a nondescript, government-issued sedan. His Mustang still sat in the Virginia junkyard, where it most likely would remain since he hadn't carried much insurance. Just the minimum, since he never anticipated that it might one day be involved in a car fight. The repair bills to restore it would be in the thousands, far more than he could afford to sink into a nearly fifty-year-old vehicle. Too bad. It was great while it lasted.

He'd slept a few hours and even had breakfast. Stephanie had called just after 7:00 A.M. and told him what she wanted him to do, providing a Germantown, Maryland, address for Lawrence Begyn, the current president general of the Society of Cincinnati.

"We need to know about the 14th Colony," Stephanie had said to him. *"All the details with no bullshit. You have my permission to be your most charming, direct self."*

He'd smiled at that last part. Normally, she would demand diplomacy. Not here, though. He'd sensed that things were accelerating and she'd told him Cotton and Cassiopeia were back in the United States, north at the Canadian border, dealing with Zorin. Stephanie still carried Anya's cell phone, which was activated, but had yet to ring. She'd assured him that they were ready if and when it ever did.

Of that he had no doubt.

Stephanie Nelle never entered a fight without being prepared. And getting fired yesterday had not seemed to slow her down. But having the current president of the United States in your corner, if only for a few hours more, had to count for something.

He found the address outside of Germantown in a tree-shrouded suburb, amid old spacious houses—Begyn's a large, wood-sided, white rectangle atop a small knob. The area reminded him of where Charon's house stood in Virginia, a similar wrought-iron gate denoting an entrance to a graveled drive. He turned in and followed the path through bare trees up to the house.

Two things immediately grabbed his attention.

A car parked in the woods just where the drive ended and the splintered front door, half opened.

He wheeled to a stop, gripped his Beretta, then hustled to the entrance, stopping short of entering, listening for any sound but hearing nothing. A glance inside revealed an entrance hall dotted with antique furniture. What was it about these Cincinnati people? They all seemed loaded. First Charon's mansion, now Begyn's.

He slipped inside and kept to the exterior wall, searching the sunlit interior for any sign of trouble. He glanced into other rooms and immediately spotted overturned furniture, slashed upholstery, armchairs gutted, and books off their shelves lying in a jumble on the floor. Bureaus were ransacked, drawers ripped out, the contents dumped and scattered about as though an earthquake had hit. Somebody had definitely been looking for something.

His attention turned to the staircase.

A body lay sprawled across the wooden risers near the top. Blood had flowed down and congealed in thick maroon patches. He climbed the stairs, sidestepping the puddles, and rolled over the corpse. An automatic rifle lay beneath, which clattered away down the steps. He came alert and looked around to see if the noise had attracted any attention.

Nothing.

The face on the corpse was of a man, mid-thirties, short hair, thick features. A deep gash had penetrated the throat with a wide smile, which explained the cause of death.

He heard a noise.

From downstairs.

Something moving.

He crept back to ground level and turned in its direction, closing his mind to all messages except those coming from around him. A dining room opened to his left where another body lay on the hardwood, the man's throat slashed nearly identically to the first. A door stood just ahead, one that swung in and out, which he assumed led to the kitchen. He approached and pressed his body tight to the wall, sneaking a peek through the half-inch space between the molding and the jamb. He was right. A kitchen did lie on the other side. With his left hand he shoved the door inward and burst in.

Empty.

Sunlight poured in through windows, glittering off stainless-steel appliances and marble countertops.

What had happened here?

He was about to check the rest of the house when he heard another noise. Behind him. He whirled and was met by a sharp blow to his windpipe, which immediately triggered a choking response. He knew the move, it was taught to him in the army, but he'd never personally experienced it.

He fought to breathe, but never got a chance.

Something slammed into his left temple.

And the last thing he saw before everything went black was the glistening blade of a knife.

MALONE SAT IN A CAFÉ LOCATED IN DOWNTOWN EASTPORT, FINishing off a plate of eggs, bacon, toast, and coffee. Zorin and Kelly had been gone over two hours. He and Cassiopeia had watched as the two men came ashore in a small dinghy, bypassing the immigration booth located near the docks. As expected, they'd entered the town and called a cab on a cell phone Kelly produced, which arrived a few minutes later. He and Cassiopeia had not followed. Instead, the drone overhead had kept a distant watch, an open phone line providing them with a running account.

The cab had dropped the two at the Eastport Municipal Airport, which sat not far from the central business district. They'd entered the small terminal and exited a few minutes later, walking over to a row of parked cars and driving one away. Malone knew what had happened. Kelly had rented a vehicle, which would be an easy thing for him to do.

Finally, they'd caught a break.

While the drone kept watch, he decided to send Cassiopeia to follow them, cautioning her to stay way back. He'd been told that the drone's airtime was drawing to a close, so Cassiopeia would become its replacement. He'd catch up to her later. The important thing was not to lose Zorin.

He'd already called Edwin Davis and told him more of what he had in mind. So while he waited, a hot breakfast had sounded good.

The waitress cleared his plate away.

Outside, Eastport remained quiet, understandable given that winter was in command, the morning skies rapidly becoming a solid mass of slate gray. Snow seemed to be on the way. Hopefully, he'd be headed south before it arrived. The café enjoyed a light business, but it was not yet 10:00 A.M. on a Saturday. A white Ford Taurus wheeled into an angled parking spot out front and he saw two men emerge, both dressed in the blue uniform of the Maine State Police.

They entered the café, found him, and introduced themselves.

"We're told you need our help," one of them said. "National security."

He caught the skepticism. "You doubt me?"

The trooper smiled. "Doesn't matter. When the state police chief personally calls on a Saturday morning and says that we're to come here and do whatever *you* want, I come here and do whatever you want."

He had to give Edwin credit, the man knew how to get things done. Malone had explained that the best way to keep Zorin and Kelly under surveillance would be a running tail. One car follows for a few hundred miles, then another takes over, then another. Hard to notice any interest that way. Right now that only would involve Maine, so Edwin had enlisted the state police's help. Most likely, Zorin and Kelly were headed south farther into New England, so more tails would have to be ready in other states. So much easier to just have a drone follow the car, but he knew messy legal issues were associated with that on U.S. soil.

No matter, the old-fashioned way should work just fine.

Along with a backup.

He finished his juice and said, "We need to go out to the airport."

The trip was quick, just over a mile, and inside the terminal he found a single rental car counter. He'd asked for the officers to come in with him just in case of a problem. Nothing intimidates more than uniforms, badges, and holstered weapons.

They approached the counter and he said, "About two hours ago you rented a car to two men. We need to see the paperwork." The attendant looked like he was going to balk so he pointed a finger and said, "And the only correct response here is, *Yes sir, here it is.*"

His stern look and the two troopers beside him made the point. The clerk handed over the rental agreement, which was in Jamie Kelly's name, on a Canadian driver's license, paid for in cash. No drop-off point noted.

"Is the car coming back here?" he asked.

The clerk nodded. "That's what they said."

But he knew that wasn't true.

So he asked what he really wanted to know. "You have GPS in all of your vehicles, right?"

"Of course. We can find them, if need be."

He gestured with the rental agreement. "We need the GPS frequency for this one. Now."

CHAPTER
FIFTY-TWO

STEPHANIE LISTENED AS THE MALE VOICE ON THE OTHER END OF the cell phone, dry and raspy, like the rattle of some creature in a pile of dead leaves, told her things she'd never known. Apparently, back in the 1980s, while she'd been engaged with Forward Pass, working covertly with Reagan and the pope, others had also been hard at work undermining the Soviet regime with more active measures designed to destabilize.

"It was quite a time," the voice said. "You have to remember Andropov was head of the KGB when they tried to kill John Paul. He would have approved that operation."

She listened as the voice explained how Andropov became convinced that John Paul's papal election was designed by the Vatican to undermine Soviet control in Poland, part of a deliberate plan to collapse the Soviet Union. Ridiculous, for sure, but ultimately, thanks to circumstances that formed outside the church—mainly the election of Ronald Reagan as president of the United States—that's exactly what happened.

"He firmly believed that the pope was dangerous, and largely because of John Paul's charm, especially toward journalists. I remember reading a memo where Andropov went on and on about how the pope went for cheap gestures with a crowd, like wearing a Highlander's hat in England, or shaking hands with people, kissing children, as if he were running for office. Andropov seemed terrified of what the pope might do."

And rightly so, since John Paul orchestrated his actions with the direction of an American stage manager. Interestingly, though, never once had either Reagan or the pope warned her about Andropov.

"The KGB went through the Bulgarians to have John Paul shot," the voice said. "That much we know. And they chose their assassin with care. Ali Ağca supplied them with perfect plausible deniability. He was weak and stupid and knew nothing about nothing. All he could do was babble nonsense, and that's what he did. I remember when the pope went to the prison and forgave Ağca. What a brilliant move."

One that she'd helped arrange.

John Paul made the decision, and Reagan approved.

So in 1983, two years after the assassination attempt, the pope met privately with Ağca who, filled with emotion, cried and kissed the pope's ring. Photographs and accounts of what happened consumed the press, which splashed the story around the world, along with those possible assassination links back to Moscow. The whole thing had been bold and assertive. A pitch-perfect example of how to make lemonade out of lemons.

Or at least that's how Reagan had described it to her.

"When Andropov assumed the general secretary's post," the voice said, "there was talk of trouble. He knew what we'd been doing in the Eastern Bloc. Funneling money to dissidents, providing logistical support, offering secret intelligence on their governments, even taking care of a problem or two."

She knew what that meant.

People had died.

"Then Andropov gets sick and he knows it's over for him. The doctors gave him eight months. That's when we got scared. He had nothing to lose, and there were people in the Kremlin that would follow him right off the cliff. When Kris called earlier and asked me about Fool's Mate, I immediately remembered it. We all thought it was going to be the old Russian's last move."

She wondered who the aged voice belonged to, but knew better than to ask. If Kris had wanted her to know she'd have told her. Most likely he'd been CIA. High up. And she knew the score. Neither successes nor failures ever were aired in public. The agency was deliberately compartmentalized, its past laced with so many secrets that no one could ever know it all. And the big ones that really mattered? They were never written down. But that didn't mean they were unknown.

"Andropov hated Reagan. We all thought the KGB was going to make a move on him. He'd tried to kill the pope, so why not a president. The writing was definitely on the wall by late 1983. The Soviet Union faced serious economic trouble. They also had a leadership problem. The whole country was in flux. The Kremlin became fascinated by American presidential succession. Kris mentioned that you read a communiqué we seized. There were several like that. The zero amendment. That's what they called the 20th."

"Do you know why?"

"Because, if an attack was done right, no one would be left in charge."

"How's that possible?"

"I'm no scholar on the issue, but I remember being told that if you can wipe out the president-elect and vice-president-elect, the Speaker of the House, and the president pro-tempore of the Senate in one swoop, before the new president and VP are sworn in, you're left with cabinet members who take power through a congressional act. That law is riddled with problems. It's unclear whether cabinet officers could even constitutionally serve. There'd be so much infighting that no one would be in charge. Infighting, by the way, that the KGB would stoke. Those guys were masters at active measures like that. They manipulated our press a thousand times, and they would have done so there, too."

"And the purpose of all that?" she asked

"That's the moment the USSR would strike. When no one is sure who can give the military orders. You'd have total confusion. The tanks would roll across Europe. We'd be busy fighting among ourselves about who's in charge. Some would say this guy, others this guy. Nobody would know for sure."

The tactic made sense.

"We picked up intel that they were working on some active measures that involved the 1947 Presidential Succession Act. Of course, to make that work, they'd have to strike at an inauguration. Some of us believed that's what Andropov had up his sleeve for Reagan's second in 1985. But thankfully, the old man's kidneys failed in early '84. And everything was forgotten since the people who took over after that were not interested in World War III. All that loyalty to Andropov vanished."

She stared across the table at Kris Cox, who was watching her with eyes the color of glacier water. Everything about her friend's countenance signaled that she was being told the truth by someone who knews.

"How many people are aware of this?" she asked the voice.

"Not all that many. It was one of those things that never happened, so it just went by the wayside. There was a lot like that back then. The KGB, if nothing else, stayed focused. Every day there was something new. It's important now only because you seem to have a problem. I remember Aleksandr Zorin. He was a competent KGB officer. Our people respected him. It's amazing he's even still alive."

She decided to learn all that she could and asked, "What about RA-115s?"

"Haven't heard that term in a while, except on TV or in the movies. They existed, of that I'm sure. Others disagreed, though. The problem was that not one of them was ever found anywhere in the world. And you would think at least one would surface. Some thought it was part of a KGB misinformation campaign. Like I said, they were good at that. A way to get us to chase shadows."

"The SVR says now that they did exist, and that five are still unaccounted for."

"Then you should listen to them. That's quite an admission."

One she was sure Nikolai Osin never should have made, considering the increasing division within his chain of command. The last thing Russian hard-liners would want would be for the United States to know anything about any possible suitcase nukes.

"Could they be here?" she asked. "In the United States."

"Absolutely. The KGB was the largest, most expansive intelligence agency the world has ever seen. Billions upon billions of rubles were spent preparing for war with us. Those guys did anything and everything. Nothing was out of bounds. And I mean nothing. We know for a fact that arms caches were placed all over Europe and Asia. Why would we be exempt?"

He was right.

"It seems Zorin may be trying to implement Fool's Mate," she said. "Apparently he was privy to what Andropov planned."

"Four KGB officers were assigned to the operation. We never learned their names. So he could have been one of those."

"But it's been so long," Kris said. "Why now?"

She knew the answer. "He's bitter about everything that happened with the end of the Soviet Union. He was an ideologue, one who truly believed. Osin told me that he blames us for everything bad in his life and he's been stewing on that a long time."

"Which makes him especially dangerous," the voice said through the phone. "My guess is that he wants to use the 20th Amendment to generate the same political chaos here that we did over there. But he needs a workable RA-115 to make that happen. You'd have to take a lot of people out at once."

A problem, for sure, but one Zorin seemed intent on solving.

"We'll have a new president in a little over twenty-four hours," the voice said.

And she knew what that meant.

The next opportunity to apply Fool's Mate.

CHAPTER
FIFTY-THREE

LUKE OPENED HIS EYES.

He was sitting up, bound to a wooden chair with tape, nearly identical to how he'd restrained Anya Petrova. His arms and legs were strapped tight, preventing him from moving in any direction. His neck was free, his mouth unobstructed. But his head hurt from a nasty pop and everything was still out of focus. He blinked to correct the problem and eventually saw that he was in the kitchen of Begyn's house.

A woman stood on the other side of the room.

Short, trim, not an ounce of fat on her. She wore a tight-fitting jogging suit that revealed highly toned muscles. He wondered how many hours of push-ups, chin-ups, and bench pressing had gone into that sculpting. He envied her dedication. It took all he had to work out. A pair of enameled, dark-hazel eyes appraised him with a look that was all alert. Her auburn hair was cut short, close to the ears, in what he thought was a military style, and that conclusion was further reinforced by her demeanor. She was attractive, the face bearing no malice, but neither did the features convey much compassion. Instead, she stared at him like an elephant. Calm, solitary, watchful, but encased inside a dangerous stillness. She held a seven-inch, stainless-steel blade, not unlike one he once carried as a Ranger.

"You military?" he asked.

"Riverine."

He knew the unit. Part of the navy, focusing on close combat and military operations within rivers. Riverine forces in Vietnam were the most highly decorated with the largest casualties. Women had been part of them for several years now.

"Active duty?"

She nodded. "On leave, at the moment."

He watched as she continued to twirl the blade, its tip gently resting against her left index finger, the right hand slowly rotating the black handle.

"Who are you?" she asked.

His wits and composure were returning. "I'm sure you already know that."

She stepped across the black-and-white-checkerboard floor, coming close and pressing the flat side of the blade to his throat. "You know it's not true that women don't have an Adam's apple. Actually, we do. It's just that the male version shows more than ours. Which is good, since I can clearly see where to split it."

Goose bumps prickled his skin. Which, to say the least, was not normal for him. She had the cool of a priest with the eyes of a jaguar, which made for an unnerving combination. He did not like the helpless feeling that surged through him. This woman could slit his throat and there was nothing he could do to stop her. In fact, one wrong move—a hiccup, a sneeze—and he'd carve a dark smile in his throat for her.

"I'm going to ask this one last time," she said. "You saw the other two in there. You understand what I'm capable of."

"I got it, darlin'."

"Who. Do. You. Work. For?"

His cool was returning as he sensed that this woman did not intend to hurt him. In fact, she was unsure about him. Which seemed vastly different from the two bodies he'd already seen. Those she'd harbored no doubt about. But the blade was still biting against his skin at a vulnerable spot. One twist and—

"Defense Intelligence Agency. On assignment to the White House. But you already know that, don't you? You got my badge."

He was guessing, but she withdrew the blade and reached into her back pocket, fishing out the leather case and tossing it in his lap.

"What does the White House want here?"

"Your turn. Who are you?"

"You should know that I have the patience of a two-year-old and a temperament not much better."

"That's okay. Most people just call me an arrogant ass."

"Are you?"

"I can be. But I also have my charms."

He kept assessing this woman, who seemed plain in speech and rough in manner. He noticed the running shoes at the end of her strong legs.

"You been joggin'?"

"Out for my daily five miles. When I got back, men were ransacking the house."

"They picked the wrong place."

She shrugged. "That's the way I see it."

"Any idea who they work for?"

"That's the whole reason why you're still breathing. Unlike you, those guys were Russian."

Now he was curious. "And how would you know that? I can't imagine they carried little ID cards in Cyrillic."

"Better. They spoke to one another. I heard them, after I snuck back inside."

Interesting. No calling the police or simply staying away. This woman moved straight into the fray. "What's your rank?"

"Lieutenant, junior grade."

"Okay, Lieutenant, how about you cut me loose."

She didn't move. "Why are you here?"

"I need to speak with Larry Begyn."

"His name is Lawrence."

"And you would know that because?"

"I'm his daughter. Why do you need to speak with him?"

He debated being coy but decided that would only keep him taped to the chair longer. "He took a call a few hours ago from a man named Peter Hedlund. I need to talk to him about it."

"On what subject?"

"The 14th Colony. The Society of Cincinnati. The state of world peace. You choose."

She stepped toward him and used the knife to cut his bindings away. He rubbed his arms and legs to stimulate the circulation. His head remained woozy.

"What did you hit me with?"

She displayed the stainless-steel butt end of the knife. "Works good."

More of that military training. "That it does."

She appraised him with coy eyes. "There's something you need to see."

He followed her from the kitchen, through the dining room, to a short corridor that led back toward the front of the house. A third body lay on the floor, this one with wounds to both the chest and neck, the mouth frozen agape in death.

She gestured with the knife. "Before that one died, he told me they were looking for a journal. He also mentioned the words *14th Colony.* Why do you and these Russians want the same thing?"

An excellent question.

Her voice stayed level and calm, never rising much above room temperature. Everything about her seemed wary and on guard. But she was right. These men had come straight here, which meant the other side knew more than Stephanie thought they did.

"You kill with a great ease," he said to her.

They stood close in the hall, she making no effort to add space between them.

"They gave me no choice."

He kept his gaze locked on her but gestured to the corpse. "Did he happen to say exactly what they were looking for?"

"He called it the Tallmadge journal."

Which meant the Russians were not two steps ahead, more like half a mile. "I need to speak with your father."

"He's not here."

"Take me to him."

"Why?"

"Because these guys aren't going away, and unless you plan to slit a lot more throats, I'm going to have to deal with this."

A wave of uneasy understanding passed between them. She seemed to believe him. And for all her coolness, she had a tenacious air that he liked.

"All right," she finally said. "I can take you to him."

"I'm going to have to call in these bodies," he said. "The Secret Service will handle the cleanup. Nice and quiet. We can't afford any attention right now."

"Lucky for me."

He grinned. "Yeah, I'd say so."

She turned toward the dining room and kitchen, walking away.

He wanted to know, "Why didn't you kill me, too?"

She stopped and faced him. "I can still smell that stench of army on you."

"Spoken like true navy."

"But I almost didn't take the chance," she said.

He couldn't decide if she was serious or not. That was the thing about her. You just didn't know.

"You found out my name," he said to her. "What's yours?"

"Susan Begyn. People call me Sue."

CHAPTER
FIFTY-FOUR

MALONE CAUGHT A RIDE WITH THE TWO MAINE STATE TROOP-ers. They'd left Eastport and headed back to the mainland across the causeway, then west. Zorin and Kelly were two hours ahead, already on Interstate 95, headed south. The GPS frequency for the rental car was sending real-time data back to the Secret Service, which allowed them to track the car with perfect precision. To be safe, though, a tail on the highway stayed at least two miles back in traffic, impossible for them to see or notice.

"These guys you're after," one of the troopers said from the front seat, "they're not real smart."

He noticed the statement contained a hook. Who wouldn't be curious? It wouldn't be a cop's nature just to come out and ask. Instead, they liked to fish, throwing out conclusions that invited disagreement in the hope he would volunteer something. But this wasn't his first rodeo.

So he kept it simple.

"These guys didn't have much choice. Stealing a car would have been dumb."

"But stealing a boat? That was okay?"

"No choice there, either. And they only needed it to get to Maine. A couple of hours on the water, at night. Little risk. But snatching a car and driving south? That could be a problem."

"They never heard of GPS?"

He felt safe in offering, "They've both been out of touch for a while."
And they had.

Last time Zorin was in the field GPS had not even been invented. Kelly probably knew about its capabilities, but neither one of them thought the United States cared about what they were doing. Certainly what happened at Kelly's house told them someone was interested, but he was betting Zorin had concluded that would be his own countrymen.

Cassiopeia had handled the tail until Bangor, then the Maine state troopers took over in an unmarked car and would stay on them until Massachusetts, then the Secret Service was waiting to assume the task. Where this would end was anybody's guess, but they had to give Zorin a long leash. Answers would come only from patience. Were there risks? Absolutely. But for the moment they had the situation in hand.

A cell phone rang from the front seat. The trooper not driving answered it and handed the phone back over the seat.

"It's for you."

He accepted the unit.

"Cotton, it's Danny Daniels."

CASSIOPEIA WAITED AT BANGOR INTERNATIONAL AIRPORT, where she'd been directed to go by Edwin Davis, once the Maine police signaled they were on Zorin's trail. She had to admit, she loved being back on the chase. It was almost as if she'd been born for this. Over the past month she'd tried to convince herself that she was something else. But the shoot-out in Canada had recharged her nerves, and the fact that she'd been there for Cotton had been important for them both. Other men she'd known would not have liked the fact that she'd saved them, but Cotton carried no prejudices. Everybody needed help from time to time. That had been what he was doing in Utah. Trying to help her. But she'd resisted. He was like a missing part of herself, and only when they were together did she truly feel complete. If the past month had taught her nothing else, it had made that point crystal clear.

She was parked outside a single-story terminal away from the airport's main congestion, where private jets and other aircraft sat. Ten minutes ago a small twin-engine jet with U.S. government markings had taxied and stopped, the pilots deplaning and entering the terminal.

Their ride, she assumed.

She thought about Stephanie Nelle and knew she had to make peace there, too. But that shouldn't be too hard. Stephanie was not one to hold a grudge, especially where she bore at least some responsibility for the mess in the first place. But she would offer no reminders.

No need.

Everyone knew where everyone else stood.

MALONE LISTENED TO THE PRESIDENT OF THE UNITED STATES, who sounded more anxious than normal.

"I think Zorin intends to make a play during the inauguration," Daniels said through the phone.

He did not disagree, but had to point out, "That would be next to impossible. No one could get anywhere close enough to do the kind of damage he'd need to inflict."

Earlier, back in Eastport on the phone, Edwin Davis had told him about the 20th Amendment and the flaws both it and the 1947 Presidential Succession Act contained.

"Experts tell me that one of those things, if it exists, would be around six kilotons," Daniels said. "To do maximum damage it needs to be deployed from up high so the overpressure would be strongest. The wind blast would level everything within a mile. And you're looking at a fireball a thousand yards wide. Of course, if it's sitting a few hundred feet from the swearing-in, that will have about the same effect. But I agree with you, there's no way to get that close."

"How high does it have to be to do its worst?"

"A few hundred feet. That could mean a plane, chopper, or drone."

"These guys wouldn't have access to drones."

"But the Russians do."

"You don't seriously think Moscow wants to start a war."

"I'm not sure Moscow has anything to do with this. I want you and Cassiopeia back here fast. It's time we have a chat with the incoming administration and I'd like you two present."

"For what?"

"They're not going to believe anything I have to say."

He was not accustomed to defeatism in this president.

"I now know what it means to be a lame duck," Daniels said. "I can do some, but not near what I once could. People know my time is over."

"What is it you want to do?"

"We have to change the swearing-in. It's the only way."

STEPHANIE REENTERED THE MANDARIN ORIENTAL. NORMALLY she would work out of the Justice Department when in DC, but in her current state of "between employers" the hotel seemed her only choice. The trip to Kris Cox's house had proved enlightening, and she needed time to digest all that she'd been told.

She entered the lobby, but before turning for the elevators she spotted Nikolai Osin, standing off to the side, still draped in a sharp, black wool overcoat.

He said nothing as she approached.

"What brings you here?" she asked.

His face remained stoic, the features as frigid as the air outside.

"Some people, who would like to speak with you. Privately. Not from the government. They are . . . entrepreneurs."

She knew what that sugarcoating meant.

Mobsters.

"They are here, though, on behalf of some within the government," he said. "A few of those people we discussed earlier. Which, more than anything else, explains my presence here."

She got it. No choice. "Okay."

"A car is just outside, rear door open, waiting for you."

"Are you coming?"

He shook his head.

"This talk is only for you."

CHAPTER FIFTY-FIVE

Zorin sat in the front seat as Kelly drove. They'd decided to split the duty between them, each resting a few hours. The route was simple, Kelly had said. Straight south on the same highway until they came to Virginia, then they'd head west, into the rural countryside about eighty kilometers west of Washington, DC.

He thought back to his time with the KGB. Canada had long been intended as a forward base for Soviet military operations. He'd personally reconnoitered several crossing points into Minnesota and North Dakota. The Flathead dam in Montana would have been one of their first targets for destruction, all part of a coordinated infrastructure attack designed to internally weaken the United States. But Canada itself had formed an important target. He'd spent two years gathering intelligence on its oil refineries and gas pipelines, determining the best way to sabotage them, all of which had been carefully detailed in reports back to Moscow.

Nearly every Canadian province and all of the American states had been partitioned into "zones of operation." Each came with a central base in a rural location equipped with a parachute landing site, clear of buildings for two kilometers, and adjacent safe houses for refuge. They'd named the landing sites *dorozhka*, runways, and the houses *uley*, beehives. KGB guidelines required that the land for both should belong to someone trusted, the *uley* stocked with a radio, money, food, and

water. There should also be police, military, railway, and forestry worker
uniforms, along with local clothing. Encrypted files on site laid out the
targeted power-transmission lines, oil and gas pipelines, bridges, tun-
nels, and military installations within 120 kilometers.

Then there were weapons.

Caches of firearms and explosives, either smuggled in or more likely
bought locally inside the country. That had been particularly true in
the United States, where firepower could be easily purchased.

"Did you personally prepare the *uley* for Fool's Mate?" he asked
Kelly.

"I thought you were asleep."

"I was."

"Yes, Aleksandr, I own it."

"Risky, was it not?"

"Those were Andropov's orders. I was to involve no one else. He
wanted me to have total control."

"It's been such a long time. How could any of that still exist?"

"That was part of my orders. It had to last. No exact date for action was ever noted. I assumed it would be sooner rather than later,
but with the peculiar weapons involved special arrangements had to
be made."

He knew what that meant. "A constant power source."

"Exactly. And I will say that proved a challenge."

"Is it booby-trapped?"

Kelly nodded. "One of the devices is designed to explode if the
cache is breached. That was also part of my orders. No detection or
anything left to find."

And the risk taken there had been enormous. What if there'd been
a breach, whether intentional or accidental, and a six-kiloton nuclear
explosion happened? That would be hard to explain.

"When did you learn what Andropov had in mind?" Kelly asked.

"Parts came from the other two officers. Then I searched the old
records and gathered more. But that archivist knew things, too."

Belchenko had tempted him for years with Fool's Mate. Telling
him about the zero amendment. That information had been gleaned
from Andropov's private papers, which remain sealed to this day. Eventually, he'd learned enough to know what Andropov had planned

for Reagan. Each time a new American president had been elected he'd pressed for more, and each time Belchenko resisted. But not this time. Finally, his old friend had come through and sent him along the right trail.

Which Moscow also seemed to be following.

"Are you hungry?" Kelly asked.

"We have to keep going."

"We also have to eat. We can buy something and eat on the road. There are several places just ahead."

Some food would be good and it would cost them only a few minutes. He checked his watch.

1:16 P.M.

22 hours left.

MALONE GAZED OUT THE JET'S SIDE WINDOW TO THE TERRAIN BE-low. They were somewhere over New York or New Jersey, headed south aboard a Gulfstream C-37A owned by the air force. At five hundred miles per hour they would be back in DC before 2:00 P.M.

Cassiopeia sat across from him. He'd caught up with her at the Bangor airport and they'd immediately boarded, leaving the two state troopers behind with their questions still unanswered. He'd filled her in on everything he knew and on Danny Daniels' apprehension about the pending inauguration.

"Zorin's down there," he said. "Heading south." He turned from the window. "Thankfully, we have him on a tight leash, both physically and electronically."

"So we let him lead us to whatever there is, then take him down."

"That's the idea. But we have the added complication of the Russians with their panties in a wad."

She smiled. "More of that southern colloquialism?"

"Just a statement of fact." He thought about things for a moment. "My guess, Zorin is headed for somewhere in or around DC. So we'll wait there for him to come to us. If not, we'll head to him. Sorry about all these flights."

He knew flying was not her favorite thing.

"This is not so bad," she said. "Plenty of room to move around. Those fighter jets are a different story. I just don't see the appeal."

He did, though. In fact, if not for a few twists of fate he would have been a navy fighter jock, now retired after a twenty-year career. Interesting how that seemed so mundane. So few ever got the chance to pilot a multimillion-dollar warplane, but that paled in comparison with his experiences first with the Magellan Billet, then on his own after retiring. He'd been involved with some amazing adventures, the current one no exception.

"I need to call Stephanie," he said.

The plane came with its own communications system, which he activated by lifting a phone from a nearby console. He dialed Stephanie's cell phone number, the one she'd provided to him two days ago.

The phone rang in his ear.

Twice.

Three times.

After the fourth ring, voice mail kicked in and a robotic message said that the caller was unavailable and for him to please leave a message.

He decided not to and ended the call.

"She told me she wanted to know the minute we had things under control," he said as he hung up the phone. "So where is she?"

CHAPTER FIFTY-SIX

STEPHANIE OCCUPIED THE BACKSEAT OF THE ESCALADE BY HER-self. Two men with no personality sat up front. The SUV wove its way through traffic, and even though it was the weekend the streets were clogged with inaugural visitors. The next two days would be jammed with celebrations, too many to count. A million-plus people from all over the country would be in town, security extra tight. Already, the White House, the National Mall, and the west end of the Capitol should be sealed to visitors. The scaffolding for the swearing-in would be patrolled around the clock. All the museums that stretched on both sides of the Mall, from the Capitol to the Washington Monument, would likewise be occupied by security teams, their doors locked hours before the ceremony. Back in 1989 she remembered climbing the north tower in the Smithsonian Castle and watching George Bush take the oath of office from there. That would never be allowed today. Too high a spot, with too clear a shot. Instead, either a military sentry or the Se-cret Service would enjoy that lofty perch.

She wasn't quite sure what was happening here and had not liked the look on Osin's face back in the hotel lobby. But she'd had no choice. What would Danny say? *Knowledge is knowing a tomato is a fruit, wisdom is not putting it in fruit salad.* She was in pursuit of wisdom. Interesting how even unemployed she managed to stay in trouble. For the first time she sympathized with Cotton, as this was exactly the situation he'd repeat-edly faced from her.

She grabbed her bearings and saw that they were headed north on 7th Street toward Columbia Heights. The car turned onto a side route. She hadn't been able to catch the street name. A small neighborhood park appeared on the right. The vehicle stopped. The man in the pas-senger seat climbed out and opened her door.

A gentleman?

She stepped out into the cold.

Luckily she still wore her heavy coat with gloves and scarf. The park stretched about a block and was deserted except for a man sitting on a lone bench.

She walked over.

"I apologize for the intrigue," he said to her as she drew close. "But it was important we speak."

He was short and plump, little more than a dark overcoat, a trilby hat, and stylish Louis Vuitton scarf. A lighted cigarette dangled from the gloved fingers of his right hand, which he puffed in the cold.

"You have a name?" she asked.

"Call me Ishmael."

She smiled at his use of the opening line to *Moby-Dick*.

"Names are unimportant," he said. "But what we need to discuss is vital. Please, have a seat."

To find that wisdom she'd have to oblige him, so she sat on the bench, the cold from the wooden slats seeping up through her clothes.

"You don't sound Russian," she said.

"I'm just an emissary, hired by a group of interested foreign nation-als. Disturbing things are happening inside Russia that concern them."

She made the connection with what Osin had said back in the hotel lobby. "Are you here for the oligarchs or the mob? Oh, I forgot, they're one and the same."

"It's interesting how we forget that we went through a similar pe-riod of maturing. The Russia of today is not all that dissimilar from us in the late 19th century, and even up to the 1930s. Corruption was a way of life. And what did we expect when we overthrew 800 years of authoritative rule? That democracy would just bloom in Russia? All would be right? Talk about naïve."

He had a point. All of that had been discussed in detail by Reagan and his advisers back when Forward Pass was active. Everyone wondered what *would* happen after communism. Little thought, though, had been given to alternatives. Ending the Cold War had been all that mattered. Now, twenty-five years later, Russia seemed more authoritarian and corrupt than ever, its economy weak, political institutions nearly gone, reforms dead.

"The men I represent have authorized me to speak frankly with you. They want you to know that there are factions within the Russian government who want dangerous things. Perhaps even a war. They hate the United States, more so than the communists once did. But most of all they hate what Russia has become."

"Which is?"

He savored a long drag on his cigarette, exhaling a blue funnel of smoke. "We both know it is no longer a global threat. Yes, it waged war in Georgia, continues to intimidate the Baltics, and invaded part of Ukraine. So what? Minor nothings. It's too poor and too weak to do anything more than posture. Washington knows that. Moscow knows that. You know that."

That she did.

Every intelligence report said the same thing. The Russian army was totally demoralized, most soldiers undertrained and unpaid. On average, twelve a month committed suicide. And while the new Russia had managed to produce some formidable warplanes, super-silent subs, and ultrafast torpedoes, it couldn't manufacture them in mass quantities. Only its nuclear arsenal commanded respect, but two-thirds of that was obsolete. No first-strike capability existed. Its global reach was gone, and even its regional capabilities were limited.

All it could really do was threaten.

"It seems that certain events over the past few days have triggered a renewed sense of pride in certain quarters of the Russian government," he said. "Contrary to what you and the CIA and the NSA think, not everyone in Russia is corrupt and for sale. Ideologues still exist. Fanatics have not disappeared. And they are the most dangerous of all."

She grasped the problem. "War is bad for business."

"You could say that. People leave Russia each year by the hundreds of thousands. And those aren't the poor and unskilled. They're smart entrepreneurs, trained professionals, engineers, scientists. It takes a toll."

She knew that to be true, too. Corruption, red tape, and the lack of the rule of law were driving people to safer environments. But she also knew, "More are coming in than are going out. You're not in any danger."

"Thankfully, people flock to the many available jobs. Which is even more of a reason why Russia can't afford all this fanatical nonsense. It should be building on what it has, diversifying from oil and gas, expanding the economy, not preparing for a war that cannot be won. I was hoping that you and I could see these truths together."

"I no longer work for the U.S. government. I was fired."

"But you still have the ear of the president of the United States. Osin told us that. He says you're the one person who can speak with Daniels."

"And say what?"

"We're here to help."

She chuckled. "You're kidding, right? Russian oligarchs. Mobsters. Here to help? What do you plan to do?"

"What you can't. Eliminate the fanatics within the government. This reverting to Soviet-like behavior must end. There's talk of suspending arms control agreements, testing NATO airspace with bombers, rearmament, even the retargeting of missiles to again include Europe and the United States. Is that what you want?"

She could see that this man was genuinely afraid. Interesting what it took to jar the nerves of someone who dealt with people of no conscience.

"No one wants a new Cold War," he said. "That's bad not only for my benefactors, but also for the world. You consider those I represent to be criminals. Okay, they can live with that. But they don't bother you. In fact, they do business with you. They have no armies and no missiles."

"But they do export crime."

He blew a contemptuous funnel of smoke skyward and shrugged.

"Everything can't be perfect. They would say that's a small price to pay, considering the alternative."

She was definitely intrigued. "Your people are going to take down all of the problems?"

"There will be many funerals across Moscow."

The United States never officially sanctioned assassinations, but reality was far different. It happened all the time. "What do you want from us?"

"Stop Aleksandr Zorin."

"You know what he plans?"

"We know what he wants."

"Which is?" She wanted to hear it.

"To make the upcoming inauguration the most memorable in history. Don't allow him to do that."

Finally, confirmation of the endgame.

There'd been lots of talk over the past few years about a new Cold War. All agreed that if it materialized it would be fought with money, oil, and especially social media propaganda. Half-truths backed by just enough evidence to make them both interesting and supportable. Easy to do today. The Internet and twenty-four-hour news had changed everything. The old rules were long gone. Large closed societies were next to impossible to sustain. Look at China, which had failed miserably. The Soviets once believed that ruthless discipline worked best, that the West could be forced down simply by standing firm and never blinking. Unfortunately, that philosophy had failed, too, since communism only bred poverty and repression. Both tough sells. So eventually the USSR had been forced to blink. Then collapse.

Now parts of it seemed to want a resurrection.

She hated herself for asking, but had to. "When will they act?"

He finished the cigarette and flicked the butt away. "In a matter of hours. There are arrangements to be made. It would be better if this was seen as an internal power struggle, discrediting both the dead and the living. Done right, they will destroy themselves."

"And you and your benefactors keep making money."

"Capitalism at its truest. I can't see how anyone here would have a problem with that."

One thing she had to know. "Is Zorin on to something?"

"Those fanatics think he is. When he moved on Vadim Belchenko, that drew their attention. They watch archivists, and that one particularly. They sent the military to kill Belchenko in Siberia. They managed to get him, but your agent left five dead Russians, three of them soldiers, in that dacha beside Lake Baikal. I hope he stays that good. He'll need to be to stop Zorin."

"There are suitcase nukes here?"

He smiled. "We know Osin told you about them. That's fine. You should know. And that was the thing about Andropov. For all his bravado, he truly believed the USSR would lose the ideological and economic war with the West unless drastic steps were taken. So he took those. He called it Fool's Mate. Everyone thought both it and him forgotten. Now here he is, risen from the grave, to wreak havoc. So yes, there are weapons here."

She felt a little numb, fatigue and the cold beginning to take their toll. Being part of an illegal conspiracy wasn't bringing her any comfort, either. But the man sitting beside her was not bluffing. His benefactors had worked too long and too hard to have idiots take it all away, so they were going to do this with or without her. Oh, yes, there'd be funerals in Moscow. But there might be a few here, too.

Already, Anya Petrova had died.

How many more were to come?

"The SVR made a move on Zorin in Canada," she said. "How much do these crazy people within the government know?"

"I'm told quite a bit. They have full access to classified KGB archives, including Andropov's personal papers. These are records few have ever seen. When Zorin brought Belchenko east, then your agent was allowed into the country, that raised alarms. It seems they already knew of Fool's Mate, but not its full potential. So they educated themselves and found out about Jamie Kelly. That's when they decided to kill Zorin and Belchenko to keep it all contained. Your agent thwarted their attempt to take Zorin out in the air, which would have ended things. They were not happy. Now they're here to tidy up all the remaining loose ends, which include Zorin, Kelly, and your agent. So be ready."

"They know where the nukes are?"

He shook his head. "That's the one thing we have going in our favor. They need Kelly to lead them, as does Zorin, by the way."

She'd heard enough and stood from the bench. "We'll handle things here."

"Keep an eye on the television. The cable news channels will alert you when it starts on the other side."

She started off.

"I can offer you a ride back to the hotel," he called out.

The thought turned her stomach.

"Thanks, but I'll find my own."

And she walked away.

CHAPTER
FIFTY-SEVEN

LUKE FOLLOWED SUE BEGYN OUT OF THE CAR. THEY'D DRIVEN
two hours east to Annapolis, then south along the Chesapeake shore.
Sue had said little on the trip and he'd left her alone with her thoughts.
Instinct and training cautioned him against revealing too much to
her. Instead he'd tried the bare minimum to see what she made of it.

Which had been nothing.

The White House assured him that all would be handled at the
Begyn house, with no traces remaining of the bodies. Sue had changed
from tight-fitting workout clothes into jeans, a long-sleeved twill shirt,
coat, gloves, and boots. She was armed with both a hunting rifle and
handgun, her father's study stocked with weapons. Apparently, Lawrence Begyn believed in the 2nd Amendment.

The rain started about halfway along their journey, a cold steady
drizzle that reduced visibility on the roads. She'd directed him along
on a series of highways, ending up at the coastal village of Long Beach.
Her father owned a house nearby, one where, she'd noted, he retreated
from time to time. Luckily, Begyn had chosen yesterday to seek solitude, ahead of the uninvited visitors to his house. But Luke wondered
about that timing. It seemed far too coincidental with Peter Hedlund's call.

"I was headed back to the base today," she said as they walked in the rain. Bare limbs rattled overhead, scattering drops of freezing water onto the nape of his neck.

"You goin' to get in any trouble?"

"I'm not officially due back until tomorrow."

Fifteen whole words. That's the most she'd said since they'd climbed into the car. Before him rose a rambling white-framed house with long verandas, landward sides, and a cedar-shingled roof. A detached two-car garage stood off to the side. It sat nestled among bare maples and beech trees in the curve of an oxbow from the bay. Sue had called earlier and told her father the situation.

Waiting for them under the veranda was a tall pencil of a man with a square face and brownish-gray hair. He wore what looked like hunting clothes and carried a Browning bolt-action rifle. Luke and his brothers had each owned one, too. His father had also been a big supporter of the 2nd Amendment.

"You okay?" Begyn asked his daughter.

"She slit three men's throats," Luke answered.

The senior Begyn eyed him with a mixture of curiosity and contempt.

"My daughter is a soldier," he said. "She knows how to defend herself."

Luke stepped out of the rain onto the covered porch. "On that, we agree."

"I just met you," Begyn said, "but I don't like you."

"I get that a lot. But here's the thing. Either we do this nice and easy, or we do it hard with a whole lot of federal agents around. Personally, I don't give a crap which one you choose. But I need answers and I need them now."

Begyn still gripped the rifle, its barrel pointed skyward, but the threat remained as the right index finger rested on the trigger.

"I assure you, Mr. Begyn, you'll never get the chance to use that. I know how to defend myself, too."

"There'll be two of us," Sue said.

He faced her down. "Bring it on, honey. I can handle you."

She stood silent, studying him with marble eyes. Whoever trained this woman should be proud. She seemed to have taken every lesson to heart. Especially the one about listening, as opposed to talking, which he'd never been able to master. But Stephanie had told him to get answers with whatever method worked.

"What do you want?" Begyn asked.

"The 14th Colony. Hedlund said to ask you about that."

The older man looked at him with a studied gaze.

"Hedlund called you yesterday. He told you, *'It has to be that. We thought all of this was long forgotten, but apparently we were wrong. It's starting again.'* The *'that'* must be the 14th Colony. So I want what, why, when, how. Everything."

"Peter said I'd probably be hearing from you."

"I love it when folks expect me. Makes the job so much easier."

Then he noticed something out in the rain, past the garage, near where the tree line began. A pile of frozen clods of dirt and a shovel plucked into them.

"Been doin' some excavating?" he asked Begyn.

"Why don't you shut up and come inside."

STEPHANIE NEGOTIATED THE SIDEWALK BACK TO 7TH STREET AND turned the corner, heading south toward central DC. The rumble and roar of car engines filled the air, the skies overhead thick with low hurrying clouds rushing in from the northeast. A cold rain and probably snow looked to be on the way, and she was a long way from anywhere warm.

Her gloved hands stayed in her coat pockets and she kept a watchful eye out for a taxi. But DC was not like New York where rides scurried everywhere at all hours of the day and night. Of course, she could always use her cell phone and call for one. She'd hardly ridden in a taxi for the last decade, ground transportation and security usually provided for her. The effects of being unemployed were beginning to set in, but she might as well get used to it.

Cotton had tried to find her, the phone noting a missed call. She needed to try him back, and would shortly. In the meantime she switched the unit off silent mode.

She'd resented Ishmael's attitude, as if they were long-lost allies, each fighting a righteous cause. Russian criminal syndicates were some of the most complex, violent, and dangerous in the world. That was in no small part due to the fact that their activities inside Russia were nearly institutionalized. Not a whole lot was different, as Ishmael had said, from the early days of organized crime in America. Still, having thieves and thugs as partners was not all that comforting. But she supposed if anyone could take down the problems within the Russian government it would be the oligarchs and their private army, organized crime.

Her cell phone chimed in her pocket.

She removed the unit and answered.

"I need you back here now," Danny Daniels said. "Where are you?"

"You wouldn't believe me if I told you."

"Try me."

So she did.

"You're right. That is unbelievable."

"Yet it happened."

"All the more reason for you to be here. Stay put. I'll send a car to get you."

"What's happening?"

"We're going to have a chat with the next president of the United States."

LUKE ENTERED THE HOUSE, IMMEDIATELY STRUCK BY ITS COZY, rustic appeal. He guessed it rambled for maybe fifteen hundred square feet over two levels. Begyn propped his rifle beside a club chair and knelt before the hearth, where he lit a fire, flames licking at the kindling, then consuming the split logs, orange light flickering through the room.

"I held this until you got here," Begyn said. "It's cold out there."

And raining, but that was not the point. "Your daughter said you left the house yesterday evening to come here," Luke said. "That's not a coincidence."

"I had no idea people would invade the house."

"I didn't say that you did. But now that you've brought it up, tell me about the Tallmadge journal."

Sue had retreated to the windows, where she gazed out past the venetian blinds, as if on guard, which bothered him.

He removed his coat.

"This is a nightmare," the older man said. "One that I thought was long over."

There it was again. A reference to something in the past.

"Maybe I didn't make myself clear," he said. "I need information and I need it quickly."

"What are you going to do?" Sue asked. "Arrest us?"

"Sure. Why not? We can start with the three men you killed. Self-defense or not, we'll let a jury decide. Just the allegations, though, will end your military career."

"No need to threaten," Begyn said.

"What was so important that Peter Hedlund tried to protect it? And what have you been diggin' up outside?"

So far he'd asked four questions and received no answers.

"Mr. Daniels—"

"Why don't you call me Luke," he said, trying to relieve the tension.

Begyn eyed him hard. "Mr. Daniels, all of this is quite difficult for us. It involves the society, and that has always been private. I'm the president general of the society. Its head. I owe it my allegiance."

"Then you can explain all of that to the FBI, the Secret Service, and the CIA, who will all want to question you and examine all of the society's records."

He allowed that threat to sink in.

"Dad, you need to tell him whatever it is," Sue said. "There's no point in keeping any more secrets. Look where it's got you."

Begyn stared across the room at his daughter. That was the first thing she'd said Luke actually agreed with. Maybe reality was finally setting in. Every high came with a low, and killing was never easy, no matter who you were.

His host motioned toward a doorway and led the way through it. They stepped into a long, narrow kitchen with windows that pointed out toward the bay. A small room opened off to the right, where a glass door led outside. Wind buzzed just past its frame, jostling the rain that continued to fall.

A mudroom.

His boyhood home in Tennessee had one, which he and his brothers had made good use of. Lying on its hardwood floor atop a layer of newspaper was a plastic box caked in mud.

"I dug it up," Begyn said.

Luke bent down and eased up the lid. Inside lay bundles of opaque plastic wrapped around what looked like books and paper.

"What are these?"

"Secrets that Peter Hedlund thought he had to defend."

CHAPTER
FIFTY-EIGHT

STEPHANIE SLIPPED INTO ONE OF THE CHAIRS SURROUNDING THE oval table within the White House Cabinet Room. Nineteen others guarded its perimeter, but only a few were occupied. Present was the current president and the president-elect, along with the incoming attorney-general-designate and Bruce Litchfield, the current acting AG. Edwin Davis was likewise there, along with Cotton and Cassiopeia, both of whom she was glad to see. There'd been no time for pleasantries. She'd walked straight from the car that had found her on 7th Street to the conference room.

This was her first time inside the room, where for decades presidents had met with their cabinets. She knew the story about the table, bought by Nixon and donated to the White House. The president always sat at the center of the oval, opposite the vice president, with his back to the Rose Garden, his chair a few inches taller than the others. Cabinet members were assigned places according to the date their department had been established, the oldest seated closest to the president. Each administration selected portraits to adorn the walls, designed surely to offer inspiration. Right now, Harry Truman, George Washington, Thomas Jefferson, and Theodore Roosevelt kept watch. But she knew those would most likely change in the coming week.

With no vice president here, President-Elect Fox sat opposite

Danny. Everyone else chose sides depending on their boss. She moved to the end of the oval at Danny's right, Litchfield between her and the president, while Cotton and Cassiopeia assumed neutral ground at the oval's opposite end.

After a flurry of introductions, Fox said, "You mentioned this was urgent."

She caught the dismissive tone of *How could anything be urgent at this late hour in your term.* And the demeanor. Like a schoolmaster encouraging a slightly backward pupil. But Danny seemed to keep his cool. She knew he and Fox were nothing alike. Physically, Danny was tall, broad-shouldered, with thick bushy hair and piercing eyes. What had one observer noted? *A great flint-eyed hulk of a man.* Fox was short, pinched, pursed, and solemn with ash-gray hair and watery blue eyes. From what she'd read, he considered himself a northeastern intellectual, a financial progressive but social conservative. Danny was southern to the core and totally pragmatic. Pundits had tried to pigeonhole him for years, but none had ever been successful. To her knowledge the two men did not know each other, and compounding their estrangement was the fact that they were of opposite parties, neither owing the other a damn thing.

"We have a developing situation," Danny said. "One this idiot sitting next to me was aware of, but decided wasn't our problem."

She smiled at his reference to Litchfield, who could say nothing.

"I understand," Fox said, "how you could be irritated that we okayed the firing of Ms. Nelle, but we had an agreement that everything would be okayed by my people, especially at this late hour."

"Last I looked Litchfield works for me. And your bird dog was all over things, issuing orders to stand down. Contrary, I might add, to my direct instructions."

Litchfield sat confident in his chair.

"He did what I told him to do," the AG-designee said. "I would have terminated her next week anyway."

"Go screw yourself," Stephanie said.

Fox, Litchfield, and the new AG looked her way. Even Cotton seemed a little shocked. Cassiopeia just smiled.

"I assume wounds heal better when not constantly reopened," Fox said to her. "My apology for that comment."

And if her disrespect offended him, Fox did not show it. Instead, he turned his attention back across the table to his equal. "Why are we here?"

Danny explained everything he knew about Zorin, Fool's Mate, and the 20th Amendment. She added what she'd learned at Kris Cox's house, and Cotton filled in what had happened in Siberia and Canada. Since Danny had said nothing about what had just happened in the park, she followed his lead and kept that to herself.

Fox sat back in his chair when they finished. "None of that sounds good."

"Welcome to my world," Danny said.

Fox glanced at his AG-designee, then at Litchfield, asking either for his opinion.

"We don't know a whole lot," Litchfield said. "Most of it is speculation. Seems the most important questions are first, whether thirty-year-old nuclear devices are still here, and second, whether they're viable."

"The Russians definitely think the bombs are here," she said. "They designed the things to last. So we can't take the chance that they're not workable."

"But you don't know they exist," the new AG said. "It could all be nothing, a wild-goose chase. A misdirection by Moscow for something else."

"We can't take that chance," Danny said.

Fox seemed intrigued. "What do you want me to do?"

"Let's move the inauguration to an undisclosed location. You take the oath there at noon, as the Constitution requires, then we don't have a problem."

No one said a word.

Finally, Fox shook his head. "I appreciate what you're saying. I really do. But moving the swearing-in at this late hour would only raise a million questions, and there's no way we could keep this under wraps. At this point we don't even know if it's a credible threat. The first month of my administration would be consumed with the cable news channels analyzing, speculating, and guessing about what we did. We'd never get on message. I can't start my presidency with that hanging over me."

"Would you rather be dead?" Edwin asked.

Which was a fair question, and coming from a man with a mind that cut like a diamond, the question should be taken seriously.

"Is everyone who works for you insubordinate?" Fox asked Danny.

"Not to me."

Fox smiled.

"At a minimum," Danny said, "move the vice president's swearing-in to another location. That way you're not both in the same spot."

"And how do we do that without raising the same questions? Everything is set for noon tomorrow with *both* of us taking the oath together."

Cotton had sat uncharacteristically quiet, watching the two giants spar. She realized that the decisions Danny wanted made suffered from the weakness of no hard evidence to support them. Fox, and rightly so, would want details to persuade him to follow the plan without adding variations of his own. But she wanted Cotton's assessment, so she asked him, "You've spoken to Zorin. You were there with Vadim Belchenko. Is this real?"

"These men are on a mission. No question."

"Then by all means," Fox said, "play this out. Do your job. But we're not delaying or changing the inauguration until you have something concrete. A true, genuine, verifiable threat. Surely all of you can see the wisdom in that? And besides it all happens tomorrow right here, in the White House. Where else would any of us be safer?"

She knew what he meant.

The Constitution mandated that the outgoing president's term end precisely at noon on January 20. Usually, that wasn't a problem. The ceremony occurred in public, outside the Capitol, high on scaffolding, with millions watching. But when January 20 fell on Sunday things had long been different. The new president and vice president would take the oath on Sunday, as required by the Constitution, and then a public celebration, which included a retaking of the oath in the more familiar public setting outside the Capitol, took place the next day.

"I checked," Fox said. "Since 1937, when the 20th Amendment took effect, three times this has happened on a Sunday. Tomorrow will be number four. I can't control the calendar or change the Constitution, but I can stick to the plan. And that we'll do, unless something drastic is discovered."

"Is that show so important to you?" Danny asked.

"That's not fair. You had two inaugurals, both extravaganzas I might add. Now it's my turn."

"You're making a mistake."

"But that assumes you're right about this. What if you're wrong and I go along with it. Then I look like a fool, following your lead, chasing shadows. Surely you can see that. And by the way, you're not all that popular with my supporters."

Stephanie was proud of Danny. He hadn't lost his temper or his cool. Understandable, given he'd moved with darting ease through political mazes for most of his life. Never had she seen him troubled by confrontation. Instead, he thrived under pressure, seeming to draw strength from it.

"I will do this, though," Fox said. "Bruce, prepare me some legal background on the 20th Amendment and the Presidential Succession Act. I confess to not being an expert on either. That way, if this materializes into something credible we'll be ready to make informed decisions."

Litchfield nodded.

"In the meantime, the rest of you keep working at what you're doing," Fox said, "and let's see what develops. I'm not oblivious to what you're saying. I just want more before I act. And we have time to make changes, if need be."

Fox pushed back his chair and he and his AG-designee stood.

Danny pointed at Litchfield. "Take this one with you. The sight of him makes me sick."

Litchfield stood.

"But before you go," Danny said. "You need to remedy something."

Litchfield glanced at Fox.

"What the hell are you lookin' at him for?" Danny said. "Don't think for one moment I won't fire your ass right here, right now. Talk about drawing attention to things."

Litchfield bristled at the insulting tone, but wisely held his tongue.

"Think about that press conference," Danny said to Fox. "It'd be a doozy."

318 | STEVE BERRY

White House reporters were a different breed, the last of the in-
telligent and tenacious. Definitely not a good place for a new president
to be challenged on the eve of inauguration.

So Fox wisely nodded his assent.

Litchfield faced her. "You're reinstated." He reached into his pocket,
found her badge, and walked it over to her.

Then the three men left the Cabinet Room.

"I told him to bring it," Danny said to her.

"I'm glad I live in Denmark," Cotton said. "Those people are fool-
ish."

"What was asked of them was entirely reasonable," Edwin said,
"given the possible threat."

"First thing a wing walker wants to know is who's drivin' the plane,"
Danny said. "Fox came to find that out, and he's right about one thing.
We don't have spit for proof. Last I heard, Zorin and his pal were still
on I-95 headed south. They're comin' our way, but for what and where?"

"They'll all be in one place tomorrow," Edwin said. "President-elect,
vice-president-elect, Speaker of the House, president of the Senate, and
all of the cabinet, except one. Right here, in the White House at noon.
Let's just say the unthinkable happens and they're all blown to bits,
that means the designated survivor would take command."

"Who is it this time?" Danny asked.

She knew the White House chief of staff made the selection.

"The secretary of transportation."

"Who's great at building highways, but doesn't know beans about
leading this country," Danny said. "Not to mention the constitutional
problems with that succession law. I had it checked out."

"Litchfield?" Stephanie asked him.

"Hell, no. The White House counsel handled it. That 20th Amendment and the succession law are a train wreck. Once the dust settled
from a bomb, there'd be court challenges, political fights, chaos."

She remembered what the voice on the phone at Kris's house had
cautioned. "And more, possibly fueled by the SVR in a misinformation campaign."

"That they would," Danny said.

She glanced at him and he nodded. "We also have an added complication."

And she reported to Cotton, Cassiopeia, and Edwin what had happened in a northern DC park.

"I thought it best to keep that to ourselves," Danny said.

"He confirmed that the bombs exist," she said. "But we have no way of knowing if that's true. No way at all."

"Not yet, anyway," Cotton said. "But Zorin is coming closer. With Kelly, and they're surely headed straight for them."

"The Russian government is about to get some chaos of its own," she said. "The people making money over there like things exactly the way they are. They have no dreams of a new Soviet Union."

Danny turned to Edwin. "Get State working on this. I want an assessment of who they might take out. Have the CIA advised and see if they can pick up anything. Since we've been given a heads-up, let's not get caught crapping by the creek."

Edwin nodded and left the room.

"Going to be quite a party here tomorrow," she said.

"My last. They're setting up the Blue Room now with cameras. It won't take long. Maybe thirty minutes. We're having a small reception for the bigwigs starting at 10:30. They'll all be out of here by 1:00."

"So there's a two-and-a-half-hour period where the whole Fool's Mate scenario could play out," Cotton said.

"Not really. Fox and his VP won't arrive until 11:30. So there's ninety minutes, at best, we have to worry about. But 12:00 noon is the perfect time. Everyone is guaranteed to be front and center."

She knew that other festivities around town would not get under way until Monday after the noontime public ceremony. On leaving the podium, finished with his inaugural address, Fox would head inside the Capitol and sign the necessary documents submitting nominations for his cabinet so the Senate could go to work on confirmation. He would then have lunch with leaders of Congress before enjoying the inaugural parade. In the evening would be celebration balls, the new president and vice president making the rounds.

"Once they're all out of here," Danny said, "it won't matter. Everybody is too scattered. No. Our Achilles' heel is noon tomorrow. Where's Luke?"

The sudden shift in topic caught her off guard.

"Checking out more leads with the Society of Cincinnati," she said. "Zorin sent Anya Petrova there for a reason. I want to know what that is."

"So do I," Danny said. "Which brings up a fascinating question. What does a two-hundred-plus-year-old Revolutionary War social club have to do with the USSR?"

CHAPTER
FIFTY-NINE

LUKE SAT AT THE KITCHEN TABLE. WATER BUBBLED IN A KETTLE
on the stove where Begyn was preparing hot tea. Sue sat with him and
Luke wondered how much of this she knew and how much she was discovering for the first time. Her comments earlier seemed to indicate
that she was more than a passive observer. He wondered about her
mother, but knew better than to ask. He'd noticed some family pictures in the other rooms—father and daughter only—which made him
wonder about divorce as opposed to being a widower.

An antique brass chronometer on the wall showed that it was approaching 5:00 P.M. The day had gone by fast. Snow had begun to sift
down from an ever-darkening sky, and the wind continued to rattle
the panes. A fire still burned in the grate, casting warmth and a golden
glow. But no more logs lay in the wood box and anything outside would
be too wet to burn. He'd already noticed a thermostat, which indicated
that the house came with central heating.

Begyn brought the kettle to the table and poured them all a cup of
hot water. Luke liked green tea, a taste acquired in the army from a
fellow Ranger. Nothing fancy for him, though. No fruit or spices or
cream. He preferred a simple blend, plain, nothing added, decaffein-
ated if available. Which Begyn had on hand.

His host sat at the table. Stacked before them were the plastic
bundles from the box in the mudroom. He'd discovered that they were

vacuum-sealed bags, the contents obscured thanks to the opaque covering.

"This may not seem important to you," Begyn said. "But some things relative to the Society of Cincinnati *are* important to me. I've been a member my entire adult life. One of our ancestors fought in the Revolutionary War and was a founding member."

"Are you the first to be its leader?"

The older man nodded. "That's right."

"And let me guess. You're the last, until Ms. Jim Bowie here gets married and has a son, since women aren't allowed as members."

"Are you always such a prick?" Sue asked.

"Only when I'm being played which, by the way, both of you seem to be doing."

"Peter Hedlund told you about the 14th Colony," Begyn said.

He nodded. "America's plans to conquer Canada. That was a long time ago. Who cares?"

"We do."

Begyn's voice rose several notches, which seemed to surprise the older man. So Luke backed off and listened about how things had been just after the Revolutionary War. A new country emerging into turmoil. Leadership at a minimum. A virtually nonexistent economy. Thirteen states fighting among themselves. No uniformity. No centralization. Both officers and regular army soldiers had been sent home unpaid after years of loyal service. There was talk of another revolution, this time a civil war.

The Society of Cincinnati, first formed in 1793, emerged from that turmoil. At first, no one paid it any mind. But when chapters organized in all thirteen states and its treasury swelled to over $200,000, people became frightened. The society had more money than the country, and soldiers organizing raised alarm bells. The fact that membership passed hereditarily stunk of a new nobility and a nation divided by classes.

"Patricians and plebeians," Begyn said. "That's how critics saw the new nation. Like ancient Rome, where the same thing happened. Between 1783, the end of the Revolution, and 1787, the start of the Constitution, this country stayed afraid. Those were difficult years the history books gloss over."

Then, as Begyn explained, when French officers, who'd been allowed to join the society, began to donate money a new worry began—foreign influence and monarchal leanings. Finally, when the society started to exercise control over both state legislatures and Congress, lobbying for causes it believed in, calls for its abolishment grew loud.

"They labeled us *'contrary to the spirit of free government. A violation of the Articles of Confederation. A threat to the peace, liberty, safety of the United States.'* If not for George Washington's personal intervention, the society would have dissolved. But in 1784 Washington proposed massive changes, which were ultimately accepted, and the threat level diminished."

Henceforth, no more lobbying. No more politics or hereditary titles. No more foreigners or foreign money. And, to quell fears of collusion, general meetings would be held only once every three years.

"Everybody seemed satisfied with the new and improved society and we were forgotten."

"So why is that not the end of the story?"

"During the War of 1812 we were called upon to help the country," Begyn said. "In a capacity that was . . . in conflict with our new charter. Many of our members had fought in the Revolution. James Madison was president of the United States. He wanted a war with Great Britain and he got it. Then he wanted Canada invaded. That was the closest British territory, so he asked the society to draw up an invasion plan."

As Hedlund had recounted. "That didn't turn out well."

"You could say that. Some of the journals here on the table, sealed away, detail those 1812 war plans. Called, as you know, the 14th Colony. They're quite detailed. The men who drew them knew what they were doing. Unfortunately, the men running the war were incompetent. The invasion was a disaster. Afterward, we hid these plans away. About thirty years ago we purged them from our official archives. It was thought best that no one ever know what we'd done. I was told to destroy them, but I couldn't bring myself to do it. Embarrassing or not, contradictory or not, they're still part of history."

He was recalling more of what Hedlund had said. "Charon knew about these journals?"

"Of course, he was the Keeper of Secrets at the time. He had them in his possession. But he violated his duty and allowed an outsider to see them."

Finally, the good part. "Do you know who?"

Begyn sipped his tea. "Only that he was a Soviet, working out of the DC embassy. I don't remember his name or position. It was back in the late 1970s or early 1980s. Brad allowed him access to our sealed archives, which was an absolute breach in protocol. We let it go the first time, but when it happened a second time, about ten years later with another man, an American this time, the president general removed him."

"You got a name there?"

Begyn shook his head. "I was never told."

"So if we open these packets up, all we're going to find is our Canadian invasion plans from the War of 1812?"

Begyn laid down his cup and began to shuffle through the ten or so bundles on the table. "It's amazing these things survived. These vacuum bags work. I remember buying the device, used for food, and adapting it. I haven't thought about any of this in a long time."

"Until Hedlund called."

"That's right. He told me about the Russian woman who'd come to his house and the gunfight."

"We thought all of this long forgotten, but apparently we were wrong."

"Is the president-general who fired Charon still around?"

Begyn shook his head. "He died years ago."

"Hedlund says you know it all. But it sounds like you're missing a lot of pieces to this puzzle."

"Our society is a closed one. We keep to ourselves and don't bother anyone. Today we are philanthropic. It's important for us to stay above politics. We breached that mandate in 1812. But that was not the only time. We've helped out presidents and the military on several occasions after that. Which means we've violated the mandate that George Washington and the society founders laid down. And, as I said earlier, that may not mean much to you, but it does to us. Brad compounded things by allowing outsiders, foreigners, to learn about that."

Luke was puzzled. "Yet nothing ever came of it."

"Not a word, until yesterday."

"It's starting again," as Hedlund had said on the phone.

Sue had sat silent, sipping her tea, listening. Daddy probably did not discuss these things with his daughter. Most of this was crap. But part of it still had to be important since Anya Petrova had come all the way from Siberia to deal with it.

Begyn shuffled through what lay on the table, then offered him one of the sealed packets. "We also did something else. More recent."

He accepted the bundle.

"You're holding an operational plan for the United States to invade Canada," Begyn said. "Dated 1903."

CHAPTER
SIXTY

ZORIN SAW THE ROAD SIGN THAT INDICATED THEY WERE LEAV-
ing the state of Pennsylvania and entering Maryland. He'd not shaved
or showered in over a day, and his mouth tasted awful. Sleep had come
in spurts but, strangely, he was not tired. Instead a tangible feeling of
success swirled in his stomach, his body charged with a sense of achieve-
ment at possibly his last chance at redemption.

He thought again of Anya, wondering what she was doing. He'd
switched on the cell phone hours ago, hoping she might call. He'd
decided not to call until after he learned what Kelly had accomplished.

Both his wife and Anya had brought him joy, each in her own way.
He'd been lucky to find them, especially Anya, who was far more ad-
venturous than his wife had ever been.

His wife, though, had been a wonderful woman.

They met when he was still in training and married in secret, her
family not approving of her choice in a husband. But his being KGB
quelled any objections they might have made. They'd lived together
nearly thirty years before ovarian cancer claimed her. Sadly, she lived
long enough to be there when their son died, and the sadness from that
tragedy never left either of them. His wife understood him, accepted
him for who he was, living most of their married life alone as he moved

from station to station. For their entire marriage she'd handled everything until she became too sick.

But even then, she remained in charge.

"You must listen to me," she said, lying in the narrow hospital bed.

On her back, arms at her side, toes pointing upward, she formed a small mound beneath the sheets. Most of the time she'd stayed sedated, but there were moments, like now, when consciousness overtook the drugs and she was lucid. The clinic, on the outskirts of Irkutsk, treated only the party elite and their families. The room was large, with a high ceiling but a gloomy feel. He'd managed to have her admitted, and though they'd never spoken of the fact, where she lay, this part of the building, housed only terminal patients.

He wiped away a thin film of sweat from her gray, pallid forehead. Her hair was dank with oil. She wasn't dirty, the nurses bathed her daily, but the odor of death she exuded seemed unmistakable. The doctors had already told him she was beyond their aid. All they could do was ease the pain and make sure he had no complaints. Though no longer of the KGB—both it and his job ended years before—his reputation had preceded him.

"I want you to do what it is you've been wanting," she said to him.

His face mirrored her pain, but he was still surprised by the comment. "What do you think that is?"

"Do not treat me like a fool. I know that I'm dying, though you can't bring yourself to tell me. Neither can the doctors. I also know that you're troubled by so much. I've watched you these past years. There's a sadness inside you, Aleksandr. It was there before our precious son died, and it remains."

Pain began to reassert itself and she no longer lay neatly in the bed, tossing from side to side, plucking at the sheet that covered her. Soon they would come with another injection and out she would go for another few hours. He'd already been told that eventually she would not reawaken.

He took her hand in his.

It felt like a small bird, delicate and frail.

"Whatever it is that consumes you," she said. "Do it. Resolve your anger. And that's what you have been, Aleksandr. Angry. More so than ever before in your life. Something is unfinished."

He sat beside her and allowed their life together to wander through his mind. She was a plain woman who had always spoken of him with respect. So many other wives he knew wore away at their husbands, some even made cuckolds—creating jealous, suspicious, agonized fools whose work suffered and reputations declined. That had not happened to him. Never had she asked for much, nor expected more than he could provide. Marrying her was the smartest move of his life.

She grew more restless and cried out. The duty nurse appeared but he waved her away. He wanted to be alone with her for just a few moments more.

Her eyes opened and she stared straight into him.

"Do not . . . waste . . . your life," she said.

He recalled how her eyes stayed open, lips curled in a half smile, the grip from her fingers vanishing. He'd seen death enough to know its look, but he sat there for a few more minutes hoping he was wrong. Finally, he kissed her cold brow before slipping the sheet up over her head. For so many years she'd been drawn into his dilemma, one blind step after another, trapped just like him. She knew his anger and wanted it gone.

As did he.

He recalled how grief had risen hot in his throat and threatened to strangle him. His mind had numbed with a sudden sense of loneliness. No longer could he think either of or about her. She and his son were both gone. His parents dead. His brothers lived far away and rarely communicated. He was essentially alone, with a long, empty, purposeless life ahead of him. His physical health remained, but his mental stability hung in doubt.

"Do not waste your life."

And that was when the thought first came back to him.

Fool's Mate.

"It's time for us to be honest with each other," Kelly said.

He glanced across the darkened interior of the car and brought his mind back to the present. Outside, snow was falling, not heavy or accumulating, but definitely in the air.

"The envelope I was given that night by Andropov," Kelly said. "I was told that in the late 1970s the KGB learned some vital information from the Soviet embassy in DC. It seems one of the staffers there made friends with a man who knew some unusual things."

All Soviet foreign diplomats and KGB officers had been taught how to elicit information without the source ever knowing of their interest. In fact, the vast majority of intelligence originated from just such innocent exchanges. They came with a low risk of exposure as no one ever suspected a thing. Just simple conversation among friends and acquaintances. What was the American and British saying from the Great Patriotic War? He'd been taught it at trade school. *Loose lips sink ships.*

"This unusual information dealt with Canada," Kelly said.

He listened as Kelly told him about the Society of Cincinnati and how it designed invasion plans for America's northern neighbor.

"The detail of the work is remarkable," Kelly said. "The early plan from 1812 was written by a man named Benjamin Tallmadge, who was a spy for the Americans during their Revolutionary War. The later plan, for the 20th century, was drafted by more society members skilled in warfare. I read both. Quite amazing what America had in store for Canada. Andropov's original source learned about this and passed it on, along with something else, something even more important, which required me to reverify. It is the second move in Fool's Mate, Aleksandr. The one you asked about, the one that wins the game."

An excitement surged through him.

"I redeveloped contact within the society with the same member who first talked to our embassy official. His name was Bradley Charon and we struck up a friendship. The fact that the society twice planned Canada's invasion was some sort of guarded secret. Only a few of the members knew. And frankly, that's of little consequence. But that other piece of information. That made all the difference. Yet one question lingered."

He knew. "Was the information correct?"

"That's right. And it was, Aleksandr. Every detail."

He felt compelled to say, "That society. I know of it. There were mentions of it in old KGB records. Also, that name, Tallmadge—there's a journal he is associated with, which the society possessed. I learned that Andropov was interested in that journal, so I concluded that part of your mission was to acquire it."

"Excellent work. You're correct."

"That Soviet contact in our embassy," he said. "He reported to Andropov about a secret room in that man, Charon's, home. A few days ago I sent someone to find that room, on the chance the journal might be there. She's been here for nearly a week, searching. At some point I need to make contact with her."

"She knows where the actual journal is located?"

"That's what I have to find out. From her."

"We don't need it, Aleksandr. I know exactly what it says."

Good to hear.

"It's actually quite amazing, and ironic. And I assure you, what that journal contains is catastrophic."

But there was one thing. "Provided a workable RA-115 is nearby."

"You sound as if that's not possible."

"Is it?"

"You'll find out, in about three hours."

CHAPTER
SIXTY-ONE

Summary of Military Options in a War with Canada
Dated: June 4, 1903

During the summer of 1898 the United States fought a conflict against Spain. It lasted a mere three and a half months and ended with a resounding American victory. The United Kingdom stayed neutral, but afterward it became increasingly concerned with the United States. Ownership and control of the coming Panama Canal has further agitated relations. America is evolving into a global power, a potent force on the high seas, and the United Kingdom, which currently fields the largest army and most powerful navy in the world, fears that competition.

For several decades now Canadian-American relations have been strained over a lingering border dispute in the northwestern region. Gold being discovered in the Yukon has further aggravated this conflict. The United Kingdom has just emerged from a costly war in South Africa and is unwilling at the present to supply the Canadians with any additional military assistance in their ongoing border dispute. Both the United States and Canada have moved troops to the Yukon region.

This secret document was requested by the War Department and details a plan concerning a possible full-scale invasion of Canada. American interest in acquiring Canada dates back to the Revolutionary War and the War of 1812. The 1783 Treaty of Paris respected Canada's (or as it was known at the time, the Province of Quebec's) independence. Of late, America's interest in Canada has again sparked from a flicker to a high flame. Absorption of its territory through nonviolent means is certainly preferable, but Canada is deemed a valuable component of the British Commonwealth, one Great Briain would clearly defend. It is the second largest manufacturing country within the British empire, with Ontario and Quebec the most important industrial centers. As tensions rise between the United States and the United Kingdom, Canada is becoming increasingly strategic and vital to American national security. Recent military successes overseas and acquisition of new territories in the Pacific and Caribbean have fostered a renewed interest in American expansion northward.

The following pages contain a detailed analysis, along with all relevant data affecting a military operation against Canada. But here is a summary of the proposed plan:

(1) A first strike on Bermuda to eliminate the island as a possible port or supply base for the Royal Navy;

(2) A takeover of Halifax. Harbor defenses in and around Halifax have recently undergone new fortification, but its armaments remain obsolete. Without Bermuda, that port would become the main entry point for any overseas British reinforcements. An on-site visit to the port (made in preparation of this study) showed that the dockyard itself seemed a place of rust and ghosts, incapable of sustaining any long-term military operations. But that situation could be remedied, so the port should be secured;

(3) Acquire western entry points. Here the aim is to sever communications with eastern Canada and prevent re-

inforcements from Australia, New Zealand, and India.
The same derelict-port situation from Halifax exists
on the Canadian west coast at Esquimalt, where American land forces could easily be sent ashore. Another
on-site visit showed that this former British base,
now Canadian, is ill equipped and poorly manned, its
dock currently in horrid condition;

(4) Additional ocean-capable ports at Yarmouth, St. John,
Montreal, Quebec City, Prince Rupert, Vancouver, Vic-
toria, Churchill, Three Rivers, Windsor, and New
Westminster would likewise be either seized or blockaded;

(5) An initial troop land thrust would cut all rail communications, with one front in Maine, another in
Montana, and a third, the main column, up through
the Great Lakes where the St. Lawrence River canals
would be seized;

(6) Control of the Great Lakes and the St. Lawrence River
is vital, but the bridge at Cornwall offers the fastest way to transport troops and equipment northward
across the border;

(7) The Great Northern Railway connecting Quebec to the
West must be taken. This would include the Pacific
terminal at Prince Rupert. From a military viewpoint
these railroads provide excellent transportation.
Once seized, Canadian prairie farmers located along
the rail lines, unable to export their crops, might be
inclined to deal exclusively with the United States.
This could cripple the Canadian economy with widespread food shortages;

(8) Highways will need to be controlled. While there are
enormous stretches of country, particularly in the
northern portion, with few or no roads, the southern
portion is well served. Some 95,000 miles of roads exist, most classified as gravel, macadam, and concrete
construction. Gravel roads will require extensive
maintenance, especially during the spring.

The full plan anticipates a possible offensive response with Canadian and British troops sweeping down into New England, and other operations targeted at Michigan, Pennsylvania, and the Pacific, the idea being to create a multifront attack. The most effective means to counter these moves is to draw Canadian and/or British forces deeper into American territory, stretching their supply routes, lengthening their lines of communications, and isolating them.

It is our opinion, though, that Canada would most likely develop only a defensive posture, similar to what happened during both the 1775 and 1812 American invasions where local patriots waged an effective guerrilla war. Montreal and Quebec City would have to be strongly defended, most likely by the regular Canadian army, while the British navy attacked American commerce in the Atlantic. This was another tactic employed during the 1812 conflict. American naval power, though, is much different today than in the early part of the 19th century. Our fleet is now fully capable of engaging its British counterpart.

Estimates are that Canada could maintain an effective defense for only a matter of weeks. Any military force sent from the United Kingdom in support could defend defined points for a limited time, but would eventually be overborne by sheer weight of numbers. Even if the Royal Navy managed to command the seas, the war would be lost on land. Canada would most likely concentrate on the defense of Halifax and the Montreal-Quebec line in order to hold its current bases of operation.

Our conclusion is that military operations by Canadians would be limited. We note that during our field visits (acting as casual tourists) French Canadians liked to boast that "we beat the Americans before and we can do it again." But a British officer said that the defense of Canada would be more difficult than the protection of India.

CHAPTER SIXTY-TWO

LUKE READ THE INVASION SUMMARY, THEN THUMBED THROUGH the pages of facts and figures used to support the suggested tactics. Sue was now scanning the summary, her reading every bit as intent as his own.

"It was a different time," Begyn said. "Manifest destiny had taken hold. We controlled Cuba, Puerto Rico, and the Philippines. To the world we had the look and feel of a budding empire. It was the era of Teddy Roosevelt, when we first flexed our muscles on a global stage."

At times like this he wished he'd studied history closer. He knew some of what Begyn was referring to, but not the details. "How did the society come to prepare this plan?"

"Notice the date, 1903. At this point the Army War College had been formed, but the first class of students did not attend until 1904. So there was nowhere the United States planned for war, whether real or imagined. No one was thinking about possibilities, planning for contingencies. Teddy Roosevelt supported the society. He needed a plan drawn, in secret, without any attention. We could offer that service."

"Except that it blows to hell that image of a quiet, benign social order."

Sue finished her reading. "It sounds like they really meant to do this."

"On May 21, 1916, the Army War College filed its own plan for the invasion of Canada. Much of it tracked this original position paper. From 1903 to 1916 the United States spent $71 million, a huge amount of money at the time, on fortifications along the Pacific and Atlantic coasts, which were recommendations we made. The 1916 report came about because of England's close ties with Japan and what the British might allow the Japanese to do in Canada. A lot of it was hysteria, but it was the kind of hysteria people back then believed."

"Then World War One changed everything?" Sue asked.

"That's right. Canada became an ally, not a threat or a prize. We all had a common enemy. Germany. But you need to know something else."

Luke listened as Begyn explained that, in the 1930s, the War College once again turned its attention to Canada. War Plan Red was approved in May 1930, similar in many ways to what had been formulated years earlier. Incredibly, in 1934, that plan was amended to authorize the use of poison gas against Canadians and the strategic bombing of Halifax, if the port could not be captured by land forces.

"Then," Begyn said, "in February 1935, the War Department arranged a congressional appropriation of $57 million to build three border air bases from which preemptive surprise attacks on Canadian airfields could be launched. The base in the Great Lakes region was to be camouflaged as a civilian airport capable of striking the industrial heart of Canada and the Ontario Peninsula. Those aren't my words. I read them in the minutes from the 1935 hearings of the House Committee on Military Affairs. That testimony was to have been secret, but it was published by mistake."

"I've never heard of any of this," Luke said.

"That's because it was top secret until 1974. The society was mentioned in those House hearings, since they analyzed our 1903 report. I was tasked with reviewing all the declassified materials to make sure there was nothing that could cause us problems."

Luke felt he had to say, "You do realize that the War College engages in a lot of hypothetical exercises, most of which are never meant to be real."

Begyn seemed unfazed. "In August 1935 we held what were, till then, the largest peacetime military maneuvers in history. Thirty-six thousand troops converged at the Canadian border, south of Ottawa. Another 15,000 were held in reserve in Pennsylvania. It was billed as a war game scenario, a staged motorized invasion of Canada."

"Which is probably what it was," Luke said.

"No, it wasn't. What that war game became was the operational basis for the final Canadian invasion plan. Once France fell to Germany in 1940 our isolationism went out the door. In August 1940 Roosevelt made a mutual defense pact with Canada. If Hitler had taken Britain in the fall of 1940, his first foray into North America would have been Canada. Our objective was to *defend* Canada by occupying it. So our 1903 plan, the War College's plan, and more was added to create the last operational directive they also code-named the 14th Colony. The society thought that was interesting—how they went back to our original label from the War of 1812—but the intent and symbolism cannot be denied. *That* plan remains classified to this day. But I talked to some of our older members who were there and helped formulate it. The idea was clear. Once we arrived in Canada to *defend* it, we weren't leaving."

Outside was dark. The wind had subsided, and things had grown much calmer and more quiet. Including Sue. She'd sat at the table like a dutiful daughter, keeping her thoughts to herself. Most of the women he attracted were the exact opposite. Bold, loud, and aggressive. Truth be known he liked them that way, but there was also something about the silent ones. Especially those who could handle themselves as deftly as this attractive Riverine.

"You always this attentive?" he asked her.

"You learn so much more with your mouth shut."

He chuckled. "That's not a lesson I ever took to heart."

The time was approaching 8:00 P.M. and he hadn't reported in all day. He should find out what was happening. But first he had to know one more thing. "How does this figure in with Brad Charon and his big mouth?"

"That's the rub," Begyn said. "Brad was aware of all this when he served as the Keeper of Secrets. This is what he allowed the Soviet diplomat and that other outsider to read, along with something else."

Now he knew. "That Tallmadge journal."

Begyn nodded. "Exactly. And whether you believe me or not, I don't know what's in it. Brad kept that journal to himself."

Not entirely, though, as the Soviets, the Russians, and Anya Petrova knew all about it.

Begyn sat back in his chair. "Brad considered these secrets more silly than anything else. Ancient history, he liked to say. He never seemed to grasp that *we* considered them important and would prefer they stay among us. I know a little about the journal. Tallmadge headed up drafting the original 14th Colony plan for the War of 1812. He also oversaw other favors we did for the government in the early part of the 19th century. He kept a record of those in the journal. When Brad was dismissed, it was not found in the archives. He was confronted and never admitted that he had it, but he did."

"Why keep it?" Sue asked.

"That was Brad. His way of paying us back. Difficult, like I said. We decided to let it pass. A way to keep the peace. When he died, we thought about retrieving it, but the probate fight made that impossible. Fritz Strobl told me you discovered a hidden archive at Brad's house. We knew about it. Brad had promised to leave those books to the society, but that was before the trouble. It was not mentioned in the gift he gave us of his main library, so we just assumed he changed his mind. Again, we made no effort to retrieve any of it. I understand, though, your superior has promised to help."

Which might now be harder to do than first imagined since Stephanie Nelle was unemployed and her remaining benefactor would shortly no longer be president of the United States.

He silently reviewed what he knew.

The Society of Cincinnati had been involved with an early plan to invade Canada, a plan that was later expanded upon and made operational during the Second World War. The 14th Colony. Nothing ever came of it, except some Soviet interest in the late 1970s, then another peek by an American in the 1980s, both of which led to the dismissal of the society's Keeper of Secrets. That same man kept in his possession an old record, the Tallmadge journal, which detailed more of what the society may have done covertly in the early years of the United States. Again, as Charon himself said, more ancient history than anything else. Or was it? Anya Petrova had come specifically in search of it, going straight to the Charon estate and smashing into that concealed room.

Finding nothing.

Which sent her to Peter Hedlund.

And led him here to Lawrence Begyn.

He stood from the table and approached one of the windows. Security lights mounted along the eaves cast purple-tinged shadows on the falling snow.

"You said the men back at the house, before you killed them, mentioned the Tallmadge journal," he said to Sue.

"They did."

Which meant Moscow knew about this supposed secret, too.

"I know for a fact that the journal was not in the secret room at Charon's estate," he told them.

"But it could be there, in the house," Begyn noted.

"What makes you say that?"

"I know Brad."

He saw it in the older man's eyes. "You know where, don't you?"

"I think so. He had another hiding place."

CHAPTER SIXTY-THREE

MALONE NEGOTIATED THE BACKROADS. HE AND CASSIOPEIA HAD left the White House over an hour ago, driving west into Virginia toward Front Royal, then north off I-66 into rural Warren County. The Secret Service had GPS tracked Zorin's rental car to a point nearby, where it had stopped. A drone with night-vision capability would have been great, but weather made that next to impossible. A winter storm had arrived, snow clinging to the windshield, the headlights receding into the unlit darkness and gold-edging the falling flakes.

"This is going to be a nasty night," Cassiopeia said from the passenger seat.

He was still bothered by the encounter with the new president. Certainly Warner Fox was no idiot—after all, he'd managed to gain election to the most powerful political position in the world. Not making any bold moves until they were sure seemed reasonable, but refusing to even shift the vice president's swearing-in to another location smacked of pettiness, arrogance, or stupidity.

Hard to say which.

He and Cassiopeia had received a thorough briefing from both Daniels and Stephanie before the Secret Service alerted them that Zorin and Kelly had turned west off I-95 onto I-66 and headed into Virginia. That had been an hour ago. Now they were driving to a rendezvous with the agents who'd been tailing Zorin for most of the afternoon.

"We need this to end here," he said. "Where we have it contained."

That was their one advantage. Zorin had no idea anyone was watching, especially not the American who should be dead beside Lake Baikal.

They'd also managed a quick bite to eat and a shower. He was beginning to feel a little grimy and a shave had helped, all courtesy of the White House. Cassiopeia, too, looked refreshed. At least they were facing this together, which he liked.

"You and I both like to avoid emotions," she said to him.

That they did.

"How about this. Let's have a no-bullshit rule. From now on, between you and me. None. Okay?"

He liked it. "Deal."

"All right. I'll start. I've been stuffed into enough supersonic planes over the past twenty-four hours to last me a lifetime."

He smiled. "It wasn't that bad."

"What if it were reversed and you'd been trapped underground in a teeny, tiny little space where you couldn't move?"

He shuddered just at the thought.

Everyone had their fears. He could take pretty much anything, except what she'd just described. He often had a recurring dream where he was caught in just such a place, no way out, encased on all sides by solid earth. The tighter the confines the worse the nightmare. Once the dream even placed him inside a sealed box where he could not stand or stretch, and could hardly breathe. That had been the worst his subconscious had ever meted out. Luckily, he'd been alone that night when he awoke in a cold sweat. He rarely spoke of the phobia, preferring simply not to think about it. From time to time he'd found himself enclosed, but thankfully never to an extreme, always with some room to maneuver. He'd never told Stephanie about his fear and, luckily, Magellan Billet agents had never been required to submit to extensive psychological profiles. Stephanie never cared for them. She preferred her own assessments.

"You know how to cut to the chase, don't you?" he said.

"You get my point?"

"Yes, ma'am. I got it."

"I didn't tell you this earlier," she said. "But when you took that fighter into a dive and let Zorin get away, there was a lot of chatter on the radio about what to do. Our pilots wanted to eject both you and me."

"And what stopped them?"

"An order from the ground. They were told to deliver us and not let on that what happened even bothered them."

"So that faction within the government was already in control."

"It would seem so. They knew exactly where this Kelly man lived. And once they realized where Zorin was headed, they went straight there, too."

And now they knew, thanks to Stephanie and her newfound friend Ishmael, that the goal had been to kill Zorin, then take Kelly alive so he could lead them to the cache.

"Just because they failed in Canada," he said, "doesn't mean they won't be here."

"I'm betting they know about a cache around here somewhere, maybe even more than one. They might even know the properties where they're located, but they don't know exactly where on those properties. A lot of time has gone by since those places were deemed useful. Not to mention any booby traps."

"So you're thinking they may have locations staked out?"

"It's a reasonable assumption."

He agreed.

Which meant they needed to stay on their toes.

"Taking out the inauguration of a new president," she said. "That borders on insane. Not even hard-liners would be that stupid. The U.S. would annihilate them. The smart play is they want this contained, kept to themselves, and those bombs held by them for the future."

Ahead, he saw the McDonald's he'd been directed to and pulled into the parking lot. Inside, two Secret Service agents, dressed like men about to head out on a winter's hunt, nursed steaming cups of coffee.

"The car stopped a few minutes ago," one of the agents said. "About ten miles from here."

"Are we it?" Malone asked.

"As you requested. Just the four of us."

The last thing he wanted was for every intelligence and law enforcement agency within a hundred miles converging here, spooking Zorin, each one intent on taking the credit for stopping the threat.

This was not about accolades.

It was about results.

"We've been tailing them since Pennsylvania," the agent said. "They
made one stop, at a Target in Maryland. We sent agents in after they
were long gone. From the security footage and register records we know
they bought a shovel, sledgehammer, two flashlights, bolt cutters, a
hasp lock, and five heavy-duty six-volt batteries."

An interesting list, the last item grabbing his attention. Edwin Davis had briefed them on the RA-115s. They needed battery power to
be portable. Zorin was certainly coming prepared.

"We have a chopper on standby at Dulles. It can be here fast," one
of the agents told him.

"Keep it there, for now. It won't be much help in this weather."

"You two going to handle this all by yourself?" the agent asked,
sounding skeptical.

"That's the plan. We'll keep it simple. We need them to lead us to
whatever there is to find, then we'll take them both down. Preferably,
alive, as we have lots of questions."

"What exactly are we looking for?"

The fewer who knew anything the better, especially considering the
widespread panic information like this might cause. Foreign nukes on
American soil? Talk about a bad news day.

So he ignored the question.

"Tell me where Zorin is."

CHAPTER
SIXTY-FOUR

Zorin sat in the parked car, listening to the patter of sleet against the roof. With the rain earlier he wondered about ice, as some had already sheeted on the windshield, the wipers scraping hard over its rough surface. He needed to stretch his legs from the ride, but was waiting for Kelly to make some decisions. Ever since they'd arrived, Kelly had been studying a map that he'd brought inside his travel bag. He liked this scenario. No high-tech gadgets. No electronics. Nothing to lead anyone to where there were. Just proven tradecraft, the kind he'd made a reputation performing.

"What are we waiting for?" he asked.

"You're becoming impatient in your old age."

"The weather is deteriorating."

"Which is to our advantage." Kelly folded the map. "When Backward Pawn told me the weapons had arrived, I wasn't fully prepared. I told the officer I was, but I wasn't. The parameters Andropov laid out were tough to meet. My orders were to be ready in time for the 1985 presidential inauguration. But Andropov died a year before that. After, everything went quiet. Then, three years later, in 1988, the call suddenly came that the bombs were in America. I was shocked that things were still moving forward. I had to hustle to have my part ready."

"Maybe things would have been different, if Andropov had lived."

Kelly shook his head. "That was not the time."

He wondered about the observation. "Why do you say that?"

"The response from the world would have been unanimous and devastating. Killing an American president? Setting off a nuclear explosion in Washington, DC? Soviet leaders far overestimated both their power and their importance. They could not have defeated the entire world."

He hated hearing about more weakness.

"History has confirmed that, Aleksandr. By the late 1980s the USSR was over. It was simply a matter of time before everything collapsed. Then in 1991 it finally did."

And he saw the other difference between then and now. "This time it's just you and me. There will be no retaliation since there is no one to retaliate against. We will achieve the effect of what Andropov wanted, but without global repercussions."

"Exactly. The timing is perfect. Like you, I've thought about this for a long time, never acting on it, just thinking. The United States emerged from the Cold War as the dominant world power, and over the past thirty years it's grown into an arrogant monster. We will finally put it in its place. Do you remember the oath we took as KGB?"

Vaguely. Such a long time ago.

Kelly found his wallet. From inside, he slipped out a folded scrap of paper, whose creases and color showed that he'd carried it a long time.

In the din of the cabin light Zorin silently read the printed words.

Of being a Soviet citizen and joining the ranks of the Workers' and Peasants' Red Army, pledging to be an honest, brave, disciplined, and vigilant fighter, to guard all secrets and obey all orders.

Then, the important part.

To be prepared to come to the defense of the motherland and defend her courageously, skillfully, creditably, and honorably, without sparing life or blood to achieve victory.

And the final sentence.

If through evil intent I break this solemn oath, then let the stern punishment of the Soviet law and the universal hatred and contempt of the working people fall upon me.

His comrade offered a hand to shake, which he gladly accepted. Pride swelled inside him as that sense of duty, of purpose, thought lost, returned. He'd long known fear and isolation, both of which had worn him down, leaving only a blind desire for some kind of action.

Like Kelly.

But here he was again, working against the main adversary, defending the motherland. Fulfilling his oath. So many had dedicated their lives to that endeavor. Tens of millions more had given their lives for the same reason.

It couldn't all be for nothing.

He heard again his wife's plea.

"Don't waste your life."

"We shall do this together," he said to Kelly.

"That we will, comrade."

CASSIOPEIA THOUGHT SHE WAS AN INDEPENDENT PERSON. HER parents raised her to be strong. But a part of her liked the fact that she felt safe and comfortable with Cotton.

Was that weakness?

Not to her.

She'd saved Cotton in Canada, as he'd done for her many times before. There was something to be said for trust, an element sorely lacking in her previous relationships. She assumed Cotton had experienced a similar lack with his ex-wife, whom she'd come to learn was once quite difficult but now much more manageable. She'd like to meet that woman one day. They had lots to talk about, and she'd love to know more about Cotton's past, a topic he discussed only in tiny doses.

Seeing Stephanie Nelle at the White House had, at first, been difficult, but they, too, made their peace. She was relieved that the rift between them had not yawned into a chasm. Too much was happening here to allow events that could not be changed to interfere with clear thinking.

What's done was done. Now was what mattered.

She liked to think she was a pro. Definitely, she possessed experience. And as she and Cotton drove deeper into the dark Virginia countryside she wondered what awaited them.

Success?

Or disaster?

That was the trouble with cheating fate.

The best odds on the table were only fifty-fifty.

ZORIN FELT THE SNOW AS IT HIT HIS FACE THEN TINGLED AWAY. Everything was so much wetter on this side of the Atlantic Ocean. He was more accustomed to the dry, Siberian variety that fell in abundance from mid-September to early May. Not much of a summer graced Lake Baikal, but he'd always enjoyed the few weeks of fleeting warmth.

He hated the feeling of getting old, but he could not escape or disguise the impressions his body was beginning to force upon him. The jump from the plane had taxed him to the max. Thankfully, he would never have to do that again. For so long the lights upon which his ambition seemed founded gleamed in isolation. Over the past few days they'd changed to definable bright bulbs, strung together, himself the cord that would prevent them from extinguishing.

But he could not escape the doubts.

That was another thing age had brought, which youth ignored.

Reflection.

He kept pace with Kelly as they walked across a drift of loose shingle, boots digging in, legs laboring. He wore his coat and gloves and held the shovel they'd bought earlier. He was careful with his steps, aware of the fragility of ankles and the price of stumbling. Kelly toted a shopping bag with some of the items they'd bought. The sledgehammer, bolt cutters, and hasp lock had been left in the car. Apparently, they were not needed here. They each carried a flashlight.

"I took control of this property long ago," Kelly said. "It was fairly isolated then, nothing around for miles. Still is, but in the 1980s there was even less out here."

He'd seen only a few farmhouses and even fewer lights on the drive.

"It's titled in a different name, of course. But I pay the taxes and the power bill."

The last part caught his attention.

"All this time?" he asked, as they kept walking.

"It was my duty, Aleksandr. We're not talking about a lot of money. The power is barely used."

Kelly stopped.

Ahead he saw where the trees gave way to a darkened clearing, where the hulks of what appeared to be a farmhouse and barn could be seen.

"It's not in the best repair," Kelly said. "But it's livable. What attracted me was a hidden extra the previous owner installed. He was a veteran of the last world war, a bit eccentric. Quite a character."

The air chilled him, but he took in the draft and allowed the cold to cleanse his lungs.

"He was terrified of nuclear war," Kelly said. "So he built a bomb shelter."

Now he realized why they needed a shovel.

"That old man died years ago. The KGB covertly took ownership from him and planned to use this as a standard cache. But once I saw it, I knew it was perfect for Fool's Mate. So I was given control."

Alarm bells rang in his head. "Then there could be a record of this place."

Kelly considered the inquiry a moment. "I suppose there could."

Memories of what happened on Prince Edward Island filled his brain. He came to full alert and found his weapon.

Kelly nodded, understanding the implications, and gripped his gun, too. "It was so long ago, Aleksandr. Maybe it's been forgotten. And even if they know of the property, they'll not find the hidden shelter."

He wasn't comforted. They'd found Kelly, so why couldn't they find this place, too?

"And don't forget the booby trap," Kelly said.

Zorin motioned for them to advance, checking his watch, the luminous figures swimming as his eyes focused on the glowing circle of numbers.

10:40 P.M.

They should hurry.

Only 13 hours to go.

CHAPTER
SIXTY-FIVE

STEPHANIE ENTERED THE JUSTICE DEPARTMENT, THE NIGHT doors staffed by the usual security teams. She'd come and gone a thousand times at all hours and the personnel there knew her on sight. She'd wondered about Litchfield. The SOB had sat smug during the presidential summit, speaking only when spoken to, but demonstrating exactly where his allegiance lay. Danny, though a lame duck, had clearly established who was still in charge. After Cotton and Cassiopeia had left she'd asked him why he did not just fire Litchfield and be done with it.

His answer was trademark Danny Daniels.

"It's always better to have your enemy in the tent pissin' out, than outside pissin' in."

Two hours later when a call came from Litchfield, asking her to meet with him, she'd begun to understand that wisdom. What could he possibly want? But Danny had insisted she go, saying *"Don't argue with an idiot, he'll only beat you with experience."* Little was happening at the moment anyway. Cotton and Cassiopeia were off to Virginia to deal with Zorin, and Luke was somewhere, she wasn't sure where, as he hadn't reported in. She tried once to contact him but the call had been immediately directed to voice mail. She was curious about what the president general of the Society of Cincinnati had to say. Danny's question about the group's interest to the former Soviet Union was a good one.

She found Litchfield in his office, alone, working before an assemblage of books and paper. Interestingly, here he wore rimless spectacles that gave his eyes a more singular, intense look.

"Please, have a seat," he said to her, his tone noticeably different.

She accepted his offer.

"I want to apologize," he said. "I've been an ass. I realize that. The president slammed me in my place back at the White House, and rightly so."

She checked her watch. "At 10:00 P.M. on a Saturday night, on the last day of the administration, you've finally realized who's in charge?"

"President Fox climbed my ass, too. He said to either work with the team or get out. And the team still includes Daniels."

"So contrition has been forced upon you."

"Okay, Stephanie, I deserve that, too. I get it. I've been rough on you. But we have a serious problem here, one that I think I can help with. We are, after all, on the same side."

You could've fooled her. But Danny had also told her, *"Turn on the vacuum cleaner, sucking in far more information than you let out."*

"I've been reading about the 20th Amendment and the 1947 Succession Act," he said. "If the president- and vice-president-elect both die before being sworn in, and there's no Speaker of the House or president pro tempore of the Senate, it definitely could generate a host of novel issues. I didn't realize, but I'm even in the line of succession. I'm not the actual AG, but when I was made deputy AG I was appointed by the president and confirmed by the Senate, so under the 1947 act, as acting AG, I'm eligible to be president, provided of course six other people are dead."

"Which is entirely possible here, thanks to Fox's refusal to bend."

"He told me after we left that if credible evidence of an imminent threat materializes, he'll make changes in the inauguration. He just wasn't going to admit that to Daniels. He wants you and me to assess things and determine if the threat is real."

Now she got it. This was a way to draw her inside *their* tent. "You know everything I know. There are no secrets."

Which was not exactly true, as she still did not know what Luke had been able to learn and she'd withheld from Fox any mention of what was about to happen in Moscow.

"I need to ask you something," he said.

She waited.

"Would you be willing to speak with someone?"

She nearly smiled, but caught herself. Danny had told her to expect a divide and conquer. One of the oldest political tricks that, surprisingly, never went out of style. And for good reason. It worked. People who made it to the highest levels of government were, for the most part, highly ambitious. At the moment those same people were also anxious. Though many were civil service and legally immune from dismissal or a pay cut by the incoming administration, that did not mean they would keep the same job or the same responsibilities. Reassignments were common and dreaded. For political appointees like Litchfield things were even worse. Their jobs hinged totally on the new people wanting them. No safety net existed. Their jobs ended at noon on January 20 unless reopted by the new people. Danny had forced her reinstatement. Now the other side was looking to find out how badly she wanted to keep it.

"Sure," she said.

"Just don't act too agreeable," Danny had warned.

So she added, "You know that I don't give a damn whether I stay or not."

"I get that. Your allegiance is to Daniels. Fox admires that."

Litchfield quickly worked the keyboard on the laptop before him. She heard the distinctive chimes of Skype activating, then its trademarked rotary sound effect as a line rang. He tapped the trackpad, then angled the machine so it faced her way. The screen blinked to life and she saw the attorney-general-designee.

"Stephanie, I want to sincerely apologize for my comment earlier. It was out of line. Yes, you were insubordinate and I went along with your firing, but an apology from you could have solved things, too."

She got it. Her turn to be put in her place. Petty, but she knew what had to be done. So she faced Litchfield and said, "He's right. I was wrong to do what I did. It was highly unprofessional."

He accepted the gesture with a nod.

"I'm glad we can get all this out of the way," the AG said. "It's important that we work together."

She wanted to say that he had no idea what it took to run an ongoing intelligence operation, especially one that involved something as volatile as the new Russia. Whatever this man may have learned at his New York law firm, none of it would help with what he was about to experience. That was why AGs needed people like her. But she kept her thoughts to herself and said only, "I disobeyed a direct order. Bruce was justified in what he did. I would have done the same to one of my people." Her stomach was churning. "With that out of the way, may I ask why you asked to speak with me?"

"I want you to stay on and work with us."

"Doing what? The Magellan Billet is gone."

"We will bring it back."

Score another premonition for Danny.

"I'm beginning to see that the Justice Department needs the unit," the AG said. "But, Stephanie, I need something from you."

Finally, the point.

"We don't want to be blindsided. We want to hear it from you, a person who plans to be part of the next four years. Is this threat real?"

"It is. But President Fox was right, we don't have all of the pieces. It's a lot of speculation. Those missing pieces are being gathered, though, as we speak."

"Which I assumed was the case. We want to be kept informed, immediately, as things happen. No filters. Direct information. Will you do that for us?"

She nodded. "I can keep my eyes and ears open and report what's happening."

"This is not about betraying anybody," the AG said. "It's just about our getting the best information from which to make informed decisions. All any of us wants is to be right about this."

Interesting how he made deceit sound so reasonable.

"Communicate directly with Bruce. He'll pass things to me and the president-elect. That keeps you out of trouble. Fox is not reckless. He'll do what's necessary, but only that. The Daniels administration is over. It's important that we start tomorrow fresh, all of us marching to the beat of a new tune. Not more of the same. But we don't want to make a stupid mistake, either."

"That would not be good, for anyone."

"I wanted you to hear this directly from me," he said. "That way there's no misinterpreting what was said. Are you on board?"

Suddenly she no longer minded that the Magellan Billet was gone—and gone it was, no matter what this lawyer might have said. This man had no intention of doing anything more, or less, than what had already been done. What he lacked was a credible spy on the inside and, to his mind, he'd just recruited one. Did they think her so weak and shallow? Clearly that description fit Bruce Litchfield. And to the next attorney general, it apparently fit her, too.

Memo to herself.

Quit at 12:01 tomorrow.

But for now—

"You can count on me. I'll make sure you're not blindsided."

CHAPTER SIXTY-SIX

ZORIN USED THE FLASHLIGHT AS THEY FOUND CLEAR PATCHES OF earth the snow had yet to whiten. The temperature remained low, but he wondered if it was cold enough for any real accumulation. Most of the ground and the bare tree limbs above them were only lightly dusted. His breath smoked with each exhale and he was puzzled why they'd not just driven all the way to the house. Then he saw why. The road ahead was blocked with downed trees.

Kelly stepped over them. "I dropped these a few years ago to discourage visitors."

Smart. So far this ex-KGB officer had shown good work. Amazing that time had not dulled a single one of his abilities. But neither had it affected his own.

"When I lived in DC," Kelly said, "I came out here regularly. Now it's once a year, but usually only in summer. Some things require maintenance. I was just here last August."

The only sound was their footsteps on the hard, rocky soil, and the only movement, the snow drifting down in a sparse procession. No sign of any other visitors so far. Ahead were more slabs of darkness without features, pricked and squared only by their flashlights. His hearing moved beyond his heartbeat, trying to take in all that surrounded him, searching for any danger, but he encountered only more silence.

They came to the house and he saw that the walls and roof were intact, the windows whole, the door closed. A brick chimney rose from one side.

"It's in okay shape," Kelly said. "I stay here when I come. Not a five-star accommodation, but it serves the purpose. I thought it was important that it not become derelict." Kelly motioned with his light. "Over here."

They rounded the house to where the clearing continued for another fifty meters before the forest began again. A black rectangular hulk, grim and sooty, stood in the dark, maybe ten meters long by five wide.

"A barn," Kelly said. "Built there for a reason."

They walked over and Kelly used a key from his pocket to remove a padlock from the doors. The inside smelled of damp mustiness. Bare rafters spanned overhead. No windows. Tools, a wheelbarrow, and a riding lawn mower lined one side. Stacked against the opposite wall were rows of cut logs. A long-handled ax angled upward, its blade buried into the wood. Back in Siberia he'd kept a constant supply of firewood, too, most dried and aged for a year or more, ready to burn in the dacha's hearths.

"It's underneath," Kelly said, scraping his shoe on the dirt floor. "No one would have any idea."

Zorin spotted an overhead incandescent fixture and stepped back outside to check on things. Using his light, he scanned overhead, noticing a power line, already thickened and white-leaved with frost, tracing its path to the roof of the house.

"The previous owner had a generator down below. I needed constant power, so I wired a line from the house through the barn wall. There's never been a problem with the power. Sure, it might go off here and there from storms, but there are backup batteries."

Kelly laid the shopping bag aside and settled his flashlight on the ground. No attempt was made to switch on the overhead lights.

"We have to clear away some of the wood."

MALONE AND CASSIOPEIA STUDIED THE RENTAL CAR, PARKED IN the center of a narrow lane between rows of bare trees. The GPS monitor had led them straight here. Neither of them spoke, knowing that their quarry was nearby. Ahead, maybe a quarter mile away, he saw the sporadic streaks of flashlights.

He recalled reading about KGB weapons caches in the Mitrokhin archives, published back in the 1990s, and the booby traps. To date, the SVR had never once publicly acknowledged that the caches existed, much less offered any assistance in their removal. All of the ones he'd ever heard about had contained only communications equipment. So he could only imagine what safety precautions had been taken to safeguard five RA-115s. Kelly and Zorin were leading the way, so he assumed they knew what they were doing. That meant he and Cassiopeia had to allow them time to neutralize the site.

He noticed something in the car's backseat.

A blue nylon duffel bag.

He eased open the rear door and unzipped the bag. Inside lay a sledgehammer, hasp lock, and bolt cutters. The agents back at the McDonald's had mentioned that all three had been bought at Target, along with a few other items, including a shovel, which was nowhere in sight.

He closed the door softly and pointed ahead.

They moved deeper into the darkness.

ZORIN TOSSED ASIDE ANOTHER OF THE SPLIT LOGS SLIPPERY WITH lichens. "Did you cut this wood?"

"Every piece. I may be getting old, but I'm still in good shape. As are you, Aleksandr."

They'd removed a section of the stacked wood near the center of the long row, exposing hard dirt beneath. Kelly found the shovel and began a careful excavation, seemingly knowing exactly where to dig. His strikes with the blade were almost surgical, as he worked the tip only a few centimeters into the ground, forming a circle about a meter in diameter.

"Close the door," Kelly said to him.

He stepped over and eased the two panels shut.

The only light came from their two flashlights pointed toward the circle. With the shovel, Kelly carefully loosened the packed dirt within the outline. Then he laid the shovel aside.

"This has to be done carefully."

He watched as Kelly knelt and began to remove the dirt, which, thanks to the cold, came away in clumps. Dark metal became visible. More dirt was freed to reveal a hatch.

"No lock?" he asked.

Kelly glanced up at him. "I didn't see the need. If this is not opened properly, six kilotons of nuclear explosives will ignite."

His spine stiffened at the danger.

Kelly surveyed the hatch. "It seems okay. Nothing has disturbed it. Could you hand me the shovel?"

He did, and Kelly stayed on his knees, using it to loosen a path half a meter away from the portal. Kelly tossed the shovel aside and reached for one of the flashlights, clearing away more dirt until he found a small plastic box. He brushed it clear, blowing away the last remnants of dirt from its domelike shape. Kelly then reached to one side of the box and twisted, freeing the lid, which opened on a hinge. Inside were three sets of wires, each separately connected with a colored twist connector.

Red. Yellow. Black.

"You have to disconnect the right one," Kelley said, "or it explodes. Disconnect all three and it also explodes."

Clever, he had to admit.

Kelly untwisted the red nut. "I change the color each time, just to be safe. Red was this year's."

Kelly separated the exposed copper wires, angling them far apart. He then reached back and opened the hatch, the metal hinges offering only minor resistance. Below was a ladder built into one side that stretched down three meters.

"Go ahead," Kelly said. "There's a light switch at the bottom."

CHAPTER SIXTY-SEVEN

LUKE DROVE AS FAST AS CONDITIONS ALLOWED, HEADING WEST ON I-66 past DC into Virginia with Sue and her father in tow. Lawrence Begyn had told him about another hiding place within the Charon mansion, one Begyn assumed Brad Charon might have used to secrete the Tallmadge journal.

"*I saw the place one time,*" Begyn had told him. "*Back when Brad and I were still okay with each other.*"

"So you have no way of knowing if the journal is there?"

"*Brad was a creature of habit. Once he started something, he kept to it. It's reasonable to assume he'd keep that journal safe, hidden, and nearby.*"

So it was worth a look.

"There's something I don't get," he said to Begyn. "If Charon was a big mouth and breached your archives with two strangers, why was he allowed to keep the journal?"

"Brad was a strange man in many ways. Keeping that journal was maybe his way of showing us that he really could keep a secret. That he could be trusted. We decided not to press the issue. And we never heard about it again, which is why we thought this to be long over."

His watch read nearly 11:00 P.M. He should call Stephanie. She'd tried him earlier and left a message, but there was nothing to report so he decided to play this out a little while longer. The night had not turned completely nasty yet, the wind, cold, and snow unaccompanied so far by ice, which was a good thing. The interstate remained a wet blacktop, snowflakes dissolving atop its surface. He sensed he might be on to something. But he was flying blind with no backup. Just himself. Which he liked. But he did have Sue, who sat in the rear seat, her father's hunting rifle cradled in her folded arms. Begyn had, at first, not wanted her to come, but relented when she pointed out that she'd already killed three men and that the decision wasn't his to make. He was glad to have her along.

He found the exit and turned left again on the same two-laned road where he and Petrova had squared off. A few miles later he passed beneath the wrought-iron entrance and sped through the woods to Charon's house.

They stepped out into the night.

Begyn had brought two flashlights and led the way inside. "I haven't been here in a long time. What a wreck this place has become. It was once a grand house."

"It's what happens when people can't get along," Luke noted.

"Can I see the archive you found first?" Begyn asked.

He didn't want to take the time, but decided a quick peek couldn't hurt. The flashlight beam he held pointed the way and they entered the study, stepping though the gash in the wall. Petrova's ax still lay on the floor where she'd tossed it. Sue stayed outside in the hall, keeping watch with the rifle.

He and Begyn surveyed the secret room.

"Amazing stuff," Begyn said. "We need to get it out of this cold."

"My boss said she'd get it for you. You can take that to the bank."

Begyn studied the book beneath the glass cover. "This is a rare volume, worth about $25,000. I know several society members who would pay that and more."

Which mattered not to him. "Finished?"

His tone conveyed that they needed to move on, so they fled the study. The older man took the lead up the stairs to the second floor, where a long corridor ended at a set of paneled doors. Luke dragged in deep breaths of the freezing air and steadied his nerves, following the two Begyns into a master bedroom.

"I read that the other end of the house is the one that burned," Begyn said.

The master suite was intact with all the furniture still there, the bed even made with a spread, but everything reeked of mold and mildew, dank as a ditch.

"In there," Begyn said, motioning to a half-open door.

"You two go," Sue said. "I'll keep watch."

He wondered about her taut nerves. "Somethin' wrong?"

"I don't like this place."

Neither did he particularly, but nothing so far had generated any pause. "Any details you'd like to share?"

"It just feels wrong."

He decided to respect her instincts so he indicated that they should hurry up. He and Begyn entered a closet larger than his apartment's bedroom. Nothing hung on the bare rods, the windowless room devoid of everything except the empty racks, wooden cabinets, and shelves.

"It was there," Begyn said, pointing at the last cabinet, a mahogany rectangle that accommodated a four-foot-wide rod for clothes and shelving above. It sat at the end of a row on the long wall, the cabinets from the short wall nestling tight to it at a right angle.

"We had a party here one night," Begyn said. "Brad being Brad, was showing off. He brought a few of us up here and grabbed this rod, which then was hung with dress shirts." Begyn handed him the flashlight and gripped the bare metal. "He twisted it this way."

They heard a click and the cabinet shifted right, revealing that the corner with the other cabinet was mere illusion. Begyn slid the whole thing farther right, exposing a dark chasm behind.

"I bet Charon liked Harry Potter," Luke said.

Begyn chuckled. "I'm sure he did. He loved mysteries. He was a bit of an actor, too. He always played Bob Cratchit in the society's production of A Christmas Carol. Quite good at it."

He shone the light into the darkness, which dissolved to reveal a small space, about three feet square. The only thing inside was a black, four-drawer filing cabinet. A lock could be seen in the upper-right corner. He hoped it would not be an impediment and was pleased when the top drawer slid open.

"What's the point of locking it," Begyn said, "when it's hidden away."

He agreed, thankful that Charon was not overly obsessive-compulsive. Inside the top drawer were papers, mostly bank records, financial statements, and stock purchases. The second drawer was full of files for real estate, lots of deeds and surveys.

"Brad was quite wealthy," Begyn said. "Worth maybe $20 to $30 million."

"And his kids and the widow couldn't figure out a way to divide it up?"

"Apparently not."

The third drawer was empty, but the bottom one contained the jackpot.

An oversized leather-bound volume.

Begyn lifted it out and opened to the first page. Luke shone the flashlight and they both read the handwritten paragraph.

> A true account of any and all activities of the Society of Cincinnati as performed for the government of the United States, and the governments of the several states, during the last and great war with Britain lasting from June 8, 1812, to February 17, 1815, meant to record and memorialize those events so that a full understanding of their many intents and purposes shall be clear to all those who might question. Let it be said that every member of this society is a true and loyal patriot and our only desire was to serve our country with honor and distinction.
>
> Benjamin Tallmadge
> August 8, 1817

"This is it," Begyn said.

A scrap of paper extended from the top of the journal, marking a page. He decided to start the examination there and gestured for Begyn to open to that point, about halfway through.

> On the evening of August 24, 1814, a shameful thing occurred, one I am sad to say I lived long enough to witness. Within the capital city cannon fire had roared for most of the day and when the explosions stopped the local residents' feelings were left in fearful fluctuation, fondly hoping that their countrymen had prevailed, then awfully fearing that all was lost. They

soon discovered that the dust beginning to rise above the forests in thick clouds, rapidly advancing, came from British forces. Sadly, American soldiers fled the capital. The cry "ruffians are at hand" could be heard from men on horseback as they rode away. The remaining militia dropped their guns and ran like frightened sheep in every direction except toward the enemy. And though they exclaimed that they had taken a good fight to the British and expended all of their ammunition, those who stole a look at their cartridge boxes noticed that not a single round had been used.

Inside the Executive Mansion Dolley Madison awaited the return of her husband, President James Madison, who had left two days earlier to visit the front. He was due back by nightfall and a meal had been prepared for both him and his contingent. But the sight of the British entering the city changed those plans. It was suggested to Mrs. Madison that a trail of gunpowder be laid to explode if the British tried to enter the Executive Mansion, but she refused to allow it to be done. When told to leave, she hesitated until certain things were readied for transport, many of them national treasures. One was a grand painting of George Washington that she urged others to save. A great fear existed that Mrs. Madison might be trapped inside the mansion with no means of escape. Eventually, she left the city by wagon just ahead of the advancing British forces, which claimed the city after dusk.

They first entered the Capitol building and George Cockburn, the British commander, mounted the speaker's chair and put the mock question, "Shall this harbor of Yankee democracy be burned? All for it will say Aye." His troops cried their approval so he declared the motion carried unanimously. Chairs, furniture, books, maps, and papers were piled high and set aflame. Soon the entire building burned. The fire raged so hot that marble columns turned to lime and collapsed. Fire burst from the windows and alighted houses to the leeward, some of which contained congressional records stored there for supposed safekeeping. The Capitol eventually became wrapped in a winding sheet of flame that destroyed the building.

Luke wondered about why this passage had been flagged. "We all know we got our butts kicked in the War of 1812."

"That we did. Tallmadge lived through it. This is an important firsthand account of things."

And it was damn important to Anya Petrova—
Four pops echoed through the house.
The sound unmistakable.
Gunfire.

CHAPTER SIXTY-EIGHT

ZORIN SWUNG OPEN THE HEAVY METAL DOOR HE FOUND AT THE bottom of the ladder. The air that greeted him from inside was surprisingly warm, but musty. He flicked a switch and fluorescent bulbs illuminated a closed, windowless space, cylindrical in shape, that stretched ten meters and about half that wide. Metal shelves lined one side and held supplies of drinking water, canned food, blankets, clothing, tools, wire, and weapons, along with both small arms and rifles and spare ammunition. He also recognized portable radio units, standard KGB issue that he'd once deployed at locations himself. Everything was stacked neatly and in order, a sparkling tidiness about the place, one that denoted a devoted caretaker.

Kelly completed his descent and entered the shelter.

He noticed that a layer of heavy plastic sheathed the interior walls. He pointed toward it and asked, "Moisture control?"

"This shelter was built with concrete and waterproofed, but I thought some additional protection was in order."

Then he saw them, lying on a metal table opposite the supply shelves. Five small suitcases, each lid nearly closed, a wire leading out of the partially shut lid to a trunk line that snaked a path toward the far end, then up and out.

"A vent back there allowed air to circulate. I sealed it off, but it was the perfect place to feed power. The electricity charges the units and gives off just enough heat to keep the air inside warm."

He was impressed. A lot of thought had gone into this.

He stepped toward the RA-115s and hinged open the lid of the first one. The case was lightweight aluminum. Not a speck of decay tarnished the exterior. Inside were three canisters joined in a cylinder about half a meter long. It lay diagonally with a battery above and a switch below, wires leading from the switch to the battery to a small transmitter, then to the cylinder. He recalled his training. Activate the switch and the battery triggered a small explosion that shot a uranium pellet forward where it collided with more uranium and sparked a chain reaction, causing a blast the equivalent of 5,000 tons of TNT.

He checked the other four.

Everything seemed in pristine shape.

"I maintain them yearly," Kelly said. "New batteries, new wiring. Of course, the cylinders are stainless steel, and all the parts inside are made of noncorrosive metals."

He knew there were no moving parts and nothing depended on gears or springs. Once the electrical charge activated the trigger, simple physics took over, generating a coffin of solarlike heat and flame that would vaporize everything within a kilometer.

"Will they explode?"

"Absolutely. They're all in perfect working order."

"You understand that the inauguration this year takes place inside the White House," he said to Kelly.

"As the one in 1985 did."

He'd not realized.

"That was the whole idea, Aleksandr. It's why Fool's Mate was initially created. At Ronald Reagan's second swearing-in they all gathered in the White House, at noon on Sunday, January 20. But Andropov was long dead by then and the bombs weren't here. I thought the whole thing over until that call came in 1988 from Backward Pawn. Then everything seemed back on. But still, no order to act was given. A shame, really. The Americans regard the White House as ultrasecure, though 9/11 probably gave them pause on that one."

But he caught something in addition to the tone. Certainty? Pride? "What is it you know?"

Kelly smiled. "They have forgotten their own history."

CASSIOPEIA NESTLED CLOSE TO THE TRUNK OF A TALL PINE, STAR-ing at the darkened hulk of a house and barn. Zorin and Kelly had disappeared inside the barn about fifteen minutes ago, and all had remained quiet ever since. Cotton had swung around to the rear of the house and should be, by now, near the barn entrance. She'd assumed a cover position to keep an eye on the big picture, and make sure they were not graced with any uninvited visitors.

The night was wintry cold, but bearable. She'd ditched the French cold-weather gear in favor of American issue, which the Secret Service had provided. She also carried an automatic pistol, the magazine full, spares in her pocket. Cotton, too, was properly dressed, armed, and ready.

And she agreed with him.

Zorin and Kelly had to be stopped here.

MALONE CREPT TO THE BARN, CAREFUL NOT TO TRIP ON ANY branches, roots, or slippery rocks. The door had been closed a few minutes ago, outlined for a while by a faint chink of light, now gone. As he came closer he noticed that it had not been latched, nor locked, just pushed shut.

He had to see inside.

But he'd already reconnoitered the entire exterior and the barn came with no windows.

There was only one way.

ZORIN REALIZED THAT WHAT KELLY WAS ABOUT TO TELL HIM formed the missing element he'd been seeking, the one Anya had come to learn.

The second move of Fool's Mate.

"You can't just walk up to the White House fence and lay down a suitcase," he said.

Kelly smiled. "We don't have to do that. There's an easier way."

He stared at the five weapons, nearly thirty kilotons of nuclear power.

"All I have to do is change the battery in one of these and it's ready to transport," Kelly said. "The batteries are only a few months old, but no sense taking a chance."

Which explained Kelly's purchase of the six-volt power sources. He knew how it worked. Activate the switch inside the case and the battery sent a charge to the detonator. The one drawback was the low voltage, which took time to build enough heat to activate the trigger, sending the uranium colliding. About fifteen minutes, if he recalled, and he asked Kelly if that was still true.

"More or less, depending on the temperature around the case."

Which meant the switch had to be flicked no later than 11:45 tomorrow morning.

But first.

"Where is the point of convergence?"

Kelly smiled. "It's a fascinating story, Aleksandr. Which started long ago, when the White House burned."

CHAPTER
SIXTY-NINE

LUKE RUSHED FROM THE CLOSET, TELLING BEGYN TO STAY INSIDE, but the older man ignored the command and ran with him. More gunfire resonated from beyond the bedroom, in the outer corridor, this time rifle fire. Sue was apparently firing back.

But at whom?

Luke stopped his advance at the double doors, assuming a position to the side of the jamb with Begyn next to him, and called out, "What's happening?"

"We've got company," Sue yelled. "Two I could see. They're downstairs but are trying to get up here."

"Stay here," he said to Begyn, who also held a revolver.

He fled his position and moved down the corridor, keeping close to the wall. Ahead, beyond where the staircase ended, past the ornate balustrade on the far side he spotted Sue, crouched low, the rifle in her grasp.

Automatic gunfire exploded from below, and the spindles supporting the second-floor railing were obliterated as metal tore through wood. Then two objects flew over the top and clattered to the floor.

He knew that sound.

Grenades.

He dove back and hit the floor, covering his head, hoping Sue had done the same.

Both exploded.

MALONE EASED OPEN THE BARN DOOR, CAREFUL THAT NO SOUND betrayed his presence. He slipped into the still interior, moving lightly, his shin brushing against a wheelbarrow. Something scuttled, which startled him. The air smelled old and used. The only light shone up from a circular hole in the ground amid a long pile of wood.

A hatchway.

Leaking from it was a mumble of voices.

A quick survey of the interior satisfied him he was alone. Apparently, both Kelly and Zorin were belowground.

He crept to the hatch and saw that it was equipped with no hasp or lock, no way to seal it shut. Too bad—that would have been perfect. But that did not mean he couldn't trap them below. Enough wood piled on top should be sufficient to keep them contained.

But that depended on there being only one way in and out.

An assumption he would have to make.

He also noticed three wires nearby in an excavated box, one set disconnected.

The booby trap.

Now disarmed.

Perfect.

He had them right where he wanted.

LUKE ROLLED ONTO HIS BACK AND STARED BACK AT THE BOILING orange flame and rising cloud of smoke and dust.

"Sue."

"I'm okay," she answered.

He glanced back toward the bedroom and spotted Begyn, who was hustling toward him.

"They're coming up the stairs," Sue warned.

He sprang to his feet and plunged into the cloud, looking left where he recalled the stairs ended, and saw a black form racing up.

He fired twice, sending the body rolling backward across the risers toward the ground floor.

That was too easy.

Then he saw why.

Flames erupted from an automatic rifle, bullets whining through the air. He dropped back and used the nearby wall for cover, but not before seeing the man he shot rise to his feet and begin his climb again.

Damn Kevlar.

Next time shoot for the head.

Something solid hit the wall ten feet away.

Then another, and another.

He heard the same familiar clatter on the wood floor and leaped for Begyn, taking the man down just as three explosions generated a bright sunshine that lit the darkness. Fire erupted with a fury, the house's dry brittle wood and plaster quickly succumbing. More smoke poured out and gouts of orange flame reached toward the ceiling.

A black silhouette emerged from the smoke, darkly clad, wearing a protective vest and aiming a rifle straight at him where he lay on the floor. He hoped to God Begyn had enough sense to not be a hero like Peter Hedlund. The man stood over them, gun pointed straight down. In the halo of light he searched the face for nerves, apprehension, or doubt. He saw none, his own gun concealed beneath his partially rolled body.

He decided to feign pain and squirmed.

"Stay still," the man warned.

His captor leaned forward, shoulders hunched, head tilted, staring down the length of his weapon in an effort at intimidation. Luke rolled a little more, his eyes now facing toward Begyn.

He screwed them up, along with his face, as if in pain.

"I have two of them," the man called out.

Luke reversed the roll, settling on his spine, the gun now exposed, which he fired into the man's thigh, dropping him to the floor. He sprang to his feet and grabbed the rifle. A spark of compassion flared, then passed. No time to mess around. He shot the man in the head.

Fire and smoke raged, making their way down the hall toward the master bedroom.

"Sue," he screamed. "Sue."

No reply.

Not good.

"Where is she?" Begyn asked.

"She's a big girl. We have to go."

They retreated to the bedroom. The window on the far side shattered as something solid passed through. Another window crackled to shards as a second projectile flew inside. He and Begyn dove toward the heavy four-poster bed.

The grenades exploded.

The room's ceiling began to rain down as a new fire started, engulfing the floor and furnishings, blocking their way to the closet where the Tallmadge journal had been left. That was the least of his worries, though. Smoke and carbon monoxide consumed the air. Both he and Begyn began to cough. He could feel a weakness in his lungs as the oxygen in the room diminished. He pointed toward the broken windows, but grabbed the older man just before he plunged his head out. Instead, he yanked a pillow from the bed and tossed it out the window.

Retorts could be heard outside.

Just as he suspected.

The idea had been to either kill them with the grenades or draw them to the windows for easy pickin's.

They were quickly running out of options.

CASSIOPEIA KEPT TIME ON HOW LONG COTTON HAD BEEN INSIDE the barn. It was not a large structure so there couldn't be all that many places to hide. He'd apparently thought it safe enough to enter, which made her wonder just exactly what was happening.

Five minutes had elapsed.

The cold had stiffened and thickened her fingers. She worked out the kinks through her gloves. Her legs likewise had tightened. A noise came from her right. In the darkness she saw snow fluttering down from where the branches of a pine tree had been molested. The rustle of a startled animal? Out in this weather? Hardly. She kept to her hiding place and remained still, her gun ready.

A shadow bobbled into view.

Followed by another.

Both had rifles angled across their chests.

LUKE RUSHED TO THE WINDOW, BUT KEPT TO ONE SIDE, MINDFUL of the snipers below. The doorway from the bedroom to the hall was completely ablaze, the bedroom itself about to be in the same condition. Begyn had assumed a position next to the other broken window, so they both could breathe, at least for the moment.

He stole a glance downward.

Shots rang out.

But not in his direction.

Two, before fire was returned, then three more.

"Luke."

His name being called from below as the shots stopped. He glanced down and saw Sue staring upward. Apparently, she'd avoided the fire and made her way out of the house.

"They're all down. You need to get out of there."

He stuck his head out the window and assessed the drop. Fifteen or twenty feet. Enough to break a bone or worse. He might make it, but not Begyn. Then he spotted a drainpipe outside another window at the corner of the building. Thick. Copper, most likely. Plenty enough to hold on to.

He dashed to the window and raised it.

"Come here," he called out to Begyn.

The older man approached, fits of coughing racking his lungs. "Asthma. This is not good for me."

It wasn't good for either one of them. "Use the pipe. Grab hold, arch your body out, and ease down using your feet as brakes."

He pantomimed what he had in mind.

Begyn nodded and did not argue, climbing out and grasping hold of the round pipe. The older man then planted his feet and angled himself outward, easing his grip on the pipe and sliding toward the ground.

Sue waited for him at the bottom.

More coughing stopped the descent.

Begyn seemed to be struggling, breaths coming and going in ragged gasps. Then hacking. A fight for air. He arched his head upward and stared straight at Luke.

"You can do it. Keep going."

"It's . . . my . . . lungs. I . . . can't breathe."

Begyn seemed to black out and his grip on the pipe released. He dropped deadweight fast, but not before his head clipped both the pipe and the outer wall. Sue tossed the rifle aside and readied herself to catch him, which she tried to do, breaking the fall, but his weight sent them both to the ground.

"You okay?" he called down to her.

He saw her emerge from beneath her father. "I got him, but he's out cold."

"Get him to the car."

He studied the bedroom. He had to retrieve that journal. Flame licked at the wall where the closet opened, everything orange and consumed by fire. He might be able to slip in, grab the thing, and get out. They'd read only a portion of the flagged pages and he had to know what other information lay inside. He surveyed the room but could find nothing to use to make his task easier.

Time to suck it up and do his job.

"Luke," Sue called out from below. "Let's go."

He stuck his head out and hollered, "I said get out of here. Call 911. I'm going for that journal."

"Let it go," she screamed.

He waved her on. "There could be more problems out in those woods. Stay sharp and move out, Lieutenant."

Then he turned his attention to the closet.

It had become difficult to see, his eyes burning from the smoke, flames shimmering through an ever-growing rolling cloud.

Something cracked overhead.

Loud. Disturbing.

He glanced up just as the ceiling began to turn black, consumed from the attic side by flames working their way downward. Heading for that closet suddenly did not seem like a good idea, but a moment of hesitation was just long enough for everything to give way.

Burning wood cascaded, filling the room.

He dove for the bed, which seemed like the only cover.

His chest tightened, heart pounding, and he was suddenly aware that he was choking on smoke. Before the world disappeared, and everything went quiet, his last thought of the intense heat that had engulfed him.

CHAPTER
SEVENTY

British troops left the burning Capitol around 10:00 P.M. on the night of August 24, 1814, marching in formation, two abreast, up Pennsylvania Avenue. Only a few timbered houses surrounded the broad street, with the last mile before the White House lined with trees. Near 11:00 P.M. a detachment of 150 crossed the road and approached the White House, which sat dark, deserted, and unprotected. The building stood as the grandest house in the city, designed by George Washington himself. The fourth president of the United States, James Madison, was nowhere to be seen, having fled on horseback hours earlier. The British thought it could be a trap, finding it hard to believe the Americans would simply allow them to advance into their capital at will.

But no resistance came from any quarter.

The British entered the White House unmolested through the front door, exploring the elegant rooms by lantern, their nostrils filled with the odors of food cooking. In the ground-floor state dining room they found a table set for forty with a damask tablecloth, matching napkins, silver, and delicate glasses. Several kinds of wine were cooling in ice on the sideboard. Everything was properly laid out, ready for use. In the kitchen, they saw spits loaded with meat turning before a fire, along with pots of vegetables and sauces. Apparently a dinner prepared for a president, not to be enjoyed. So they sat at the table, drank the wine, and ate the food, repeatedly toasting "Peace with America, war with Madison."

Afterward, the soldiers helped themselves to mementos and souvenirs, nothing of great value to earn any charges of looting. And there was much there that was valuable. Sofas, writing tables, and cushioned chairs filled the rooms, some collected by Jefferson while in France, others belonging to Washington and John Adams. Most of the Madisons' personal possessions had also been left behind. A portrait of Dolley Madison was stripped by a soldier from the wall and confiscated for later exhibition in London. The president's dress sword became the possession of a young Scottish lieutenant. An admiral took an old hat of Madison's along with a chair cushion, which he proclaimed would help him remember "Mrs. Madison's seat."

Once they were done with their feasting, roaming, and pillaging chairs were piled onto tables and the remaining furniture stacked close together. The windows were broken open, the bedding and draperies soaked with lamp oil. Then fifty men assumed positions around the outside carrying a long pole to which was affixed a ball of rags soaked in oil. Each was lit and, on command, the poles were thrust like javelins through the broken windows.

Conflagration was instant.

The whole building burned in unison, consumed by flames and smoke. Only a hard rain, later in the night, extinguished the inferno and saved the outer stone walls from collapse, leaving just a hollow shell.

Zorin knew little about American history, though they'd been required to study aspects of it as young men during their KGB training. He'd never before heard the story of the British burning the White House that Kelly had just recounted.

But he liked it.

"One of the soldiers wrote later that they *were artists at the work*," Kelly said. "They were quite proud of what they did. The raid was designed to deliver a message to Madison. It was Madison and his cronies that had wanted war in the first place. At the time Britain was busy with Napoleon and considered a fight with America an unnecessary distraction, one they resented. But there was also an element of payback. Not only for the American Revolution defeat but earlier in the war for when America had invaded Canada and burned Toronto. They returned the favor."

All of which he liked, too.

"It took two years to rebuild the White House, and a dozen more years after that to finish everything completely. Imagine, Aleksandr, the British totally humiliated them."

Impressive, but, "What does that have to do with now?"

"Everything, for you see something else came into being at the same time the White House was rebuilt."

By 1814 the District of Columbia had become the seat of the national government. Though there was an Executive Mansion, a Capitol building, and other government edifices, life within the district came with limits. The nearby towns of Georgetown and Alexandria were far more comfortable. Roads were few and unpaved, dust and mud constant problems, as were the marshes and flooding from the creeks and the Potomac River. Residential neighborhoods slowly developed, though, and houses began to appear. People settled down and lived there. Religious services were held in the Capitol itself, the Treasury, or one of the other executive branch buildings.

Finally, though, freestanding churches arrived. Two were Episcopal, one near Capitol Hill, the other farther out in Georgetown. After the destruction by the British, a cry arose for a third Episcopal church to be built in the west end. On September 14, 1815, the cornerstone was laid for that church, on Square 200, directly north of the White House.

Its design was simple. A Greek cross on four equal sides, without a tower, porch, or nave. Inside rose a gallery supported by columns. Box pews lined the brick floor. The center was crowned by a dome with a cupola and lantern. Half-moon-shaped windows at the end of the four transepts provided sunlight. The chancel was shallow, bringing the altar close to the congregation.

Consecration of the building came in December 1816.

The church still stands, expanded over time, at 16th and H

Streets, on Lafayette Square, just a few hundred feet from the White House.

St. John's Episcopal.

Its yellow façade, colonnaded portico, and tall steeple have become local landmarks. Every sitting president since James Madison has attended at least one service. Madison established the tradition of a "President's Pew." John Tyler paid for its use in perpetuity, and Pew 54 still accommodates the president.

"St. John's," Kelly said, "is the key."

"Is that what you learned from the Tallmadge journal?"

Kelly nodded. "The church offers public tours all the time. I made a point to know its caretaker, and he showed me every nook and cranny. That's when I verified what Tallmadge had written about in his journal from 200 years ago. The KGB searched all the time for American legends. Then Andropov himself managed to find one from the War of 1812, one that people here have simply forgotten."

He saw the excitement in Kelly's face.

"Tell me."

MALONE HAD TRIED TO LISTEN TO THE VOICES BELOW BUT HAD been unable to hear anything. He could not risk climbing down closer so he decided to take command of the situation and slammed the metal lid shut. He then piled cut wood atop, more than enough to make it impossible to shove the hatch upward.

They were now Spam in a can, sealed tight.

CASSIOPEIA WAITED AS LONG AS SHE COULD, WATCHING THE TWO black smudges, listening to the sqeak of their soles on the snowy ground as they approached the barn.

She could take one, but probably not both.

So she opted for the smart play.

"Cotton," she called out. "You've got company."

Both forms halted their advance and turned.

Then one headed her way, the other toward the barn.

Exactly as she'd hoped.

MALONE REACTED TO CASSIOPEIA'S WARNING AND DOVE TOWARD the end of the wood pile, using it for cover toward the door, which burst open.

Gunfire began.

A rapid rat-tat-tat from an automatic rifle.

He hunkered low behind the wood which, thankfully, offered ample protection, rounds whining by, hammering into the outer walls, shredding the logs. The man was firing indiscriminately in the dark, trying to take out anything and everything, which meant they wanted no one left alive.

Including him.

CHAPTER
SEVENTY-ONE

ZORIN HEARD THE HATCH SLAM SHUT, THEN THE RATTLE OF heavy objects pounding its exterior. He surmised that someone had sealed them below with the wood, but he rushed to the ladder and climbed, confirming his suspicions. He cursed himself for being so careless, but the excitement of the moment had overridden his usually cautious nature.

He eased back down to where Kelly stood and asked, "I'm assuming there's no other exit?"

Kelly shook his head, but no look of concern filled his comrade's face. "I have PVV-5A."

He smiled. Plastic explosives.

Perfect.

Kelly moved toward the shelves where two ice coolers sat, their lids sealed with thick tape. He removed the bindings, and inside lay several bricks of an olive-green material wrapped in thick plastic.

"It's been here a long time," Zorin said. "Is it still good?"

"I've kept it stored like this since the beginning. I was told the material had a long shelf life, if properly protected. We're about to find out if that's right."

CASSIOPEIA STAYED BEHIND THE TREE TRUNK, REALIZING THAT the man headed her way had no idea where she was located. Nothing but thick woods surrounded them, so advantage her. Cotton, on the other hand, was under fire. She could hear the barn being sprayed with rounds. She needed to head that way, but first there was the matter of her own pursuer.

She reached down and found a rock that filled the palm of her right hand. The shadow was twenty meters away, headed toward the trees off to her left. She lobed the rock upward, ahead of the man, and it clattered through the branches, sending some of the accumulated snow drifting down in silent showers.

The gunman did not hesitate.

He opened fire in the direction of the commotion.

Bad move.

She swung around, braced her gun against the tree, and pulled the trigger.

ZORIN CLIMBED THE LADDER TO THE EXIT HATCH, CARRYING ONE of the green bricks. It had been a long time since he'd last used explosives. One full brick seemed too much, but there was no time to worry about power or effect.

Kelly had found a spool of copper wire and cutters. Thankfully, the cache was stocked with all the right tools. But that had been the whole idea. Everything had to be there, ready to go.

He could find no good place to lodge the brick except just above the final rung, a few centimeters beneath the closed lid. He assumed whoever had trapped them had piled wood atop, making it impossible to shove the hatch upward, but that would not be a problem for the force he was about to deliver.

Volleys of gunfire raged above him.

Odd.

Like back at Kelly's house. Something was happening in the barn. But it didn't concern him at the moment, not until he was free of this cage.

Kelly came up the ladder behind him to hand over the exposed ends of two copper wires. He wrapped both around the brick, then inserted the bare metal tips through the plastic covering the explosive. He then relaid the bundle close to the hatch and climbed down, careful not to jostle the wires. Kelly had already snaked them across the shelter to its far side.

"Ease the door shut," Kelly told him. "As far as you can without hurting the wires."

He understood the wisdom. The explosion would certainly blast upward, but there would be a downdraft, too, and it was important that the RA-115s stayed protected. Not to mention himself and Kelly. He managed to nearly close the door, which opened outward. The blast would only slam it further shut. But there was still the matter of air compression in the confined space. Kelly had thought of that, too, grabbing two wool blankets and tossing one his way.

For the head and ears.

Not 100 percent protection, but enough.

They retreated beyond the shelves and the table with the five nuclear devices, and huddled in a far corner. The other end of the two copper wires lay before them, as did a six-volt battery.

Touch the exposed ends to the terminals and the charge should be more than enough to ignite the night.

MALONE WAITED UNTIL THE FIRING STOPPED, LYING STILL BE-hind the woodpile, out of sight of the man in the doorway. That was the problem with bursting in without thought. Somebody else on the inside just might be thinking. Especially after a warning. But this guy had not seemed to mind, choosing to see if he could kill everything quickly.

The firing stopped.

For an instant.

Malone sprang up on his knees, found his target in the dark, and fired three shots, dropping the man to the ground. Quickly, he advanced to the doorway, gun still aimed, kicking away the rifle, then checking for a pulse at the neck.

Dead.

CASSIOPEIA HEARD THE SHOTS AND SAW THE MAN AT THE BARN door collapse to the ground. Apparently, Cotton had been ready for him. A form stepped from the barn, its outline unmistakable.

She hustled across a patch of scruffy grass, calling out, "You okay?"

"Any more out here?"

"I took the other one out."

She was ten meters away.

ZORIN HELD ONE WIRE, KELLY THE OTHER, THE BATTERY LYING on the floor between them, blankets wrapping their heads, insulating their ears from what was about to bang through their underground prison. This was what KGB officers lived for, what they spent years being trained to do. Finally, he'd awakened from an agonizing, self-induced trance. For so long he'd blundered around like a drunk, staggering through life, his stomach hollow with loathing and disappointment, but now he'd finally achieved locomotion.

He was moving. Forward.

And nothing would stop him.

He nodded at Kelly.

They touched their wires to the terminals.

Sparks.

MALONE HEADED TOWARD CASSIOPEIA, ABOUT TO TELL HER THAT he had Zorin and Kelly sealed tight when the barn exploded.

Everything rushed outward and up, air surging past both him and Cassiopeia, blowing them backward, upended, then crashing them to the ground. His head immediately hurt, all sense of balance gone. He rose and tried to find Cassiopeia. She lay a few feet away. He crawled toward her, forcing his muscles to work. Debris from the barn began to rain down. He seized what final bits of strength remained and thrust his body across hers.

His muscles pained to numbness.

Then reality vanished.

ZORIN REMOVED THE BLANKET FROM AROUND HIS HEAD, AS DID Kelly. The explosion had sent nearly all of the blast upward, the shelter's door forced shut, clanging hard metal to metal and keeping most of the force away from them. A deep subterranean rumble had rocked the walls, coming in shocks and waves, but it had now subsided. Everything had held. The electricity still worked and the overhead lights burned bright.

They stood.

All five weapons remained on the table and appeared fine.

He moved toward the door and shoved it open. The ladder well was clear, the overhead hatch gone. He listened and heard nothing. The barn above no longer sheltered anything. Snow rained down.

"Get one of the weapons ready to move," he said to Kelly. "I'll check above."

He grabbed a flashlight, found his gun, and climbed to ground level. Only about half the barn remained, the rest scattered out twenty meters in all directions. The weak beam wavered as he jumped on top of the debris. He flicked the light across the ground and saw a body. He rolled the corpse over, seeing three bullet wounds to the chest.

This one died before.

In the gunfire he'd heard.

He washed the light over what was left of the barn and spotted another body. He went close and dropped into a crouch, tossing aside the pieces of old wood. No. Two bodies. One above the other. He rolled the top one over. In the light he saw a face he recognized.

The American. Malone.

Here?

A woman lay beneath him.

Concern swept through him.

How could this be?

"Aleksandr."

Kelly had emerged from the shelter, a briefcase in hand.

Was the other dead man with Malone? Or against? The gunfire he'd heard earlier seemed to indicate a battle. Was the other one SVR? Possible. No, more probable. His mind was suddenly flooded with doubt, a sense of traps laid and not sprung.

Kelly came close. "Are they American?"

"This one is."

"How do you know?"

"He was supposed to have died in Siberia. That one over there could be Russian, like at your house."

"The rental car," Kelly said. "It's possible they found us through it. Technology allows that. I simply assumed no one here was watching. You should have told me everything back at my house. I would have done things differently."

Too late now.

He stood, hearing nothing from the darkness around them. Surely the explosion would have attracted reinforcements.

But nothing.

Maybe these were the only ones.

"It's ready," Kelly said, motioning with the case. "The battery will handle things for at least a few days. More than enough time for to-morrow."

His mind swirled with new possibilities. Contingencies to deal with the Americans that might assure success. Just in case.

Improvise. Think.

"We're taking all five weapons."

"They're heavy, Aleksandr."

He recalled. About twenty kilos each. "We can manage."

And they should leave with a change of vehicle. He searched Malone's pockets and found keys.

"We'll need the things that are inside our car," Kelly said.

And he wanted his knapsack. "I'll get them. Prepare the other weapons. I'll be back to help carry them up."

One other thing.

Kelly never had the chance to explain about St. John's Church, the White House, and what the Tallmadge journal had revealed.

"You need to finish telling me what you started to say downstairs."

"And you must explain about Siberia and the Americans."

CHAPTER SEVENTY-TWO

MALONE OPENED HIS EYES.

Snow covered his face, more trickling down the opening at his collar. Someone was shaking him, calling his name. He recognized the face. One of the agents from McDonald's. Cold lay tight around his temples and he struggled with numbed senses, but just feeling anything seemed a good sign considering what he recalled happened.

The barn had exploded, covering both him and Cassiopeia. He was lying next to her, the other agent rousing her awake. He pushed himself up. His head ached, his neck stiff. Everything flashed woozy. His mouth was dry, so he sucked in some of the snow. His breath clouded around him in puffs of distress and relief. He checked his watch. A little after 5:00 A.M. They'd been out a few hours.

"We waited as long as we could," one of the agents said. "Then we came and found you."

Cassiopeia sat up and stared at him. "That hurt."

"You got that right."

"What happened?" an agent asked.

He hobbled to his feet and sucked in more cold air, trying to rid the staleness from his lungs. "Zorin did not appreciate being trapped underground. So he blew his way out. You didn't hear it?"

"We were ten miles away, inside a building."

"What about the other two we took down?" Cassiopeia asked.

"Both dead," an agent reported. "We're still trying to determine how they tracked Zorin."

Not all that hard, really. As Cassiopeia had surmised earlier, they knew generally about weapons caches, just not the details, especially any booby traps. So they kept watch and got lucky. But they weren't the problem anymore.

He stared over to where the barn once stood. "We need to take a look at something."

His adrenaline, sluggish at first, now pricked and prodded him into alertness. He borrowed one of the agent's flashlights and led the way through the dark, finding the underground entrance from earlier, its cover gone, leaving a neat hole in the ground.

"That metal hatchway kept the explosion directed upward, like a cannon, instead of outward," he said. "Otherwise we'd be dead."

It had to be a bomb shelter of some sort, or perhaps a facility built specifically by the KGB. His head still spun, so he stopped a moment and allowed the cobwebs to clear.

"You two keep an eye out up here," he called out. "And nobody heard the explosion?"

"This is the middle of nowhere. The next farm is several miles away."

He climbed down into the blackness, hoping for no more booby traps. At the bottom he found a half-open metal door, which he closely examined, determining that nothing seemed out of the ordinary.

He eased the door open and pointed his light inside.

A switch was affixed to the rounded outer wall, a conduit leading up to overhead bulbs. He wondered about flicking it on but decided, what the hell, and did.

The tubes shone bright.

He switched off the flashlight.

Cassiopeia followed him inside.

He was impressed with the array of stored materials. Anything and everything an enterprising spy might need. Inside an ice cooler lay bricks of plastic explosives, which explained how Zorin had managed to free himself. He took inventory of the small arms, rifles, and ammunition along with survival supplies.

But no RA-115s.

A table did stretch down one side of the shelter, its top empty, nothing there to indicate that nuclear weapons had once been here.

"Just great," he muttered. "He's gone and we still have no idea if he's a threat or not."

Being unable to hear the conversation earlier now became a big problem. He banged his palms against the wall in impotent fury. Anger surged in him like nausea, filling his throat. He'd messed up. Big time. The two agents on site should have been included as backup. But he was trying to keep the information trail contained. The mockery of the shelter seemed evident, and though roomy he still did not like the enclosed feeling. With nothing further to be learned, they climbed back to ground level.

"Is the other car still up there in the road?" he asked one of the agents.

He was told that it was, so he and Cassiopeia broke into a trot, finding it parked in the lane beyond where trees blocked the path. She seemed to know what he was after and they both stared into the rear windows. The nylon bag, there earlier, was gone.

"So they apparently needed a sledgehammer, bolt cutters, and a hasp lock," she said.

That they did.

The other two agents caught up to them.

"Is our car here?" he asked one of them. "Back near the highway."

"Didn't see one."

Just wonderful.

"He has several hours' head start," Cassiopeia said. "So he's certainly wherever he meant to be by now."

"Even worse, no one has been looking for him."

Time to report the bad news.

STEPHANIE SAT AT THE SMALL DESK INSIDE HER HOTEL ROOM. She'd returned here from the Justice Department, after calling Danny and telling him that he should open a fortune-telling business. He'd just chuckled and said it didn't take a psychic to read these people. Sleep had proved impossible. Outside, four stories below, amber lights illuminated the hotel's main entrance, taxis and cars-for-hire coming and going. Light snow had fallen through the night, leaving remnants but little ice. That would hurt later today. Better weather meant more crowds, more distractions, more opportunities for Zorin.

Her phone rang.

"I hope it's good news," she said, answering.

"It's not," Cotton said.

And she listened to what happened.

"We have cameras all over this city," she said to him. "I'll have the footage checked. That car has to appear somewhere."

"Assuming Zorin is coming into DC. He may be planning an aerial attack from the outside."

"We have the skies covered better than the ground."

"I'll leave that to you. We're headed back to the White House."

She ended the call and decided to play out her deal with Fox, dialing Litchfield's cell phone. The moron answered quickly and she told him that they had nothing and Zorin was still on the loose.

"No proof he has a nuke?" Litchfield asked.

"Afraid not."

"Fox will want to keep to the schedule."

"I understand."

"I'll be at the White House around ten," he told her. "If there's any change let me know and I'll make sure he acts immediately."

"You'll be the first call I make."

She clicked off the phone, hating herself for even appearing to cooperate. She still planned to quit later today. The thought of working for these people turned her stomach. Hell, Litchfield was bad enough. She could find something else to do somewhere. Maybe she'd follow Cotton and move overseas. That had always carried an appeal to her.

Her phone rang again.

Luke.

Finally.

She answered and a woman's voice greeted her.

"My name is Sue Begyn. My father is Lawrence Begyn. Luke Daniels came to talk to him."

Nothing about this seemed good. "How do you have Luke's phone?"

"He's been hurt. I finally managed to get his phone from a nurse. You were the last call he made, so I just redialed. Do you know Luke?"

Dread swept through her.

"I'm his boss. Tell me where you are."

CHAPTER
SEVENTY-THREE

ZORIN FELT BETTER. THEY'D MANAGED TO STEAL MALONE'S CAR and make their way into DC without incident. Dawn had arrived with weak sunlight and a gusty wind driving leaden clouds in low. They'd removed all five weapons and any electrical evidence that the bombs had ever been in the shelter. On the trip into town he'd explained to Kelly what had happened at the dacha, leaving out nothing about the American, Malone. Kelly had then told him some astonishing information, and he could now easily understand how Andropov had been excited about a historical tidbit from an obscure American Revolutionary War society, stumbled upon forty years ago by an astute Soviet attaché.

A truth, like Kelly had said, that people had simply forgotten.

They'd parked in a garage adjacent to Union Station among a zillion other cars. Hopefully, no one was looking for theirs or, if they were, they would not think to check there. Inside its trunk lay four RA-115s, ready to be activated. An idea had occurred to him back at the shelter, a way to divert attention and occupy the Americans, tossing them one last false feeling of security.

Before finding an open diner, they'd scouted St. John's Church and discovered something astonishing. The building was closed for renovations and had been for the past year, an extensive remodeling that involved scaffolding stretching up to the top of its bell tower. No services were being held there today. Kelly had worried about that, thinking they would have to make their entrance early before people arrived. Now that would not be necessary, the entire perimeter enclosed by a tall temporary fence. Once past that he should not be disturbed. The lack of anyone around the site had also offered an opportunity to hide, among the debris, the nylon bag they'd retrieved from the rental car.

Lafayette Park sat just across the street from the church. Past that stood the White House, only three hundred meters away. The impressive building had been lit in the early morning, readying itself for a new president to assume office. Finished with their survey, they'd quickly retreated several blocks away to the diner and ordered breakfast, which had just been delivered.

"There's something else we must discuss," Kelly said, his voice low.

The tables were rapidly filling with customers straining to be waited on. Zorin caught snatches of tourist conversations, political debates, and gossip. Once again he was surrounded by the main adversary. But this was no ordinary Sunday morning. History was about to be made.

And in more ways than one.

He worked on his eggs, sausage, and toast.

"We won't be leaving here today, will we?" Kelly asked, his voice low.

He stared up at his comrade. No purpose would be served by lying. "I won't."

"From the moment I opened the door and saw you," Kelly said, "I knew that my time had come, too. Then that incident at my house told me things. I'm too old to go on the run, looking over my shoulder every second. Wondering if today is the day they finally find me."

He understood that paranoia. Every foreign service officer experienced it. Living a lie came with the liability of the truth. But there'd always been a bailout. If exposed, or in trouble, all you had to do was make it back home to the USSR.

But that option no longer existed.

"We have nowhere to go," he muttered.

Kelly nodded. "No one wants us, Aleksandr. We are all that's left of what once existed."

He thought back to military school, then the KGB training center.

Never then would he have imagined that he would be the last man standing.

"I realized," Kelly said, "that this was a one-way mission for you. I want you to know that it's a one-way ticket for me, too. When it goes, I'll go with it."

"You are a good and loyal officer."

"I was born into the KGB," Kelly said. "My parents were both officers and they raised me to be one. I've known no other life, though I've lived a fiction for a long, long time."

He'd also lived that contradiction.

Which was not good.

He was surprisingly hungry, the diner filled with an inviting smell of brewing coffee. So he motioned to the waitress that he'd like another order.

Kelly smiled. "The condemned always seem to be able to eat."

"Now I understand why. There's a peace in knowing that it will all soon be over."

"My one regret," Kelly said, "is that I never married. I would have liked to have experienced that."

"My wife was a good woman who died far too young. But now I'm glad she's gone. I might not have had the courage to do what must be done, if she still lived."

Then there was Anya.

He should call and say goodbye. He'd been putting that off, knowing that he could not tell her the truth. She'd volunteered to look for the journal. The fact that it was now irrelevant mattered, and she should be told. He still carried the cell phone he'd acquired in Irkutsk, switched on the past few hours, but she'd not, as yet, tried to contact him either.

"You brought all five for a reason," Kelly said.

That he had, and one rested at his feet, beneath the table, safe inside its stylish aluminum case.

"It's time you tell me why."

"We need to ensure that the Americans are occupied," he said. "Now that I know your intentions, there is something you can do to ensure our success. A penultimate surprise for the main adversary."

Kelly seemed to like that. "Tell me."

CASSIOPEIA WALKED INTO THE BLUE ROOM. SHE AND COTTON had come from Virginia straight here, to the White House. The oval-shaped space lived up to its name, adorned with striking blue carpets and matching draperies. Doors opened into adjacent rooms and another set with glass overlooked the south lawn where a portion of the Rose Garden could be seen, along with magnolia trees veining a pale sun. The furniture had been removed, replaced with rows of cushioned chairs facing a podium before the room's only fireplace. A television camera stood opposite the podium near the exterior doors. No one was inside, all of the doorways blocked by velvet ropes.

"A lot will happen in here soon."

She turned and saw Danny Daniels.

"We didn't get to say much when you were here a few hours ago," he said.

"It's good to see you again," she said.

The president stepped beside her.

"Cotton is speaking with Edwin," she said. "I decided to come have a look."

"It's an impressive space. Today it will usher in a new president."

"You don't sound excited."

"I'll miss this job."

"And your plans for the future?"

She knew about him and Stephanie, one of a handful who were privy to the truth. That closed circle included only the president, the First Lady, and Edwin Davis. She'd gained entry by accident through another crisis a few months ago. Cotton had sensed she knew something, but she'd resisted all his efforts at learning more. If nothing else, she could definitely keep a secret.

"Pauline and I have said our goodbyes. We'll be moving on from each other," he said to her, his voice barely a whisper. "But like they say, you don't need a parachute to skydive. You need a parachute to skydive twice."

"You always could place things in their proper perspective. I'll miss that."

He shrugged. "Nostalgia ain't what it used to be."

"Cotton's pretty pissed at himself."

"It's not his fault Zorin decided to blow his way out. The question is, do we have anything to be afraid of?"

On arrival they'd been told that the Secret Service had swept the bunker for radiation, not detecting enough to draw any conclusions. They'd also been told that Luke Daniels had been hurt and was in the hospital.

"Any word on Luke?" she asked.

"Stephanie's there. We should hear something shortly."

She watched him as he studied the empty room. "Does the swearing-in take long?"

He shook his head. "The chief justice will administer the oath, first to the vice president, then the president. We all stand there and gawk for the cameras. Fifteen to twenty minutes tops. No speeches. That's all for tomorrow and the public ceremony outside the Capitol. Half hour and we're clear. But Fox plans to hang around a little longer."

She had to say, "We still have no concrete evidence that nukes are here."

"They are. I can feel it."

Her instincts were likewise pricked.

"We'll need you here to keep a watch," he said. "You and Cotton are the only ones who can positively ID Zorin and Kelly."

They'd both snuck a peek through the window on Prince Edward Island.

"Are you going back to Tennessee tomorrow?"

He nodded. "Back home."

He seemed not here, off somewhere else, far away.

"I got a bad feelin' about this," he muttered. "A real bad feelin'."

ZORIN FINISHED EXPLAINING HIS PLAN, PLEASED THAT KELLY agreed with the tack he'd decided to take.

The waitress brought their second orders.

"You realize," Kelly said, "that we will be the first to strike a direct blow against the main adversary."

That they would, which meant something to him.

A sense of accomplishment.

Finally.

He extended his hand for Kelly to shake. "Together, we shall do this for the motherland."

They clasped each other in a tight grip. Comrades, both seemingly glad that it would end this way.

"Eat your food," he said to Kelly. "I must make one call." He found his knapsack and retrieved the phone. "It will only take a moment, and I'll step outside."

He stood from the booth and caught sight of a wall clock behind the counter.

7:50 A.M.

4 hours left.

CHAPTER
SEVENTY-FOUR

Stephanie found the hospital in Manassas, Virginia, using a car supplied by the White House. On learning about Luke she'd called Danny, who'd urged her to head that way immediately. At arrival she'd met Sue Begyn and learned that Luke had suffered a concussion and bronchial trauma from severe smoke inhalation. He was unconscious, his lungs being cleansed with oxygen. Thankfully, no burns. He'd dived beneath a heavy bed, which had collapsed, protecting him long enough for Sue to get him out. Apparently, the woman had risked her life to make the rescue. Amazing, until Stephanie discovered she was a Riverine.

Stephanie stood beside Luke's bed and stared down at the younger Daniels. He'd been a good hire, urged onto her by his uncle, but he'd proved himself with exemplary performance. Even Cotton spoke highly of him. The doctor had told her he should be fine, but he'd be out of commission for a few days. What she had to know was what he was doing back at the house in the first place.

Sue had been called to her father's room. During the escape the older man had suffered a severe asthmatic attack, and was now in a semi-coma, but he should come out of it. Luckily, paramedics and the county fire department had arrived at the scene in time, quickly transporting both men straight to the hospital. She hadn't pressed Sue, seeing she was upset over her father, and she'd wanted to check on Luke.

But time was running out.

Noon was coming fast.

A description and license plate of the government car stolen in Virginia had been provided to all police within fifty miles of DC. Traffic camera footage was being studied on the off chance that the vehicle might appear. But she knew that kind of luck happened only on television. So many people were in town. Too many cars. And there were hundreds of cameras and even more hours of footage that would have to be reviewed.

The Secret Service had control of the weapons cache, but no sign of any RA-115s had been detected. Even worse, they had no idea what Zorin looked like. No photos existed of him in U.S. data banks and the Russians had not been willing to offer one, assuming they even possessed a current image. The man had not been a player in a long time. But Cotton and Cassiopeia could recognize him on sight. Kelly, too, had proven difficult since they knew little to nothing about him. No current American passport, or a Canadian driver's license, was held under the Kelly name. Not unusual, as this man had been trained to be invisible. Canadian authorities had interviewed his neighbors and employer, finding no current photographs of him. Apparently, he was camera-shy.

The door opened and Sue entered Luke's room.

"How's your dad?"

"He's going to be okay. But he'll be here a few days."

"I have to know what happened."

"Three men attacked the house with incendiary grenades. I managed to escape out a window. I heard some shots from inside. The firemen told me they found a body, so Luke must have taken one of them out. I shot the other two outside. We got my dad out, but he had an attack. Luke stayed inside."

"You know why?"

Sue shook her head. "I wasn't where my dad and Luke went. I was on guard outside the bedroom. They were after the Tallmadge journal, but I have no idea what they found, if anything."

Yet Luke had risked his life to stay inside a burning house.

A phone rang.

Not hers.

Petrova's.

Which sent a chill down her spine.

"Could you wait outside a minute?" she asked.

As Sue left she found the phone in her pocket, which she'd been carrying ever since Luke had retrieved it from Petrova's destroyed car.

"Anya," a male voice said when she answered.

"No, Comrade Zorin, this is not Anya."

Silence.

"My name is Stephanie Nelle. I work for the U.S. Justice Department. We know what you're doing."

"I doubt that."

"Can you be sure? I do have this phone."

"Where is Anya?"

"She's dead."

More silence.

"How did she die?"

"In a car crash, trying to evade us." She decided to expand her bluff. "We know you're in DC and that you have a weapon. We now control that cache in Virginia."

"It's of no consequence. As you saw, it is empty."

"Did you take all five with you?"

"Five of what?"

He wasn't bending, but what had she expected? This was a man who played the game back when there actually was a game.

"You won't make it to the White House," she said.

"I'm already there."

And he was gone.

Call over.

Truth or fiction? Impossible to say. She'd tried her best to rattle him, but he'd kept his cool, even when learning that his lover was dead. But she had no idea how close that relationship had been. And even if it had been something special, a man like Zorin would not have conceded anything.

She glanced down at Luke.

What he knew had just become even more important.

In fact, he was the only lead they had left.

ZORIN STOOD OUTSIDE THE CAFÉ, IN THE COLD, TRYING TO KEEP his composure.

He switched off the phone.

Anya, dead?

He'd not experienced such a sense of loss since his wife died, but now the familiar pang returned to his gut. Anya had willingly taken up his cause, making it her own, becoming an active partner. Had they loved each other? That was hard to say since neither one of them ever expressed much emotion. But the relationship had been satisfying. Learning that she lived no more only reinforced what he'd already decided.

This would be his last mission.

The woman on the phone—Stephanie Nelle—owned only bits and pieces. He'd been around long enough to read a bluff. She knew about the RA-115s, but she had no idea if any had been there in that bunker. And she certainly had no idea where he was currently located.

But she did know the target.

The White House.

Unfortunately, it would do her no good.

They would never see him coming.

STEPHANIE KNEW OF NO WAY TO REESTABLISH CONTACT. ZORIN was gone, still loose somewhere, his phone surely off and soon to be destroyed.

"Sue," she called out.

The younger woman reentered the hospital room.

"There's no way to talk with your father?"

"He's going to be out until at least tomorrow. The doctor said he was lucky the smoke didn't kill him."

Which narrowed her options.

The monitor beside Luke's bed continued to bump its green charted line across a video screen, the soft blipping like clockwork. She reached down and pressed the button that would summon someone. Time to throw her weight around. The nurse appeared and she told the woman to find Luke's doctor. When she was met by resistance a flash of her badge emphasized that it was not a request. Finally, the nurse relented and left the room.

"Tell me all that you know," she said to Sue. "As you can see, I'm not in the mood for bullshit."

"Dad told Luke about a journal from the society, written by Benjamin Tallmadge. He said that Charon may have it hidden somewhere in the house. Dad thought he knew where that might be, so we went to check."

Petrova had been after the same thing, so she now understood why Luke had risked his life. "And you have no idea as to its significance."

"Dad never spoke of this until the past two days. But he told Luke that a long time ago some Soviet may have got a look at the journal."

Which Peter Hedlund had also reported.

The doctor entered the room and she told him that she wanted Luke revived.

"That's impossible," he said. "Much too dangerous. He needs to come out of it himself."

She'd known that would be the response so she displayed her badge again and said, "I can only say, Doctor, that what's at stake here is vital to this country. I have less than three hours to figure something out and I have to speak with my agent. I assure you, Luke would want you to do this."

The man shook his head, holding firm.

She had to know, "Is there a stimulus you can give him that will bring him out of it?"

"There is, but I'm not administering it."

Sue stepped toward the bed and yanked Luke upright, slapping him hard across the face.

Okay. That'd work, too.

The doctor moved to stop her, but Stephanie cut him off with her drawn weapon.

"Get out," she said.

Shock came to the man's face as he fled.

Sue slapped Luke again, then shook him. Luke began to cough, opening his eyes like someone roused from sleep, his pupils slow to focus and darkly stained beneath. More than a two-day stubble dusted his chin. He did not look or act like himself.

"It works in the field," Sue said.

Stephanie smiled. That it did. "Luke, I need you to wake up."

She could see that he was trying hard to do just that.

"I have to know if there's anything to find in that house."

She glanced at Sue and decided there was no choice, so she nodded and another slap popped the side of his face.

His eyes went wide, looking straight at Sue. "Did you . . . smack me?"

She grinned. "Only with the greatest of respect."

He rubbed his cheeks. "That hurt."

"Did you hear what I asked?" Stephanie said.

"Yeah, I got it. But I'm having a hard time breathing."

Oxygen lines wrapped his head and fed air straight to his nostrils. She gave him a moment to savor a few breaths of clean air.

"The roof collapsed," he said. "How did I get out?"

Stephanie pointed at Sue. "She saved your ass."

"Looks like I owe you one."

Stephanie found her phone and dialed. When the connection established she hit SPEAKER. Danny had been waiting for her call, he too knowing they were dead in the water except for what Luke might know.

"That Tallmadge journal is . . . in the house," Luke said. "We were reading it. Begyn and I." He rubbed his head. "But we . . . didn't finish . . . before the shooting started."

"The house burned bad," Sue said. "But it is still standing."

"So the journal is gone," a new voice said.

Danny. Through the phone.

Luke saw the unit in her hand. "No, it's not."

"Talk to us, Luke," Danny said. "I got the entire U.S. government coming through the gates. Do I need to get them out of here?"

"That journal," Luke said, "is inside a fireproof cabinet in the master bedroom closet. A secret chamber Begyn knew about."

It seemed to take all he had to get that out.

She gestured that he should take it easy.

"Stephanie, you're the closest we have," Danny said. "Petrova wanted that journal in the worst way. We need it."

And Zorin doesn't have it, yet he continues to move forward.

"I'm headed there now."

"I'll send some help by chopper. But get there first and check it out."

MALONE STARED AT DANNY DANIELS. WHEN THE CALL CAME from Stephanie the president had walked across the second-floor hallway into the sitting room where he and Edwin Davis had set up headquarters. Downstairs was far too busy, with too many people for even a semblance of privacy. New staff were eagerly beginning to claim their assigned posts as the old closed out their desks.

"I should go to that house," Malone said to the president.

Daniels shook his head. "You and Cassiopeia are the only ones who know exactly what Zorin and Kelly look like. I'm going to need you both in the security center. We have cameras everywhere. See if you spot either one of them outside the fence."

"That's not much of a defense."

"It's all we've got."

"Shouldn't you be downstairs greeting guests?"

"Like I give a damn. And by the way, they don't give a crap about me. I'm yesterday's toast."

So far they hadn't been able to locate the car Zorin stole, but agents were still examining traffic cam footage. A be-on-the-lookout alert had been issued to every law enforcement agency, but estimates were that nearly a million people would be in town today and tomorrow.

"He's got a bomb," Daniels said. "You and I both know that."

Malone agreed. "He might even have more than one."

"He's going to try and blow this whole place to kingdom come," Daniels said. "And we can't do a damn thing about it short of causing a panic. And if we're wrong? There'll be hell to pay." Daniels glared at him with a look of resignation.

The lack of concrete evidence of a definitive threat continued to make their case next to impossible to press.

"I don't know why we don't just do this damn swearing-in at the Capitol, Sunday or no Sunday. If the idea is to respect the Lord's day, we're working harder today than we will tomorrow."

Malone heard the frustration.

"The experts tell me Zorin's got to get close," Daniels said. "Which means he has to tote that case with him."

Along with a sledgehammer, bolt cutters, and a hasp lock, which Zorin had made a point to retrieve. Daniels was right. Monitoring the perimeter cameras seemed like a smart thing.

He stood.

So did the president, dressed in a sharp suit and tie. Tomorrow it would be black tie and tails for his last appearance on the platform before the Capitol.

"They also tell me that it ain't like on TV," Daniels said. "There's no digital counter on these things beeping away. They were made long before those ever existed. In fact, there's no counter at all. That's too many moving parts. They kept it simple. To shut it down just flip a switch inside or pull the wires from the battery. That stops the charge, which builds the heat, which triggers the reaction. But if there's enough heat and that trigger snaps, there's no way to stop anything."

He did not like the sound of that.

"Thought you should know," Daniels said. "Just in case. I'll be downstairs. Doing what lame ducks do."

Malone glanced at his watch.

10:20 A.M.

1 hour and 40 minutes to go.

CHAPTER
SEVENTY-FIVE

ZORIN FOUND ST. JOHN'S.

He'd made his way toward the church through myriad back streets, blocks from the White House, staying off the busy thoroughfare that fronted the main doors. He'd hunched in his overcoat against the chill and stayed alert, looking for surveillance cameras, or someone stumbling upon him by chance, or anything that might stop him, intensely aware of his vulnerability. Especially after the call to the American woman. This was definitely the most precarious moment.

Luckily, the area behind the church came with trees and hedges that offered plenty of cover. Earlier, while it was still dark and before anyone may have been on alert, he and Kelly had secreted the bag with tools. He now carried the aluminum case, something else that made him obvious, but he'd been able to hustle down an alleyway behind an adjacent building, then slip unnoticed through the fence onto the construction site.

He took a moment and peered at Lafayette Park, less than a hundred meters away, a heavy blanket of noise billowing up from the crowds there and filling the closed portion of Pennsylvania Avenue that fronted the White House. Vehicular traffic had not been allowed there in twenty years, but pedestrians were free to come and go.

Today it would be a busy place.

The fence encircling the church offered perfect cover as it was sheathed with black plastic that prevented any views through. At spots, bare trees flanked the barrier, their trunks black as iron. He considered the fact that the church was closed for repairs a sign, not from the divine, as God was never a part of his life, but more from fate. Perhaps a gift from fallen comrades, watching his progress, urging him on.

Kelly had told him all he needed to know about the church and he quickly moved to the north side of the building, carrying the heavy aluminum case and nylon bag. He kept careful with his steps, his boots occasionally skidding on the accumulation of snow. Beneath the scaffolding, among the trees and shrubbery, past a black iron railing, he spotted the basement entrance. He laid the case and bag down and found the bolt cutters. The way in was blocked by two hinged metal plates, bound by a shiny lock. Kelly told him about his tour of the church and how the curator had taken him into the basement. The belowground space was surprisingly roomy, added to the building about twenty years after the church had been built.

He snapped the hasp and the lock clattered away.

He replaced the bolt cutters in the bag, then thrust open the two panels, exposing a set of concrete steps. Originally, Kelly would have replaced the lock with the new one bought earlier, sealing him inside. With Sunday services happening, it would have been a way not to draw attention to the fact that someone was below. He would have entered hours ago and simply waited for noon to come. The church being closed changed things and had also allowed for Kelly to perform a much more vital function.

Still, he decided a little subterfuge might be wise.

First, he carried the bomb and nylon bag below. Then he attached the new lock to one door panel, bringing the two together, slowly allowing them to close onto each other from below. Only up close could it be seen that the lock was not fully engaged to both panels.

He descended the steps and found a switch, activating overhead lights. The brightly lit space was about fifteen meters square, littered with equipment and entangled with ducts, pipes, wires, and valves. Most of it appeared to be for electrical, heating, and cooling systems. Machinery purred, churning out warm air up into the church, some of which also heated the basement.

He removed his coat and gloves.

And stared across at the wall.

STEPHANIE DROVE OUT OF MANASSAS AND, USING HER SMART-phone's navigation, found the Charon estate. Sue had been right. The fire had gutted the house. Most of the roof was ash, one wing collapsed, but the central section and a second wing still stood up two floors. The whole thing had become a charred, smoldering mess no longer scream-ing affluence.

The firefighters were gone, the scene almost funereal. The gutted-out window frames that remained hung like gaps of dark shadow in the sooty façade. Clouds scudded in the wind, soiling pale sunlight and threatening more snow. She hurried toward the hulk, turning up her collar to the cold wind. Yellow crime scene tape stretched across the perimeter, understandable given that three people had died here last night. Investigators would probably return sometime today, so she should hurry.

Time was running out.

MALONE AND CASSIOPEIA STEPPED OUT OF THE WHITE HOUSE gate onto Pennsylvania Avenue. The pedestrian-only segment of the street that stretched before the North Lawn was packed with people, so many that the perimeter cameras had proved useless. Nor-mally, this gate was used sparingly, sealed off for security reasons. On television and in movies, though, it was the one always filmed, the supposed way in and out. He'd been told that the distance here from the fence to the White House front door was a mere 180 feet. Not far at all. The opposite side of the building was buffered by several acres that formed the South Lawn, the East and West Wings protected by Executive Avenue. Vehicular traffic used other gates located on the east and west sides of the property, far from the building itself.

They decided to patrol together since there was no telling how Zorin and Kelly might make their approach. Agents were still scanning the video cameras for anything suspicious, the entire White House security force on heightened alert. Getting a car near would prove next to impossible. Here, on the north side, a sea of people offered a solid buffer, the streets in and around Lafayette Park closed to traffic. The south side had numerous gates, all equipped with elaborate measures to stop any incursion. But with a six-kiloton nuclear weapon, just getting to the gate would do the job.

He recalled what Daniels had told him. Flick the switch inside off. Provided the heat had not reached critical mass, all would be good. If not? Then, boom.

"So many people," Cassiopeia muttered.

"But he's got to be carrying the case, so focus on that."

Everyone was bundled to the cold in winter gear, few carrying anything larger than a shoulder pack. Many children rested atop their parents' shoulders, catching a glimpse of the iconic white building beyond the black iron fence. The chatter was all of excitement and awe at being here. He knew that on the south side of the building dignitaries were pouring in. Power was about to shift, and so were allegiances.

His phone vibrated.

He found the unit and answered.

"We have the car."

He stopped. "Talk to me."

"On 15th Street, headed south. Cameras tagged it."

He knew the huge Treasury building shielded the White House from 15th Street. But just past that iconic building the road ran directly adjacent to the South Lawn and the Ellipse. A gate allowed vehicular access to the grounds.

"You sure?"

"We just got a shot of the tag. It's the car. Moving fast."

STEPHANIE PICKED HER WAY INTO THE BURNED-OUT SHELL AND saw that the staircase was gone, but a ladder had been left in place allowing access to the second floor. That meant investigators would definitely be returning.

She climbed the aluminum rungs, realizing that this was the first time she'd been on a ladder in decades. Interesting how on the last day of her career she'd become a field agent, doing what the men and women who'd worked for had done. There seemed an irony in this finale, one she'd wished had never occurred.

The second-floor balcony that once overlooked the entrance foyer and connected the wings was gone, the ladder angled upward to a still-passable corridor that led past burned-out doors to another room at the far end. Luke had told her that would be the master bedroom. Sue reported that firefighters had arrived in time to douse the flames before they consumed that side of the house. Almost everything was now exposed to the elements, the roof nearly gone, snow dusting portions that had cooled enough to host it.

She checked her watch: 10:46 A.M.

74 minutes left until noon.

Though the floor appeared secure and the walls relatively intact, she took each step with caution, the wood creaking from the wind around her. She made it into the bedroom without incident and saw that its ceiling was no more, most of the furniture charred lumps. She found the door to the closet and made her way inside, climbing over blackened ceiling joists that blocked the way. Smoke still smoldered from a few hot areas. She spotted the secret compartment Luke had described along with the filing cabinet, which appeared intact. He'd told her that when the shooting started he'd dropped the journal into the lowest drawer and slammed it shut.

A good move from a cool head.

She picked her way over more debris and managed to get hold of the handle for the bottom drawer, which she yanked outward.

The prize lay inside.

Not a scratch.

Luke's assessment that the cabinet was fireproof had been correct.

She removed the journal and stepped back out to the bedroom where there was more light from the gray, cloudy day. A slip of paper marked a spot, just as Luke reported. She opened and read about the burning of the Capitol and the White House by the British in 1815.

Tallmadge seemed appalled at how American infantry abandoned their posts and fled the city, leaving both the town and its residents defenseless. She kept scanning the dark masculine handwriting that had not faded much in two centuries.

Flipping the pages.

Then a passage caught her eye.

> *The Executive Mansion shall be rebuilt, but President Madison is insistent that measures be incorporated to address its occupants' protection. Mrs. Madison had come close to being trapped inside the mansion, becoming a British prisoner. Only providence and good luck had saved her. The president has ordered that a more secure means of escape be provided and he called upon me to both fashion and construct that means.*

She read, no longer skimming, savoring each word that had been written by the spymaster. Every American intelligence officer knew about Benjamin Tallmadge. Now here she was reading his private thoughts. *Careful,* she told herself. *Get it right.*

Her eyes scanned down.

She turned the pages and the information crystallized.

"My God," she whispered.

She heard the baritone thumb of rotor blades beating through the air and knew the helicopter Danny had promised was approaching.

Reading further, the implications became clearer.

She now knew what Zorin planned.

The chopper swooped in over the trees, the noise of the rotors swallowing her. It swung toward a clearing in the front of the house.

She had to leave.

Now.

And would call in from the air.

CHAPTER
SEVENTY-SIX

MALONE BOLTED ACROSS THE WHITE HOUSE GROUNDS, CASSIO-peia at his side. They'd reentered through the north gate and raced over the frosty lawn, rounding on the east side where the Treasury building with its huge columns and portico could be seen. On the far side of that monstrosity stretched busy 15th Street. They kept moving through the trees across the winter rye, heading for a gate that allowed vehicular traffic into the Ellipse. He still held his cell phone, receiving reports that the car was headed for the intersection of 15th Street and Pennsylvania Avenue. Earlier, guards all across the grounds had been alerted to their presence and told by Edwin Davis not to interfere with them in any way, particularly the snipers and lookouts on the roof who'd been placed on the highest alert since they still did not know if the threat might come by air.

They ran down a lane identified as Executive Avenue, then cut across more grass, past a monument to General William Sherman that Malone had long known was there. Overhead, ragged clouds kept scuttling across a dim sky. The 15th Street vehicle entrance lay directly ahead.

"He's nearly at the gate," the voice on the phone said. "Local units intercepting."

Sirens could now be heard, as the Treasury building no longer shielded anything. Here the roadway ran close and parallel to the White House fence.

They came to the gate.

Their government car from earlier, stolen by Zorin, roared into the intersection, braking, rear end sweeping around in nearly a full circle. Then it leaped the curb and vaulted into Pershing Park across the street.

"There's an ice rink in there," Malone said. "Lots of people."

The sirens roared into view and blocked the intersection to traffic, blue lights swirling. He and Cassiopeia bolted past the gate into the fray. The stolen car was angled up on a brick-paved walk near the curb, away from the ice rink. Thank goodness. He saw no casualties, which was good.

Everything went still.

The three police cars were positioned around the car, fifty feet in between, the officers out with guns unholstered and aimed. He and Cassiopeia approached from behind.

"Get back," the officer screamed, keeping his head directed across the street. "Now. Get away."

Malone held up the phone.

"This is the Secret Service," the voice said through the speaker. "Please do exactly as he says."

"Get real," the officer said.

Two uniformed Secret Service agents had crossed the street and ran toward them, flashing badges, assuming command, ordering the locals to stand down.

"You get that," Malone asked the cop.

The man lowered his weapon and turned. "Yeah, I got it."

"Gentlemen," Malone called out. "We're going to handle this. Not you. So everybody stay calm."

The driver's-side door of the stolen car opened.

A man emerged.

He recognized the face.

Kelly.

ZORIN REMOVED THE SLEDGEHAMMER FROM THE BAG. THE BASEment walls were formed of old brick, held in place with rough mortar.

The painted concrete floor seemed much newer. His objective was the south wall, about three meters away from the southwest corner, a rectangle the size and shape of an oversized doorway, its brick a tad different from the rest. Exactly as Kelly had described. The difference, though, was not enough to arouse any suspicion. More like a patch in the wall.

There. But not important.

He stepped close, planted his feet, gripped the wooden handle, and swung wide and hard, driving the sledgehammer into the brick.

Which absorbed the blow with a shiver.

Another blow sent cracks radiating.

Two more and chunks dropped away.

According to Kelly, the basement was not original. It was added years after the church had been completed, when a larger nave above became needed. So a pit was dug beneath to hold a central furnace, replacing old woodstoves that had heated the interior. Prior to that the entire church had sat on solid earth. It still did, except that now, inside its foundation footprint, lay the basement.

More pounding and a section of the wall crumbled onto itself, crashing down among dust and shards.

He cleared out a path.

Sweat moistened his hairline.

He laid down the hammer.

Before him, past the wall, opened a dark chasm.

STEPHANIE CLIMBED INTO THE MARINE CHOPPER, WHICH IMMEdiately powered up and lifted into the midday air. She carried the journal and told the pilot to head for the White House.

"We'll need clearance," he told her.

"Get it. Let's go."

She had to be absolutely sure, so she gave the journal one last look.

January 1817. President Madison inspected today and complimented our ingenuity, pleased that his request had been honored. His specifications had called for a concealed escape path from the Executive Mansion that would lead to a defensible point of safety. Our task had been to locate, design, and construct such a route. Several options were considered but the most viable came when we were able to join the reconstructed Executive Mansion with the recently consecrated St. John's Church. The distance was not unreasonable and the tunnel was easily disguised as a drainage outlet for the North Lawn and a nearby marsh. No questions were raised during its digging. Other similar structures exist throughout the capital city. We chose a brick façade both for longevity and to keep water from flooding in. The entrance from inside the Executive Mansion is concealed beneath a piece of movable furniture. At the church the exit opens through a section of the brick floor near the building's southwest corner. Only the president and his immediate staff are aware of the precise locations. Three within the society are likewise privy. Reference is made here, along with a map and sketch of its precise location, for future use. Maintenance and repair may be required from time to time and the President has asked us to assume that task. This escape route will provide the chief executive with a measure of protection that has been heretofore lacking. We consider it an honor to be asked to assist.

So a tunnel once existed between the White House and St. John's Church. She knew the building, located a few hundred yards away, north of Lafayette Park. The White House itself had been renovated many times, new rooms and basements dug beneath it, yet she could recall reading nothing about anyone ever discovering a brick-encased tunnel.

But it was there.

Zorin had to be at St. John's.

Her watch read 11:05 A.M.

She dialed her phone, trying to reach Edwin Davis. No luck. She tried Danny's phone. Only voice mail. Both were probably now involved with the reception and preparing for the imminent arrival of the president- and vice-president-elect. So why not cut out the middlemen and go straight to the source?

She dialed Litchfield's number.

Two rings and he answered.

She pressed the phone tight to her ear and over the rotor's roar yelled, "Bruce, a bomb's going to be planted beneath the White House. Zorin is at St. John's Church, across the street. There's a tunnel there somewhere. Send agents, now. He's probably shooting for noon on the dot. Find him."

"I hear you, Stephanie. Where are you?"

"On the way, by chopper," she yelled. "Get everyone out of the White House. There might still be time."

"I'll handle it," he said.

She ended the call.

And dialed Cotton.

MALONE LAID HIS CELL PHONE DOWN ON THE HOOD OF THE PO-lice car and stepped out, catching Kelly's attention. Crusty, sooty snow from the street crunched beneath his feet, the cold gusting air sharp with exhaust fumes.

He found his gun and brought it out. "Can we help you?"

"Smart-ass," Kelly said. "Nobody likes one."

"His right hand," he heard one of the Secret Service agents say from behind him.

He'd already noticed. Kelly's arm waggling against the thigh, hand out of sight, between him and the open car door, as if it held something.

"Okay," Malone said, "let's try it another way. These policemen would like nothing better than to shoot you dead. Give me one reason why they shouldn't."

Kelly shrugged, a gesture that signaled disdain, disinterest, and dismissal. "Can't think of one."

The right arm swung around and revealed a gun. Malone, though, was a second ahead of Kelly and aimed a shot to the legs. They needed this man alive.

But the other officers had a different idea.

A din of gunfire erupted.

Bullets slammed into Kelly, piercing his coat, plucking him back and forth as if in convulsions. Kelly tried to spring away, but failed, his body slamming the pavers and settling atop the snow.

Malone shook his head and glanced back at Cassiopeia. Only they realized how bad this had just gotten.

Their best lead was dead.

ZORIN FOUND THE FLASHLIGHT HE'D ADDED TO THE NYLON BAG and shone its light into the opening. It extended about two meters, to where the floor ended and another black maw opened down. He investigated and saw how the tunnel once came up here, at the church, then extended toward the White House at a level about a meter farther down.

He grabbed the RA-115, entered, and carefully stepped down. The path ahead was U-shaped, lined with brick and mortar, including the floor. He had to stoop in order to walk, the ceiling less than two meters high. But the path was relatively clear. He'd taken an estimate earlier of the distance from the church to the White House fence. All he had to do now was keep track of his steps. If he was off a little, it didn't matter. He'd be more than close enough to obliterate everyone.

Who were all the main adversary.

He started walking.

And counting.

CASSIOPEIA RUSHED WITH COTTON TO KELLY'S BODY. THE WIND swirled loose snow into a crystalized mist. No need to check for any signs of life.

Cotton was infuriated. "You were told not to fire. What part of that order did you not get?"

"We saved your ass," one of the officers said.

"I didn't require your saving. I had it under control. We needed him alive."

The Secret Service was on the radio reporting in.

He read his watch.

11:20.

Cassiopeia checked the car's interior.

Nothing.

Then she found the lever and released the trunk.

Cotton moved toward the rear of the car. She followed. Four aluminum cases lay inside. Cotton didn't hesitate. He lifted one out, laid it on the ground, and opened it, revealing a switch, a battery, and a stainless-steel cylinder lying diagonally. All three items were linked by wires and padded with black foam so they could not move about. The switch was labeled in Cyrillic, which she could read.

"It's off," she said.

Cotton felt the battery and the cylinder. "Cold."

Quickly, they removed the other four and discovered the same thing. None of the RA-115s had been activated.

"Are those bombs?" one of the cops asked.

"Get them the hell out of here," Cotton said to the Secret Service.

The police were hustled away.

"Kelly wanted to die," she said.

"I know. And he brought these four toys to keep us occupied."

She remembered what Stephanie had learned. *Five* RA-115s were unaccounted for. That meant Zorin had the last one.

But where?

"Malone," someone called out. "Somebody on your phone says its urgent."

He'd left the unit on the hood of one of the patrol cars.

They ran across the street, still blocked to traffic, and Cotton took the call. He listened for a moment, then ended the conversation.

"It was Stephanie," he said to her. "Zorin is at St. John's Church with the fifth bomb. Get back to the White House and make sure they get everyone out fast. Stephanie said she's already alerted Litchfield. Help him out. I'd say we have maybe twenty to twenty-five minutes tops."

"I need this car," he said to the cop.

He leaped into the driver's seat.

"Where are you going?" she asked.

"To stop the SOB."

CHAPTER
SEVENTY-SEVEN

ZORIN HAD COUNTED HIS STEPS AND WAS SATISFIED THAT HE WAS now directly beneath the White House grounds. He was smeared in dirt, the confines in the tunnel progressively tightening as he'd ventured farther and farther into the earth.

But he'd found Kelly's point of convergence.

Andropov would be proud.

His vision was about to become reality.

He lay flat on his belly, the ceiling here only centimeters high, the flashlight beside him illuminating the aluminum case. He released the catches, only able to open the lid halfway. He knew that once the switch tripped there'd be fifteen or so minutes before the trigger engaged, maybe a little more thanks to the underground chill.

He checked his watch.

11:40.

Kelly should have accomplished his diversion by now, which, for at least a few minutes, would keep people surprised, confused, puzzled, and, most important, inactive. Finding four RA-115s should also calm them long enough for the fifth to strike a blow.

Everyone should be inside the White House by now, ready for the ceremony that would start promptly at noon. He'd read enough about American tradition to know this one would not be altered. The U.S. Constitution said noon on January 20 so noon, today, it would be.

A shudder ran through his tired arms and shoulders. His thighs and calves felt weak. Yet lying here, alone, encased by earth, he felt at peace. His end seemed prescribed. Fitting that it all had led right here. Perhaps his ashes would fertilize a new seed, a new fight, maybe even a new nation. The resentment he'd so long harbored seemed to have vanished, replaced by a rush of relief. No more was he a weary, aged, defeated man.

Instead, he'd succeeded.

Fool's Mate.

Two moves to victory.

Kelly was probably dead by now.

One move done.

His right hand reached inside the case and found the switch.

How many more would leave this world today? Tens of thousands? More like hundreds of thousands. About time the main adversary felt what Soviets had long ago grown accustomed to experiencing.

Defeat.

Two fingers gripped the toggle. A surge of exultation streaked through him. This spark would ignite the world.

"For the motherland."

He flicked the switch.

MALONE FLOORED THE ACCELERATOR AND SPUN THE WHEEL, speeding the police car north on 15th Street past the Treasury building, weaving in and out of traffic, using the siren and lights to clear a path. At H Street, which was one way in the wrong direction, he turned left anyway and sped around a few oncoming cars for quarter a mile to where St. John's Church sat overlooking Lafayette Park. He wheeled the car up on the curb and partially into the park, as far as he could go before a barrier of in-ground iron pedestals blocked the way. He fled the vehicle. People were everywhere between the park and Pennsylvania Avenue. Stephanie had told him about a tunnel between here and the White House, most likely directly beneath where he now rounded a corner to the church's front side. The whole site was closed off, under construction, a fence encircling it, but he leaped over. Folks out on the sidewalk gave him a strange look, but he had no time to explain anything.

And no time to evacuate them either.

The only chance was to stop the thing before it exploded.

CASSIOPEIA RAN BACK TO THE WHITE HOUSE, ONE OF THE SECRET Service agents that had been at the scene of Kelly's shooting with her. Immediately, she noticed that no one seemed to be leaving. They entered through the East Wing and were told by agents inside that the ceremony was about to begin.

"Why aren't they evacuating?" she asked.

A perplexed look came to the man's face. "For what?"

She brushed by him, intent on heading into the main house.

Two uniformed agents blocked her way.

"You can't go in there," one of them said.

"We have to get this place cleared out. You're not aware of anything? The attorney general. Litchfield. Find him."

The agent used his radio and called in the name.

A moment later he faced her and said, "Mr. Litchfield left the building half an hour ago."

ZORIN HAD WANTED JUST TO STAY WITH THE DEVICE AND DIE AS it exploded, but he decided that the smart play was to head back to the church and stand guard, making sure nothing interrupted. He'd still die, being only a few hundred meters from the epicenter of a nuclear blast, but at least he'd be doing his job to the last.

He crouched and made his way through the old tunnel, which smelled foul but had held up remarkably for its age. The flashlight beam licked a dim path across the brick floor. Only back where the weapon lay had the tunnel collapsed onto itself, so he doubted that the route all the way to the White House even still existed.

He came to the end and stood from his haunches, hopping back up into the church basement.

His watch read 11:47.

Five minutes since he'd activated the device.

MALONE SEARCHED THE GROUNDS, WHERE A THICK SCATTERING of debris and a thin layer of snow registered little trace of any passage. He spotted a set of metal doors that would certainly lead beneath the church. He ran over and saw a hasp lock holding them closed, but as he approached closer he noticed that the lock secured nothing, attached to only one panel.

He wrenched the handles, felt no resistance, then flung them open, leaping down a steep set of concrete steps. Before him stretched a lit basement full of electrical and HVAC equipment.

On the far side stood Zorin, carrying a flashlight.

He rushed forward and heaved his frame against the big man, using his shoulders like a linebacker to lift them both off their feet.

ZORIN HAD AT FIRST BEEN SURPRISED, THEN SHOCKED TO SEE Malone. The American seemed impervious to dying. Twice now a resurrection. The clatter of the metal doors opening had struck him like a call to attention. He did not carry his gun, having left it with his coat that lay a few meters away.

But Malone gave him no time to react.

His body slammed the concrete floor.

CASSIOPEIA STOOD SHOCKED. APPARENTLY, INSTEAD OF SOUND-ing the alarm, Litchfield had fled, saving only himself.

It was now too late to do anything here.

And explanations would waste precious time.

"Where is St. John's Church?" she asked.

One of the agents told her.

She ran out the door she'd entered, calling, "Tell the north gate I need to be let out."

MALONE HAD TO END THIS FAST.

He'd seen no aluminum case and the destroyed brick wall could only mean one thing, that the bomb was in place, the trigger heating.

Zorin broke free and came to his feet.

He did, too, but was met by a fist that twisted his head and sent a jolt through his jaw. Another punch to the solar plexus buckled him. But he shook off the blow and butted his head into Zorin's nose, hearing a groan, then followed it with his right fist.

Zorin staggered back, but quickly regained control, lunging, his thrusts cobra-quick. Atop a concrete block sat a length of thick steel chain, which Zorin quickly grabbed and whipped his way. He ducked, the metal whizzing by so close he felt its wake. Chips of brick flaked off the wall where the chain struck, sending out a shower of dust. Zorin whipped the chain again in a wild arc, which he dodged with leaps back.

This man knew how to fight.

But so did he.

He planted his feet and punched, planting blow after blow. Zorin tried to muster the strength to swing the chain again, but an upward palm thrust into the jaw stunned the big man, then two blows to the kidneys caused Zorin to lose his grip and the chain dropped away.

Malone's knuckles hammered away at the face and he tore a gash above one eye. Blood continued to pour from Zorin's nose. He sensed that his opponent was weakening, so he focused on the midsection and slammed a fist into the stomach, catapulting Zorin off his feet and to the floor.

He leaped down and wrapped his right arm around the throat and clamped his left hand tight in a choke hold. Sweat poured from his brow. He blinked away the wetness and increased pressure. Zorin tried to break free but he held firm.

He squeezed tighter.

Breathing became jerky, then rough.

The grip from Zorin's hands, locked onto his arms trying to break the hold, slowly weakened. Blood pounded in his ears as if he heard Zorin's heartbeat rather than his own. He'd never killed a man with his bare hands, but an urgency drove him forward. Zorin had to be eliminated. With no question, no remorse, no delay. In his head he was counting down the time and knew that he had only a handful of minutes left.

Zorin's muscles tightened, the body tugged with fluttering fringes at the iron vise. He heard gagging, then the feet shuffled in a gallow's dance. The head lolled to one side, then everything went limp.

He released the hold and crawled from the body on all fours, gasping for air. Drums drowned his ears, purple curtains blocked his vision. Zorin lay still, the mouth agape, blood still oozing from his nose, the face covered in pits and shadows.

He checked for a pulse.

None.

Then he realized.

Zorin had made a show of protest, struggling, but only for form's sake. Like Kelly, this KGB officer had booked a one-way ticket. He planned to die here in the blast, so having the life choked from him accomplished only one thing. More time for the bomb to prime itself.

He cursed his stupidity.

Dangerous seconds had ticked away.

He brushed aside the cobwebs and sprang to his feet, rushing toward the maw in the cellar wall. Sharp pain ached in his ribs, a duller version radiating in his back. He found the flashlight Zorin had discarded, then climbed down the tunnel's entrance.

Hurry, he told himself.

He entered the blackness.

CHAPTER
SEVENTY-EIGHT

STEPHANIE COULD SEE CENTRAL DC AHEAD. THE CHOPPER WAS flying in from the west, past the Pentagon over the Lincoln Memorial. Many thousands of people filled the National Mall, all within the blast range. No way to get them to safety. She could only hope that Litchfield had cleared the White House of Fox and his vice president. Knowing Danny, he hadn't gone anywhere.

"Do we have clearance?" she asked the pilot through the headset.

"Yes, ma'am. Straight to the North Lawn."

"Make it fast."

She caught sight of the White House.

CASSIOPEIA RUSHED OUT OF THE NORTH GATE ONTO CROWDED Pennsylvania Avenue, where the babel of thousands of indistinguishable voices rose from people waiting for noon. But above it all she heard the sound of a helicopter cutting through the air. Turning back, she saw a military version swoop in over the White House and descend quickly, flurrying up snow in its downdraft before landing. Its rear door swung open and she saw Stephanie hop out, carrying what looked like a book. She raced back to the gate, which the guard reopened, calling out and grabbing Stephanie's attention.

"Litchfield told no one and left the premises," she said as they drew close.

Shock filled Stephanie's face. "They're all still in there?"

She nodded. "Cotton is after Zorin at the church. I'm going there now."

"I'll do what I can inside."

They hustled off in opposite directions.

MALONE KEPT PRESSING AHEAD, THE WEAK BEAM FROM THE flashlight barely leading the way. The tunnel, though tight, remained relatively unobstructed. What he did not like was that he would have to go several hundred yards into the ground—a long way—nothing ahead or behind but utter blackness. If he switched off the light he would not even be able to see his finger touching his nose.

His watch read 11:50.

Zorin probably activated the trigger somewhere between five and ten minutes ago, surely planning to keep the explosion as close to noon as possible. He tried to focus on that urgency, fighting a rising swarm of panic that was rapidly taking control of his mind and body. Never had he experienced any trouble in an elevator, revolving door, or tiny bathroom. Not even inside the cockpit of a fighter, crammed into its tight space, unable to see the ground. Just beyond the canopy had always been open sky, and the force of acceleration from the afterburners had never triggered any feeling of being trapped.

Quite the opposite, in fact.

There he'd felt freedom.

He'd read a lot about claustrophobia. How adrenaline surging through the body triggered either a run or a resist impulse. But where neither act was possible, only panic resulted.

Like now.

He stopped and absorbed a few seconds of breathless silence. The darkness seemed even more profound, the air cold and cheerless.

The first time he ever recalled this feeling was as a teenager. He and another friend had hidden in the trunk of a car, sneaking into a drive-in movie. He'd freaked, kicking out the backseat and escaping. Years of occasional recurrence had made him realize that it wasn't a fear of tight places. No. More a fear of restriction. Of being stuck. Never had he liked the window seat on a commercial flight. And where he kidded Cassiopeia about her *fear* of flying, he'd always known that his weakness was more than a fear. Fears could be overcome. Phobias were paralyzing.

Acrid bile filled his throat.

Tendrils of fetid air swirled in his nostrils.

He doubted this tunnel had seen much ventilation in a long time.

He started moving again.

But a fireball ripped upward from his belly and assaulted his brain.

The terror was starting.

STEPHANIE ENTERED THE WHITE HOUSE THOUGH THE NORTH doors. The building buzzed with quiet conversation and an aura of expectation. The swearing-in was only a few minutes away. Edwin Davis waited for her, surely drawn by the helicopter's arrival.

"It's underneath us," she said. "A tunnel dug by the Society of Cincinnati, after the War of 1812." She gestured with the journal she held. "It's all in here. I alerted Litchfield, but he left, telling no one."

And then she realized.

"Bastard. He told me that, under the 1947 Act, he's in line to succeed. I'm betting that the AG is higher on the list than today's designated survivor. If this place goes up, Litchfield is president."

"Then let's make sure it doesn't go up."

She stared out through the glass doors, past the portico, over the North Lawn, to the fence and the people beyond. When she'd called Litchfield there'd been a chance to protect Fox and at least some of them.

Now nothing could be done.

A six-kiloton blast would annihilate everything within a mile.
"It's all up to Cotton now."

MALONE COULD NOT STOP. HE HAD TO KEEP GOING. BUT AN AP-
palling sense of dread had invaded his mind and clouded all thoughts
save one.

Escape.

Weakness crept into every muscle. He clamped his eyes shut and
retreated into himself, trying to quell panic's irrational bloom. He
hadn't experienced this helplessness in a long time.

But the familiar panic had returned.

A suffocation, as if his clothes fit too tight. Dizziness. Disorientation. The walls closing in, compressing by the second. Someone told
him once that it was a control issue.

Bullshit.

It was like a cage, within a cage, within a cage.

Horrible.

The only saving grace was that no one would see him like this.

The tunnel had begun to narrow, the ceiling definitely inching
closer. Some compression and collapsing here. He hadn't counted his
steps, but he was a long way in, surely past Lafayette Park, maybe even
Pennsylvania Avenue. How had this thing escaped detection all these
years? Amazing. Yet here it was. Intact. The farther in he went the
more deterioration he saw. He tried to focus on that and trick his mind,
but no luck. The tunnel felt like a python squeezing the sanity from
him. Terror shot out of the darkness and struck him like a dart.

Ahead, he saw where the path had caved in, the space no more than
three feet square. He'd gone from hunched over on two feet, to crouched,
to now scrambling on all fours. But before him, only a few feet away,
stretched a space where he'd have to wiggle on his belly.

Like a slit in the ground.

He shone the light inside.

And saw an aluminum case.

Ten feet away.

My God.

But getting to it?

In every nightmare he'd ever experienced this was the worst-case scenario. The one that always jarred him awake in a cold sweat.

But he had no choice.

CASSIOPEIA FOUND ST. JOHN'S CHURCH, THE GROUNDS WRAPPED by a tall construction fence, which she quickly scaled. On the other side she swung around to the north end and spotted steel panels swung open. She made her way to them, then down concrete steps, through an open door, into the church basement. A warm, sickly aroma instantly made her stomach queasy. She spotted its source. A body on the far side.

She rushed over.

Zorin.

Dead.

Cotton was nowhere to be seen, which meant he had to have headed into the tunnel.

So she followed.

MALONE INCHED FORWARD ON HIS BELLY, HANDS THRUST AHEAD pushing the flashlight along. The confines were so constricting he could not even bring his arms back to his sides. He was easing his way toward the case, clutches of dirt coming away in his grip with each inch of ground gained. His throat choked up, his lungs felt as though they were filled with fluid. He coughed, trying to get air. Dirt from the ceiling cascaded and caused him to stop. He wondered if his efforts might cause a cave-in.

That thought paralyzed him.

He reminded himself that a nuclear bomb lay just a few feet away.

If it exploded he would be utterly vaporized. The only saving grace would be that this torture—and that's what it was—would be over. But he could not allow that to happen. Too many people above were counting on him. So he kept crawling, shoulders passing his elbows, kicking with his toes.

He made it to the bomb.

The chute here was maybe twenty-four inches tall at most. Not much room to even open the case. Jostling it around, trying to pull it back for more room to work would take time and could be catastrophic. He saw that its latches were free. He laid the light where it held the case in its beam and carefully opened the lid enough so that his hand could enter.

He felt the stainless-steel cylinder.

Hot.

He recalled what Daniels had advised and flicked the toggle but, to be sure, his fingers probed and found the wires springing from the battery poles.

He yanked them free.

Sparks triggered inside.

His eyes went wide.

He waited for a blast as hot and bright as the sun, a blinding phosphorous light he'd see only for a millisecond.

But nothing.

Another few seconds.

Still nothing.

His prison was ice-cold, the air nearly impossible to breathe. He was truly in the bowels of the earth. He lay still and stared at the case, his hand resting inside. He moved his fingers and again found the cylinder. Already not nearly as hot. Only warm and fading fast. He kept touching, then gripping. Touching, gripping.

The cylinder was definitely cooling.

He'd made it.

The damn thing was disarmed.

Time to leave.

He tried to back out, but couldn't. He tried again, but the ultra-tight space restricted his movements. When he tried to force it, dirt fell, clogging the air. Suddenly everything around him seemed to be contracting even more, bearing down, crushing him.

More earth rained down on his spine.

The chute seemed to be resenting his intrusion.

He was stuck.

Mother of God.

What the—

The chute collapsed.

And he screamed.

CASSIOPEIA HUSTLED AS FAST AS THE TUNNEL WOULD ALLOW, us-ing her phone for illumination. She could only imagine what Cotton was experiencing. He hated tight places. This was tough even for her, and she wasn't necessarily bothered by them. She'd moved a long way into the ground, maybe a hundred meters, the tunnel becoming pro-gressively smaller, when she heard a shriek.

From ahead.

Not far.

She increased her pace and finally saw where the tunnel became more of a slit, closed onto itself.

There was movement.

Shards of light seeped out.

Oh, God.

Cotton was buried.

MALONE LOST IT.

He could not remember the last time, if ever, he'd screamed. He felt silly and weak. The stink of his own fear had finally hammered him into submission. He closed his eyes as the reality of the situation washed over him. He heaved at his leaden body, arms and legs cramp-ing with pain. He was buried, barely able to breathe, his brain locked with only one thought.

Get out.

How could—

"Cotton."

He grabbed hold of himself.

A voice.

Firm, resonant, authoritative.

And familiar.

Cassiopeia.

Just hearing her yanked him back from the precipice.

"I'm here," he said, trying hard to keep control.

Hands grabbed his shoes. The sensation of her touch calmed him. The dual grip on his ankles told his addled brain that he might be okay.

Hold on. Take it easy. Help is here.

"I'm sealed. I . . . can't get out."

"You can now," she said.

CASSIOPEIA HAD DUG HER WAY IN, TOSSING DIRT OUT BEHIND her, burrowing furiously until she'd found Cotton's feet. She now kept a firm grip on his ankles and wiggled herself back out of the chute. Being smaller gave her a few more precious centimeters in which to maneuver.

The scream had been his, and she knew why.

If there was any concept of hell, which she did not necessarily believe in, this would be Cotton's.

MALONE WIGGLED HIS WAY BACKWARD, CASSIOPEIA HELPING things along with solid pulls on his legs. Just a few more feet and he'd be free of this coffin. He'd left the case and flashlight. Others could retrieve them later. He just wanted out. His feet and legs escaped the chute, back into the cramped three-by-three-foot tunnel, which seemed like Grand Central Station compared with where he'd just been.

He was on his knees, his breathing ragged but calming. A light came on from a phone and he saw Cassiopeia's face. Like an angel.

"The bomb?" she asked.

"I got it."

"You okay?"

He heard the concern and nodded.

But he wasn't.

He dragged air into his aching lungs and fought a coughing fit, his whole body heaving, throat still filled with bile and fear.

She reached over and clasped his wrist. "I mean it. Are you okay? It's just you and me here."

"I was . . . buried."

He knew his dirty face reflected pain and pleading, his features clawed with terror, but he did not try to hide any of it. Why? She'd heard his scream, revealing a vulnerability that someone like him would never want exposed. But they'd made a pact. No more bullshit.

So he decided to honor it.

He stared into her eyes, grateful for what she had done, and said what he felt. "I love you."

CHAPTER
SEVENTY-NINE

WHITE HOUSE
MONDAY, JANUARY 21
5:45 P.M.

STEPHANIE STUDIED THE OVAL OFFICE, THE ROOM NOW CLEAR OF anything to do with the administration of Robert Edward Daniels Jr. Warner Scott Fox had taken the oath, as prescribed by the Constitution, yesterday at 12:00 noon. She'd stood just outside the Blue Room and watched, everything broadcast live to the world. The whole time both she and Edwin had wondered if they'd all be blown to dust from an underground nuclear explosion, but nothing had happened.

Cotton had done his job.

Which had allowed for the second ceremony today outside the Capitol. Fox had spoken in the cold for half an hour with a surprising eloquence, energy, and courage. The new president had enjoyed the inaugural parade, then returned to Blair House to prepare for an evening on the town, he and his wife moving from one ball to another. But first Danny had asked to speak with him, choosing here, in his old haunt, for a final conversation.

The gang was all there.

Cotton, Cassiopeia, Edwin Davis, and herself.

She'd reported everything to Danny yesterday, just after the swearing-in. She'd wanted to tell Fox, but Danny had vetoed that idea.

Not yet, he'd said.

A partial report, she knew, had been provided on the incident with Jamie Kelly and the four cases that had been found. She imagined that information would have sent shivers through Fox. Luke was doing fine, wanting out of the hospital, but the doctors had told him one more day. The younger Daniels had been informed, though, as to what had happened, and was pleased things worked out.

The door opened and President Fox entered the office alone, decked out in black tie and tails, looking quite dapper.

"You know," Fox said to Danny with a smile, "you do have to leave at some point."

The Sunday twitch in things had made the customary departure of the outgoing president a non-newsworthy event. Usually, just after the Capitol ceremony, the former president was seen waving to reporters and flying off from Andrews Air Force Base. Not this time. Danny had watched Fox take the oath yesterday, spending a final night in the White House, then gawking a second time today before retreating here to leave with his things.

"I'm on the way out the door," Danny said. "But first we need to have a chat."

"I feel a little outnumbered," Fox said. "Should I ask my staff to join us?"

"Let's keep this between the few of us."

"I'm sensing that everyone here knows something I should."

"We tried to tell you things were bad and you wouldn't listen," Danny said. "Instead, your people went behind my back and tried to recruit my girl over there as a spy. And, yes, on my orders, she was playing them."

Fox said nothing. But men like him did not appreciate being cornered. In fact, they spent their whole lives avoiding right angles. This was classic Danny Daniels, though. The Tennessee Torture, as members of Congress and the cabinet had called it.

"Are you referring to the four bombs seized yesterday?" Fox asked. "I was briefed. They weren't even activated."

"They were decoys," Danny said.

And the Secret Service had done a good job diverting public attention from them, labeling Jamie Kelly as some sort of exhibitionist, trying to prove a point, who ended up dead. The "bombs" found were fake. "Security teams doing their job" had also been the explanation used for the helicopter landing on the North Lawn.

"There was a bomb," Danny said. "Six kilotons, placed directly beneath the White House in an old tunnel."

"And I wasn't told?" Fox asked.

"I wanted that privilege."

"I'm going to have to speak to the Secret Service about their loyalty. Since noon yesterday, I've been in charge around here."

"Not on this operation. You told us to handle it. We did. Now it's over, so we're reporting back, as you requested."

Hard to argue with that logic, since it was all true.

"Okay, Danny. I get your point. As to recruiting Stephanie, that was a clear miscalculation on my attorney general's part. When he told me what he'd done I was not pleased. That's not my style."

Danny nodded. "I get that. I've had Lone Rangers, too."

A couple even tried to kill him, she thought.

"But I am wondering," Fox said, "how no one knew a tunnel existed beneath this building."

Stephanie nearly smiled. Fox was trying to score a few points of his own.

Danny reached down to the Resolute desk and retrieved the Tallmadge journal that she'd handed over to him yesterday. "This is some interesting reading."

And Danny told Fox about the Society of Cincinnati, then said, "It all started with the War of 1812. We wanted Canada to be our 14th colony, to be part of the great United States. But the British didn't want us to have it. We burned Toronto, so they came and burned DC. We've done some checking and discovered that, a long time ago, we did know about the tunnel. Records show it was shut down during the Civil War. By then it had collapsed beneath the White House, so they sealed it on this end, then went over to St. John's, dug it out from the cellar, and bricked up that side. No one at the church even knew it existed. Not wanting to draw any attention to its presence during a time of civil war, they just quietly got rid of it. If not for the fact that the Cincinnati Society kept a record, it would have stayed forgotten. And if not for the excellent work of the people in this room, along with my nephew who's in the hospital thanks to all this, we'd be dead. Cotton stopped the bomb maybe seconds before it would have exploded."

Fox glanced at Malone, but said nothing.

Danny went on. "And to top it off, the guy you specifically wanted as the go-between to keep you informed decided he wanted to be president. So he didn't tell you that a bomb was there. Instead, he ran like a dog on fire and got as far away from here as he could."

Surprise now filled Fox's face. "What do you mean?"

Stephanie said, "I called from the helicopter and told Litchfield to warn you and everyone else. There was time then to get away. But Litchfield used that time for himself. If we'd all died in a nuclear blast, he'd be president right now. He was at the swearing-in, saw that the secretaries of state, treasury, and defense were all there—each of whom are ahead of him in the line of succession—so when I called and told him what was happening, he just left."

The implications hit home.

"That sorry son of a bitch."

"Can you imagine," Danny said, clearly enjoying this. "The designated survivor comes out from his assigned hiding place, ready to take command, then Litchfield shows up and says, 'Excuse me, I'm still here and you're not the one. The AG outranks you on the list, and the succession law says the highest qualified person on the ladder wins.' I guess he figured he'd pay us both back."

"He's fired."

Danny chuckled. "He's worse than that."

Fox seemed puzzled.

"Cotton found him a few hours ago," Danny said. "He owed him one for wanting to leave him to rot in Siberia. So I had him pass on both his own and our collective displeasure. How many broken ribs?"

"More than one," Cotton said. "We had a spirited discussion on presidential succession. Along the way, Mr. Litchfield decided that he would be pursuing other career opportunities and tendered his resignation. Then he went to find a doctor."

"You beat him up?" Fox asked Cotton.

"Absolutely."

The new president seemed pleased. "Then that's that. Everything is tied up."

"Not exactly," Danny said. "Stephanie here quit yesterday, which you may or may not know."

"I was told."

"You need her, Warner."

Danny's deep tone had changed. Lower. More conciliatory.

"This a shakedown?" Fox asked.

Which she was wondering, too.

Danny shrugged. "Call it what you want. But I don't think you want me tellin' the world that we all came within moments of having hundreds of thousands of people vaporized, all because you wanted to be sworn in on live TV inside the White House at noon. Not to mention that your people actively tried to interfere with an ongoing investigation that was working to reveal the plot. Then, when I add in the conspiracy with Litchfield and his betrayal, wow, we've got ourselves a TV series. It'll run for weeks on every news outlet in the country. What was it you said on Saturday? *'We'll never get on message.'*"

Danny hadn't explained what he planned, but she'd suspected.

"Cotton," Danny said, "Litchfield will make himself available for interviews, right?"

"He gave me every assurance that as soon as the pain subsided, he was at our disposal."

"See? There you are. We even have a witness."

Fox smiled. "I was told you could be terribly persuasive, when you want to be."

"You're going to learn that's a valuable skill to have around here."

Fox considered things for a moment before saying, "So we're clear, I didn't jump on your parade Saturday because you offered no concrete evidence of anything. I wasn't oblivious to the risks, I just wasn't prepared to bet everything on *your* instincts. But I was ready to move when, and if, you had proof. Now, with Litchfield, that was my mistake. We listened to him. My AG was dead wrong and, as Mr. Malone describes, we had a spirited discussion, just without the violence." Fox looked at Stephanie. "Litchfield convinced us you were something other than what you clearly are. My apologies for that wrong assumption. The Magellan Billet will be restored, with no interference from me or the new AG. And though we all know this idea was forced onto me, I agree completely with Danny. I want you watching my back."

"I'll do my best, Mr. President," she said, deciding a little concession of her own was in order. "You'll find me a loyal soldier."

"And who am I to argue with a man leaving office with a 65% approval rating?" Fox said.

"I didn't realize you were a fan," Danny said.

"Since it's just us here," Fox said. "Let me say that I think you did a good job running this country. I even voted for you. Twice. Of course, political correctness prevents me from saying any of that in public. That meeting here Saturday was a show for my people. We all have to do it, from time to time. But I want to keep this country safe, just as it's been for the past eight years. To me, that's the number one job of this office. I know I'm new to this league, but I'm a fast learner."

She appreciated the mea culpa, unusual for presidents.

Warner Fox certainly wasn't Danny Daniels.

But only time would tell if that was good or bad.

"To all of you," Fox said. "Thank you. Great work." Fox pointed at Cotton and Cassiopeia. "Especially you, Mr. Malone. You should get a medal."

Cotton shook his head. "Just pay me for my time, and let me get a few days' rest. That'll be more than enough."

MALONE STEPPED FROM THE WHITE HOUSE BENEATH THE NORTH portico. Blades of sharp sunlight stabbed through the retreating cold clouds. The city remained abuzz with inaugural fever, Lafayette Park and the pedestrian-only areas beyond the fence hectic with camera-toting visitors. Cassiopeia stood with him, Danny and Stephanie following quickly behind.

"I didn't want to say anything inside," Danny said, "since this is our little secret. But Stephanie's pal from the park was right. People are dying fast in Moscow. It started yesterday. Three killings. Another a few hours ago. Various ministers, some at a high level, others midlevel. I imagine the message is ringing there loud and clear."

Danny wrapped his arms around both him and Cassiopeia, slapping affectionate blows to their shoulders.

"Thank you both for what you did. Great work. And I wasn't

bullshittin' in there. This new administration needs all of you. Help them out, if you can."

A dark sedan waited under the portico.

Danny produced a set of keys. "I borrowed it. I've been waiting a long time for this. I finally get to drive."

"What will the Secret Service have to say about that?" Stephanie asked. "You have a detail assigned to you, right?"

"I took a cue from the first George Bush and refused any further protection. Don't want 'em. Don't need 'em. Just me from now on."

Stephanie shook her head. "God help us. He's loose on the world with no adult supervision."

"I wouldn't say that," he said. "There's you." He motioned to the car. "Shall we?"

"Where are we going?"

"The hospital in Virginia, to see Luke. You can start rebuilding the Magellan Billet tomorrow. I also need to shake the hand of a brave navy lieutenant named Sue Begyn."

Stephanie held the Tallmadge journal, which he'd told her to bring from the Oval Office. Danny pointed at it and said, "We need to return that to the older Begyn. Our people have gone through it and could find no more secrets to cause us problems."

She was relieved to hear that. "And I owe the Society of Cincinnati that library from the Charon estate."

"It's already being handled," he said. "I'm told that, amazingly, it survived the fire." Danny reached for the car door. "And I have a present for my nephew. I'm having his car repaired, good as new. On me."

She knew Luke would like that.

They climbed inside and the engine revved. Before motoring off Danny wound down the window and said, "You two take care. And don't be strangers."

The car peeled away and headed toward the south vehicle gates, disappearing around a curve and into the trees.

"What did he mean," he asked Cassiopeia, "when he said to Stephanie, 'There's you'?"

"It's a long story. But I think it's okay to tell you now."

He was intrigued.

"I doubt we've seen or heard the last of Danny Daniels," she said. He agreed. No way.

They walked from the building toward the pedestrian gate in the north fence. The RA-115 had been retrieved from the tunnel and experts had verified that, as Danny had said inside, it had been only seconds away from triggering. The subterranean cold had prolonged the process for enough extra moments to allow its disarming. Inspection also revealed that the weapon, along with the other four, was totally viable. The Secret Service had already sealed the tunnel entrance beneath the church with tons of concrete and planned to fill in the entire remnants beneath the North Lawn.

They strolled down the paved lane toward the guard station. He couldn't help but stare out at the manicured lawn of winter rye. Yesterday, he'd been encased beneath it. Neither one of them had reported anything more than that the bomb had been found and deactivated. So only he and Cassiopeia knew what really happened.

"You know that you can tell me anything," she said, "I hope that's true for me to you."

He faced her. "Always."

They'd both seen the other at their most vulnerable. He with her in Central Asia, then again in Utah. She, just yesterday, in the ground beneath their feet. Shame coursed through him at the thought. But he was glad that it had been Cassiopeia who'd heard him. He could still feel her reassuring grip on his ankles, the dirt wrapping him like a mummy. Nothing had ever reassured him more. He was surprised at how emotional his thoughts had become. But she had that effect on him.

As he'd said. He loved her.

And what was wrong with that?

He pointed off beyond the gate toward Lafayette Park. "The Hay-Adams hotel is just past the trees, across the street from St. John's Church. I've always wanted to stay there. Robert Ludlum loved to use the place in his novels—some spy always having a drink in the bar at the Hay-Adams. It sounded so mysterious."

"I hear hotel makeup sex is pretty good, too."

He smiled. She knew just how to work him. But that was okay. He liked being worked by her.

"How do you plan to get a room?" she asked. "It's Inauguration Day."

"We have friends in high places. As I was leaving the Oval Office, Fox slipped me this." He displayed a key card for the Hay-Adams. "It opens the Federal Suite. He said it's the best room in the house. We have it for two nights, compliments of the new president of the United States, who is, as we speak, moving his clothes from there to the White House. The hotel has been his temporary quarters for the past few days."

She liked his proposal, but had to say, "You're pretty sure of yourself, agreeing to all that, without asking me."

He offered his arm, which she accepted.

"That I am."

WRITER'S NOTE

For this novel Elizabeth and I made a memorable journey to Prince Edward Island, Canada, three trips to Washington, DC, and an excursion into rural northwestern Virginia.

Now it's time to separate fact from fiction.

The meeting between Ronald Reagan and John Paul II happened on the date noted in the prologue, the first time a pope and president ever spoke alone. The only twist I added was altering the time frame of John Paul II's scolding of the Nicaraguan priest, which, in real life, did not happen until after June 1982. Most of the dialogue contained in the prologue accurately portrays these two men's respective thoughts and feelings. They talked alone for fifty minutes and, to this day, no one knows what was said. As to an active conspiracy between them to bring down the Soviet Union, we have no evidence that such an agreement was ever made. But there is no doubt that tacit cooperation developed, each applying pressure to the USSR in different ways (chapter 30). Special envoys did in fact pass between them, delivering messages, but operation Forward Pass is wholly my invention. And the tens of thousands of nuclear weapons each nation possessed in 1982 (as numbered in the prologue) is correct.

The An-2 is an actual single-engine biplane, and does possess the ability to fly backward in a strong headwind (chapters 1, 5). Lake Baikal (chapter 1) is the largest freshwater reservoir in the world, and each winter its ice becomes a superhighway for cars and trucks. The deaths of hundreds of soldiers during the Great March and the building of a railway across the winter surface during the Russo-Japanese War happened (chapter 1). The observatory noted in chapter 10 is real, though I moved it from the west to the east shore. The village of Chayaniye is entirely my creation. But *Kozliks,* nicknamed Goats, are actual Russian military vehicles (chapter 21).

Cassiopeia's castle reconstruction (chapter 4) is modeled after two real-life efforts. One is Guedelon in France, the other is the Ozark Medieval Fortress in Arkansas. Both have websites where you can learn more.

Black baths existed in abundance all across Siberia. The one in chapter 6 is described from a historical account. Abandoned houses are common in Virginia (chapter 8), though Brad Charon's is purely imaginary.

There are varied locations throughout the novel: Annapolis, Germantown, St. Andrews by the Sea, Eastport, Maine, and Long Beach, Maryland. Each is described correctly. The Mandarin Oriental is a superb hotel in Washington, DC. Both Stephanie and I enjoy it from time to time. The city of Ulan-Ude sits in Siberia, along with a huge bust of Lenin (chapter 22). Prince Edward Island, Charlottetown, and Stratford are stunning Canadian locales, and a national park does stretch along the island's north shore (chapter 37, 38). The Confederation Bridge, connecting the island to the mainland (chapters 40 and 45), is likewise real.

Spetsnaz units (chapter 11) still exist today and the information about them noted in chapter 19 is correct. Leaping from a high-altitude plane in the middle of the night is something any *spetsnaz* officer could accomplish. The jump described in chapter 37 is taken from real-life experiences. Soviet forward attack plans against an enemy, using these specialized units (chapter 55), existed.

The KGB became a master at both active and passive intelligence measures, its tentacles stretching into every corner of the world. Especially the United States, which was the USSR's *glavny protivnik* (main adversary). The vast majority of Soviet espionage activities were channeled into preparing for an inevitable conflict with America (chapter 10). The Woods (chapter 49), where its most feared First Directorate established its headquarters, was a magnificent facility. Its rise and fall, as told in the story, are accurate. KGB employees did in fact receive a multitude of special privileges, becoming insulated from the suffering of ordinary Soviets (chapter 49). That privilege would also explain how it was able to so easily inflict so much pain on so many of its own people. Intourist still exists (chapter 45), though now privatized, no longer the official state travel agency.

The Society of Cincinnati continues to be America's oldest home-grown fraternal organization (chapters 14, 18). Its beginnings, and the apprehensions about it described throughout the story, are taken from reality. George Washington himself eventually saved it from dissolution. Benjamin Tallmadge, America's first spymaster (chapter 34), was an original member, but his keeping of a journal and his involvement with any war plans of the United States and a secret tunnel beneath the White House are my additions to history (chapters 14, 18, 20, 23, 34, 39, and 60). Anderson House, though, is real and can be toured (chapter 18, 20). It still serves as the society's national headquarters. The basement library is there and contains one of the finest Revolutionary War collections in the world. The ballroom and orangery are stunning, but the video room on the second floor (chapter 23) is fictional.

Yuri Andropov existed as described (chapter 33), except for Fool's Mate. He hated both Reagan and John Paul II (chapter 52). The West did fear him (chapter 50) but, thankfully, he died after only 15 months as general secretary. The ten-year-old American girl mentioned in chapter 33, who wrote a letter to Yuri Andropov, published in *Pravda,* was Samantha Smith. Her actions, and Andropov's response, became a 1982 media circus. Andropov did in fact use the opportunity to lie to the West, proclaiming he was stopping all work on a missile defense system (chapter 33). Lies like that, part of a more widespread disinformation and propaganda campaign, were all too common from the Soviet Union. In 1983 Samantha visited the Soviet Union, but Andropov was too ill to greet her. Sadly, she died in a 1985 plane crash.

The Strategic Defense Initiative (SDI) existed (chapter 29), created as detailed in chapter 30. Historians disagree, but some assert that its main purpose was not to develop a workable missile shield, since that was way beyond the scope of technology at the time. Instead, the idea had been to convince the Soviet Union that it *might* be possible, driving it to spend billions of rubles that it could not afford (chapter 30).

And that was exactly what happened

Which only hastened the regime's downfall.

Along the way the United States acquired a multitude of innovative technological advances, but a complete and workable missile defense shield remains only a dream.

The U.S. Navy Riverine Squadron was one of the most decorated units from the Vietnam War, suffering huge casualties. Women being a part of the unit has only recently become a reality (chapter 53). George Shultz (chapter 18) and Cyrus Vance (chapter 9) served as secretaries of state. John Paul II did visit and forgive his assassin (chapter 52) and the USSR is still, to this day, the most likely candidate to have ordered the 1981 papal assassination attempt.

The White House grounds, Lafayette Park, and Pershing Park (chapter 76) are correctly laid out. The Cabinet Room inside the White House is there, and Nixon did purchase and donate the table (chapter 58). The burning of both the Capitol and the White House by the British in 1815 happened (chapter 59 and 70). The War of 1812 was regarded as "Madison's War" and the British hated having been forced to fight it (chapter 39). In August 1815 American troops did flee the federal district without putting up a fight. Contrary to legend, on that day Dolley Madison did not save Gilbert Stuart's famous painting of George Washington (which now hangs in the Smithsonian's National Portrait Gallery) (chapter 67). Instead, that feat was accomplished by others.

St. John's Church arose at the same time the White House was reconstructed (chapter 70). I came across this fact during a tour of the church (which anyone can take) and immediately decided that a connection between the two events made sense. The President's Pew inside the church is real (chapter 70). I was also able to venture down into the church basement (not part of the tour), which is described accurately in chapters 75 and 76—with one exception. There is indeed a difference in the wall, but not with contrasting brick. Instead, the actual break is of concrete, supposedly where a former coal chute existed to fuel the boilers, now sealed. Its presence, though, spurred my imagination, so I added a tunnel from there to the White House. Also, on occasion through its two-hundred-plus-year existence, the church has been closed for renovations, just as in the novel (chapters 73 and 75).

This story addresses the 20th Amendment to the Constitution along with the 1947 Presidential Succession Act. Both are riddled with legal flaws and inconsistencies, creating Supreme Court–ready issues that Congress has been unwilling to address (chapters 42 and 48). The USSR's fascination with those problems is my addition, but the former Soviet Union did study every aspect of our society, searching for weaknesses. January 20ths that fall on Sunday have always been treated differently, with two swearing-in ceremonies occurring (chapter 58)—one on Sunday, the other Monday. In 1985 that was the case with Ronald Reagan's second inauguration. The designated survivor is real (chapter 58), he or she chosen by the White House chief of staff. It's also true that the highest person in the line of succession (per the 1947 act) who survives an attack becomes president, whether that person be the designated survivor or not (chapter 48 and 79). Also, unlike in the novel, on those rare Sunday occurrences the vice president is always sworn in separately and at a different location.

RA-115s remain a mystery. No one has ever seen a suitcase-sized nuclear weapon produced by the Soviet Union. However, Stanislav Lunev (chapter 11), a former Soviet military officer and the highest-ranking intelligence operative to ever defect to the United States, describes them in his memoir, *Through the Eyes of the Enemy*. In the 1990s Congress held hearings on their existence, and the description used herein for the weapon is taken from those hearings (chapter 68). The trigger-warming aspect (chapter 68) is my addition. And there was a *60 Minutes* story, as recounted in chapter 11, which the Soviets tried to discredit with misinformation about its producer.

KGB weapons caches have been found across Europe and the Far East (chapter 19), but none has ever been located in this country (chapters 66 and 68). Former archivists have proved to be the best source of information. The definitive account is the *The Sword and the Shield: The Mitrokhin Archive and the Secret History of the KGB*, published in 1999 (chapter 11).

Finally, there is Canada. The Founding Fathers desperately wanted it to become our 14th colony. The Articles of Confederation did contain language that would have allowed it to automatically join the new nation (chapter 39).

But that never happened.

And two invasion attempts failed.

Canada again came onto our radar in the early part of the 20th century. The invasion plan from 1903 is real (chapters 59, 61, 62), and most of what is recounted in chapter 61 is quoted verbatim. On May 21, 1916, the War College filed its own invasion plan and all of the money spent and preparations detailed in chapter 62 happened. The massive war game at the Canadian border in August 1935 occurred. More concerns about Canada arose during World War II, particularly if England fell to Germany, and a ninety-four-page document was prepared on how best to secure control. There's even a 1977 book on the subject: *The Defence of the Undefended Border,* by Richard A. Preston. Of course, the Society of Cincinnati having anything to do with that is fiction.

Unlike my other novels, this one deals with a more recent historical period. The Cold War. It was fascinating to learn some of its secrets, which are only now beginning fully to come to light. At its peak the KGB employed over 700,000 people scattered across twenty-plus directorates.

Sharp of Sword. Tough of Shield.

That was its motto.

Both the CIA and the NSA were created in direct response to its presence. KGB agents posed as diplomats, reporters, businessmen, professors, even ordinary citizens, infiltrating anything and everything. Nothing was sacred. Once, even the piano tuner for the governor of New York was reputed to be a KGB asset. In the memoir mentioned above, Sanislav Lunev made a comment that Stephanie Nelle thought profound enough to never forget (chapter 11).

It's good advice.

Both frightening and instructive.

The best spy will be everyone's friend, not a shadowy figure in the corner.